WAT.

Please renew or return items by the date shown on your receipt

www.hertfordshire.gov.uk/libraries

Renewals and enquiries: 0300 123 4049

Textphone for hearing or 0300 123 4041
speech impaired users:

L32 11.16

Helen Russell is a British journalist, author and speaker. Helen has previously worked for the Sunday Times, Take a Break, Top Santé and on new launches for Tatler Asia, Grazia India and Sky. She joined Marie Claire as editor of marieclaire.co.uk in 2010 and was BSME-shortlisted in 2011 and 2012.

Helen now writes for magazines and newspapers around the world, including Stylist, The Times, Grazia, Metro, and The Wall Street Journal. Helen is a columnist for the Telegraph, a correspondent for the Guardian and author of Leap Year. Her first book, The Year of Living Danishly, is now a bestseller.

Gone Viking

Helen Russell

EBURY
PRESS

3 5 7 9 10 8 6 4 2

Ebury Press, an imprint of Ebury Publishing
20 Vauxhall Bridge Road,
London SW1V 2SA

Ebury Press is part of the Penguin Random House group of companies
whose addresses can be found at global.penguinrandomhouse.com

First published in the UK in 2018 by Ebury Press

www.penguin.co.uk

A CIP catalogue record for this book is available from the British Library

ISBN 9781785036491

Typeset in India by Integra Software Services Pvt. Ltd, Pondicherry

Printed and bound in Great Britain by Clays Ltd, St Ives PLC

Penguin Random House is committed to a sustainable future
for our business, our readers and our planet. This book is
made from Forest Stewardship Council® certified paper.

Author note

This is a work of fiction.

Purists: I have played fast and loose with Viking heritage –
from a place of love – to convey the *essence* of Viking culture
in modern-day Scandinavia. Deal with it and put your 'proud
face' on.

For everyone else: come on in, the water's lovely (if cold, see:
'Scandinavia') – and get ready to go berserk …

Prologue

Twigs snap beneath my feet as I bat away branches and run. Really run. Heart pounding so hard it's threatening to break free from my chest and outstrip me at any moment. The rain is relentless and I'm wet through. The kind of wet that would normally chafe, but I'm so cold I have no sensation below the waist. What I am conscious of is my brain rattling around in my skull with every bare foot hitting bracken and I've been tangled in the limbs of so many trees that I'm carrying a campfire's-worth of kindling in my hair.

A mist descends and I hear an eerie noise as I hurtle through the semi-darkness. Crows caw and thunder rumbles. This isn't the sort of woodland populated by princesses and talking creatures keen to lend a hand. Less *Snow White*, more *Blair Witch Project*, I think.

Then I slip on something brown and slimy.

Let it be a slug, let it be a slug, please let it be a slug, I beg, but don't stop to analyse. *Must get to the clearing,* I think, limbs pumping. I reach peak adrenaline and feel as though I'm – almost – flying. Then I trip on an exposed tree root that sends me crashing down with a thud.

So this is how I die, I muse, face full of mud. *So long, world, it's been quite a ride.*

I wait for a bit, but nothing happens.

Damn it, I'm not dead! This means I'll have to do more running ...

Some ancient self-preservation instinct kicks in and I summon the strength to move. Nothing appears to be broken (apart from, perhaps, my nose ...) so I scramble up. Touching my lip, I realise it's bleeding a vivid red. But that doesn't matter right now, and I keep moving, towards the flickering light.

'*Arghhh!*'

I hear a voice in the distance and redouble my efforts before another wail sounds out.

'*Arghhhhh!*'

I stagger on, until the verdant canopy becomes patchy and light dapples a carpet of leaves. Fire-lit torches give off a welcome heat and my clothes start to steam.

'Hello?' I haven't spoken for twelve hours and I'm not entirely sure I remember how. I try again, voice like porridge.

'Is anyone there?'

I hold my arms out, allowing my chest to expand, then shout.

'*Arghhh!*'

Two muddied, feral-looking women emerge from behind the foliage and scream back. 'Arghhhhhh!' One is short, dark-haired and heavy set. The other is tall, model-esque and offensively young – sporting glossy, caramel-coloured hair that seems to shine, despite the mud.

We lock eyes and an understanding passes between us: whatever happens next, life is never going to be the same again. After a few seconds of guttural screaming, a third figure limps into view – an older blonde, hair backcombed by bushes, skin the colour of mahogany.

She gives a half-hearted growl before flopping down and holding on to her knees to steady herself. 'Oh god, cramp ...'

She grasps at a calf, heaving to get more air in her lungs. 'I need ...' I worry she's about to say '*medical attention*' and I'll be called upon to do something, but then she gasps '*gin*', and we hear a slow hand clap.

A barrel-chested man wearing nothing but harem pants deftly descends from a tree. He swings down branches with simian grace, then strides across the clearing. His hair is in a bun and he readjusts an ill-advised fishhook necklace.

Wanker.

I have long been distrustful of men sporting buns, placing them in the same category as women who wear bandanas and moan a lot.

'Well run, Vikings,' Man-bun says now in softly accented English. 'So, who's feeling fantastic?'

My legs are shaking like a shitting dog, I'm pretty sure I'm having a heart attack, and there's a strange tingling sensation spreading from my scalp.

I choose not to answer him.

'Oh, you have *insects* in your hair!' the younger model-esque women pipes up, helpfully. 'Awww, a spider! He thinks it's a web!'

'Great. Thanks.'

'Let me hear you roar!' semi-naked man demands.

Three of us give him a look as though we might wallop him but the model-esque spider-informer obliges.

'Ahhhhh!' she hollers beatifically.

'Come on, the rest of you!' Man-bun moves towards me until he's almost touching my face and bellows, 'Arghhhh!'

I wipe spittle off my cheek.

'Taste the freedom!'

Is 'freedom' supposed to taste like mud and pickled mackerel?

'Commune with the ancient forest!'

I just want to commune with a hot shower right now … I think, looking down at my soiled clothes, bruised limbs and bloodied knees. *How did I end up here? Life used to be so … clean. So ordered. So … insect-free,* I muse, scratching at my head. *And yet …*

I look over at the shorter woman with the scraped-back brown hair, the girl I've known forever. Her eyes narrow as she approaches me, dimples on show, betraying just how much she's loving this. Cheeks flushed, fists clenched, she opens her mouth and lets out a primal wail. Thirty-five years' worth of primal wail. A wail so loud that I recoil slightly and have to take a moment to compose myself before I can muster the strength to scream back. But then I muster. Hard. And all the tension and fear and pain of the last few days – as well as the past few years – is expelled from my lungs in one, long, warrior cry.

'ARGHHHHH!'

Man-bun looks impressed. 'That's it, go berserk!'

We carry on until we're the last two shouting.

I may not have her lung capacity but I've given birth. Twice. I'll be damned if I'm letting her win at wailing …

Her roar morphs into a growl, then a splutter and shoulders heave as she shakes out her arms, spent.

But I keep going.

With more roar in me than I'd ever have thought possible, with nearly four decades' worth of berserk to unleash, I yowl: *'ARGHHHHHHHHHHHH!'*

As I scream into the empty woodland, my vision begins to blur from the periphery.

'ARGHHHHHHHHHHHHHHHHHH!'

My head starts to swim and soon it feels as though the top has flipped off my skull like the lid of a boiled egg.

'ARGHHHHHHHHHHHHHHHHHHHHHHHHHH!'

And then I'm floating. Up and up, higher and higher, until I can see our assembled grouping from above. Trees turn into blobs. People: to ants. Until finally ... my knees buckle and my head hits the ground with a thud.

All is black.

And I pass out.

One

Three weeks earlier …

'It's spelled R-A-Y – "Ray".'

A thunderously bored woman scratches the top of her head with a pen as I argue my case and the strip lighting hums. My 'smart shoes' are pinching and I can feel my phone vibrating in my pocket (not unpleasant), reminding me with each new pulse that there are important messages I may be missing while wasting *literally* seconds on this exchange.

'One more time?' the woman sighs.

So I go through the problem again, watching her eyes glaze over as I speak.

'This says "Rat".' I dangle the laminated rectangle to illustrate. 'My name is Alice Ray.'

'Not "*Rat*"?'

'No.'

'Huh …' She scratches again, then inspects the end of her pen for any excavated treasure. 'Couldn't you just make do?'

'You want me to walk around for two days wearing a lanyard that says "Alice Rat"?'

'Yes?'

'At a conference called "How to have a winning smile"?'

'No?'

'No.'

She adjusts her weight in the plastic chair and then, without looking at me, extends an arm in my direction.

'Thank you.' I offer up the badge, softening my tone. 'I don't want to be difficult; it's just these are my colleagues – my professional peers – and I'm *speaking* ...'

My voice trails off as I watch her select a permanent marker from a Tupperware container. She bites off the cap and crosses out the letter 't'. Then she adds a 'y', followed by :)

Really? That's how we're fixing this?

'Couldn't I just have a new one?'

She gives me a look of such hatred that I feel myself repelled as though by a force field. Reluctantly, I back off, but not before retaliating with a death-stare that I hope implies *'you're going on my mental list of Total Arseholes who deserve to step in puddles and have doors slam in their faces.'* She scratches her head again. *'And get nits.'*

'Next!' she barks, and I'm dismissed.

There's time to spare before I'm due to join my panel discussion and I swore to myself that I'd make an effort and mingle, rather than looking longingly at the sugar-free biscuit table while mainlining carrot sticks and overpriced Paleo bars, like I've done every other year.

I should network, I tell myself; *I should smile at people and appear 'approachable'.* It's not that I'm scared of interacting with other human beings ... it's just that—

'Oh, hi!'

Oh, crap.

'Alice?' A man in glasses squints at the lanyard now grazing my breasts, and I remember reason #142 why I hate conferences: some joker always makes it so that the name badge hangs conveniently at mammary-height. This gives CSPs ('conference sex pests' – reason #141) the perfect excuse for a gawp, and, occasionally, a fondle (reason #143[1]). Now, Glasses Man performs a strange sort of squat, bending his knees so that he is on eye-level with my A-cups before looking up at me quizzically. 'Alice … Rat?'

'It's "Ray".'

'Right! Yes! We met last time!' He extends a hand to shake mine.

'Oh, yes, I remember!' I don't.

After one of those handshakes that last about five minutes, he starts telling me about some new dental floss his company is promoting ('*Flossed in Space* was developed by NASA! It's the *future* of hygiene filaments!'). I nod politely, before feeling my phone quiver in my pocket and taking it as my cue to escape. 'I'm so sorry, would you excuse me? I have to take this, then my session's about to start.'

In fact, '*How Do You Solve a Problem like Major Root Canal Surgery?*' isn't for another half an hour, but there are only so many aspartame-laden Rich Tea biscuits a woman can *not* eat. Plus I'm a social leper trapped in the body of a dentist.

'You hanging around after? There were rumours they'd got Malala for the keynote but I just saw that magician we had last year so we might be in for Cavity-In-A-Hat 2.0 …'

The fluorescent tube above my head flickers and the idea of another twenty-four hours in a venue totally lacking in natural light, where delegates subsist purely on processed food and dentistry puns, makes me weary. I promise to try and make his 'Return of the Plaque' session, then leave. I've missed

---

[1.] Otherwise known as 'doing a Thornberry' after Jeremy Corbyn's Most Awkward High-Five Ever post-2017 election …

the phone call, but that's OK. I don't like talking on the phone any more than I relish 'a natter' in real life.

I wasn't always like this. But lately I've become worn out. As though I've used up all my 'nice' in the consultation room or on parenting, until there's nothing left. That's what almost eight years of childrearing along with fifteen years at the plaque-face of dentistry can do to a person. *Not to mention a life-sentence of marriage* ...

'Excuse me?' I ask a large man with an already sweaty moustache guarding the entrance to the hallowed back stage area where, I've been assured, privacy, Wi-Fi, and 'the good coffee' are located. 'Can I come in?'

'This is for VIP pass holders only, madam,' he tells me.

Jesus, I'm a 'madam', now am I? Aka 'past it' ...

'I've got a special blue lanyard ...' I dangle it hopefully.

'Rat?' He frowns at me and then at an iPad, dabbing at it with fleshy fingers. 'No "Rat" on my list ...'

'It's Ray.'

'It says "Rat".'

'I know. But it's Ray.'

'Sure?'

'I'm pretty sure.'

He has a long hard stare at my chest, presumably to verify this, then stands aside to let me pass through to the inner sanctum. It smells strongly of sandwiches and the pheromones of several other 'experts' enacting various rituals to see them through the next ninety minutes.

A woman click-clacks past in full, precise make-up and trousers so tight they almost certainly necessitate a cranberry juice drip afterwards.

'Are you ... ?' she asks, then tries to frown through Botoxed brows and points instead at my name badge.

'It's a typo. I'm Alice Ray. Hi!'

'Oh! Lovely. You're on the panel I'm chairing.' She claps her hands together but her fingers don't touch.

Weird …

'Oh, great.' *Say more*, I tell myself, *say something else. Quickly. Do 'talking' like normal people.* 'Umm …' I try to think of something to say. 'Are those Viennese Whirls over there?'

There I go again, captivating people with my effortless charm and chat …

'Err, well, yes. Help yourself!'

'Thanks.' I won't. I would no sooner eat a Viennese Whirl than I would the plate they're arranged on.

You see, officially at least, I don't eat sugar. Or bread. Or potatoes. Or pasta. Or rice. Or dairy. Or trans fats. Or saturated fat. Or meat. Our canines may have been designed for tearing the flesh of animals from their bones, but I've dealt with enough oral cavities to be put off the stench of rotting meat wedged between teeth for life. Mainly though, I kept reading about how it might be making my gut sluggish – and I haven't got time to be sluggish. In any department. Of course, there's the occasional blip. Like last month, with the quarter-pounder … but that was under the cover of darkness and the kids weren't with me. *And if you eat it in your car, with no one watching, it doesn't count. Everyone knows that.* That's how I like my meal deals: with a side order of shame.

'Right. Well, lovely to meet you,' Cranberry Pants says, bringing me back from my reverie.

'Lovely,' I reply with a nod in response.

She tilts her head to one side and purses her lips, as though I'm a stray cat that's just dragged something dead into the house. 'And good luck, OK? We've got fifteen more minutes of "The Only Way Is Airflow", then a loo break before your session.' She pats my arm and scissors off.

'Lovely ...' I repeat, scanning for the quietest, darkest corner where I won't have to interact with anyone. I wedge myself between a black curtain and a wall to watch the editor of *Dentistry Magazine* karate chop the air to get in the zone, while a celebrity hygienist I've seen on *This Morning* hops up and down on a mini trampette. The speakers from 'New Trends in Sinus Care' come off the adjacent stage and an 'alternative oral therapist' opens his mouth like a baby bird, tilting his head back so that his miniature assistant (*Child? Wife? Child-wife?*) can dispense a pipette of some magical unction.

Just another day at the office, I think, keeping my head down and willing my fellow speakers to keep their distance. But in reality, this is an honour. *A privilege*, I remind myself: *I'm representing the surgery – as well as speaking on behalf of grassroots dental practitioners at the gravel pit of oral care.* It was a coup to be asked. This is what all the hard work – all those hours overtime and putting myself forward for extra training and more responsibility – has been aiming for. *I'm finally being taken seriously in my field*, I tell myself.

Then the theme tune from *Frozen* starts up.

I don't react straight away as my daughter's game of 'changing Mum's ringtone to something different every day' means that I can't be sure it's me who's blasting out Elsa (last week it was Little Mix). But then the editor stops air-fighting and baby bird pipette man is looking over and I realise that the only person the sound can be coming from is ... me.

Arse ... I fish out my phone and peel off a squashed raisin before answering.

'Hello?'

'Hi,' says the Eeyore-like voice on the end of the line. 'It's just me.'

It's always 'just me'.

'Hi. I'm about to go in to my session; I can't really talk now. Everything OK?'

'Yeah. Just wanted to check when you'd be back—'

'I'll be back tomorrow, as soon as I can. As planned ...'

'It's just the trains—'

'I've booked a ticket—' *Amazingly, I can organise my life ...*

'—are cancelled.'

'Oh.'

'There's a replacement bus. I saw it on *South East Today* after a feature on parking restrictions in Brent.' We don't live anywhere near Brent, but my husband likes to have the TV on AT ALL TIMES in case he misses something 'really important'. Probably parking related. 'So anyway,' he goes on, 'you're best off getting a lift from someone ...'

'I'll work it out. Thanks.'

'You could always call—'

'Yes, I know I could call *her*. But I'd rather not.' He means Melissa. A woman who doesn't normally loom large in my life but is, as sod's law would have it, *local*. I have no intention of calling Melissa. We've barely spoken in months and the last thing I'll be in the mood for after two days at a dentistry conference is an in-depth analysis of why this might be. Or even worse – having to feign interest in her latest obsession. Or conspiracy theory. Or animal acquisition.

Greg does a loud sigh, then offers reluctantly, 'I mean, *I* could always—'

'No, no, I'll be fine.'

'OK, if you're sure,' he responds – far too quickly – sounding relieved.

'Yeah. Listen, I've got to go. There are people here on trampolines; I should probably be preparing in some way.'

'Right ...'

'Right then. Well ... bye.'

'Don't you want to know how the ki—'

Cranberry Pants is coming towards me with a beanbag in her hand and a rictus grin. She taps her watch to hurry me along.

'Got to go—'

I'm just about to press the red receiver icon to 'End Call' with 'Greg Mobile' when I hear a rushed, 'The kids are fine, thanks for asking.' And then he hangs up.

Shit ... I am A TERRIBLE PERSON.

I love them. Of course I love THEM. *Even though they haven't let me sleep beyond 5.30am since 2009 ...*

I add my own name to the *Total Arseholes* list then feel an overwhelming compulsion to scratch my head. *If Ms Itch-a-lot has given me lice,* I think ... *well, then, that's karma.* But then Cranberry Pants is showing me all of her very large teeth and attempting to raise her eyebrows at me in a 'shall we go?' expression before frogmarching me out. And we are on.

It should be noted for the record that a panel discussion on root canal surgery is every bit as much fun as it sounds.

Afterwards, it's hard to say who's more relieved – audience or panellists.

'Lovely ...' Cranberry Pants sounds strained now as she attempts to save the celebrity hygienist from the editor of *Dentistry Magazine* and walk in a way that doesn't splice herself in two. 'Now then, lunch?'

She gestures towards several plates packed with neatly arranged cakes and sandwiches, sweating slightly. The backstage area is stuffy and, despite the lack of windows, an alarming number of flies have appeared and are now congregating atop a plate of '*Tooth Friendly!* ☺' branded fairy cakes. The hygienist bats away a bluebottle as a catering assistant crunches several more with the back of a spoon, flicking them off the plate before she thinks anyone's noticed.

I've noticed.

There's nothing here I can eat. Or rather that I'll allow myself to eat. So I don't. This is a mistake. Because what I do instead is drink. And I soon discover that the warm white wine on offer doesn't taste so bad after a couple. Then an overly hairsprayed woman gives me a pink '*Dentists Rule!*' glass suspended on a chord that can be worn around my neck. The larger, beer-glasses on a man-ribbon have presumably been reserved for the male delegates, lest they break my fragile *female* mouth. But I don't care. *Because now I have WINE to hand At All Times! Not even 'to hand'*, I think, giddy with novelty ... *hands-free!*

This makes the 'Wave Ta-Ta to Tartar' seminar much more interesting and even the Cavity-In-A-Hat magician doesn't seem quite so crap when I'm partially inebriated ('*How does he DO that with the doves?!*'). I also find the awards ceremony ('the pinnacle of the dentistry year!') less painful than usual, and start a secret game of cliché bingo, drinking every time someone says 'raising the bar', 'recognising excellence', or 'giving a hundred and ten per cent ...' *It's like* The Apprentice, I marvel, *but everyone's got fractionally flatter hair!*

Soon, the comforting blanket of fog descends and wraps itself around me so that my senses are dulled and I feel slower – softer, even – than usual.

Ahh, alcohol, I think, fondly. *Hello, old friend ...*

I'm a lot more sociable when I'm drunk. But after some surprisingly pleasant exchanges with the celebrity hygienist and a woman who runs a practice in Peckham, I get stuck with a man who looks as though he's been on a lot of caravan holidays, and another who's clearly wearing bronzer (and possibly mascara). Mascara Man proceeds to cup his hand around my elbow and tells me he's a life coach.

'I specialise in pre-surgery visualisation,' the melted, latter-day Simon le Bon insists enthusiastically. 'Close your eyes, I'll show you!'

Because I'm overly obliging, socially awkward and inebriated, I do.

When I open them, I pray inwardly, *please don't have your penis out*. After some gubbins about 'pelvic breathing', I squint to find the male member still, thankfully, concealed beneath some flammable-looking trousers but I'm alarmed to note the white ghost of a wedding ring. This happens a lot at trade events: the lanyards go on and the wedding rings come off.

I politely decline melted Simon le Bon's suggestion to go on a cocktail-menu crawl but then he slurs something about 'lady dentists' being 'really sexy'.

Oh dear lord …

This is: a) gross; b) a patronising affront to my feminist principles; and c) gross. Because no one over the age of twenty-five should ever use the word 'sexy'. Ever.

I scroll through my mental rolodex of excuses to get the floss out of there, but my mind isn't able to function as swiftly after five glasses of hands-free wine, so when a tall, handsome man with truly excellent teeth butts in and suggests we all move through to the next room 'for the disco', I comply.

'Urggh, thanks,' I whisper, swaying slightly despite my best efforts to walk in a straight line. 'You saved me from another demo of his hypnotism skills. On top of his life coaching. And his making-wedding-rings-disappear trick ...'

Mr Teeth makes a joke about 'watching out for the pampas grass lobby' at these events, and I laugh, always impressed when the seriously good-looking are also funny – as though they don't have to be. *They already have so many advantages the rest of us lack. And Such. Nice. Teeth ...*

Under the influence of alcohol, he blurs out of focus, then multiplies by two, crossing over himself, before swinging back again in an odd sort of Shiraz-induced optical illusion. This makes 'walking' even more of a challenge but, somehow, we make it.

Roxy Music are playing in the 'party room' (not in person, FYI – dentistry budgets don't stretch that far ...), and it's around about this time in the proceedings that my glass of Shiraz starts whispering to me, conspiratorially.

Shiraz: '*Oh, hey you! Wouldn't it feel good to throw some shapes around about now? Shake things up?*'

Me: '*No. Go away. You're drunk—*'

Shiraz, interrupting: '*No, YOU'RE drunk! Trust me: you're a brilliant dancer ...*'

Me: '*No. Must stay in control. At all times. That's my thing. Along with hiding in the loo at social events.*'

Shiraz: '*Pah! That's the old you. The bor–ring you that works all the time and is stressed and hasn't smiled in weeks! This is the new, FUN version!*'

Me: '*I am NOT dancing ...*'

Shiraz: '*Horse shit!*' (My glass of Shiraz has quite a mouth on her.)

I'm drowsy and confused and the music is loud. So, really, everything that happens after this point is Bryan Ferry's fault (and the wine. Did I mention the wine?). But what *I think* happens is this:

1) Mr Teeth takes my hand and we move to the side of the dance floor.

2) The hands-free-glass hanging around my neck is refilled and Mr Teeth even procures a straw for me so that all I have to do is dip my chin and suck (so to speak ...) to get my Shiraz on. Naturally, this means I drink All The Wine until Mr Teeth offers to top me up. I gratefully accept and drink some more. This happens, on repeat, until I feel numb. *Do I still have toes?* I wonder, in an abstract sort of way. *I haven't felt them in at least half an hour ...*

3) Many more dental practitioners flood the room until we are all pushed up against each other.

4) And then ...And then ...

I'm looking down at a woman wearing the same ten-year-old Zara skirt suit as me, with the same ten-year-old hairstyle as me, and the same nervous laugh as I've been trialling for the past decade (spoiler alert: it's me) and I'm shouting at her: YOU'RE ABOUT TO KISS A MAN WHO IS DEFINITELY NOT YOUR HUSBAND! STOP IT! STOP IT NOW! THIS IS ABSOLUTELY, INCONTROVERTABLY NOT THE FATHER OF YOUR CHILDREN! CEASE AND DESIST!

But she doesn't.

For about twenty seconds I don't know how I feel about this. *How should I feel? Horrified? Guilty? I should feel guilty around about now. Shouldn't I? Shouldn't I be breaking away and running off in tears? That's what would happen in a Richard Curtis film, wouldn't it ... ? Quick! Someone check ...*

But I'm tired. So tired. And it's so unlike me. Because, well, who wants to play *that* part? The married mother of two who snogs strangers while listening to Bryan Ferry at a dentistry conference just off the M42?

Then I remember all the cumulative rows that Greg and I have had over the past decade – rows over who does more (*me* ...) and whether or not the other partner appreciates it (*he doesn't* ...). And I think, *Is that it?* Is that what it'll be like? For the next eighteen years? Or longer? What with house prices and financial uncertainty and kids living at home for ages ... (*Damn you, economy!*) After which we can look forward to a future of staring at each other in silence, wondering what to talk about and counting down the hours until we can go to sleep? I promised to hang out with him until death us do part. But people live forever these days, don't they?

I can almost picture a messenger on each of my shoulders, trying to sway me:

Good Angel (a miniature blonde in a metallic dress. Essentially, Kylie): 'You can't split up – you've just had the bathroom done! You're booked in for an extension next spring; you have two wonderful children – and you don't want to be "the woman who ended her marriage at a dentistry conference"!'

Less-Good Angel (aka Shiraz): 'Greg-Schmeg ... What you really want is for someone to hike up your skirt and shag you senseless. And that hasn't happened in quite some time. Definitely not post-Brexit ...'

And then ... nothing.

I wake up at the convention centre's Premier Inn, naked but for my 'Alice Rat' lanyard, on top of a dubiously stained hotel 'comforter'. I appear to be alone. And the colour-coded toiletries arranged in perfect symmetry on the bedside table confirm that I'm in my own room. But still ... things aren't looking great.

I feel jagged and raw, and I can barely lift my head it's so heavy. Instead, I have to prop myself up on my elbows, then execute a sort of commando roll to get to the side of the bed and sit up. The room spins a full 360 degrees so I decide it's probably best to keep low and slow, slicing off the divan and onto the floor. There's an acrid tang in my mouth and a vague stench of stale self-loathing emanating from my every pore. I crawl to the en suite, splash my face with water, then look up to see a woman whose mouth has set to a thin line, with a complexion like pea soup and a mop of dry, straggly hair. She's thin from exhaustion – the cleft of each rib can be made out, clearly – but she's flabby around the middle from not having had time to exercise since 2009. And possibly the late-night sugar/meat-patty sessions. Her eyes are small red slits and she has what the magazines call 'wine-face'.

'I never want to look that tired,' I say out loud, as the mirror-hag mouths the words back at me.

Ohhhhh …

I don't recognise this new reflection. Or rather, I don't want to. But my mind feels ragged. Threadbare, even. I force myself to breathe slowly and to try not to vomit as the air curdles around me. I turn on the shower and make the water as hot as I can until steam obscures the reflective glass and saves me from myself. Then I peel off the lanyard now adhering to my clammy chest, curse the cellulite blooming in my thighs, and scrub – hard – with a hotel flannel that's seen better days.

Washing feels good, I think. *Really good. I should wash more …* I wish I could do my insides, too, but make sure I give all available surfaces a thorough going over then scrape the heck out of my cheaty-snogger-mouth that so betrayed me last night with a new, goodie-bag box-fresh, firm-headed toothbrush. This initiates a small gag-reflex but I rationalise it's a price worth paying for a clean(er) mouth.

And then the guilt comes.

It descends like lead, crushing my chest first, then sinking to my stomach, until I think it might be a good idea to just let my legs crumple and lower myself down again onto the hotel bathroom's cold, tiled floor.

Charlotte and Thomas.

Seven and five.

Laughing. Puffy-eyed from sleep first thing in the morning. Tumbling downstairs, dressing gowns flapping. Eating boiled eggs and soldiers. Having their faces flannelled until they're pink and glowing. Or, I calculate, if everything's running to schedule, smelling sweetly minty around about now, after two minutes each with the electric toothbrushes they got for Christmas. I miss them. And the thought that I might have done something that could hurt them pierces like a thorn. Because whatever problems Greg and I may have, he's their dad. So I'm going to have to get on with him. Somehow. Better.

It was easier when he was working. He had something to get up for in the morning. He made an effort, and shaved and ironed his shirts occasionally. Staying at home was only ever supposed to be temporary. 'Just until I find something else,' he'd said. So I took on more responsibility at the practice and worked longer hours. I got promoted and my new role came with the 'honour' of occasionally speaking at events like these. Greg said he'd look after the kids and use the opportunity to make a start on his 'Seminal Guide to Stonehenge': a project he'd apparently started as a student but had to postpone because of, well, *life*. So the spare bedroom became a shrine to druid temples, pictures of rock formations and academic journals. Only he didn't do much of the 'looking after the kids' bit. And I still cooked and cleaned and dropped them off at school. And he'd just about remember to pick them up from the child-minder before coming home to slump on the sofa or fall asleep in his 'study' on his 'day bed'. Which, increasingly, was becoming his night bed too.

He hasn't applied for a job in months now. And when I offered to read the book – or at least the chapters he'd written so far – he became suddenly sheepish. He told me something about it being better to 'read it all in context'. And that was that.

So although, yes, I am technically a terrible person, I'm pleading mitigating circumstances. And I'm quickly becoming convinced that this morning's monumental hangover is Punishment: Part I.

I scrabble around for painkillers, find some in my bag, take two, then remember that they're the special ones from work with big shouty letters on the packaging that read: *One a day. DO NOT EXCEED RECOMMENDED DOSAGE.*

I try regurgitating one. Or both. Which, obviously, doesn't work and just makes me feel more anxious and dizzy.

Smart. Really smart ... I scold myself, before deciding that perhaps I should try eating something. Ordinarily, I don't do breakfast, but I rationalise that this might be one of those days that calls for an exception. *Fruit, maybe? Half a grapefruit?*

The 'restaurant' – another windowless room – is crammed with children and their parents, all bound for the nearby theme park. It smells of wet wipes and despair and the decibel level is deafening.

'Araminta? Do you want cow's milk on your cereal today? Does Mummy usually give you half fat or full fat? Try this and tell me if it tastes normal ...' a man wearing a blazer and cufflinks to a Premier Inn breakfast buffet addresses his two-year-old. Another woman loads as many bagels as she can into her handbag while a third dissects five hard-boiled eggs to extract the yolk and discard the rest.

People are ridiculous.

The sounds of several dozen spoons bash against bowls as though competing to give a toast and various pre-schoolers are congratulated loudly on their Weetabix intake ('Four, Felix? Clever boy!'[2]).

My skull is going to split open, I think. *Right here and now. That, or splinter internally and haemorrhage in some way ...* I decide, nursing my cranium. *But at least I'm keeping full-throttle nausea at bay for now. Well done, me ...*

I'm just approaching the 'cereal 'n' fruit station' when I experience the first lurch: a fish hook in my stomach threatening to wrench up the single raw food bar I found in my bag and the only solids to have passed my lips since 11am yesterday. My head continues to pound as I contemplate the small spheres of soft fruit bobbing in murky liquid. I decide I would very much like to hollow out my brain with a melon baller, but take a bowl anyway and convince myself, '*You can do this!*'

Only it turns out I can't.

It comes up – faster than I can stop it and with a force I didn't know I had in me. The salad bar sneeze guard proves no match and offers little resistance. Great chunks of paleo-mush, stomach lining and Shiraz (*damn you, Shiraz ...*) surge out of me and spray the fruit, the cereal, and onlookers. Liberally.

I can see the headline now:

'*Drunk mother of two vomits on breakfast buffet in front of dozens of startled diners. "I'm a disgrace," Alice Rat, a dentist from Streatham, admits ...*'

---

[2] Post recession, even the Waitrose brigade loves a Premier Inn

'Oh god, I'm so sorry.' I cast around for things to mop up with, taking it upon myself to dab at the spatters of sick nicely coagulating on cufflink man's suede loafers. *Bet he wishes he'd stuck with the cereal now,* I think. *Probably rues the day he offered Araminta a fruit parfait …* 'I'm a horrible human being,' I mutter, to no one, as I clasp a hand over my mouth and realise the ordeal isn't over. *There's more?* And then, I confirm, decisively: *There's more.*

'I think perhaps you should leave, madam,' a weedy man in a too-big suit and a badge that reads *'Here to help!'* suggests.

I agree, wholeheartedly, then flee for the lifts – hoping to make it back up to my room before the next bile-a-thon makes its presence felt.

I'm back in the privacy of my own en suite, holding my hair back to execute what I hope is a final heave over porcelain, when I hear a familiar voice.

'Well, this is cosy.'

No. My. God. You have got to be kidding me …

Wiping my mouth on the back of my sleeve, I turn around.

A broad brunette in wellington boots is leaning against the doorframe, arms folded, smelling strongly of the outdoors and judging me.

'What are *you* doing here?' I croak, pushing back hair and attempting to make myself presentable. I had been in such a hurry to hurl, I realise now, that I may have *ever so slightly* forgotten to shut the door. Or rather, forgotten that it was likely to remain wedged open by the complimentary copy of the *Daily Mail* looped over the door handle in a see-through plastic bag (*damn you, terror threats and new pictures of Helen Mirren on holiday!*)

'You sound rough!' the short, dark-haired woman broadcasts.

'You sound *loud*.' I wince at the throbbing in my skull.

'Greg called.'

I stand, unsteadily, and try very hard not to breathe booze-'n'-bile on her as she envelops me in a non-consensual and extremely vigorous bear hug before punching my arm in a gesture that presumably passes for an appropriate salutation in her world, but that *really hurts* in mine. She is only five foot two inches tall, but the woman has arms like a butcher and guns of steel. For someone who subsists solely on Shepherd's Pie and sponge pudding, she's in surprisingly good shape. Her hug-'n'-left-hook combo takes the wind out of me and the heady aroma of 'horse' she habitually carries around with her sends me right back to the toilet bowl.

'Nice to see you too,' she says as I hurl, again.

I don't like people seeing me like this. Ever. Even her. She knows this and I suspect that a part of her is enjoying it.

'Sorry,' I mumble, and then, 'How are you?'

Her mouth twitches at this. 'Better than you. Come on, let's sort you out.'

Mortified, I am hoisted up and a flannel is flung at me to 'mop up'.

This isn't right ... I'm the grown-up. I'm the one who makes sure everyone's been to the loo before they leave the house. I keep four Sainsbury's bags-for-life in my car. At All Times! I'm the in-charge-person. Not her ...

Once we're both satisfied that I'm unlikely to puke again – or indeed have anything left to throw up, save perhaps a kidney – she tells me to get packed so we can 'hit the road'.

'I can't leave!' I tell her. 'I've got another day of conference left. I'm booked in to "Combat Cake Culture" and "Take My Breath Away: Giving Halitosis The Heave Ho" ...' I hear myself saying this out loud and realise there's no way I am spending the morning in an airless room surrounded by dental practitioners. 'OK, so maybe that bit's not happening. But I don't need a lift, thanks. I'm getting the train.'

'Not until tomorrow you're not: cancelled.'

Bollocks. I had forgotten this, what with all the hands-free wine and Mr Teeth and the sick ... *Oh god, Mr Teeth ....*

'Well, lucky for you,' she goes on, 'I'm heading down south today.' It grates the way she always says 'down south' as though I've abandoned our northern roots. I haven't: we're from Leamington Spa.

And this is Melissa. My sister.

'I'm seeing a man about a dog,' she goes on. I don't doubt for a moment that she means this literally. 'So what happened last night? Get drunk all by yourself?'

'No,' I say, far too quickly. 'With a friend.'

'Was your "friend" tequila?'

'No!' I snap again, then add in a very small voice. '*Shiraz ...*'

She gives a hint of a smile, flashing her dimples.

'What?'

'"*What*?"' She mocks me, looking as innocent as a Botticelli cherub. 'By the way –' she points '– your shirt's on inside out and you've got carrot chunks where your cleavage should be.' She gestures to her own impressive décolletage to underline my failings in this area.

'Oh, for fuck's sake!' I begin scooping out chunks of ... I can't say what exactly. 'I'm very slightly hangover, that's all.'

'Really? Because the man on the front desk said I was "welcome to remove the crazy lady from room 204", and those rings around your eyes say this isn't a one-night thing. They say –' here she adopts a high pitched voice '– "*Oh hi! My name's Alice and I work all the time and I may or may not be losing it ...*"'

'That's what my *eyes* say?'

'That's what they say.' She nods as though she can't be held responsible for my eyes betraying the current state of my mental health. *If I was a photograph, she'd be drawing a moustache and a monocle on me round about now ...* I pinch the bridge of my nose, unsure whether I'm going to be sick or cry. 'Listen,' she goes on, 'how about you get dressed properly and have your existential crisis on the road? Parking costs a bomb round here ...'

Feeling too rough to object, I change out of my vomit-stained clothes into my only other outfit, the ten-year-old skirt suit from the night before. Then I draw on as much make-up/camouflage as is seemly before, in a moment of madness, asking Melissa if I look OK.

'You look like someone who wants to share "How you too can make money in real estate ..."' she tells me in an American infomercial voice.

'Thank you. I now feel far more confident about going back downstairs and facing the world,' I mutter back. *Just because I haven't started shopping at the 'I've given up' clothes shop of elasticated waistbands and body warmers. Who died and made her the mayor of fashion town?*

I pack up my right-angle arranged toiletries and stuff each sick-stained garment in one of the complimentary shower caps provided in the en suite to avoid cross contamination in my overnight bag. Then, wrapping a few extra tissues around each bundle of disgrace, just in case, I zip up the holdall and leave.

I avoid eye contact – with anyone – until I've completed my walk of shame and we're safely ensconced in the underground car park. I'm led towards a once-white pick-up truck that is apparently to be my chariot and clear the passenger seat of sweet wrappers, old newspaper ('*the dogs like to ride up front ...*'), and a half-eaten pasty.

'Oh god, that stinks,' I reel, repulsed

'Of deliciousness, you mean!' is her response.

'—of type two diabetes ...' I murmur.

'I'll have that thanks. Waste not want not ...' She crams the Cornish pasty in her mouth. 'What?'

'Nothing. You're looking ... well ...'

'Thanks. It's my post-break-up revenge body,' she mumbles through a mouthful of flaky pastry, dry mouth clicking slightly. I'm eating like Elvis after Ramadan.'

I nod as though this explains everything. I don't tend to ask about her love life any more. I rationalise that if there's anyone important, she'll tell me. *If there's anyone important, she'll tell everyone*, I think. So I'm presuming the 'revenge' is for a minor fling who doubtlessly failed to treat the dogs with adequate reverence or was allergic to the horse. Or the 'house bunnies'. I shudder at the thought. ('You know rabbits eat their own poo?' I once told her after reading an article about them online.[3] 'So?' was her response).

Melissa reaches an arm behind the passenger seat headrest to reverse and we judder backwards. As we're queuing to exit the car park, I become conscious of her looking at me. Really looking.

'What? Why are you staring?'

'Are you OK?'

'Yes!' I shrill, at a higher pitch than intended. 'I'm fine! Absolutely fine!'

[3.] Also: naked mole rats, chinchillas, mountain beavers, baby elephants, hippopotamus calves, orangutans and rhesus monkeys, according to the *Cornell Veterinarian Journal*.

This shuts down the conversation and so we drive, out of the car park and blinking into the light. I paw at my bag until I can locate sunglasses – huge bug-eye-lensed affairs that thankfully conceal half my face but look rather as though I'm being whisked away from an illicit encounter to avoid paparazzi. I couldn't look more out of place in a muddy white pick-up truck if I tried.

'Bit bright, is it, Jackie O?' Melissa asks. Loudly.

I merely whimper in response.

The low humming sound interspersed with warbling – a noise I had taken to be the ancient engine – becomes amplified once were clear of the multi-storey car park and reveals itself to be none other than Celine Dion.

Melissa assures me that this isn't her choosing. 'Local radio.' She nods at the stereo as we stop and start, jerking our way through congested city streets, livid with traffic and alive with car horns that do nothing to salve my hangover. I retrieve my phone, realising I haven't checked it since sobering up enough to remember that I *have* a phone.

It's switched off. *Switched! Off!* I never switch my phone off ordinarily. *Never.* I shudder, holding down the tiny doll-sized button to turn it on again and waiting for the black apple icon to appear, silhouetted against a bright white background. I enter my password with fumbling fingers, then feel my stomach sink yet further with each missed call notification.

Ping!

Ping!

Ping-ping-ping-ping-ping!

A torrent of new alerts come through, notifying me of voicemails.

'*You have ... TWELVE ... new ....messages. First message, sent yesterday at four sixteen pm ...*'

Nooooooo ...

That's the thing about making yourself the kind of person who's always in control – the kind of person people can depend on: you become eminently dependable. Indispensable, even. People rely on you – at least, that's what I tell myself. And then on the (very) rare occasions when things aren't running entirely to schedule or, just for example, you go AWOL at a dentistry conference, people notice. Had I married a man who could locate the Hoover and knew his way around a Tupperware drawer, I very much doubt I'd have had three missed calls from home already this morning. Had I delegated rather more at work, I'm *fairly* confident that the nine memos from the surgery could have been dealt with by colleagues (albeit to an inferior standard ...). But, as it is, they've come through to me. All of them ...

I hit the red button to hang up, unable to face the onslaught yet. Ordinarily, I have one-to-two days to decompress from all the 'talking' that is apparently necessary as a functioning professional in the field of dentistry. Usually, I spend at least twenty-four hours restoring order to my home after the working week in virtual silence – ignoring my husband and merely conversing with teenage-esque monosyllabic children. This means that by the time Monday rolls around, I have built up reserves of energy to embark upon yet another week of human interaction. But it's only Saturday. I more than fulfilled my 'chat' quota yesterday and haven't got anything left in the tank, as it were, apart from a flitting, choking anxiety. In short: I can't face it.

If they want me to do an extra shift today, they can whistle, I think, nursing my head. *If Mark's got a bad back again, it's his hard cheese; I can't cover for him. I'm in no fit state to breathe Shiraz on patients at close range today ..*

If it's important, they can text me. Or email. Or send a blimp. Really, anything but the 'talking' ...

I check my email and fire off replies to as many work-related memos as I can, to make me feel marginally more useful and in control of my life – dealing with admin during 'dead time' like a productivity machine. But this ushers in an unwelcome return of the churning sensation in my stomach.

Mmm, car-sickness on top of a hangover? Lucky me ...

I wind down the old-school window to gasp at some not-at-all-fresh city air as Celine's 'Think Twice' belts out. At full volume ...

'Do you mind?' I point at the radio dial. 'I'm not feeling great.'

'No shit ...'

'I just mean, couldn't we listen to something less *shrieky*.'

'We can have Celine, UB40 or Ronan Keating.'

'Or "nothing"?'

'Nuh-uh.' She shakes her head and gives the ancient stereo a firm shunt with the heel of her hand until UB40 starts up. 'The off button's missing and you can only get local stations.'

'How do you *know* what they'll be playing?

She looks at me as if I'm a fool. 'It's *always* Celine, UB40, or Ronan Keating.'

'Oh.'

'We don't all have *digital* ...'

I respond with a spontaneous sneezing fit, thanks to all the animal hair in the car. My eyes start to water and my breathing becomes shallow and I can't quite tell whether I'm about to suffocate or spontaneously combust. *Or both?* I'm grateful for the sunglasses concealing my reddening eyes and then my phone starts up again.

Oh, shit off, Elsa!

The caller ID announces that the 'Surgery' is summoning me, so I switch it to silent mode.

I'm already feeling guilty that I haven't checked in as promised after the panel discussion yesterday. *But seriously? On a Saturday? I bet it's Steve, the practice manager. Get a life, Steve ...*

A third call rings through, from a mobile number I don't recognise.

At first I worry that it's from *him.* Not Steve, but *him.* Mr Teeth.

I didn't give him my number, did I? What am I? Sixteen? Although when I was sixteen, mobiles had barely been invented so it would have been Melissa or Dad picking up on the landline. I cringe at the recollection – both of last night and the years of social awkwardness when I was 'supposed' to be getting into boys. It's little wonder I remained remarkably chaste until leaving home.

The caller gives up after a few flashes of green and I allow myself to exhale.

It was Steve, wasn't it? I bet he was calling from his wife's phone. Or his personal one that none of us are supposed to know about for all the Tinder he Definitely. Doesn't. Do. Despite Beverley on reception catching him swiping right at least twice last week ...

But then the number flashes up again. I press 'End call' as a cool panic trickles through me – that not only have I made such a massive error of judgement last night, but that it can still haunt me. That it might ... follow me. Home.

Let him not text, let him not text, I pray – to whoever it is I believe in since I stopped believing in ... well, anything ... sometime in the mid-1990s.

I check the messages on my phone and am further alarmed to see the familiar *dot, dot, dot* to suggest that someone is composing a message.

He's typing something ...

'*You OK?*' is all it says. I look up at the horizon to quell my mounting queasiness before glancing back at the phone and studying the mystery number.

'*Who is this?*' I type back.

Nothing.

Then the *dot dot dot* starts up again and keeps going, pulsating ominously. I have another horizon break to stop the bile coming up again, before looking back down at my phone.

They're still typing? That can't be good, I think. But then it stops.

They've gone. And I am left in peace. Or as close to an approximation of 'peace' as a married mother of two who has just done something horrendously stupid and is now regretting it is ever likely to achieve.

At the next traffic lights, Melissa, seeing that I'm finally off the phone, gives me a dead arm by way of appreciation and tells me to help myself to a Fondant Fancy from the glove box. This, to her, is love.

'No, thanks.'

'There might be a Scotch egg in there, if you'd prefer?'

'I'm fine. Thanks.'

'Your loss,' she mutters. 'You've still got some sick on your neck by the way.'

Oh brilliant ...

'Well, you've got minced beef on your cheek from the pasty,' I respond. But it's a shallow victory. *Melissa probably doesn't care that she's walking around covered in meat. Probably thinks it makes her whacky and eccentric in her enormous truck. Whereas I'm a dentist. With sick on her ...* I put a hand to my collarbone and press to ease the uncomfortable sensation.

'What's up?'

'It's nothing,' I manage, voice thin. 'It's just … my chest feels a bit tight.'

'Is your bra on the wrong hook? I get that.'

'No. My bra's fine.' I don't tell her about the four heart scares in the past two years. Apparently that's not normal for a woman in her thirties. So said the male consultant in his fifties. *I'd like to see him get two kids out of the door, on time, with shoes on, after five hours' sleep and then put in a sixteen-hour shift before collapsing in bed with a man who thinks Stonehenge is hotter than she is. Then we'll see whose heart's under strain …*

Another volley of sneezes takes over and I become convinced that my insides are about to burst. Again. Either that, or I'm about to have another of those panic attacks where it feels like I'm drowning and falling all at the same time.

I haven't got time for this …

There is nowhere in my schedule – a colour-coded rolling spreadsheet covering every conceivable area of modern life – that says, *'self-sabotage by getting drunk and then ending up at the mercy of your little sister.'* I've got things to do. The kids have swimming. *Which I bet Greg's forgotten about …* Then there's piano. And possibly a play date. *I can't remember whether it's today or tomorrow … bugger …* I'm just looking at my phone to check when the unknown number calls again. I press 'End call'. Again. But then another call comes through that reads '*Surgery*'.

It was probably just stupid Steve, I tell myself. *The unknown calls were probably just stupid Steve. Weren't they?*

I still don't answer. Then Esme, the big boss, starts calling. *You should really answer this one,* I tell myself: *It's your boss, it's your boss, it's your boss …* And yet …

They can't fire me: I'm the only one who knows how to work the new polishing machine. And where we keep the spare X-ray plates. And the coffee … Basically, they can't fire me. Can they?

I hit 'End call' again. And again. And again. Until soon, I'm jabbing at buttons frantically to make it stop, like some stomach-knottingly tense game of whack-a-mole. *Just. Can't. Do. Talking. Today …*

'Can't you put your phone away for five minutes?' Melissa complains. 'So we can chat? Like *normal* people – like we used to.'

Melissa, if she were honest, would like everything to be as it 'used' to be. I have a sneaking suspicion she even thinks electric light is overrated and is forever trying to drag me back into conversations about things that happened when we were kids. Just as she's doing now …

'Remember when we found frogs in the front garden and made up a whole swimming-pool complex for them out of ramekins?' she starts. 'Or the time we played hide and seek on our bikes in the woods …'

I shudder. I hate woods. *Too many spores. And shadows. And bugs …*

' … and you got lost, then freaked out because I didn't "find" you in time and so started making owl noises as a distress signal?'

I look blank. *I don't remember, but the whole expedition in general sounds awful …*

'You *know*! It was the same summer the boy next door offered to show us his penis and we told him "no, thanks" because *Rentaghost* was on?'

Nope. Nothing. I appear to have whitewashed vast swathes of our collective past. From childhood hijinks to being forced to grow up before I was ready, there are things I can't remember even if I wanted to. And I don't, for the most part. I'm not sure that childhood was a condition that particularly suited me. *Besides, there's no point always harping back, is there?* I prefer to look forward. Like now …

My heart start to gallop as I seize the wheel. 'Watch out!'
'What?'

'Look where you're going!'

The car swerves around a bollard and mounts the kerb before I can right it, bringing us back down with the crunch of a hubcap.

'All right, cool your fetlocks. It's fine. We're fine!'

'*Just ...*' I mutter, as a pigeon squawks and skirts the windscreen.

After this we travel in silence. Well, with Celine, Ali Campbell and Ronan Keating for 'entertainment'. It's better for everyone this way.

Melissa and I are as dissimilar as it is possible to be. I have booby-trapped my life with people who need me, all the time, whereas she has made very sure that she has no (human) dependents and is free to do as she pleases. She lives largely like a character from an Enid Blyton book or one of D. H. Lawrence's gamekeepers (think Sean Bean, but with bigger breasts), living a simple – some might say simplistic – life. The last time I visited her at home, I had to wait *eight minutes* for her on-the-hob kettle to boil and even then she insisted on using loose-leaf tea. *Not a pyramid bag in sight!* I asked for the Wi-Fi password, since the reception was terrible, and she told me she 'didn't believe in Wi-Fi'. She'd once read about a man in Leicester who was allergic to it and had to wear a body suit made of tin foil to 'repel the waves'. I bought her a microwave the Christmas before last, but she only uses it for storage ('I don't want radiation with my jacket potato, thanks very much!'). She shuns 'the new', loves anything 'old' ('Including rickets? How about hanging?' I asked once in a moment of frustration) and occasionally likes to 'opt out' of the 'fat-cat system' by closing her building society account so 'The Man' can't trace her. All this, under the umbrella ambition of being 'free'.

But freedom has always seemed overrated to me. I prefer order. And the indoors. *And clean, disinfected surfaces*, I think, as I touch something alarming in the passenger seat footwell that I'm dearly hoping is a banana skin (rather than anything more sinister).

In fact, the only thing my sister and I have in common is that we share some genes. *And not many, at that*, I think, eyeing up my driving companion.

It's fair to say that I wouldn't have chosen Melissa as my sister even in a nuclear fallout. Nor she, me, for that matter. But apparently there 'definitely wasn't a mix-up at the baby unit' and no one was 'secretly adopted' (she checked this, aged twelve). So Melissa and I are stuck with each other. Normally, this doesn't prove too much of an issue. Normally, I can get on with my life and all the 'looking after people', merely adding Melissa to the end of my 'list' during our twice-yearly meetups or quarterly phone calls. It is manageable; neat; contained. Just the way I like it. But all this is about to change.

Two

The children, welded to an iPad, barely look up when I come in. Fun Aunt Melissa elicits more enthusiasm. She is tackled to the floor within five seconds flat and is soon, from what I can make out, wrestling with them in the hallway. Greg appears, frowning at a smartphone, which he hastily puts away when he sees us.

'Oh. Hi ...' he says in his most Eeyore-y of Eeyore voices.

'Are those pillow marks on your face?'

'I ... I may have fallen asleep.' His cheeks colour.

Dad of the Year Award in the post, I think.

'I love a nap,' Melissa offers generously. 'It's like two days in one.'

'Err ... yeah. Tea?'

'Thanks. Green,' I tell him as he slouches off to put the kettle on. There's no sign of a swimming bag, nor has the satchel containing Charlotte's piano practice moved from its spot in the hall where I left it yesterday. *Greg evidently forgot both activities in the 'rush' of demolishing the Kellogg's' Variety Packs I bought for the kids yesterday ...*

I lower myself tentatively onto a kitchen chair, still conscious of the nausea ripples in danger of returning to tsunami-like proportions at any moment. *I just want to hide under the duvet with a bottle of Lucozade Zero*, I moan inwardly. *But I'm a mother of two; I have responsibilities. And possibly some sick still lodged in my bra* ...

When I've done some slow breathing and swallowed hard to put any bile back in its place, I look around at the assortment of half-empty takeout containers and sandwich wrappers scattered over the kitchen surfaces like a modern-art installation.

'I see you've been nailing your five-a-day ...'

'Huh?'

'Did you even look at a pan while I was away?'

Greg settles into his customary mask of resigned fatigue while I adopt a steady expression of well-practised tolerance. It's a heady combination that's got us through the past few years. *No point rocking the boat now*, I think, getting up in search of paracetamol. *Or a lobotomy. Or a stomach pump*, I think. *I'd take either right now.*

It's then that I notice the trail of crusted mud (earth? Manure?) meandering around the white tiled kitchen in hot pursuit of ... my sister.

'You! Shoes! Off!'

Reluctantly, she relinquishes her boots and at the same time, unleashes a blast from the past.

'Jesus Christ, your feet still stink.' I cover my mouth with a hand, fearing a further episode of vomiting.

'What? They're my lucky socks!'

'Do you ever *wash* your lucky socks?'

She looks at me, appalled. 'I'd wash the luck off!'

'I don't care! Put the boots back on.' I point at the doormat. 'I'll get you clean socks.'

'They're not dirty; they're unwashed,' Melissa objects.

'There's a difference?' I ask, incredulous and Very Nauseous Indeed by now. My sister looks at me as though I'm a fool.

It doesn't matter. Just stay there. I'll lend you a pair of mine. I need to change, anyway.'

Sprinting upstairs as fast as my hangover will let me, I pass duvets pulled over piles of washing and a fusty-smelling study, blinds still down. Fear flickers behind my eyes and I feel the familiar tightness in my throat. Instinctively, I reach into my pocket for my phone in need of a soothing pellet of ... something. *Bugger, it's still in my bag* ... I feel bereft. Pulling on some jeans and a fresh shirt, I start to worry that the mystery caller or texter will have started up again. Or worse, that Greg will have answered it. I realise I have no option but to get the socks and go back downstairs. *To my life* ....

'What's for lunch?' Greg greets me as I deliver the clean socks and return to the kitchen. I slip my phone from my bag and check: two more missed calls, one from the surgery, and a message.

'*It's me* ☺'

I feel sick.

'*From last night?*' the follow-up text reads.

So that's definitely not Steve from the surgery. *Mr Teeth* ... I don't want to know his real name. I don't want to know anything about him. What I want is to vomit again and then hide under the table with my fingers in my ears until everything and everyone goes away. But I can't. *Because I'm the grown-up here* ...

'*Don't contact me again*,' I type back swiftly before adding as an afterthought, '*please*.'

Manners cost nothing.

I ram my phone in my pocket so that I can keep it close to me from now on and practise my best 'unruffled face'. The kettle has boiled and there are mugs on the draining board. This, clearly, is as far as Greg's tea-making is going to extend today.

'I said, "what's for lunch?"' he asks again.

'I don't know,' I snap back. 'What wholesome, nutritious dish have you been slaving over?'

'Err ...'

'Right then.' I yank open the fridge and analyse the contents. 'I'll do it then, shall I?' I begin pulling out packages of various shapes and sizes and arranging them in an order that I hope might constitute a meal. 'Kids? Food! Melissa? Stay ... if you want ... ?'

I'm hoping she'll say no.

'I could eat ...' she peers at the packaging ' ... some "tofu ragu" ...'

I can already tell she's having second thoughts as I stab the film of the plastic tray with a fork and throw it in the microwave.

'Don't worry,' I assure her. 'A couple of "micro-waves" won't kill you. And there's a meat version for whoever wants it.' I watch her shoulders lower with relief. Greg slopes off to do whatever Greg does and Melissa reluctantly adds her 'lucky socks' to the washing pile. While I wait for the food to 'ding', I attack a cling-filmed head of broccoli – my one concession to home cooking – and steam it over a pan of spaghetti.

'Right. Food. Everyone!'

There is no response.

'Lunch!' I try again.

'No!' one child yelps, followed by giggling.

'Yes!'

'No!'

'Right ...' I do some deep breathing and press my fingers to my temples in an attempt to quell the throbbing as the saucepan boils over.

'We're watching a Taylor Swift video!' the eldest calls out plaintively.

'Taylor who?' My sister isn't great on pop-culture references.

'Swift. Long legs. Lucrative break-ups.' I bring her up to speed while draining pasta and scalding myself on the steam. 'The kids like to watch her videos on YouTube.'

'Bit young, aren't they? It was a dolls house and farm sets in our day.'

'Was it?' I say, distracted by the pain that now seems to be lodging itself in my eye sockets as well as my newly burnt wrist. *FFS ... this isn't a hangover; this is torture ...*

'Of course *we* didn't have all this *technology* ...' Melissa pronounces this as though it's a new fancy word for something she refuses to have any part of.

'Come on!' I try again. 'Who's for broccoli?' There is silence. 'Mmm! Broccoli ... I *love* broccoli!'

'Said no child ever ...' Melissa jokes. I give her a look that says: *don't you dare come into my home and criticise my cruciferous vegetables.* 'Sorry. Sorry. OK, deal me in.'

So I do. Even laying out knives and forks and napkins and condiments on the table in the hope of pulling back control of a day that has already gone seriously off track. *We can all sit down and share a meal. Like they do in films. Like the magazines tell me we should. We will talk. And eat. And a convivial time will be had by all,* I decide.

Greg appears in the doorway and smirks slightly. 'Why have you laid the table?'

'Sorry?'

'Why aren't we eating on our laps in front of the TV like normal people?'

'Because it's a lunchtime on a Saturday, for once we're all home, and –' my voice catches until I reign it in, sharpish '– I *thought* we could eat together. That it would be *nice*. But the food's there. Do what you want with it.'

So he does. Loading up a plate and conveying it to the sofa where he can shovel it into his mouth with only the television for company. Taking their cue from 'Dad', Charlotte and Thomas come in giggling and do the same, seizing the bowls I'd served up for them and lolloping back to their Taylor Swift sound-tracked lair. Only Melissa sits down with me at the table and tucks in, appreciatively.

'Do you know what the most important ingredient of the meal is?' she asks, mid-mouthful.

I look at her plate, puzzled. 'Beef?'

'No!' She raises a fork in appreciation and clinks her water glass against mine. 'Good company!'

'Oh.' I can tell she's trying to make me feel better but it's not working.

She has flecks of food in her teeth, I observe, *and it doesn't look like ragu … or pasty … I bet she hasn't been using the multipack of floss I sent her …*

I eat without pleasure or appetite. Broccoli with a drizzle of tofu sauce: because I should. Because it's what a responsible, health-conscious mother of two who *didn't* have a rollicking great hangover would do. It takes some more aggressive swallowing than normal and a battle of wills with my oesophagus about what's going *down* and what's still intent on coming *up*. But I win. I usually do. Or at least, I used to. Then I chase the children around the house with a pan full of broccoli (the usual) before giving up.

In lieu of a family mealtime, I treat myself to unloading clean dishes from the dishwasher (Greg thinks a House Elf does this …) and replacing them with newly soiled ones, along with a surplus collection of crockery that has built up on the windowsill.

Finally, once order and symmetry have been restored, it's time to move on to upstairs. Melissa follows me.

'Is that normal then? Greg just eating and watching TV and the kids on iPads?'

'Well ... not normal exactly ...' I flounder.

'They didn't seem very happy to see you.'

'Thanks for that,' I say as I ascend the stairs. *My sister: human truth grenade.*

At the top of the stairs, I feel a strange sense of vertigo as I survey the carnage. *You can do this*, I coach myself. *Just tidy up, get the laundry sorted, do some work, do dinner, do bath time, get the kids to sleep, then you can go to bed.* This way, I rationalise, I can make the day be over sooner. I feel sluggish and fatigued now, so pinch the fleshy part of my left hand to regain focus. *You just need to keep going, laying the path one paving slab at a time in front of you ...*

So what if I spend my life loading and unloading a dishwasher? Or putting on the washing machine then emptying it and hanging it up (the worst part). I'm getting things done, keeping my career going and looking after my family until some magical point in future when things will get easier. Like retirement. Or death ...

I'm just grappling with a double duvet cover while simultaneously trying to check emails (Esme wants to know why I've gone AWOL; I could, if I wanted, have my penis enlarged at a *'low, low price'*[4] and our library books are late; but on the plus side: I've got two new endorsements on LinkedIn!) when Melissa pipes up.

'Have you ever thought maybe modern life is life too convenient?'

Inside my tent of Egyptian cotton (wedding present), with both arms outstretched in a crucifix position, mid tricky

---

[4] Really, very reasonable, were I in the market ...

manoeuvre of holding-on-to-the-inside-of-the-duvet-cover-corners-for-dear-life pre sheathing action, I seethe.

'No.' I'm hoping the irritation in my voice is muffled by my vast cotton shroud. 'I have never thought my life is "too convenient" ...' I execute a 'flip and shake' motion with all my might and woman-wingspan to force the duvet into covered submission until, finally, I'm free – newly static hair giving me an attractive, electrified appearance. Melissa misses my triumph and is now occupied leafing through old photographs that she keeps in her wallet, like it's the 1990s.

'Well, then riddle me this,' she starts and I brace myself. 'Look at this picture of Nanna, smiling, looking totally content.' She waves a yellowing curled square showing a sepia-tinted image of a woman neither of us really ever knew. The woman has Victory rolls in her hair and wears a sundress. She's posing on a pier somewhere, standing up very straight. 'She doesn't care about how many likes her Facebook posts get, or what her inbox looks like,' Melissa goes on. 'She's just happy because war is over and she's about to be reunited with Grandpa and have twins!'

I bet she wasn't smiling like that once they arrived, in the days before disposable nappies, I can't help thinking.

'Her life was simpler!'

'Yes, well, lucky old grandma – some of us are paying a mortgage.'

I can say this because Melissa lives in a gardener's shed on an estate that she pays tuppence a year for. From what I can tell, her 'job' mainly consists of swanning about with animals in tow like a latter-day Dr Doolittle to earn what funds she needs for 'essentials', like pasties and the upkeep of a 1980s white pick-up truck.

'Anyway, I'm happy,' I protest. 'We go on holidays ...' In truth, I can't remember when the last one was. Holidays

have always seemed to me something of a time-hungry indulgence – a distraction from getting on with work/being a
grown-up. 'And there's a Starbucks opening near here soon,'
I add.

Melissa doesn't look impressed and I'm annoyed that she's
bearing witness to the moment I realise my life to date has
proven underwhelming.

'Do you hang out with people from work much?' she asks.
I shake my head. 'Old school mates?'

'What old school mates?'

Melissa folds her arms and gives me her over-the-garden-
fence face, as if to say, 'I rest my case'.

My insides shift uncomfortably and for a moment I wonder
whether I'm going to vomit again. But then I identify the
sensation: *it's not nausea, it's sadness ...*

I can't remember the last time I spent an evening with
girlfriends. Or even went for coffee. Or had a phone call. *Is
it me?* I think. *Have I let things slide? Is it them? Or have we
all been a bit crap?*

'Do you and Greg get out much? On dates and things?'

'God, no!' I scoff, then feel embarrassed by this admission
of marital failure. 'I just mean we're busy. I'm busy. And there
are always ... better things to do.' I realise as soon as I say this
that it's further ammunition for Melissa's campaign of hating-
or-my-life. 'All right, so we're not yabadabadoo happy,' I go
on. I haven't heard Greg laugh for months now. He just watches
News 24 and eats junk. The kind of food that makes him
smell a little like a decaying, milky cow. And it's not just the
quality of what he shovels into his unsmiling Eeyore mouth
that irks me, it's the quantity, too. I married a hungry man. I
shudder at the thought of the stack of pizza boxes I found
around the back of the bins last week. Or the chocolate bar

wrappers stuffed into trouser pockets and just left there, to ferment, stickily, until some mug (me) thinks to empty them before doing the laundry. I had presumed that this was normal – the average flotsam of an ordinary marriage.

But what if I've been wrong?

I'm not some naïve teenager in her first flush of love: I'm not stupid enough to think you can go through life fancying only one person. We've been on separate tracks since the kids came along – but that's life. Isn't it? And I find ways to cope. Ways to prevent a knot of stress developing in my stomach every time a new book idea goes awry or he gets overly involved in a news story on political strife in a country I couldn't pinpoint on a map. Like in bed the other night, when I'd shaved my legs and hadn't even put in my retainer yet (two kids in, this is foreplay ...) and he told me that the Czech Republic has an unemployment rate of only 3 per cent. I asked him if he was joking and he told me, 'It's a very buoyant economy.' And so I listened to a podcast on women who kill their husbands, went to sleep facing away from him, and deliberately burnt his non-Paleo, nutritionally bereft *white-bread* toast at breakfast. He slept in his study the night after that.

There might be time for romance when the smoke's cleared, I tell myself. *When he gets a job, or gets back in shape, or when we start liking each other again ...*

It's never been exactly *Casablanca*. I've never had time for long piano solos or Vaseline-lensed close-ups. Greg was meant to be my sensible life partner who could hold down a job, liked me enough to put up with me, and was prepared to build a life together and be a good father. I know, it's the stuff of Coldplay songs. Greg came along after *that* boyfriend, the one we've all had. The one I met at Fresher's Week, who played the guitar, wore a lot of product in his hair, and dumped me at the end of every term so that he could be single for the holidays. You know the sort. So when I met Greg – safe, predictable Greg, who smelled of Right Guard – I was ready. He seemed *OK*. And by the time I started to harbour doubts about this, I felt as though it was already too late. As though maybe I was just one of those people who see problems where there are none. But just recently, everything has seemed up for re-evaluation. Recently, I've started to wonder what will happen if we never like each other again.

What if this is it? A hardening fist settles in my gut at the thought – but what's more terrifying, even, is that I can't imagine an alternative. I was a daughter, then a wife, then a mother. And a dentist. That's all I've ever been.

I was destined to be a dentist from the age of five. There was something about sitting in a clean, white room – quiet but for the occasional hum of the electric blinds that closed with the touch of a button – that appealed to me. Even when I had braces fitted as a teenager, I didn't mind the bimonthly appointments to tighten the screws on my train tracks. It hurt, of course, but in a good way. And in a way that was a distraction from the gaping, hollow kind of pain that was starting to engulf me at home. Early on, my course was set: I would wear white clogs for a living and operate a hydraulic reclining chair. So I became a dentist. And now, that's what I do, in addition to running a house/crèche. Like a finely tuned machine. I work hard and keep working until each item on my to-do list is ticked off in turn. Until lately. When the day's activities have started to overlap, like the scales on a fish.

Suddenly I feel terribly tired of being a dentist. And a wife ...

'You should do something different,' my human Labrador of a sister suggests. 'You need a break.'

'It's not *Sliding Doors*,' I tell her. 'This is my life! I chose this. I've got two kids who ignore me and bills to pay. I can't just get a pixie crop and open a tapas bar …'

Melissa looks at me like a wounded puppy and I want to cry again. But I don't. Because I never do. I excel at the art of 'taking care not to make a scene'. Some may call it 'bottling up'. I prefer 'breeziness'. *We can't all fall apart …* No matter how much I want to shout and cry and scream, I always do my utmost to keep it together and never succumb to The Rage. This is a policy that has seen me through tragedy (our mother dying), humiliation (breakfast buffet barf-gate; being married to someone who prefers *Question Time* to sex …) and the impossible (root canal surgery on an exceptionally stubborn gum; getting the kids to eat vegetables at least once a month, before scurvy strikes …). My only way of coping is to keep it together. I can't lose it. Because … well, then everyone will have lost it.

And I'm the one with the four bags for life in her car …

After Mum died, everyone told me, 'Take time to cry'; 'Make space to grieve'. But I didn't. Because Melissa did enough for both of us. I couldn't compete with her extravagant displays of anguish. So I just had to get on with things. That's what was best for all of us, I decided. And I am, largely, *fine*. And if there's ever a glimmer of doubt about this, I remind myself, on loop. *'I'm fine; I'm fine; I'm fine …'* So when, very occasionally, it all gets too much, I *im*plode. My heart breaks inwards, mess-free. Fuss-free. I'm considerate like that.

There are many things I'm good at: I can check your oral cavity; I can carefully examine your soft, fleshy parts in a position and circumstance where the majority of people feel at their most exposed and vulnerable. I can plan a family calendar two years in advance; prepare a ready meal for four in five minutes flat; and remove splinters with a 100 per cent success rate. I know, just call me Peggy Lee.[5] I can clear up other people's messes and inflict pain when necessary, when it's The Right Thing To Do. But if you want someone to reminisce for hours about The Good Old Days while eating ice cream and watching *Beaches*? You're looking at the wrong woman. I'm busy. I've got stuff to do. In fact, next on the list ...

'Kids?' I croak down the stairs. 'Come and do the pillow cases, please.'

'Blimey, it's a hoot round your house ... broccoli *and* bed linen?!'

'Professional success in life has been linked to doing chores as a child,' I tell Melissa, ignoring the sarcasm. 'Starting as early as possible.'

'Yawn!' She does an exaggerated stretch then pretends to fall asleep.

I decide that now might not be the time to mention the twenty minutes of maths I do with them each night or my mantra that 'every moment of the day represents a learning opportunity'. Instead, I share my other favourite adage. 'Effort is like toothpaste – you can always squeeze out a little more.'

She mimes hanging herself in despair.

'Greg didn't know how to work a washing machine when we met!' I persist, defending myself now. 'Do you really want that inflicted on anyone else?'

'No,' she concedes, then mutters, 'though I'm not sure I'd want Greg inflicted on anyone ...'

[5.] Having a bad day/dealing with idiots? Put on Peggy Lee's 'I'm A Woman'. You're welcome.

'You know that thing where you talk out of the side of your mouth? You know I can still hear you, right? You're not speaking any more quietly,' I inform her before trying another yell: '*KIDS!*' The exertion sends me back on my heels, dizzy. So I keep quiet after this and go on folding the piles of (I hope) clean laundry, agonising for a moment as to whether one pair of blue pants belongs to me or my daughter. I hold them up to my face for further inspection.

'What are you doing?' Melissa looks at me as though I'm insane, so I explain.

'These – I wore them last week but now I'm thinking that maybe they're Charlotte's.'

'They're child-sized ...' She lets the ellipses hang.

'They were a bit snug ...' I admit. *Things were rather chafe-y ...*

Melissa continues to look at me as though I'm insane.

'Yeah, that's creepy.'

'No, it's not!'

'Yes, it is.'

'No ... ?'

'Yes.'

'Oh.'

'There should never be any doubt,' she clarifies, 'as to whether a pair of smalls belongs to a six-year-old girl—'

'She's seven, actually. Nearly eight—' I interject, but Melissa carries on.

'Or a *grown woman*. It means a) your bottom's too small; and b) you need to eat more. You barely touched lunch. What do you run on? Vapours? Do you plug yourself in to the wall every night then power down like one of your devices?'

I tell her that this sounds tempting round about now and she does a very bad face at me then puffs out her cheeks.

'There's a lot of wood to be chopped here ...'

I explain that I'm not familiar with her ye olde worldy fairy-tale woodchopper metaphors so she paraphrases, 'It's just that your life sounds a bit bollocks at the moment. And I say this with love ...'

'Bloody hell! What would that have sounded like without love?'

She holds her hands up as if to say 'don't shoot the messenger' and I want to protest. But I'm becoming increasingly suspicious that she might be right. I work. All the time. I'm often so exhausted that I feel sick. Even when I haven't bathed in a vat of Shiraz. My visible hipbones, which had been a source of pride post childbirth and were admired by the other mums struggling to lose baby weight, now jut and hurt when I accidentally bash them on things. Which I do. With growing regulatory (see 'exhausted'). And there have been times recently when the sight of Greg on his day bed, watching *News 24*, or staring at the Breville toastie maker, have made me want to headbutt a wall, so acute is my loathing of him.

'How can I put this kindly?' Melissa goes on. 'I can't, OK: your husband's an idiot.'

Melissa has never had a high opinion of Greg so this isn't a total surprise, but I feel compelled to defend my life choices in some way.

'I ... I think he might be depressed.'

'I think he might be an idiot.'

'OK, maybe. But he's my idiot. Contractually speaking, at least.' I reach automatically for the next pair of pants to fold, then realise that they are Greg's and that they're definitely not laundry fresh.

'Urgh, are those skid marks?'

'Uh-huh,' I say, expressionless. Mystery: thy name isn't the man you've been married to for years.

'That's disgusting!'

This? From the woman who trod excrement into my house and eats leftover pasties? Good grief ...

'You don't understand; it's all part of family life.' I toss them into the laundry pile, attempting to convince myself, then try one last time to summon my offspring: '*KIDS!*'

'Oh, I'm sorry, just because you remembered to have children.'

'No! No, I didn't mean that, I ...' I tail off. A large proportion of what little time I spend with my sister is occupied with trying not to rub her nose in the fact that I have a family and she hasn't. Yet. She's always maintained that she doesn't want children, but, well, how can she *know?* I think benevolently. So I try to keep kids off limits.

There's an awkward silence after this. So that by the time Melissa finally speaks, she catches me off guard. 'Well, listen, robot woman. Why don't you get away for a while? Have some time off work and the kids and Skid Mark Greg? It'll be good for you!'

I find I'm so grateful for a respite from the awkwardness that I respond in the positive. 'Mmm, maybe, one day.'

I plan to do a lot of things 'one day', knowing full well there isn't an allocated 'self-indulgence' slot in the two-year family calendar.

'Great.' Melissa seizes on this. 'We could do something together. It'll be like Brownie camp!'

'What, being picked on by the Guides and then eating burnt baked beans?'

She looks hurt. 'You might have fun!' she retorts.

Yeah, that's not going to happen, I think. *'Not enjoying things' is my forte ...*

'Don't you want to come away for a week with me?' she says, pleadingly.

A week? So long ... is what I want to say. But instead I try another tack. 'I'll come away with you once you get your wisdom tooth taken out.'

We both know this is unlikely.

Melissa has a phobia of medical professionals that she puts down to Mum sending her to a dietician briefly when we were growing up.

'If you'd been weighed like a prize heifer each month, you wouldn't like specialists either,' Melissa says.

'That's not the same thing at all!'

I then start down a well-worn path of defending accusations against the dead, of which neither of us have proof either way and I have scant recall. 'If you get your tooth sorted, it won't hurt any more!'

'It doesn't hurt,' Melissa corrects me, 'it *aches* occasionally. And twinges.' She cradles her jaw. 'I just don't like medics, no offence.'

'Plenty taken.'

'Plus, I'm healthy as an ox.' Maddeningly, wisdom tooth aside, she probably is.

'Shame. There might have been a sticker or a toy dinosaur in it for you.'

Melissa perks up. 'Really?'

'No, you're not five years old.'

'Then I'm definitely not going.'

'Fine. You stick with your slowly decaying tooth that's making your gums swell and your soft tissue inflamed and I'll stick with my usual routine.'

Dodged a bullet there, I think.

'Is it lonely being right all the time?' she snaps.

'I *really* wouldn't know.'

She reflects on this for a while, during which time I fit sheets to two single beds, make piles for three different loads of washing (whites, coloureds, delicates), and run the Hoover around, reeling now, from the enervation. Finally, Melissa does a really slow blink. *It's like taking a holiday in the mind of a Teletubby,* I think.

Then, she speaks. 'OK. I'll do it.'

'What?' I've got one hand up a single duvet cover and a fist full of feathered down in the other.

'I'll book an appointment. Next week. And a trip. For the two of us.'

Oh crap.

'Sort you out.'

I'm planning to remonstrate that I don't need 'sorting out', when I remember several distinct indicators that I may be ever so slightly unravelling of late. These include, but are by no means limited to:

- Googling *'Best of Bublé'* the other night.[6]
- Administrative errors and/or typos. Like signing off an email to a pharmaceutical rep with a kiss, and telling the new, male, orthodontic therapist that I was 'very busty'. I'm not. I meant 'busy'.
- Failing to be cross, or even surprised, when Greg ate the sandwiches I'd made for Thomas's birthday party because he thought they were 'going spare'.
- Taking showers sitting down.
- *Mr Teeth* ...

---

6. 'Haven't Met You Yet' is incredibly catchy ... OK, shoot me. Shoot me now ...

The churning starts up again in my stomach at the recollection. So I do what I always do: I bury it. Gone. *There! Ta da!* There are a lot of bad feelings buried in my back garden. But my private unspooling of emotions makes me think that maybe, just maybe, I might be losing it a little. Like a frog in a pan of water that's slowly being brought to the boil. *What if I'm having a breakdown without anyone actually noticing? That's just the kind of thing I'd do.* I silent-panic for a few moments more before tuning back in to hear Melissa say, ' … you can get some great help these days, too—'

'"Help"? I don't need therapy!'

'Who said anything about therapy?'

'Oh …' My voice is a little tighter now. 'No. No one …'

'I meant help to *book* something. Ooh, we could go ultimate-paintballing!'

'No.'

'Go Ape?'

'No.'

'Pony Painting?'

'Painting? ON a pony?' *Is she on glue?*

'Yes! They don't mind, apparently. They find it relaxing, like a massage.'

'Oh. How about a spa?' *I could handle a spa,* I think; *It would be quiet. There would be robes. And I wouldn't have to talk to anyone.* After this, I'm physically present, but mentally I'm in a white fluffy dressing gown somewhere listening to whale music. Alone.

'OK,' I tell her, surprising even myself. 'I'll go away with you.' *What's the worst that can happen?* A spa might be just what I need, I reason.

'Great! Leave it to me,' she says.

'Are you sure? I can organise it.' I'm just whipping out my phone – to a) check there aren't any messages from work or Mr Teeth; b) add this to my To-Do list; and c) plan how to scale it back to a weekend – when Melissa interrupts.

'Don't you trust me?'

Are you mad? I don't trust anyone! After last night, I barely trust myself!

My hand vibrates to alert me to a new message on my phone and I find that every sinew has tensed. *Don't let it be him, don't let it be him* ... I start up my most recent internal mantra, followed by the habitual advice of my cardiologist: ... *and remember to breathe* ...

'Of course I trust you!' I lie to Melissa.

'Well then. I'll sort it.'

'A spa, right?'

'Sure.' She shrugs.

'OK, then. Done.'

I check my phone: it's someone asking if I've been wrongly sold PPI insurance. My lungs deflate and my heart begins to return to its normal pace.

'It's settled then!' Melissa beams, and I do my best to smile back.

And breathe.

Once I've handed over the reins I'm filled with a rush of something unfamiliar. *Relief? Could it be?* I'm becoming increasingly aware after last night's performance that something's got to give. *And if all it takes to get back on track – by which I mean IN CONTROL AT ALL TIMES – is a spa break with my sister, well, then perhaps it's a price worth paying?* Sure, I've just entrusted a weekend of my life to someone who thinks pot noodles are a delicacy and likes to shovel animal shit for fun. And yet there's a sort of warm, wobbly feeling in my throat as though maybe ...

'You're about to cry!' Melissa stands up, looking alarmed. I last cried in plain sight of another human being in 1992 – and that was when a limb fractured in four places. 'Is that a ... tear?'

'Definitely not.' I dab at an eye. This is a lie. I can now feel my armpits sweating Shiraz with the effort not to weep. 'Do you mind leaving?'

'Okaaaay, I'll go,' she says, getting up and giving my arm a hefty right hook for good measure. 'Well, see you soon – I'll aim for some time in the next fortnight.'

'The next *fortnight*?' I nurse my arm. At least it's distracted me from the urge to cry. 'I don't know about the next *fortnight*,' I tell her. 'I'll have to check my calendar. I can't just drop everything ...'

She's not listening. Instead, she's nodding as though I'm a small child.

'You worry too much, it'll be just like the good old days,' she tells me.

'Ha! Great!'

That's what I'm afraid of, I think, ominously.

Three

Two weeks later ...

'I've got us a great deal,' she said.

'It's better value to go for a week,' she said.

'Bring your passport,' she said.

I had assumed that this meant we were staying somewhere swanky. Somewhere the concierge needed extra security and liked to take down your particulars, swiping a credit card before your stay in case you raided the minibar for nuts that cost £500 or stole the towels. I hoped that this meant 'five stars' and 'luxury' and embossed complimentary stationery with the word '*bespoke*' scattered liberally around the in-room literature. I laboured under this misapprehension and kept on dreaming of infinity pools and massage chairs until our day of departure, when the muddy white pick-up truck pulled off at the junction for Heathrow's Terminal Five.

'A *plane*? We're going on a *plane*?' I bleated.

'Uh-huh.' Melissa responded with a dimpled smile, glimpsed in profile from the passenger seat.

'You never said ...'

'You never asked,' she retorted, still grinning infuriatingly before assuring me that she'd let Greg know and that, 'Scandinavia's great at this time of year'.

'Scandinavia? Wha— Why?'

'Don't worry, you'll love Denmark!'

'Denmark?' I squawked. 'Wait, and you've been before?' This was the first I'd heard of it.

'Oh yes, loads! Copenhagen's wonderful – better than the song, even!' Melissa enthused.

'Right. OK, then.' I tried to stay upbeat and reconcile myself to a city minibreak. 'So you can be our tour guide—'

'Oh no, we're not going to Copenhagen,' she corrected me.

'We're not?'

'No,' she said. 'Not quite ...'

We had already checked in our bags before she revealed our final destination. But by then it was too late.

'*WHAT?*' I struggled to contain my ire on learning that we were headed as far from the style-saturated Danish capital as it was possible to travel. Melissa tried to placate me with the biggest coffee they sold at Costa, before breaking the news that not only was there unlikely to be a fluffy towel in sight, but that there were other people involved. '*Group* travel? "Roughing it"? That wasn't what we agreed!' I hissed, trying not to make a scene.

'Wasn't it?' Melissa adopted her best 'innocent' expression. 'I must have remembered it wrong. That or you were still drunk ...' she'd added, tartly. Then, in an attempt to appease me: 'Here, I got you a present.' Rummaging in her rucksack, she pulled out what looked like the costume for a hen do: a bulleted silver plastic dome topped with two comically large horns.

Slowly, and through gritted teeth, I asked: 'What the flying fuck is that?'

'It's a Viking helmet!' She beamed, ramming it on so hard that the rough plastic moulding scraped my forehead and the bulleted rim dipped below my eyes, obscuring my vision. 'Whoops! It's a bit big. You always did have a pea-head!'

'At least I haven't got a swede-head,' I countered once I could see again and spotted the matching hat perched atop her cranium.

Melissa, unperturbed, continued. 'We're going on a *Viking retreat*! This is what *they* wear!'

There were so many things wrong with this statement, I wasn't sure where to start.

'OK, firstly: Vikings never wore horned headgear—'

'Yes, they did! I've read *Asterix the Gaul*!'

Apparently she wasn't joking.

'That was a cartoon! Drawn by a Frenchman!' I half spluttered. 'Horned Viking helmets are a myth!' Melissa looked sulky on hearing this. 'And you know Vikings don't exist any more, right? They've been out of action for a thousand years!'

'Have they though?' Melissa countered.

'Yes!'

I'd watched enough History Channel output with Greg to feel fairly confident on this one.

'Or is that just what they *want* you to think?'

'What?'

'Otherwise *everyone* would want to move to Scandinavia!'

'*Would they*? Would they *really*?' Exasperated, I removed my scratchy hat, at which point Melissa put it back on me. There ensued a very unbecoming tussle between two grown women over an item of fancy dress until our flight number was called and we passed the duration of the journey in silence.

It had been arduous enough explaining to Greg that he was going to be in sole charge of himself and two children (essentially: *three* children) for a whole week, with only an arsenal of takeaway menus for backup.

'But you never go anywhere?' had been his response.

'Exactly!' I'd told him. 'That's why I'm going away now. I've *earned* this.'

I bought up as many ready meals as our freezer could handle, then instructed Charlotte and Thomas on how to defrost them if necessary. I briefed the childminder that we might need extra hours in case Greg 'forgot' to pick up the kids (again) and asked her to call me in case of emergency.

'Because I'll only be an hour or so away,' I'd told her. 'I can easily come home'.

Ha!

What I hadn't banked on was travelling 1000km to spend a week with strangers.

I hoped that the kids would be OK.

I hoped that Greg could keep them fed and watered and generally alive and unbroken.

For Seven Whole Days ...

Now, I'm crouching in a field with a wet bottom and knees that feel as though they're going to give way at any moment. It's raining. Again. That kind of persistent drizzle that makes the world smell like a portaloo. And we're being shouted at. Again.

'Squat down: get low! Channel your inner primate!' the man-bunned hipster in harem pants is barking at us as he walks up and down, supervising our attempts at 'chimp walking'. 'This is natural movement,' he tells us while scratching at facial hair in a manner that screams 'monkey'. 'You're relearning basic mobility skills!'

That's as may be, but I feel like a fool. I'm also cold, fed up, and inherently suspicious of people who substitute a beard for a personality. I'm already pretty sure that this trip is A Bad Idea.

'See? No horned helmets,' I hiss at Melissa.

'Maybe they only wear them for special occasions,' she responds mid-squat, unwilling to meet my eye.

'Right. Sure. That'll be it,' I mutter and do some grade-A swearing under my breath.

Man-bun tells us to call him 'Magnus' and that he'll be our 'spiritual and physical guide' for the next seven days.

Well, that sounds like a lawsuit waiting to happen … I think.

'Now I want you on all fours!' he demands, prompting sniggering and a side-eye from the busty, older blonde next to me. 'I need your legs wide and your butt low!' Cue guffawing. 'I want you crawling, chest to the ground!' he says.

And by 'ground', he means 'mud'.

In a rain-sodden no-man's-land on an island somewhere in the North Sea, I finally wave goodbye to the last shreds of my dignity. And as someone who's been stooped in the trenches of early parenthood for years now, this is a new low.

I want to stand up and shout, 'What are we doing here? Surely nobody is enjoying this?' But I don't. Because I'm me. *Stupid old 'me'.*

'Next: crab walk!'

'I've done that one,' the older blonde mutters, pulling at the gusset of her leggings. 'Horrendous.'

Magnus ignores this and demonstrates a sort of mobile bridge, pushed up on his hands and feet, torso upwards, moving around with apparent ease, as though 'walking' this way is perfectly normal. 'You need to be prepared for any potentially injurious situation you might encounter!' he barks, still in position. I can't imagine *what* potentially injurious situation might necessitate a crab walk. *Perhaps a sociopathic megalomaniac with a finger on the nuclear button who says he*[7] *will destroy the*

[7.] Let's face it, it'll be a 'he' …

world unless everyone starts walking like a crab. Or a real-life version of that Catherine Zeta-Jones scene in Entrapment *where we all need to limbo under lasers ...*

Magnus goes on. 'Look up, see the sky! There's a whole world out there! Just look!'

I try. But it's raining, *hard* now. So I'm forced to squint.

'I'm very, very wet,' I hear myself whimpering, to no one in particular.

'It's just water!' Melissa scoffs. 'Don't you wash?'

'*I* wash. *You* don't wash ...'

'No, *you* don't wash'

Oh god, this is ridiculous, we can't regress to childhood insults on day one. Where will we have left to go?

'It doesn't matter.' I stop myself, too tired to spoil for a feud and damned if I'm doing it in public. 'I just hoped we'd end up somewhere ... warmer.'

Melissa inclines her head, still in crab pose. 'I'm a woman whose face gets sweaty in the Midlands! I can't go to a hot country.'

'It's just so ... *bleak*.' My crab collapses as I look out beyond our rucked-up field to the forbidding woodland behind us and a wind-churned sea – the colour of Farrow and Ball Elephant's Breath. My fluffy-robed, manicured-lawn fantasy now seems a long way off. 'It's like we're in a black-and-white film,' I say, taking in our fifty shades of grey surroundings. 'The sea, the sky – even the clothes – everything's monochrome,' I whisper.

'We're not in black and white,' she corrects me 'We're in *Scandinavia.*'

'Oh.'

My knowledge of the region prior to arrival was muddy, at best, but I have already gleaned that it does indeed boast latter-day Vikings, along with bad weather and an allergy to colour. Even the hostel we stayed at last night was largely unicolour: that colour being grey. Everything about the place could be described as 'functional'. Clean, tidy and minimalist, certainly – but a spa, it was not. Now I'm chilled to the bone and mourning disposable slippers, medical grade facials and a mini-break filled with small food on big plates.

'OK, now stand up and take off your shoes!' our leader shouts to be heard over the whistling wind.

He must be joking.

'But it's freezing!'

'It can be blowing half a pelican, I don't care. You need to reconnect with nature, *feel* the earth beneath your feet.'

I look down and see rivulets of water meandering through patches of lichen. I don't feel much like reconnecting with that. *I'll get trench foot! Isn't there some sort of health and safety directive against this?* But Magnus will not be moved. 'You won't meet the – how do you say it? – "Health and safety brigade" here. We're *Vikings.*' He goes on: 'Our work has moved from cow to computer – we've forgotten how to live. We don't even feel our bodies any more unless we're on holiday and then we get ill, because we're so run down.'

This is true. I've been on antibiotics every half-term and school 'holiday' for years.

'We're afraid to get back to the earth! Afraid to get our hands dirty—'

'Not me,' Melissa mutters.

My nose wrinkles and I find myself wiping my hands on my trousers, wishing I'd packed hand sanitiser.

'We're gym rats who have forgotten how to jump or sprint. Office hamsters who've forgotten how to climb a tree!' I'm pretty sure that now isn't the time to mention that I have never been able to climb a tree. Nor do I enjoy being compared to vermin. But Magnus goes on. 'Man – *even* woman – has been fully domesticated, and we're miserable because of it!'

'Even' woman? Rude, I think.

'You!' he jabs a finger at me, as though sensing dissent.

Oh bollocks: I'm going to be required to do something. Or worse: say something …

'Can you honestly tell me you're strong enough to carry her –' here he points at Melissa '– out of the woods when she breaks her leg?'

'"When"?' Melissa looks alarmed. 'You mean "if"?'

'Or that you could swim, cross current, when you fall in the sea?'

'Again, "when"?'

'Or jump out of a second-storey window and land unharmed?'

'No …' I falter, though feel fairly sure this isn't going to happen any time soon – the only buildings I've seen since arriving are bungalows.

'I'm sure a few of you are familiar with a treadmill.' Here he looks at our youngest participant, the model-esque twenty-something with the caramel-coloured hair. 'But *free* running is the most essential life skill we can possess.'

This seems a bit strong. *What about the ability to tear the film off an M&S ready meal while sending an email, doing a seven-year-old's homework and disciplining a five-year-old, all at the same time? Or dentistry, just for example?*

'As the saying goes: you "run for your life", you don't swim or climb for it. So here, you'll learn to run as nature intended. You will learn how to sprint up hills, carry boulders—'

'Boulders?' FFS …

'Climb trees, crawl through brush, balance on logs – all the skills our distant ancestors had to have in order to survive, back before reality TV, pensions and Wi-Fi took over. You will learn,' he continues to bark, much like an army major, 'the transformative power of PHYSICAL ENDURANCE –' he half spits these last words '– as well as the instinctual movement patterns built into our PRIMAL MEMORIES. You will reconnect to the elements; to yourselves; and ultimately, to the *UNIVERSE*.'

'Blimey,' I whisper to Melissa, 'are we in a cult?'

'Shh!'

'You will pass through the SEVEN STAGES of Viking training.' He holds up a finger to illustrate each of these. 'STAGE ONE: shelter. STAGE TWO: foraging. STAGE THREE: handicrafts—'

'"Handicrafts"?' Melissa's lip curls.

'Handicrafts,' Magnus repeats, looking irked. 'People always talk about the plundering but handicrafts are a crucial part of Viking-ing! You want to look your best going into battle, right? Well, Vikings – especially men – took extreme pride in their appearance and adorning themselves.' He strokes his beard.

This explains a lot, I think.

'Non-Scandinavians often presume all the men here are gay, but no, we just know how to look after ourselves.' He touches his necklace protectively, then smooths back his hair.

The Viking protests too much, methinks …

'STAGE FOUR: weaponry—'

'That's more like it!' Melissa grins.

'STAGE FIVE: boatbuilding. STAGE SIX: navigation. And, finally, STAGE SEVEN: going berserk.'

Magnus is dismissive when the chesty, older blonde asks him to elaborate on this last one and more than a little thrown by having his 'YOU will' speech interrupted. 'Later!' is all he says, before continuing, 'As well as mastering essential life skills, YOU will learn to embrace the Viking code of conduct—' I'm willing him to keep marauding and pillaging out of this and thankfully, he obliges '—prioritising truth, honour, discipline, courage, hospitality, self-reliance, industriousness and persever-ance.' A quick mental tally tells me I'm in need of help with at least two of these. 'By the end of the week, the four of you will never be the same again!'

We are SO in a cult, I think.

'Sorry,' the older blonde pipes up again, hand raised. 'Did you say it's just the four of us?'

'Yes.'

'That's *it*? No others?'

'Another woman was supposed to come but she twisted her ankle at a military fitness boot camp.'

Boot camp? What is wrong with people?

'No ... err ... men?'

'This week? No. Now, shoes!'

The older blonde gives a deep sigh in response, before being gee-d along to remove her shoes and place them in a hessian sack.

'Socks too?' she asks, reluctantly.

'Socks too.' Magnus nods before 'treating' us all to a demon-stration of the sorts of skills he'll be demanding, namely sprinting to the forest. His hands slice the air, Usain Bolt style.

'Feet underneath hips!' he calls out as he disappears into the distance. 'Lean forward!' He shouts now to be heard across the void. 'From the ankles! Make your heels kiss the earth,' is his penultimate yelp, before adding, 'LAND ON YOUR BALLS!' and shimmying up a tree.

'Bloody hell,' I mutter under my breath.

'Is he ... ? Was that ... ?' Melissa's eyes swivel as he vanishes into the undergrowth, then she turns back around to look at the rest of us. '*Why*?'

'I think he's showing us his technique,' announces the model-esque twenty-something with the caramel-coloured hair and the ass that just won't quit.

'You can say that again,' says the older blonde, fanning herself. She raises her non-fanning hand in greeting without taking her eyes off Magnus's lithe form – now scaling the upper branches of a tree. 'Hi, I'm Tricia.'

'Alice,' I respond.

'And I'm Melissa!' My sister bounds over and extends a paw to shake hands.

As Magnus disappears from view, Tricia turns to give us her full attention, readjusting her ample bosom as she does so.

'Marvellous to meet you both. *That's* Margot.' She points at the model-esque younger woman, who's now perfecting her 'crab walk', looking determined, drenched, yet somehow simultaneously devastatingly beautiful – despite the Old Testament weather.

'She looks like a child's drawing of a lady,' Melissa marvels.

She looks like a pain in the arse, I observe.

Balancing on her hands and feet, enviably flat abdomen raised to the clouds, head back and hips thrust effortlessly upwards, she takes a few crabby steps backwards and forwards. She moves tentatively at first, before building up speed and then stopping to look around her. Then, seeming to remember that she's supposed to be a crab, she resumes her scuttling from side to side instead. The rest of us curve our necks and tilt our heads in sync in an attempt to follow her movement.

'How does she … *bend* that way?' I wonder out loud.

'It's like magic,' Melissa murmurs.

'It's *like* being twenty-three years old,' Tricia corrects her.

We look up as Tricia gives us a rundown, as though delivering a news bulletin. 'That's her natural hair colour – I know, it's enough to make you sick. And yes, she's been scouted as a model on more than one occasion. She's also a Pilates regular – fit as you like, minor aristocracy and nosebleed rich.'

Melissa and I stare, nonplussed, wondering how Tricia knows so much about the new arrival – and whether we're to be subjected to the same level of scrutiny.

Thankfully, Tricia elucidates. 'Shared a cab with her from the airport. Clocked her luggage. And gold cards. Plural. Plus her skin elasticity is Out Of Control ...'

I glance over at Margot and her amazing skin, as well as her amazing caramel-coloured hair. *Just the kind of confident girl that wears hats indoors,* I think, *and culottes.*

'Wow! Do you think she knows the royals?' my sister asks. As well as eschewing modern technology and pop-culture post 1997, Melissa has the cultural tastes of a woman twice her age. Her favourite things include: Julie Andrews (in, well, anything), shortbread and the queen. She occasionally refers to Fergie as 'a bit *fast*' and still hasn't got over the death of Diana. Dad got her started on commemorative crockery when Edward and Sophie got hitched, so by the time Kate and Wills rolled around, she lost her royal-mug mess. In short, she's as ardent a monarchist as one might ever have the misfortune to encounter.

Tricia stoops to nurse an already uncomfortable and cold bare foot so I take the opportunity to hiss at Melissa. 'Stop being so weird and impressed by posh people.'

'I *can't*,' Melissa whispers back, shaking her head. 'I love the word "cummerbund".'

'Who doesn't?' Tricia springs up again, evidently overhearing. 'I'm particularly fond of "lacrosse". So, are you two friends?'

'Sisters.'

'Ahhh ...' She nods, before adding, 'Oh, here we go', as Magnus descends from a tree and does a backflip for no conceivable reason. 'No one has any business to be that flexible post twenty-five,' Tricia adds dreamily. 'He's like spaghetti ...'

He's, 'like', a massive show off, I think.

'Phew! Hot work, hey, ladies?' Magnus is back by our sides and before any of us can respond, the New Romantics shirt has come off and he's doing sit ups. Just because.

Tricia begins salivating. Visibly.

'Look at him, all laid out there. Like a banquet!' She preens under his gaze.

'Oh, come on ... !' This is too much and I feel morally obliged to break my vow of conversational reticence with people outside of my immediate family.

'What?' Tricia demurs as he embarks on a series of star jumps. 'He's seriously hot! I could tear those harem pants off with my teeth ...'

'You're mad,' I mutter. 'He looks like Aladdin ...'

She snorts slightly and smiles at me, so I smile back. Then Magnus begins strumming on his chest like a Scandinavian silverback and announces he'd like to assess our 'initial equilibrium' by testing us on our slack lining. Tricia starts tapping under her chin.

'That's something I've struggled with for years now,' she confides. 'My chap in Harley Street calls it wattle.'

'I don't think he means your neck,' I whisper, then incline my head to the tightrope Margot is helping Magnus string up between two giant fir trees.

'Oh! Good. Well, I'll give anything a go once.' She adjusts her breasts as if to check they are evenly aligned before stepping up to take her turn. It doesn't go well and she clings to Magnus for support, tighter than might be strictly necessary.

'How old do you suppose Tricia is?' Melissa hisses now the older woman is out of earshot.

'Which bit of her?' I say, but Melissa is too nice to pick up on my meaning.

'Reckon she's had her teeth done?' she goes on.

'And the rest!' I make my intent more overt by miming 'grapefruits' but am caught out, mid motion, by a loud, 'You!'

'Me?' I drop my fake-boob charade as swiftly as I can.

'Yes, you!' Magnus is pointing at me. 'It's your turn.'

Shit . . .

He instructs me to 'find my balance' on the hastily assembled outdoor tightrope. Which, despite being a mere two feet off the ground, is terrifying.

What if I fall? What if I get hurt? What if I look silly? My heart pounds as I step up . . . and fall. And get hurt. And look silly.

'Keep trying!' Magnus commands. 'Always!' So I do. But I'm just as bad at balance on a slack line as I am at 'balance' in every other area of my life. And starting the week joint 'bottom of the class' with Tricia doesn't make me feel a whole lot better about our excursion, either.

Then Magnus takes my smartphone away. And it hurts. Physically.

I was supposed to have relinquished my device on arrival but conveniently 'forgot'. Thanks to a handy pocket in the only vaguely exercise-appropriate trousers I own, I've managed to secrete the phone about my person until now – when a Facebook Messenger notification sets off a bright, unnatural sounding '*ting*!' and I am hoist by my own electronic petard.

'In the bag!' Magnus the Merciless demands.

Dropping my precious white phone/mobile Internet connection/life-organiser/entertainment/sustenance/sanity into a hessian sack feels like giving away a beloved pet. If I'd ever had a beloved pet. Or could bring myself to compare my smartphone to a close relative or a child. Which, of course, I never would. Obviously. But still, it smarts.

'Now, it's time for you to be baptised by this life-giving rain with your new Viking names!' Magnus bellows.

Cult, I think, *Definitely a cult.*

'You!' He hones in on Tricia. 'You shall be "Proud Chest".' She thrusts out her enhanced bosoms, delighted.

'For you—' he looks Margot up and down '—I'm feeling "Ulf", which means "Night Wolf".' Margot nods very seriously as though adjusting to this new persona.

'Here, we have Strong Legs!' Melissa looks pleased, adopting an unfortunate Peter Pan stance to illustrate.

And finally, he comes to me. 'I'm getting … "Aslög".'

I look at him. *Is he serious?*

'"Ass Log"? As in Ass Log?'

'Aslög,' he clarifies, making exactly the same sound as I have just made. 'It means "engaged to God" in ancient Norse.'

'I don't care what it means in ancient Norse, I am not being called—' I start, but he's already swinging the hessian sack over his shoulder and striding off.

Proud Chest and Strong Legs attempt to console me, and Night Wolf tries to persuade me that being crowned 'Ass Log' is a compliment ('*Oh bugger off, you get to be Night Wolf, like some hot TV Gladiator!*' I want to snap back). I assure her that I will not be operating under the name of 'Ass Log' for the next five days. *And I don't plan on using your daft 'Viking' names either*, I think.

'I wouldn't worry about it,' Tricia offers. 'We're in for a muff-heavy week, so it doesn't much matter whether or not you sound like a stool sample.'

'What? I didn't come here to … to … *hook up* with someone!' I'm not confident of the terminology here (what would Taylor Swift say, I wonder?) but I'm hoping my meaning is clear.

'No? No. Of course. Well ... well done, you.' Tricia flaps slightly and I feel bad, so I'm grateful when Melissa leaps in.

'Have you been on many of these types of retreats?'

Tricia nods. 'A few. The last one I went on was all chia berries and colonic irrigation. Before that it was transformational breath – "feeling up my clavicle" and bothering my abdomen. Then there was "family constellations", where I shouted at a woman from Watford pretending to be my ex. Made her cry. Felt awful. I did crystal therapy in Croatia last year. Detox in Arizona. Yoga in the Himalayas. And, of course, Ibiza boot camp. And now, this.'

'Wow.' Melissa looks slightly overwhelmed.

'So what made you come to this place?' I can't help asking.

'Oh, it was a last-minute thing. Didn't read too much about it. Just looked at what was available within the dates and booked.'

'You're lucky – took tonnes of arranging and anal calendar management to get Alice off work so she could come.' Melissa overshares as usual and I worry instantly that Tricia will now think I have an actual 'anal calendar' – like a period tracker for the faecally retentive. So I'm relieved when she presses on.

'I just had some holiday to use up ... Well, I was given some time off,' Tricia contradicts herself. 'So, here I am ...'

That's odd, I think. The only time I've ever encountered someone being 'given time off' at the last minute was when Steve from work was caught in a compromising position with Janet, the pharmaceutical rep, in his new reclining dental chair at the Christmas party. Esme told him to have a holiday with his wife, 'pronto'. 'And make sure you take her somewhere snazzy,' she'd instructed. He'd had to do a lot of grovelling at the clinic to be allowed back – as well as paying for the chair to be deep cleaned – before his 'holiday' (aka suspension) was deemed spent.

I look at Tricia, curiously. *Could it be that she has her own dentist's-chair/trade conference style indiscretion to hide?*

I'm curious to know what she does for a living but I let her quiz Melissa first on her own 'professional status'. Just for kicks.

'Err … I do grounds-keeping type things,' is the vague answer she's giving these days. Then she turns to me.

'And how do you pay the bills?' Tricia asks.

The admission that I'm a dentist invariably makes people speak like a ventriloquist for a good ten minutes for fear of judgement, followed by a hushed outpouring of their dental history and any oral problems currently being experienced. Tricia is no exception and we talk tartar for a while before Melissa finally asks:

'So, what do you do?'

Tricia squints at her as though assessing whether this question is for real. Then seeing the guilelessness in my sister's expression (see 'Teletubby') answers, 'Oh, radio. Just local, these days.'

'Cool,' nods Melissa. 'So why do you always play Celine Dion, Ronan Keating or UB40?'

'What?'

'On local radio!' Melissa goes on. 'Is there, like, a law or something?'

Tricia looks suitably baffled but is saved by a holler from a hundred yards away.

'Viking rule number one: Keep moving!' Magnus thunders.

'Sorry!' Melissa shouts back, and then, 'Where are we going?'

'Where are any of us going?' is his reply. 'That's the journey! That's the adventure!'

'Sure, but really, what are we supposed to be doing right now?' Tricia enquires. I suspect that she's used to her retreats having a little more structure and is missing the security of *'manicures at 1600 followed by cocktail hour at 1730 ...'*

'OK,' Magnus concedes, realising he's dealing with a bunch of namby-pamby Brits here rather than hardy Nordic types. 'I'm presuming many of you will be tired after your journey.' This is the first sensible thing he's said since we arrived. 'So we'll make a start on building shelter for the night in the forest.'

We're spending the night in the woods? We're spending THE NIGHT? In THE WOODS?

This is rapidly turning into my worst nightmare. And, it turns out, I'm not alone.

'You want us to build a shelter *ourselves?*' Tricia blinks.

'Yes.'

'But what if we don't know how?'

'I'll guide you.' This doesn't fill me with confidence. 'You will be empowered to use your hands and build something,' he says, looking at me before adding, 'You'll be reminded that there's more to life than spreadsheets! Like the sun, the sky and the earth!'

How does he know about my colour-coded schedule? I think, enraged. *And when might the sun be putting in an appearance?* I grimace at the slate-grey sky.

'It's a buzz like no other,' Magnus goes on, 'sleeping in something that you made yourself. You don't get that from Excel. So come on! Let's do this!'

There is grumbling (me), gossiping about whether or not Magnus has been on a tanning bed (Tricia, to a puzzled Melissa) and skipping to keep up with our hallowed leader (Margot, who has a fizziness about her that somehow annoys me. *She ... bounces. Everywhere. Far too much pep,* I think, testily).

We're led to a mountain of logs, neatly stacked and arranged in a giant pyramid.

'There you are!' Magnus points.

'That's it?'

'That's it.'

'I can't even do flat-pack furniture!' Tricia looks concerned. 'Plus, these hands have modelled ...'

'Ooh, who for?' Melissa asks.

'*Saga Magazine.*'

'Oh ...' My sister has no idea what this is.

'And, err, what do we do for beds?' I ask, optimistically.

Magnus points at the sodden earth and I gulp.

'Ha! Not really. I am just making a fun joke with you!' he says. *Oh, how we laugh ...*

'Wait here.' He retrieves a pile of distressingly 'rustic'-looking grey blankets from behind the wood-stack, along with four rudimentary lilos that he sanguinely describes as 'air beds'.

'What if there are bugs?' The words come out of me in a small, strained voice.

'There aren't any dangerous insects in Scandinavia,' Melissa assures me. 'Or even scary ones.'

'She's right,' says Tricia. 'This isn't *I'm a Celebrity*. There are no deadly spiders and no kangaroo scrotums will be harmed in the making of these Vikings. I checked ...' This too passes Melissa by.

I look around at the woodland surroundings that are apparently to be my home for the next week. Apart from a few rabbits, flashing a streak of white backside as they tear about, we are completely alone.

A shiver trickles down to the base of my spine.

'Right then.' Melissa gives my arm a punch. *I wish she wouldn't do that ...* 'Let's get going.' She knocks on the nearest trunk, then says authoritatively. 'Yup, good trees, these ...', then heaves a log onto her shoulder and nods at me to take the other end. Reluctantly I move towards it and embrace the cold, wet wood, crawling with insects.

I wish I had some of the latex gloves from the dental surgery with me now, I think, kicking myself for not having packed a few pairs. Like I normally do, in case of emergencies, along with the anti-bacterial lemon-scented hand gel.

In lieu of such necessities, I use my bare, unsanitised hands and pull. The log's damp, brown outer layer flakes away in my hands, but other than that, it does not move. I pull some more. But nothing happens.

'Come on, put your back into it,' Melissa cajoles.

'I'm trying,' I remonstrate, feeling my face colour and my heart race with the effort. *Keep. Your. Shit. Together,* I coach myself as I use all my strength to move the log ... precisely nowhere.

'Jeez Louise, you really are weak! I said you needed a good meal inside you,' my sister commentates helpfully.

Margot comes to my aid and is sickeningly strong for a girl with such a tiny bottom. *She's got ... triceps,* I gape, as she rolls up her sleeves to reveal perfectly sculpted arms: *A bit 'look at me' though, isn't it? Like a sort of, 'Have you met my superior gene pool?' *Arrow here ... **

Tricia joins in, too, but is – as predicted – about as much use as a carpet fitter's ladder. Somehow, between us, we manage to get the blasted thing up onto our shoulders. Which, when you have four women of varying heights from semi-midget (Melissa) to me (once reviewed by an ex as 'gangly'), makes for quite an achievement.

With one log in place, there is a sort of unspoken confidence that we can therefore get another log in place. And another.

And another. Until, maybe, hopefully, we'll have built something that keeps us dry. Ish. We've also been instructed to find a boulder for the 'door' in accordance with Magnus's strangely biblical vision for our inaugural shelter.

At least, that's the plan.

Twelve hours later, I wake to find Melissa spooning me from behind and someone's toes tickling my nose.

'Arrgh ... wha—? Go away!' I bat off feet, then Melissa's leg, which has been flung over my torso. 'I was having a very detailed dream about being at a spa ...'

A tousled head looks up from the other end of our tiny shelter and Margot blinks into consciousness.

'Morning!'

'Oh, hi ...'

'Oh ... God ... what time is it?' Tricia's voice growls, as the feet in my face stretch and flex.

'I don't know,' I reply tightly, realising that I will have precisely zero privacy for the next week. I'm also cold, dirty, and uncomfortable, lying under a scratchy blanket while my airbed gently seeps ... *I'm definitely touching earth*, I think, scanning my body for areas of severe pain and finding several. There are stones the size of a small island under my spine, my head is throbbing, and someone has broken wind.

'Oh, sorry,' Melissa apologises with a waft of her hand to clear the smell.

Urgh, gross.

'Isn't this snug?' she continues, propping herself up on an elbow.

I have never liked camping. That was always Dad and Melissa's thing. Mum and I preferred the indoors. And beds. And sheets. Dad still likes to go and stay with Melissa in the countryside and the pair apparently go off on adventures into the wild. I am not invited, but then, neither do I wish to partake. I see Dad once a year, sometimes twice, and always invite him to spend either Christmas or Easter at ours. I never go to his. Because that would mean going 'home' to a house crammed with sentiment and sadness. The house where Mum died. And I don't do sad, as a rule.

Dad has never complained about this arrangement, but then, Dad never complains about anything. You'd barely even know he was there half the time. It's as though a part of him stopped when Mum did. Like he got sick at the same rate as Mum, just in a different way – with a prognosis that was chronic rather than terminal. He demanded less from life and took less pleasure out of it. No matter what options he was presented with. This is a state of affairs that continues to this day. But it means I can at least persuade myself that he doesn't mind things the way they are. That everything's fine. That everyone's fine. I get to stay 'down South', *inside*, immersed in a life I have created for myself – while he and Melissa get to play at roughing it in the 'great' outdoors or wallowing in nostalgia in the house haunted by memories. Either way, I don't do wallowing and I do not camp.

'I am far too mid-thirties to sleep on the floor,' I grumble.

'It's the ground, actually,' clarifies Melissa. 'And technically you're now late thirties ...'

I give her a look that makes her stop right there.

Margot offers to go and start 'fire stoking' duties as the rest of us come to from our semi-slumber.

'I'll be honest, this isn't quite what I had in mind when I booked, either,' Tricia admits. 'I suspected that there might be a few Mads Mikkelsen types, around, loosely tethered. Or a lot of hot people, whittling stuff. Maybe some sword forging. But not this. Never this.' She pats the area of skin underneath her eyes to 'de-puff', as she tells us, and begins a series of bizarre facial exercises that make her look as though she's doing a very bad lip synch ('What? The render's good but we can all use some structural support after a certain age ...').

'I thought the place would be riddled with pastries, but there you go,' says Melissa. 'Still, it's exciting, isn't it? To try living like they did hundreds of years ago?'

What? On lilos marked 'Made in Taiwan'? is what I want to say but find I have lost my appetite for sarcastic asides.

Tricia is shaking her head and I'm comforted by the thought that I might have a kindred spirit in Viking-despair.

'I miss a cloud-soft bed and silk pillowcases,' she says now. 'And an external coffee.'

'External?'

'Not homemade. In a paper cup.'

'Ah.' I nod. 'I miss my phone,' I confess, then add hastily, 'and my kids. Obviously.'

'Oh, yes. And the dogs.' Then Tricia also reassesses her list: 'And my son.'

'Ahh, you have dogs?' Melissa perks up.

That's her take-home from Tricia's statement of priorities? The sodding dogs? I'm intrigued by Tricia's parental and domestic arrangements. But Melissa, clearly, isn't

'What breed?' my sister goes on.

'I've got four little Shih Tzu.' Tricia beams.

'Huh ...' Melissa sounds disappointed. I suspect she was hoping for something a little tougher.

'And your son?' the question slips out.

'Ed? Oh, he's all right. Grown-up now, but, you know, nice, really.'

I'm no earth mother, but this seems a strange evaluation of one's offspring ... Were I a normal, conversationally-at-ease person, I'd request all sorts of additional information about what GCSEs he has or whatever it is people are supposed to ask in these situations. But I'm not. So I don't.

Instead, still wearing the same clothes I arrived in, I gather a blanket around me and wriggle to my feet among the stray limbs. I can see my breath inside our 'shelter' on account of us running out of the time and energy to source anything resembling a 'door' – biblically boulder-based or otherwise. Now, I merely have to duck under a precariously balanced beam before I'm officially 'outside'. Tricia and Melissa follow and we poke at the embers of the fire Margot has successfully reignited, attempting to get some much-needed heat out of it.

Tricia is just coughing up some viscous-sounding phlegm ('Stopped smoking three months ago. Lungs playing catch up,' she explains) when Margot appears, looking pale and walking like John Wayne.

'What happened to you?' Tricia hacks and Margot blushes crimson.

'Ants' nest. Wee,' is all she says.

'Ouch!'

'I thought there were no dangerous bugs around here?' I look at Melissa.

'I don't think they'll kill you, just make you itchy,' she replies.

'And we've all been there,' Tricia says, her jaw stiffening at the recollection.

By 5.30am, according to the old-school watch that Melissa insists on wearing in lieu of my smartphone-as-clock approach, the fire is going at full lick. We're beginning to warm up as the dawn encroaches and a bluish light percolates through the trees.

I rub my hands together to get some sensation back in my fingers until Melissa intervenes.

'Here, let me help,' she says, as I adjust to the realisation that in addition to having no privacy this week, any semblance of personal space has now been utterly eroded, too. 'You've always had crap circulation. You get that from Mum.'

'Great. What did you get?'

'Slow metabolism and big bones.'

'Bitch.' Tricia shakes her head. 'I got bunions.'

'Do you mind? That's our late mother you're talking about!' I object.

'Sorry, yes. I was projecting.'

'Don't worry,' says Melissa, 'she was a bit of a c—' Then seeing my expression, she stops. 'Well, they were different times ...'

Magnus strolls into view at this moment, putting an end to any further dispute. Despite the cold he is shirtless, again, with 'nipples like bullets', as Tricia feels obliged to announce. This morning, his beard has been plaited into a long braid that reminds me of an old-fashioned bog chain.

He tells us he hopes we 'slept well in the fresh air' and that 'infrared from the fire is very healing for the body'.

'Is it?' I ask doubtfully, then inform him that it's still brass monkeys out here and I feel like death.

'Here, drink this.' He removes a flask from one of the vast, voluminous folds in today's pair of black harem pants as well as four plastic cups that he proceeds to fill with a Kermit-coloured liquid.

'What *is* that?' Melissa asks.

'Green juice!' he announces. 'Made with nettles and healing plants.'

'Mixed with Shrek piss?' Tricia asks Magnus and his pecs. 'I love a Shrek's piss drink. I've done vegan, caveman, clean'n'green, the Wellness deficit diet ...' she tails off. Melissa looks at her as though she's speaking Russian. 'What? If it's good enough for Jessica Biel ...'

Melissa nods as though this is a fair point but still looks confused. She couldn't pick a non-Royal celebrity under the age of fifty out of a captioned line-up so, for once, I take pity on her. 'Think 'a latter-day Olivia Newton-John'. Or maybe Elisabeth Shue,' I explain and Melissa makes an 'ahhh!' sound of recognition.

Our green juice is just as disgusting as it sounds and so naturally I drink it all, certain that it's doing me good (*I'll probably look like Margot by morning ...*).

Afterwards, we're led to a stream on the outskirts of the forest for a 'prison wash'. Yes, that's right: this 'retreat' is now so far from a spa it's practically a jail sentence. But once we get clear of the forest, despite being disorientated, dazed and more than a little tired, we're treated to the sight of a painfully beautiful expanse of cobalt sea that quite takes my breath away. The clouds look as though they've been painted on with a sponge and a bright, growing orb is trifling with the horizon – brighter and clearer than any sunrise I've ever seen.

Pens and paper are produced from another pocket in Magnus's palatial pants ('What else has he got in there?' Tricia's eyes are like saucers as she allows her imagination to run wild) and we're told to write a letter to our 'future selves'.

'Minimum of two sides,' he tells us, 'to be posted to your home address in six months' time.'

This all sounds very *Blue Peter* time-capsule but my fellow retreatees get on with the challenge without complaining, so I get my head down and try to do the same.

Only I'm dizzy with hunger by now – despite the Shrek piss – and the headache that's been lurking for the last couple of days is now establishing itself across my cranium. I find I have trouble concentrating and can feel my stomach contracting. *Maybe my body's digesting itself*, I speculate. *Interesting*.

'Think about what you've learned so far, what you want to get out of this week, and how you'd like your life to be different by the time you receive this letter,' Magnus prompts us.

This is hard because: a) I try not to think too much about my life in case I'm swallowed up in an existential vortex of self-reflection and indulgence (then who'll look after everyone else?); b) the mounting hunger is distracting; and c) I'm scared. Scared that in six months' time, life might be exactly the same as it is now.

Frightened, in fact, that it might even be the same in six *years'* time. This would be bearable if I just stumbled along and came across this nebulous date during the course of everyday life: working and keeping busy. Because then it would just be Getting On With Things. Coping. At which I am a strong eight-out-of-ten. But I suspect that the way I like to plan for the future (i.e. 'micromanage' and fill up a colour-coded schedule) isn't quite what our Viking leader has in mind. We're being asked to contemplate the big questions on a wider canvas. *On day bloody two* ... Which, I convince myself, is hugely unfair. But I have a go.

When I think I've finished (*does a bullet point about setting up online supermarket deliveries to save time at weekends count?*), I look up to find everyone else still hard at it. So I try again. And somehow, my pen starts moving, dancing almost, across the page. The words flow until my brain feels empty and the sun has turned a hot pink. I realise, with delight, that I'm finally warm. And I'm the last one writing. Time has vanished, without my even realising it.

Magnus collects up our offerings before secreting them in his trousers ('I've never wanted to be a letter so much in my life ...' Tricia murmurs). Then he announces that it's time for breakfast. Which is excellent news because for the first time in months (years?) I've got an appetite (See 'body digesting itself').

'Great! Where's the food?' Melissa enquires, with some urgency now as I hear her insides gurgling.

Magnus doesn't say anything, but raises an arm and points at the forest.

'I didn't see anything when we came this way.' My sister puckers her brow.

'That's because you have to find it.' our leader announces. 'You will forage like the Vikings did – in the ancient forest and scrubland.'

Crapsticks ...

I really hope the ancient forest is ready to deliver. Or that there's secretly a drive-through hamburger outlet in there. Because, for once, I'm starving.

Four

We trudge to the forest, famished and foggy from caffeine withdrawal (on my part, at least). I'm also patting myself down every few minutes in the manner of an aeroplane security guard, convinced that I can feel vibrations and that these must have a physical source. But alas, my phantom smartphone is just that.

'Shame ...' I shake my head and mutter to no one.

Tiredness has made me woozy and hunger is now slowing my brain so that I'm not entirely with it when Magnus begins his briefing on the brave new world of edible plants.

'The easiest things to start with are chanterelle mushrooms,' he says, glancing around to see if he can find one to show us, then giving up and waving a hand in a sort of *'ah, you'll be fine!'* dismissal. 'Basically they're yellow and a bit frilly. Nothing like the red and white spotted ones you see in kids' books! Don't eat *them*, they'll kill you!' He chuckles. 'But chanterelle don't look like that, so they're usually OK to pick.'

'Usually?' I echo. *Brilliant ...*

'Then ramson, or wild garlic, is easy to find,' he goes on. 'Look for long, leaves: thick in middle, narrow at the ends.'

I am none the wiser after this description, but Magnus assures us that they're a 'delicacy', delectable in wild garlic pesto.

'For breakfast?'

It's hardly a fruit plate and a large Americano ...

'Our forefathers would just have foraged for whatever they could find,' is his reply.

Maybe so, but I bet our foremothers were more discerning ...

'Vikings eat what's in season – and right now, this is ramson. You just grind it down,' Magnus says, executing an unconvincing mime in the manner of a man who is totally unfamiliar with a pestle and mortar. 'Really pump it –' I already know that Tricia is smiling at this before I look '– then substitute the foraged herb for the basil, find some hazelnuts to use instead of pine nuts, and just *imagine* the parmesan—'

Oh, FFS ... If we're 'imagining' food I may as well go for an Egg McMuffin ... Or do a Sainsbury's sweep ...

I spend a few moments visiting an imaginary supermarket in my head and filling my imaginary trolley with all manner of imaginary carbohydrates and meat-based products.

'Ground elder is also good – really fresh and bitter,' Magnus goes on. 'And of course a lot of the berries are in season.'

Finally, a foodstuff I've heard of.

He rounds up by recommending we scour the shallows for mussels, since the tide is low round about now.

Mmm, molluscs at dawn ...

But Melissa has more practical concerns. 'And you want us to do all of this without shoes on?' She looks down at our bare feet.

'Wet feet are better than wet shoes,' says Magnus.

'Well, yes, but what about wellies?'

'Willies?'

There is a snort.

'Wellingtons. As in boots. Made from rubber ...'

Tricia struggles to keep it together.

Really? We're laughing at the word 'rubber' now? Hunger has made us hysterical.

'Ah, I see. Well, do you think our forefathers wore wellies?'

Melissa looks meek and shakes her head as I contemplate that our fore-*mothers* would doubtless have invented them pretty swiftly had they been liberated from the patriarchal tyranny of constant childbirth ... or had access to a moulding plant ... I'm feeling more irritable than usual. Probably because I haven't eaten in ... I give up on the mental arithmetic before I even get started, the anticipation of effort exhausting me ... *many hours* ...

'So we forage barefoot,' Magnus continues.

'Weeing on your feet is supposed to toughen them up,' volunteers Margot with alarming eagerness. 'We could try that?'

If anyone pisses on my feet I will punch them in the face, I vow, experiencing full-voltage *hanger* now.

'If all else fails, just remember what you learned at school!' Magnus ends. 'Spending time in nature and learning about plants is something little children are really good at. Then, as time goes on, we're supposedly "civilised" by life and we forget these essential skills.'

The Scandinavian early-education system sounds slightly different to that of the Midlands in the early 1980s. Unfortunately, all I learned about nature at preschool was the difference between dog poo and Play-Doh (the hard way), and that stinging nettles and shorts don't mix. The best that St Mary's CoE primary school had to offer was a mangy 'nature table' sporting cress-heads in eggshells and – once – a dead vole that Jonathan Harris's dad ran over on the way to work. Leamington Spa locals seldom foraged for their supper beyond the confines of Asda and didn't typically possess – let alone pass on – the knowledge and skills to find food in the wild. Although Melissa did once find a Double Decker in the bushes at Newbold Common. Mum told her not to eat it, saying it probably belonged to a drug addict ('Why, Mum? Why would a drug addict chuck out a chocolate bar in a wetlands centre?'). But Melissa wolfed it anyway, despite the fact that Mum had just put my twelve-year-old sister on The Hay Diet.

'Just explore!' Magnus exhorts. 'Try things out! Taste! If you see something interesting, try a little of it. If it tastes bitter, probably don't eat it. But otherwise, most things won't hurt you. Except the toadstool mushrooms. Or yew seeds. And, obviously, try not to eat shit …'

Wait, what? Is he deranged?

Once we've all composed our faces again enough to assure him that we hadn't planned to, he adds, 'It's just we have to mention it, *legally*. There's this tapeworm that thrives in foxes and raccoon dogs around here—'

'*Raccoon dogs?*' Melissa asks.

'Is that a thing?' Tricia looks perplexed.

'Yes,' Magnus assures us. 'A very real thing. You don't have?'

'Not in Lewes, no …'

He goes on to explain that we're unlikely to come across one during our trip – especially during daylight hours – but that if we do we'll know them because they 'look like a raccoon that got old and maybe a little bit diseased'.

'Right, good to know.'

'But the risk of infection is relatively small and can only happen if you get shit in your mouth. Which, of course, should be unlikely.'

'One would hope.' Tricia looks at Magnus as though perhaps the gloss is wearing off those oiled, pumped muscles, and

I can't help thinking that, on reflection, my preschool nature training served me well.

'But in the case of a real S-H-T-F situation—'

'S-H-T-F?' Tricia asks.

'"*Shit hits the face*",' Magnus clarifies, as Margot flinches. 'We can lure it out – the worm, that is – with a flashlight up the butt and some sugar. But let's hope it doesn't come to that ...'

'Yes, let's,' I murmur in astonished agreement.

'And of course watch out for wolves,' he adds.

'What?' Tricia snaps, again.

Magnus sighs, as though aware that the 'W' word was going to cause a bit of a fuss and already wishing he hadn't mentioned it. 'It's just that *some people* think they've seen wolves around these parts, looking for food. But sightings are *very* rare and, really, you have more chance of being killed by a runaway train.'

Melissa gulps.

'If I see a wolf, I'm going to pee my pants ...' Tricia says decisively, as though this should be a warning to any passing predators.

Lesson over, we're each given a cross body satchel in uniform-grey hessian ('I feel like I'm in the Scandi branch of Chairman Mao's army,' Tricia observes. '*The Hunger Games*, more like,' I mutter) and given our orders.

'So now we're going to pair you up,' announces Magnus. 'Proud Chest, you go with Strong Legs.' *Crap.* 'And Aslög, you can go with Night Wolf.'

Great. Excellent.

Margot beams and moves closer, so close that I note her every flawless pore. She's so young and naturally lean that I can see the muscles *in her actual face.* Her skin is luminous, even after a night in a rudimentary log hut. *And that hair! Close up!* It's lighter and thicker than expected, with more shine than a Pantene ad. *Rich people have Really Good Hair,* I think. She oozes health and has a fresh, natural beauty that makes me want to peel off my own skin. Or wear a balaclava for the rest of my life. *Or steal her face and wear it as a mask ...*

The dental surgery started doing Botox recently, under the rational that while they've got you in a chair in a sterile environment they might as well jzuz up your whole face. I'd be lying if I said I hadn't been tempted. *Expressions are overrated,* I think, *I don't want anyone knowing when I'm worried or angry or anxious. And really, when you think about it, Botox is the ultimate in bottling it up – for three-to-four months at a time. Which is just ... efficient ...*

I think about asking Tricia about her experiences but then remember that the woman can't raise her eyebrows effectively and so may not be the best guide. *Perhaps it's a case of 'less is less'.* But still, I feel I need to do *something.*

I glance down at my papery hands with their Irish-blue skin, then look across at Margot's neatly manicured, plastic-looking ones. *And her arms!* I continue my assessment: *The girl has Michelle Obama arms, chiselled shoulders, a torso untroubled by childbirth, and long, slim legs. Urghhh ...* I pull down at my T-shirt self-consciously.

I looked like her once. Only it took a monumental effort on my part and I starved myself so much that my periods stopped. For ten years. It was the stupidest thing I've ever done, on paper – but a part of me has never been able to let the proclivity go. Generally, I do OK. I can drown out the voices in my head and hold it together (See 'four bags-for-life in the car at all times'). But the chorus of self-loathing is still there. Like a low-rent Greek tragedy.

As a teenager, I had the whole 'Victorian waif' thing going on – a sort of 'consumptive chic' – that I think people assumed was my natural pallor. And all the while, Melissa was looking ruddier by the day, fuelled by mugs of strong tea, fried eggs and bacon. If my sister ever noticed I was looking a little more street-urchin than usual, she'd say, 'You know what's good when you're feeling sad?' and then hold up a brown paper bag of some baked goods or other.

There was always this feeling that, because we were sisters, we were naturally similar. That we 'worked' the same way and should do everything together. That's what happens in films. But it didn't 'work' with us. After Mum got sick, the ignominy of having to repeat 'Obesity Clinic, please ...' increasingly loudly to a partially deaf receptionist at the doctor's surgery and deliver my sister to her monthly meetings fell to me. I felt I'd be judged in the harshest terms imaginable by a waiting room of flu-sufferers were I to have expanded even a millimetre in between sessions. So I went the other way. I ate less and exercised more.

It was work that finally saved me, a decade later. You can tell a lot about someone from their teeth, and red, swollen gums were the first giveaway. My body started to de-prioritise my mouth – as well as my reproductive functions – in an attempt to salvage the nutrients needed to keep the rest of me running. I didn't have enough vitamin D in my body to absorb calcium properly, my first boss told me with a look of distaste. The next step, he said, would be receding gums, then gum disease. 'And no one wants a dentist with gingivitis,' he told me. If I wanted to work at 'the cutting edge of oral hygiene', I had to 'sort myself out'. So I started eating again. Within reason. And I stopped looking like bloody Margot ...

'Are you listening, Aslög?'

Oh god, he means me ...

'Yes, err ... foraging?'

'I was explaining where to look ...'

'Yep. Got it. Thanks.' I assure him I'm totally up to speed (I'm not) and we're sent off on our merry way.

The wind has been getting up and now whistles around our ears as we move to higher ground. Combined with the yawning emptiness in my stomach, this makes for a distracting tramp, barefoot, through scrubland up a small incline to an area Magnus has assured us is 'prime pickings'.

The smell of sheep dung hangs heavy in the air as we walk – Margot striding purposefully; me, eyes flicking nervously from the horizon to where I'm putting my feet, amidst rocks and unfamiliar thistle type plants that hurt nearly as much as stepping on the kids' Lego bricks in exposed feet. *Which should have been good preparation for a week of roughing it, Danish style ...* Melissa and Tricia peel off towards the coast but Margot seems so confident in her mission that I don't dispute her course and merely follow, treading as swiftly as I can.

'So, what's it like being a dentist?' she's asking me as I look up, frowning, and promptly step on a thistle. 'I always love going up and down in the chair! And those little sinks for spitting mouthwash in!' She's speaking rapidly, either to match her pace or ... *could it be ... that she's nervous?* I can't tell. 'Does anyone ever swallow?'

'Sorry?'

'The pink mouthwash, I mean!' she bobs, hair swishing.

Oh great. I'm stuck with the genetically gifted, model-esque, perfect, and so-young-she's-practically-an-embryo girl who also happens to have verbal diarrhoea ...

'It must be very rewarding work!' She is still talking. 'I hope I'm really established in my career by the time I'm in my forties!'

I give her a brilliant glare and find that all my muscles have tensed, as though ready to take flight or fight this exotic creature. 'I'm thirty-seven,' I correct her.

'Oh! Right! I just thought –' she gives a tinkly laugh '– since you're so *settled* and everything … sorry …' She tails off, shaking her head, and assumes an expression that I can only presume is intended to convey, '*I'm such a klutz!*'

Play it cool, I tell myself while fuming inwardly. *Just Play It Cool.* I remember how I, too, used to be terrible at deciphering the age of anyone older than me, assuming they must all be ancient. *I am an emotionally stable adult … I am an emotionally stable adult … I am an emotionally stable adult … who is going to KILL her …*

Margot does a really slow blink, which I naturally interpret as a declaration of war, before turning and continuingly nimbly up the hill. She's already hard at it when I puff my way to the top – stuffing things into her bag at speed, as though she's in a Nordic nature-lover's version of *The Crystal Maze*. So I do the same, or at least, *try*. The trouble is, I've already forgotten everything Magnus taught us.

Because, really, I don't care.

Other than getting through the next few days, these are not skills I need.

I'm a busy woman, I justify my reluctance. *There are better things I could be doing right now. Like root canals. Or extractions. Or denture fittings, fillings, implants, crowns – hell, I'd even take a teeth-whitening procedure around about now over this.* With an average of thirty minutes per routine dental examination and most treatment appointments taking a minimum of an hour, I calculate that I've already neglected approximately twelve patients today, or twenty-four in total taking in yesterday's tally, by dent of my Viking detour. I often work six days a week, so by the end of this debacle I will have missed ... *seventy-two appointments*, I estimate. In short: I don't have time for this.

I never plan on living or working more than a hundred yards from a Tesco Metro and so 'foraging skills' are not – nor have they ever been – high up on my list of priorities. I'll play along, but I'm only here for Melissa. I'm here because she made me come. I'm here because, apparently, there were 'no spas available' ...

But they can't make me *care* about any of this.

What I can do – what I'm pretty good at after years of practice and a millennium (or so it feels) of marriage – is *dial it in*. I'm adept at 'getting through things'. *It's only a week,* I rationalise, *what's the worst that can happen?*

I cast about, looking at what 'nature's bounty' has deigned to offer in the way of snacks in the patch of scrubland that Margot has led me to.

There was something about pesto, wasn't there? And poisonous mushrooms ... ? But which ones? I study a few shabby specimens in front of me that look distinctly grey. *Like everything else in this country.*

I'm scouting around for inspiration (aka spying on what Margot's picking) and trying to avoid stepping on the small black pellets that seem to be decorating the ground when I come face to face with an enormous, terrifying, horrific-smelling, hundred-kilogram *beast*.

I haven't seen sheep in the flesh since childhood – this being one of the advantages of living in a city and outsourcing any manure-smelling outings to the kids' school and/or Greg, back when he could be bothered. I know, vaguely, from reading farmyard stories that sheep are not supposed to be scary. That accolade is reserved for elephants, tigers, lions, rhinos, dinosaurs etc. – some of which, apparently, aren't even a threat any more. Sheep, I've been assured, are benign by contrast, with a reputation for following the herd. *So why has this one gone rogue? Separated itself, like some sort of Mad Max of the ovine community?*

The creature looks me straight in the eye as if to say. 'You haven't got a clue, have you? We all know it ...' Then it emits a loud, low sound, possibly to alert others to my failings.

Baaaaaaa! It yammers, a little aggressively, then takes a tentative hoof towards me, chewing something intently and seemingly unconcerned by the Malteser-esque pellets currently falling with ease out of its arse.

Don't eat shit, don't eat shit, don't eat shit. My addled brain repeats the only piece of information from Magnus's tutorial that I have apparently retained.

Baaaaaaaa! The creature bleats again and Margot turns around with fresh fists of foliage.

'Are you OK? Do you need a hand?'

'I'm fine!' I smile tightly, embarrassed to have been caught having a standoff with a sheep. I keep smiling until I'm satisfied that she's not looking any more. *God, I miss the city,* I think, *the perpetual glow and hum and regular opportunities for coffee in cardboard cups ... Beats sodding nature any day ...*

The sheep couldn't care less about my metropolitan longings and, instead, continues to emit round balls of barely digested plant matter from its nether region. I'm planning to take my leave, when I notice that behind my adversary is a bush, heavy with bulbous, crimson berries.

Food! Actual food! That I could eat!

My mouth floods with saliva at the thought. It's the only thing vaguely resembling a foodstuff that I've seen so far and I'm now so hungry, I'd pretty much do anything to get my hands on them. There's only one thing for it.

'Here sheep! Here, sheep sheep sheep!' I try to lure the thing away with a handful of admittedly not-very-appealing-looking grass, but it doesn't budge. *Am I going to have to have a showdown? Dentist vs. sheep? Has it come to this?*

The clusters of dusty red fruit look a lot like the actual, *official*, 'raspberries' I'm used to seeing on supermarket shelves. Rationalising that a sheep probably won't kill me (*it might maim me*, I think, *which might mean a few weeks recuperating in hospital somewhere. Could be worth it for a bit of a break*, I tell myself. *At least there'd be food* ...), I decide to go for it.

If you've never charged a sheep, I recommend it. Bracing myself, I rock back on my heels, then throw caution and barefootedness to the wind before rolling forwards, advancing until momentum takes over and I've leant so far that I'm either going to have to break into a run or keel over. Feeling slightly mad and seriously exhilarated, I take one stride, then another, then another – covering ground without realising it, until the ewe appears larger and larger in my mental viewfinder. There is a moment when I'm not sure it's going to move and its compact horns suddenly seem incredibly sharp and treacherous. But by then, it's too late. I'm propelled by my own velocity and there's no stopping me. In the strangest game of chicken ever played, the sheep gives way at the last moment ... and the berries are mine!

All mine!

I carefully liberate a couple of soft, velvety globes and study them, with no real idea of what I'm looking for. But feeling emboldened by my farmyard-face-off and, frankly, starving, I stuff them into my mouth ... and am delighted to discover that they taste a lot like raspberries, too.

I cram in a handful. And another. And another. *I'm doing it!* I think, *I'm foraging ... !* I wish there was someone around to witness and so validate this minor victory, but Margot is busy, halfway up a tree, harvesting some sort of nut.

Once I've eaten a decent M&S-punnet sized quantity of berries and then picked a second and third, lain carefully in my satchel for the others, I look around to find Margot, weighed down with produce, watching me.

'How did you get on?' she asks, brightly.

'Good, thanks,' I say, as confidently as I can.

'Good,' says her mouth. But I can't help thinking that her eyes are saying. '*Damn it ...*'

'You?' I ask back. Because, well, you *have to*, don't you?

'*Great*,' she emphasises the word, before adding, 'thanks.'

'*Great ...*' I try to strike just the right note of sarcastic ambiguity, so that if anyone called me out, they couldn't be sure there was any uncharitable intent.

Melissa and Tricia are already back at base camp when we return, sitting on logs and poking at a vat of something. Tricia is swaddled in several Scandi-issue grey blankets and executing an impressive yoga move in an attempt to give her feet what has always been known in our family as a 'hot potato' – blowing on them and rubbing intermittently.

'Musselling,' she explains. 'Semi-successful, on Melissa's part at least, but *extremely* cold.' She swaps feet and funnels hot air on the other one to revive circulation.

Melissa, by contrast, looks in her element – trousers rolled up around her ankles, disproportionately large Hobbit feet remarkably unscathed by the sub-zero Baltic sea, closely resembling a latter-day Bilbo Baggins.

'Pull up a chair!' Magnus barks, and I look around, hopefully.

'There are *chairs*?' I miss chairs.

'Sure!' He points at the log pile. 'Over there!'

'Oh, I see ... ha!' I say, trying to raise a smile while deflating on the inside. But Margot is already on it, rolling a log towards the campfire before going back to fetch one for me. 'It's OK, I can do it.' I smile, weakly.

'No problem, it's here now.' Margot trundles 'my log' into place and brushes off some of the moss with her sleeve before presenting it to me. 'There you go!'

She even offers me an arm to lower myself down, as though I am some sort of elderly aunt.

If I had shoes on, I'd throw one of them at her ...

'Thank you,' I manage, as graciously as I can. But inwardly, I'm livid. And feeling every one of my thirty-seven years.

Then we eat.

On the menu are stewed mushrooms served with mystery leaves that now look and taste Very Brown Indeed. This is followed by a feast of precisely four mussels each. My face must betray my surprise at this because Tricia becomes defensive. 'We were out there forever! I've only just got any sensation back in my extremities!' Finally, the group is treated to a handful of hazelnuts and several dozen berries.

The foraged food is a hit, of sorts. Or everyone's so ravenous that they'll eat anything by this point, and within minutes bowls are empty.

'Well, that's barely going to keep the wolf from the door.' Tricia rubs her stomach, then adds, 'No pun intended!'

It's surprisingly satisfying (though sadly not in a hunger-quenching, physical sense) to have created a whole 'meal' for free, from nothing but our wits.

You hear that, world? I've got 'wits' now! To survive! In nature!
Without a Tesco Metro for MILES!

I catch my caffeine-deprived brain in this mode of thinking
and have to remind myself that I don't care about any of this.

Or do I ... ?

'You did very well, Night Wolf.' Magnus rests a hand on
Margot's shoulder.

Creep, I think. *No, I definitely don't care. Definitely.*

Once we're fractionally 'less famished' than before – Magnus
suggests heading to the beach again.

Tricia pulls the blanket around her more tightly and looks
dismayed. 'I'm only just thawing out!'

'Not to go in the water this time,' he assures her. 'To look
on the shore. We can start to collect things for the next stage
of your Viking education – tomorrow's craft session!'

The excitement literally never ends ...

'Where the Baltic Sea meets the North Sea, you can often
spot a holestone – or "*hulsten*" – beach stones that have a hole
in them. This happens when a big wave—' here he extends
his arms up above him and does an admirable impression of
what a wave might look like in man-bunned, human form
'—washes over a stone.' He swoops on Tricia, catching her
face in the nook of his armpit. I spot her inclining her head
to sniff at a pheromone.

Urgh ...

'The wave carries with it many small pebbles, and as it
comes crashing down—' Magnus loops his arms around a
now-beaming Tricia, then adds, with an entirely inappropriate
thrust '—then pushes its way in—'

All right, easy ...

'Until a small pebble makes its way through another stone
by wearing it down.'

'And, err ... when we've collected the stones?'

'Well.' Magnus releases a swooning Tricia from his embrace and straightens up, flexing one pectoral muscle and then the other in turn. 'You might wear one for good luck.' He fingers his latest piece of man-jewellery, drawing attention to the new monstrosity around his neck, just below a small tattoo of interlocking triangles in his hairline ('a Norse symbol' as Tricia later informs me). 'It's very soothing to feel the smooth stone and a way to connect with nature – wherever you are.'

If I weren't so concerned about conserving limited food reserves, I would probably retch at this point. *Nature can bog right off.* But our lack of sustenance seems to be resulting in rising levels of hunger-related-irritability and mild disorientation all around, so I'm not taking any chances. It turns out woman cannot survive on foraged raspberries alone. Or even foraged raspberries with a four-mussel amuse-bouche.

'Then of course we can use them for weaving tomorrow to weigh down the warp – so you can all make some very special Viking adornments!'

'It's like all my Christmases have come at once,' I mutter to Melissa.

'You'll have some trouble returning this year's present from me,' she fires back.

After this, we comb the beach, only to find two dead crabs and a washed-up ballpoint ('*handy ...*') So instead we take up position on the pier in an attempt to 'catch' something that will comprise our next excuse for a meal.

There are a few nets already in place that we're encouraged to 'have a go' with but, after twenty fruitless minutes, Magnus takes pity on us and retrieves some flimsy-looking rods and a jar of something from a small cave up-shore. Two of the 'fishing rods' are little more than pieces of doweling with a line attached – the kind that children might make for a school play. The other pair, I recognise, have the 'special wind-y-up-y bit', as I'm calling it, and look as though they've been made by someone who has at least *seen* a fishing rod.

I'll be buggered if I'm sitting here for the rest of the morning with what is essentially a garden gnome accessory, I think, and so plump quickly for one of the 'official' metal rods. Tricia does the same, leaving Margot and Melissa to slum it with the stick-'n'-wire version.

'Now, you just have to find some bait and sort of throw the line into the water,' says Magnus.

'Where do we find bai—' Margot is starting to ask, but Magnus shushes her by pressing a finger to her mouth, squashing her lips.

Bit familiar, I think.

'I have a present for you all!' Magnus replies, proffering a jar of wriggling grubs that force me to clasp a hand to my mouth and Tricia to dry heave dramatically.

'A *present?*' Tricia is still reeling. 'What's wrong with a book token?' she mutters. 'Giant Toblerone, even?'

Fortunately, Melissa is made of tougher stuff and volunteers to be the first to attempt to spear her hook through a worm's still convulsing body.

Gross ...

Margot does the same but when Tricia and I make no attempt to move towards the squirming jar, Magnus offers to 'maggot us up'.

'I ...' Tricia falters. 'No, I've got nothing ...' Even Tricia can't make an innuendo out of larvae.

We cast our lines on a count of three. And then we wait. Forever.

'Welcome to fishing,' Melissa says, still semi-brightly, though I can tell by this point she must be starving. 'They do this on the estate every weekend. The wait is all part of the experience ...'

When it becomes abundantly clear that we're catching nothing and the line on the wooden rods can't even be flung past the base of the pier, Melissa takes over the 'official' rod and the other two women opt to forage inland instead – or rather, Margot does and my fellow Viking-sceptic Tricia follows, whispering to me that she's going to try and sneak in a power nap.

We sit in silence for several minutes after this until I become conscious of Magnus jogging his leg on the rickety pier and find I'm grinding my teeth. *Must remember to wear my retainer for a few extra hours tonight ...*

'You should be able to get a good catch here,' Magnus insists, as though trying to justify the exercise. 'Another of the really good places is right by the point, over there.' He gestures to a rocky outcrop. 'In fact, I might just go over there and try for some herring. Or mackerel! Good for fatty acids – for the skin and hair – eh, ladies?' He draws this word out until he sounds like a 1970s DJ ('lay-deeees') before leaping to his feet and bounding off.

Once he's out of earshot I let out an *urghhhh* that's been fermenting in me for the past ten minutes.

'What are you moaning about now?'

'What do you mean what am I moaning about? We're hungry, cold, and we've been sitting here for over an hour, miles from civilisation—'

'Oh, you and your civilisation,' Melissa scoffs.

'*What?*'

'It's overrated, that's all.'

'Right ...' My sister is officially a Luddite. 'All I'm saying is, it's a long way to go for some casual sexism and herring.'

'I like herring ...' Melissa says, defensively.

'Do you like it served by a man with a monstrously big ego?'

'I'm not fussy.' There is a pause before she adds. 'You know your problem?'

'No, but I have a feeling that I'm going to find out. Hang on, let me get comfy. OK, shoot.'

'You're too *crabby*!' Melissa looks pleased with herself.

'I've just spent a morning drowning worms, I'm hardly feeling Zen ...'

'No! Crabby? Get it? Because we're fishing.'

'Christ ...'

Melissa has always enjoyed a dad-joke. More specifically, *our* dad's jokes – puns so painful they would put cracker manufacturers and 90s lolly-stick makers to shame. I don't doubt for a moment that there's at least one tome entitled *Hundred Funniest Fart Jokes Ever!* loitering somewhere in her home.

'Would you like another one?'

'No, thank you.' Really: *no*.

'What kind of music should you listen to while fishing?'

'I don't know. Or *care*—'

'Something *catchy*! What do you call a fish without an eye?' She's near bouncing now with glee. 'A *fsh*!'

'OK, now – quiet time,' I command, more sharply than I had intended, but Melissa complies so I decide I can always apologise later if necessary. Then I do more sea staring in between bouts of rod wriggling and run through my mental to-do list.

This ever-changing catalogue of concerns currently consists of: *update periodontitis patient list; talk to Esme about idea for mouthwash information campaign – if I've said it once, I've said it a thousand times: mouthwash is no substitute for effective brushing nor should it be used immediately after brushing as this removes the fluoride in the toothpaste used to protect teeth. I know, basic, right? But you'd be amazed how many patients don't know this ...*

Next, I move on to some habitual fretting about all the domestic things I can't get on to until I get home. I wonder what Charlotte and Thomas are doing now and whether they like the new pyjamas I bought them as an 'I'm going away and I feel guilty' present. I wonder whether Greg managed to get a brush through Charlotte's hair this morning[8] and if he's been doing their maths practice. I wonder whether Thomas is eating properly. I wonder what they're both having for lunch, and then start running through the possibilities in my head until I realise that what I'm *actually* doing is running a 'fridge porno' of all the foodstuffs I would gladly throttle a raccoon dog to get my hands on around about now.

'I suppose this is the real, traditional Nordic experience,' Melissa says to console herself while rubbing her stomach. 'Foraging, I mean.'

Roused from my daydream, I feel compelled to object. 'Yeah right!'

'What?'

'You mean not providing us with any food. Think about it ...' Melissa does for a moment, though her expression remains

---

8. Will my husband remember to use conditioner when washing his daughter's hair, as instructed? Will he buffalo ...

unchanged. 'It's the perfect scam,' I explain. 'I can almost hear the ker-ching noise ...'

'No!' She looks horrified. I arch an eyebrow and she rubs her stomach again, less sure now. 'I mean, surely not ... Do you always have to be so cynical?'

I think about this for a while before answering. 'Yes. Yes I do.'

'Remember that time when Dad took us to the aquarium when Mum was in bed with one of her migraines and you wouldn't believe the fish were real?' Melissa asks me now. 'You kept yelling "they're puppets!" to everyone and looking for strings attached. Then, when you couldn't find any, you demanded to know who had a hand up their bum?'

The muscles at the corners of my mouth twitch, because, for once, I do have a vague memory of a ten-year-old storming around a glass box, convinced the whole thing was fake.

'You were suspicious of everyone even then. Did you ever believe in Father Christmas?'

'I don't remember,' I tell her (see 'whitewashed our collective past'). But since Melissa instinctively distrusts medics whereas I distrust everything else, I suspect the answer's 'no'. 'Probably not,' I tell her.

'Exactly! That's what I mean!'

Then she gets back to the business of fishing/pole-holding. The sun emerges from behind the clouds and for a few moments a slice of bright, white light spreads over the water. I close my eyes and bask in the warmth – for as long as it deigns to last.

'What are you smiling about?' Melissa asks.

'Smiling? I'm not smiling.' My eyes snap back open, self-conscious now.

'Not often you're not, no,' Melissa concedes, shuffling over. 'But I saw a little smirk there! Were you secretly having a nice *millisecond* on this trip?'

'No!'

'OK ...' she says in a voice that implies she doesn't believe me.

And I realise that she just might be right, not to believe me.

Margot looks slightly less composed than normal when she returns to camp and Tricia half limps to catch up with her, dodging burrs, pinecones and, probably, sheep poo, in bare feet.

'We've got food!' Melissa hollers as she grapples with the entrails of one of the fish Magnus caught, pushing back hair from her face with an arm, and smearing guts on her forehead in the process.

I gallantly offered to take on fire duties (I don't do guts ...) and so prod at it now with a stick to pretend I'm doing something useful.

'Are you OK?' I whisper to Tricia, clocking Margot's punctured expression.

'Oh, yes, it's just that we haven't found much. She just kept muttering to herself, "history is told by the victors". God help us if there's a war ...'

I get it. This, I mean. *Margot's cross because she didn't 'win' at foraging, this time.* She strikes me as a girl who's used to winning. Someone who's phobic of failure. And I should know.

I'm aware that this isn't one of my most attractive qualities. Some days I'm not sure I have any of those sort left. But getting things wrong is a luxury I haven't felt able to afford for a long time now. I wonder what that must feel like to be free to make mistakes and muck things up and gambol through life, doing whatever you please. Without consequences. Without people depending on you. And then my eyes fall on Melissa and I see. *Ahh, that's how.* It makes her a nicer person, I'm becoming convinced. Less prickly. Less tense. Jollier, certainly. Better able to chase her own pleasure. *Whatever that is*, I think, forlornly. But then we eat. And I take a mouthful of warm, slightly charred fish that tastes better than any fish I think I've ever tasted before ... and promptly chastise myself for being such a self-pitying loser. *Maybe that's all pleasure is: small, seemingly insignificant moments of enjoyment ...*

We eat until we're sated this time – a strange feeling for me, although not unpleasant. The afternoon follows loosely the same rhythm as morning, but Magnus is incapable of being still and so goes for 'a quick 10k-er' around the island, pursued by an overly keen Margot.

I scour the beach again with Melissa and Tricia, who manages to endure a few moments of quiet contemplation before taking us on a blow-by-blow account of a hot flush she's currently experiencing and then filling us in on the perils of perimenopausal dating. 'I mean, the insomnia, the irregular periods ... you don't know where you are. And it's tough out there. I'll be honest, I've almost given up. People are always asking me, they say, "Tricia, how's the love life?" And I have to tell them: arid desert. Total cobweb lulu. It's been literally *weeks* now since it's seen any action. And I'm a woman with considerable sexual zip.' At this last confession I turn crimson. 'But still, I groom! God knows, I groom. Waxing, sunbeds. And I mean *all over*.' I nod, taking in her alarmingly nutty hue. 'But really, it's no country for old women. The younger men don't know anything; then the older ones either go young or get curmudgeonly if they can't – furious with life. You're damned if they do and damned if they don't. Basically, you're damned. God, give me the confidence of a middle-aged white man ...'

'Right, yes.' Melissa nods, adding, 'I see ...' I wonder whether she's reflecting that she got off lightly with her last 'eating like Elvis' break-up. But I realise that Tricia's predicament is something I get scared about, too: becoming invisible – outside of the window of anyone's romantic interest. *Which is probably why*, I think with a shudder, *Mr Teeth* ...

My neck mottles with shame. I shake off the thought before it has a chance to lodge itself in my brain and start producing another bout of the guilt that's been coursing through my veins like adrenalin at odd moments ever since Premier-Inn-Gate. Instead, I compress my lips into a tight smile. *Because everyone knows that if you smile through the pain and bury it, deep down, everything's fine*, I tell myself. Over and over. *Put sad, angry, confused Alice in a box and pretend she doesn't exist ... Ta da!* She's just threatening to pop back up, like a jack-in-the-box, when I'm distracted by a vision, emerging from the water as if in slow motion: an awe-inspiring figure, clad in short shorts and a sports bra, knife in one hand and several shells in the other.

'Is that—? Are we—? Can you see what I see?' I blink several times to check it's not a mirage brought on by mystery mushrooms.

'I think so ...' Tricia mutters. 'Either that or we're in a Nordic version of *Dr No*.'

Scandi Ursula Andress-alike strides through the shallows with strong, tanned calves that lead into strong, tanned thighs – actual thighs that look like *thighs*, rather than a twelve-year-old's arm (the kind I've been aspiring to have for years).

'Wow.' Melissa staggers back slightly.

'She's like a magazine,' is all I can murmur, because by this point, there, standing before us, is a coltish, Wonder-Woman glossy-mane-d warrior of a woman – an Amazonian goddess in human form.

'Inge.'

She speaks!

'Sorry?' Tricia asks.

'Inge,' she addresses us. We have no idea what this means. 'I'm Magnus's wife.'

Magnus has a wife? THIS is Magnus's wife?

'He didn't mention me?' She looks faintly amused by this, rather than royally pissed off. 'No, well, he often *forgets* ... but here I am. I saw he'd left the food parcel behind. Again. Probably told you that you could only eat what you find in the woods, right?' We nod, dumbly. 'Yeah, that's not quite true. He likes to make a joke with new arrivals.'

Bastard! I think, *I'll kill him ... I'll bloody kill him! And then maybe eat him.*

'Anyway, there's a hamper with oats for porridge, flour, eggs, a few essentials.' She gestures up shore. 'And I like to free up any bad mussels.' She nods to the shells in her hand. 'Don't want to kill any of you!'

'No,' I manage. '*Quite ...*'

'So how are you finding the retreat so far?'

'Um ...' Melissa stalls. 'Good, although I thought there might be a few more Viking helmets around—'

Oh god no, not this again.

I will her to stop. She does not.

'You know,' Melissa goes on, 'with horns?'

'Vikings didn't wear horned helmets,' Inge says flatly.

I nod furiously, keen to convey that I haven't been buying into the *Asterix the Gaul*-hoax.

'Not even "for best"?' Melissa isn't giving up that easily. 'They didn't even dress up on special occasions?' she asks, still hopeful.

'Being a Viking isn't about dressing up,' Inge replies, studying Melissa. 'It's about what's inside. It's finding your North Star,' she says, slipping the knife into a holster.

'My what?' Melissa asks.

'Your guiding principle,' Inge explains.

'Is that like the seven stages?' Tricia asks. 'Handicrafts and going berserk and all that?'

'Sort of,' says Inge. 'Going berserk and being stripped back naked, is all about getting to your essence—'

'Oh,' say Tricia, her tone thoughtful, but I'm forced to interject.

'Sorry, what was that last part ... ?'

'You mean getting to your essence'?'

Well, yes, but also ...

'I mean the *other* bit?'

'Being naked? Stripped back?'

'Uh-huh ...' I tremble.

Inge looks confused, as though this can scarcely be a source of concern. 'You're afraid of *being naked*?'

Yes, I'm afraid! What fresh hell is this?

Tricia and Melissa both strive to look completely at home with the idea – and, in fairness, probably are – so it's just 'uptight Alice' who's suddenly losing her mind at the idea of losing her pants.

'That's just "who you are", underneath it all. There's a freedom in nudity,' Inge says matter-of-factly as she loads up Tricia and Melissa with supplies to take back to base camp. 'You could be a CEO or a cleaner, it doesn't matter. Everyone's equal when they're naked – and we all need to be comfortable with ourselves in our natural state, obviously.'

Obviously. I try very hard not to look like a woman on the verge of a nervous breakdown.

You see, I don't do naked.

There hasn't been any need in a long time now. Even in the shower, it's more of an 'in, out and try-not-to-catch-sight-of-own-corporeal-form-after-two-kids-in-the-full-length-mirror' type thing. On the few occasions I've been forced to set foot in a public changing room, I execute the 'shimmy into underwear while holding up a towel with my chin' move with well-practised aplomb.[9]

I don't do naked.

'What about pants?' I ask still hopeful. 'Could I go berserk in my pants? Maybe a bra—' but she cuts me off.

'No. Carry this.'

I'm handed a basket of eggs and it becomes clear that no further explanation is likely to be proffered – nor is there any discussion to be had on the matter.

I crumble on the inside while attempting to appear cool, calm and collected on the outside – and fail on all three counts.

Melissa never mentioned anything about taking our clothes off! I'm going to be forced to be naked! In front of women who were strangers just yesterday! In approximately – I try to remember what day it is and how many hours stay of execution there are until I am excruciatingly embarrassed, and fail. Again. *Sodding maths. Sodding naked countdown sodding maths. Oh, and did I mention? We're all going to have to be NAKED?!*

'If she really wants to worry about something,' Inge is now joking to Melissa, 'most people crap themselves at the getting lost in a forest part!'

I stop breathing.

What the merry fuck?

[9.] My PB [personal best] for this is six seconds. Yours?

Forests and I are not friends (see 'spores'). But getting lost in one? This has only happened once before, on account of the experience being so horrific and etching such an indelible impression on my adolescent mind that I have made damn sure it's never happened since.

I was fourteen and railing against the world for letting Mum get sick. But because I liked to 'rail' solo (or rather, I had been raised to do it this way), I took myself off and thought I'd try what I believe outdoorsy types refer to as 'a walk'. It got dark (I also don't like the dark. Give me a light-polluted city any day) and I got scared. I thought I remembered a shortcut home from reluctant participation in family rambles, so I tried to get back through a forest. And it was probably the most terrifying six hours of my life.

I've never had a great sense of direction – in any respect – and the thing about sodding nature is that it all looks the sodding same. There were no handy shops or houses or land-marks to let me know that I'd already passed a particular section of woodland, twice, or that I was now doubling back on myself and prolonging my torture. There were just more trees. And bugs. And, latterly, bats. I tramped around in circles, getting cold to the core and afraid that I was going to be stuck there forever. Afraid that I would miss out on the remainder of my time with Mum.

This was when I had my first panic attack.

Lost and alone in dark woodland, I crouched down among the leaves, trying desperately to breathe and willing my legs to work again. They did, eventually. And I cried with relief. I don't know how long it took, but when I finally found my way to a break in the tree-hell, I saw a house in the distance Despite years of 'Stranger Danger' education at school, I rationalised that my best – or 'only' – hope was begging its inhabitants for help. I mentally prepared for the fact that they would probably kidnap and/or murder me afterwards, but thought that if they at least let me call home first, it would be a price worth paying. Turned out it was where our French teacher, Madame Dean [The Sex Machine[10]], lived with her husband Clive. They were midway through a game of Boggle and more than a little surprised by the apparition of a white-as-a-sheet fourth former peering in through the conservatory window. They allowed me to phone home at once and gave me peppermint tea while I waited to get picked up. Mum was livid – incensed with that strange, parental anger of 'relief' that I only recognised years later. I was so consumed by snot and shock that I couldn't speak for two hours after that. But at least no one murdered me.

Since then, nature and I haven't got on. It's no wonder Inge's words strike a splinter of ice into my very soul.

'Well, would you look who I found,' she hollers as we stumble back to basecamp to find Magnus and Margot competing to see who can do the best lunge, post run. He springs up and away from Margot on seeing his wife, then his hands vanish into his harem pants for a quick readjustment to conceal what I suspect might be a modest erection.

'You forgot the welcome hamper,' Inge tells him tartly, before adding, 'Again.'

I'm reassured to observe that even Amazonian goddesses experience marital disharmony. Or rather, exasperation.

[10.] Her official title. No one knows why, but it rhymed, so it stuck. That's secondary school folklore and the wit of a bunch of pubescent mid-1990s Midlanders for you. Mme Dean [TSM] apparently hailed from Basingstoke and had never so much as set foot on a cross-channel ferry or the Eurostar. *C'est la vie …*

'Anyway, here you go.' Inge hands over her bundle and encourages the rest of us to set down our provender. 'I'm going to head back, find the kids.'

'OK,' Magnus mumbles, looking chastened.

'Oh, you have kids?' Margot is asking.

'Three.' Inge raises her eyebrows. 'Magnus didn't mention?'

'No, he didn't!' Margot shakes her head, oblivious to any discord she may be contributing to.

Inge says nothing but gives a small smile.

'Where are they now?' I can't help asking. 'The children, I mean.'

'Oh, they're around.' Inge waves a hand dismissively. At this, my face clearly contorts in something approaching horror, because she adds, 'They're playing – kids should be free-range. We call it "healthy neglect".'

At this moment there is a roar and a flaxen-haired mini Viking tears into view. Magnus crouches down to receive him with open arms then flings him into the air, to squeals of delighted laughter.

'Watch out, he's been berry picking,' Inge starts, clocking her son's stained hands, but Magnus ignores her, slinging the child skyward again before dangling him upside down by his feet. 'Magnus, the kid probably just ate his own bodyweight in berries,' Inge says again. 'I wouldn't if I were you ...'

Magnus continues to ignore her, so Inge turns and begins walking away, muttering under her breath, 'Three, two, one ...'

As if on cue, the child erupts, projectile puking purple berries-'n'-bile down his father's legs.

'*Urghhh!*' Magnus drops his son and attempts to scrape sick off his harem pants.

Inge sucks in her cheeks to repress a smile before saying, 'I did try to warn you.' She addresses the now-deflated child.

'Come, come with me.' Then she tells the rest of us, 'I'll see you all soon, I'm sure.' And with that, she's gone.

'Wow, she's ...' Tricia is, for once, lost for words.

'Isn't she ...' I've never met anyone like her.

Melissa, however, has other things on her mind. 'What's in this hamper then? Shall we dig in?'

So we do.

As dusk approaches, we cook up some of the leaves that Margot and Tricia found earlier and Magnus shows us how to make dough from the worthy-looking flour in the hessian sack. We're going to make bread, he tells us, that we'll cook around the campfire.

I'm just about to protest that I don't eat bread and make something up about being gluten intolerant (this is a lie; only my thighs are) when Melissa gives me a dead arm. I'm so startled (*this isn't how grown-ups behave!*) and in such agony (*ow ... !*) that I clamp my mouth shut and nurse my arm instead.

'Leave the fads where you found them and just eat the fucking food,' she hisses.

I contemplate a comeback, but I'm bushed. And hungry. So I resolve to 'just eat the fucking food' (I can just see the new Instagram hashtag now: *#justetff*) and put my no-carb principles on hold.

Magnus shows us how to wind ribbons of dough around sticks to make *snøbrod*, as he calls it – or 'winding bread' – traditional style.

'We have a saying here,' he tells us. 'When someone needs to calm down, we say they need to "*spis lige brød til*" or "eat some bread".' At this, he tears off a corner of raw dough and begins chewing to demonstrate. 'Because carbs help most things,' he explains, through a mouthful, as Melissa nods vehemently in agreement.

I knew it! I think, *Carbs = sluggish. Must do a double cleanse when I get back to civilisation.* But for now, I'm in.

Sitting on logs in a circle around the fire, we rotate our sticks slowly until the dough cooks to a perfect golden brown (Margot), or to a congealed blob, blackened on the outside and stodgy, possibly raw, on the inside (the rest of us). But it doesn't matter. Because we're famished and we've cooked it ourselves and so it's – almost – the most delicious thing I have ever eaten. Hot mouthfuls of doughy goodness send steam escaping from our mouths into the cool evening air, and huddled around the fire as the black, damp night draws in, it occurs to me that perhaps this might not be so bad after all. Then Magnus gets on to what lies ahead of us in our training and just what 'going berserk' entails. And I change my mind.

'Berserk comes from "Berserkers" – the name of the fierce Viking warriors who wore wolf skins and howled in battle like wild animals,' he explains casually, as though he's telling us how he likes his herring (pickled, I presume).

'Ri-ght.' Melissa tries to get her head around this. 'And so, err, what are we going to be doing?'

We all hold our breath during the seemingly interminable pause while Magnus composes his reply. 'Wellll ...' he starts slowly, dragging the word out in a manner that doesn't inspire us with confidence.

'*Well?*'

Magnus explains that he doesn't like to go into too much detail about berserking in case people find it intimidating.

At this, the anxiety-inducing Valhalla chorus starts up in my head and Melissa thoughtfully relays that 'Alice is already intimidated after what Inge said!'

Thanks, Melissa ...

Magnus looks miffed at having his thunder purloined, so agrees to throw us a few more nuggets of information. He tells us that his version of berserking involves 'running for hours', 'being at one with The Rage', 'nudity', 'sea swimming', and 'free dancing'. Each phrase would, individually, be enough to strike fear into the heart of a sober Englishwoman; together they have the effect of something akin to paralysis.

Once Magnus departs for home and – presumably – the recriminations of his wife and child after puke-gate and failing to acknowledge their very existence, we're left alone to our thoughts. Which is never a good place to be left, in my experience. Ruminations predominantly centre around the specifics of what's to come on day seven of our training.

'I heard berserking was a shamanistic ritual,' Tricia tells us, claiming she'd met a chap who'd tried it once in a yurt in Arizona. 'You take drugs and hallucinate and stuff,' she says, becoming vague around the 'and stuff' part.

'Isn't it like an extreme triathlon?' asks Margot. 'I thought it was a naked Iron Man/woman with a disco at the end.'

I'm not sure which sounds worse: this or the hallucinations.

'Aren't there bears involved?' Melissa pipes up as I turn white. 'Don't you have to wrestle a bear? Or at the very least a wild animal? Maybe one of those mangy racoon dogs?'

Now, I'm terrified.

A bear? A fucking bear? Or, best-case scenario, a ringworm-infested racoon dog that may or may not attempt to defecate in my face to finish me off? I've already tackled a sheep. Isn't that enough? Surely animal-wrestling isn't allowed ... even in Scandinavia. Aren't there health and safety rules about this sort of thing? Then I remember Magnus's counsel: 'Vikings don't worry about health and safety'.

Turning in to our 'shelter' soon after and preparing to embrace the chill of a second night's camping, I find my mind is racing.

Is it all going a bit Lord of the Flies? I worry. *And if so, which character am I?* This is probably something worth considering, I think. *Am I Ralph? I'd be Ralph, right?* I bet a modern-day Ralph would have four bags-for-life in his car. *But then, what if I'm secretly Piggy? Or one of the actual pigs? And what if the ship never comes? What if I never see the kids again? What if I end up on* News 24 *and that's how Greg finds out I've gone?*

I lie very still, agonising over these questions and trying to get warm, but find I can't stop shivering – my muscles incapable of relaxing. I can feel the pressure building up behind my eyes.

Anyone else for a cry? Anyone? I feel like saying. But never would. Or could.

And then from somewhere, a hand extends in the semi-darkness and gives mine a comforting squeeze.

'It'll be OK,' Melissa whispers.

I swallow hard as a tear rolls down my face, pooling in my ear.

'Thanks,' I manage finally. She gives my hand one last Melissa-style crush then lets go, and I drift off to sleep to dream of pigs, carrying bread on hand whittled fishing rods, chasing me through unfamiliar woodland.

Five

Chickens squawk and scatter as we approach and I spot what may or may not be a mouse out of the corner of my eye. Magnus flings open the double doors of a rickety-looking shed and announces with a flourish, 'Welcome to the workshop!'

It's another flannel-grey morning at camp and we've walked for what feels like an Iron Age to reach a circle of huts further along the coast for the next stage in our Viking education. Rustic, weather-beaten, and puffing out black, carcinogenic smoke, the sheds are basic, at best, and I'm not filled with hope for the day ahead.

'Is this how they'd have looked in Viking times?' Margot asks, relentlessly upbeat as usual.

'Sure.' Magnus shrugs. 'Only with more flies. We used to chuck old bones and rubbish outside, like Vikings did, but environmental health found out and we had to stop.' He looks crestfallen at the recollection, although, to my mind at least, the scene still looks alarmingly rustic. *I half expect to stumble across someone playing a lute.*

Today, I'm amused to note, our leader's beard is plaited into two braids as though Pippi Longstocking is attached to his chin.

Could Magnus be 'peak' bell-end? I ponder, now, taking in the bearded, harem-panted creature before me. *I think, perhaps, yes.*

He lights a lamp that does little to lift the gloom and I can just make out a primitive-looking wooden frame with some string and treadles attached. There's also a blackened stone stove, and various baskets of fabric and what I'd term 'clutter' but Melissa would probably describe as 'useful bits and bobs'. All in the same indistinct colour spectrum we've come to expect from around these parts.

'Help yourself!' Magnus holds his arms wide. We stand motionless apart from Margot, who approaches the 'loom', as I'm informed it's called. After giving it the once over, she sits at a small wooden stool and rolls her neck and shoulders in the manner of a concert pianist about to give a recital. Then, she sets her hands upon the mechanism and starts pumping furiously at the pedals. Her right hand deftly feeds a spool of thread through a spider's web of string, then back again, as the contraption claps back and forth, holestones jangling.

'What—' Melissa starts, but Tricia finishes her sentence for her: '—is she doing?'

'Ahh, I see Night Wolf is a natural weaver!' Magnus looks pleased. 'I wondered whether any of you would know your warp from your weft!'

FFS! Who gets to have perfect upper arms, the nut-retrieval skills of a Disney sodding squirrel AND be good at bloody weaving? How is this possible? Aren't twenty-somethings too busy taking selfies? Or learning coding? How have they got time to master the art of WEAVING? What is WRONG with her? I'm determined, now, to find *something*.

Margot looks up, but doesn't break her treadling stride. 'Oh this? It's just something I picked up on my Duke of Edinburgh Award. Gold,' she adds, casually. 'I did alpaca-handling for my silver and I was going to do ballet appreciation or aerodynamics for the gold but then I switched to weaving and spinning instead.'

She spins too? Who spins?

'Did you say, the *Duke of Edinburgh*? As in the Queen's mister?' Melissa's monarchist interest has been piqued, 'Do you, like, *know* him?' she asks, wide-eyed.

'No,' I start. 'She doesn't know him. The Duke of Edinburgh awards are just a thing posh schools do—' but then I notice Margot looking bashful. 'That's right, isn't it?'

'*Well …*' Margot wavers.

Are you shitting me?

'It's just that my father paints landscape with Phil, sometimes,' Margot shrugs with a flick of her glossy caramel mane, as if to say, '*But no biggie …*'

This is too much.

'Wow …' is all Melissa can manage, in wonderment.

'Well, aren't *you* well connected!' Tricia looks similarly impressed. 'I was on his subs bench for *It's a Royal Knockout* but I needed Toyah Wilcox or Barry McGuigan to fracture something before I'd get a look in. No such luck. Never got so much as a gloved handshake with any of them,' she adds, wistfully. 'Though Duncan Goodhew did save me a vol-au-vent from the green room.'

'Duncan Good-who?' Margot wrinkles her brow.

'Exactly.' Tricia sighs. 'Big in the eighties. Before you were born. How depressing … And how swiftly our stars fade …' She tails off and starts tapping at the underside of her chin in an attempt to turn back time. 'But then, a lot of the names who were huge around then turned out to be paedos … So, you know, swings and roundabouts.'

I try to move the conversation on from this disturbing image and Margot's fancy social circle. 'So what else can we do craft-wise?' I ask.

'Well, there's sewing,' he says.

Melissa looks as though someone has just offered her a bucket of cold sick, but Magnus perseveres. 'A woman who wanted to indicate romantic interest in a man in Viking times would make him a shirt.'

'Not for me, darling,' says Tricia. 'I didn't host a televised makeover for the protestors at Greenham Common[11] to sew a man a shirt.'

Ha! I think. *Good for her!* Then I remember the four buttons I sewed on for Greg last month. *Oh ...*

'There's always leatherwork,' Magnus goes on. 'You could make coin pouches – or a belt to keep my trousers up!' He gestures to his harem pants, now slung so low that his 'Brad Pitt circa *Thelma and Louise* pelvic bones' are on show. I catch Tricia moistening her lips.

FFS ... what about Greenham Common?!

'Or there's jewellery making. Vikings wore a lot of bronze, and brooches were very popular,' he explains. 'You make a shape out of wax, put clay around it, fire it in the oven, wait until the wax melts, fill your mould with bronze, then put it in a sock and swing it around your head while it's still molten.'

'Really?' Melissa asks doubtfully.

'I never joke when it comes to molten metal,' says Magnus, offering what I'm certain is a pretty good motto for life.

Our socks haven't been used for much other than sleeping in since Magnus took our shoes away, so procuring some requires a trip back to base camp. Margot volunteers and sets off at a jog.

[11.] 'A lot of anoraks and Deirdre Barlow glasses to tackle ...' is how Tricia explains her own personal contribution to the 1981 peace camp protest against nuclear weapons at RAF Greenham Common in Berkshire.

'Bagsy not Melissa's,' I call after her, remembering the 'lucky sock' fiasco with stomach-curdling clarity.

'Rude!' Melissa observes, then yells, 'Ignore her!'

But Margot is already out of earshot. And so we begin.

It's surprisingly physical work and within minutes of pummelling wax to make a mould, I'm peeling off layers – unprecedented on the trip so far, with my circulation and the Scandinavian climate.

'Good grief, how much are you wearing?' Tricia asks.

'Me? Oh, I feel the cold—'

'That's because she doesn't eat enough,' Melissa chips in.

'Thanks,' I reply.

'It's true. You look like an extra from *Les Mis*.'

'Err ... there's hardly been a Toby Carvery on offer.' I don't know where this comes from. I haven't been to a Toby Carvery since 1998. When Mum died. Melissa knows this.

'Less talking! More crafting!' Magnus interjects and we shut up.

I squish clay around my waxwork ... err ... beetle ...

Is it a beetle?

It's a beetle, I decide. Then I pack it, tightly with clay, slide it into the oven, and burn myself – completely missing the helpful tongs hung to the side of the stove for just this purpose. Magnus tells me to plunge my wrist into a bucket of not-hugely sanitary-looking water he keeps on hand for just such an emergency, while I do a lot of swearing.

By the time Margot returns, her own, high-quality hockey socks in hand, Melissa has made an impressively elaborate dog mould, Tricia appears to have made what I take at first to be a flower, until she tells me it's a 'self-portrait' of her genitalia, while my beetle mould is ... well ... more of a general oval shape.

'Ready?' Magnus asks, socks in hand.

'Ready.' Melissa nods, demanding first dibs on the 'sock slinger'.

'Do you think perhaps we should do that outside?' Tricia asks.

'That ... might be a good idea,' agrees Magnus, with a fleeting glance to the rafters where several blobs of bronze cleave to the undersides of the beams, suggesting previous Viking delegates haven't had quite Tricia's foresight. Or Margot's sturdy socks.

We get outside and Melissa starts to swing, building up quite a momentum.

'That's great, Strong Legs, good job!' Magnus applauds. 'I think you've probably done it now,' he adds. But Melissa isn't slowing down.

'Woo hooooo! I'm like Clint Eastwood! I'm Yosemite Sam! I'm Billy Crystal in *City Slickers*! I'm ... give me a girl one?' she hollers as a sock full of molten metal swings dangerously close to my head.

'Jesus—' I duck, just in time.

'Um, Calamity Jane?' Tricia suggests.

'Or Jessie from *Toy Story 2*?' Margot offers, looking a little afraid of my sister.

'Yes! I'm them! Jane and the other one[12]! Yee-hah!' Melissa continues to swing.

'OK, let's all just back off a little here.' Magnus begins ushering us backwards like spectators at a firework display as my whirling dervish of a sister starts simultaneously running

---

[12]. Toy Story 2 came out after my sister's moratorium on popular culture and is thus unbeknownst to her as a frame of reference. But you probably guessed that by now ...

and sock-lassoing. 'I've seen this happen before,' he confides. 'The slinging goes to their heads. That and the molten metal fumes. We just need to let her spin it out.'

From a safe distance, the four of us watch Melissa execute a sort of gyrating, hula-hooping motion, then give the sock one final revolution before staggering backwards, dizzy and drunk on endorphins.

She fishes around in the toe of Margot's sock, like a child looking for a satsuma in her Christmas stocking, until her hand emerges, triumphant, holding a clay ball that we all hope contains some sort of dog. She holds it above her head, dashes it on the ground to break the mould, then seizes the still-warm bronze creation and clasps it to her bosom. 'Look!' she shows us as we all try to make appreciative noises.

'Mmm ...'

'Has your dog back home only got three legs?' Margot asks, innocently.

Melissa turns the figurine over in her hands and counts. I know this because her mouth still moves when she does this (and when she reads). There is a moment of hesitation before my usually straight-as-a-die sister for some reason decides to style this one out.

'Yes,' she says. 'It has. This is *exactly* what I was going for.'

'Great.' Tricia claps her hands together. 'Me next!'

I'm sorry to report that her 'self-portrait' has a rough ride in the slinger, but Tricia assures us that with some touch-ups it will be 'tight as rain'. My beetle is similarly abstract, with a hint of the joke shop poo about it as Melissa informs me. But still, it's mine. And I have made something from scratch.

Next, we get wood. Literally. Magnus shows us examples of whittled figurines or carvings inspired by Viking designs, all interlocking ropes, ornate circles and patterns that looks distinctly phallic.

'Just draw them on with a Sharpie, then tap them out with a chisel,' he explains.

'Were Vikings big on Sharpies?' Melissa asks, doubtfully.

'They would have been. Had they had access to them,' Magnus says firmly. 'Besides, they smell really good.' He takes a long hard sniff. 'Probably would have used them in a shamanistic ritual or something ...'

'I knew it!' Tricia hisses triumphantly as I start to worry. *Can berserking really entail nudity, free dance, forests and Sharpies? Shit ...*

'Want a go?' Tricia is asking now as she wafts the Sharpie under my nose. I recoil on reflex. 'What?' She notes my expression. 'I haven't had a drink in days. I'll take a Sharpie hit.'

'Oh, go on then.' The words slip out of my mouth.

Once we're all suitably high on permanent marker fumes, Margot chips away at a block of pine in the manner of a crazed Rodin while the rest of us craft in silence – or rather, what would pass as silence were it not for the frog chorus of stomach gurglings that start up round about now. We breakfasted like Queens on porridge and eggs this morning, but something about the fresh air and physical activity combined with the effort of learning something new means that we've all developed alarmingly healthy appetites of late. (Even me!) I can hear Melissa's internal organs protesting from here, and she finally cracks. 'I think we've got the fundamentals now.' She downs tools. 'So what about food?'

'Well, there's the forest,' Magnus starts, as hearts – and stomachs – sink.

'Or you could just ...' Tricia tries a new approach. 'I mean you really seem to have a knack for catching herring.' *A sentence*

I bet she never thought she'd utter. 'I wondered whether you could catch a few more – and show us how you made them so *tasty,* yesterday ...'

Magnus, it becomes clear, is a man easily won around by praise. After a half-hearted demurral ('Oh, it was just a few fish ... !'; 'I mean, that isn't really how it's supposed to work ... but if you lay-dees are sure ... ?') he is persuaded and sets off, whistling.

Tricia waves him goodbye, victorious, then turns to address us, carved creation, which looks a lot like a Viking dildo, in hand. 'We came, we saw, we whittled!' She whoops as I wonder whether she's had an extra sniff of Sharpie. *'Sisters are whittling for themselves ...'* Tricia starts singing to the tune of the Annie Lennox and Aretha Franklin duet and I can't help smiling. *She's definitely had another sniff of Sharpie ...* 'Standing on our own two feet ... whittling wo-od ...' she goes on.

'That's terrible!' I mutter, laughing.

'Don't tell Lennox that.' Tricia breaks off. 'She'll sing at you. Loud. We used to hang out in the 1990s, for about eight minutes. Then I did something to offend her in some way – I forget – and we weren't friends any more. Anyway, I once had tinnitus that lasted a week after a night round hers.'

'You've worked with them all!' says Melissa, without irony.

We go on crafting to distract from the hunger pangs and I find I get lost in the experience, enjoying the smoky-smelling curls and cuts of my carving. This is an interesting experience for someone who kept away from anything creative throughout school and adult life, for fear that I'd be bad at it.

And I am bad at it. But what I discover is that, actually, it doesn't matter. There's a satisfaction in using my hands in a totally non-dental way and making something – just *because* – with no end purpose in sight. While I'm doing it, I'm not indulging in my normal worry rotation and it's as though the experience presses pause on the familiar brain whirring.

I've never understood the point of hobbies before. Even at school, when Melissa persuaded our parents to sign us up for after-school clubs or macramé, I always felt as though there were other things I could be doing. Like homework, or overtime, or online banking. Back at home, I barely have five minutes to myself to go to the loo. Especially for a proper sit-down one. Once, I went a week without a 'motion'. I was literally too busy to shit. My 'hobbies' these days seem to be confined to tidying up the living room and doing laundry.

For as long as I can remember, the hamster wheel of life has sapped all my time and energy. I don't have any free blocks in the calendar or spare colours in my coding system to use up on non-essential activities. I don't do anything for the heck of it. Because to surrender to a hobby would be to do just that: surrender. So when people ask me about my pastimes, I tend to stare at them blankly.

'Any hobbies? Or are you more of a "going around to your mate's house for a mid-week bitch and a carbonara" in your spare time kind of girl?' one overly chatty woman asked at the surgery last week as we were trying to administer anaesthetic.

'I haven't got any spare time!' I wanted to fire back. Instead, I jammed the needle in to shut her up, sharpish. But I began to realise then that I haven't got many friends, either, as Melissa so thoughtfully pointed out to me when she first mooted the idea of a mini-break. I can't remember the last time I hung out with a group of women, like this.

Friends don't always wait for you, when you're busy working too much or in the quagmire of early childrearing. I'm out of sync with the ones who had kids earlier than me, as well as the ones who had them later – or not at all. Old friends moved away as house prices, jobs, families or the general grind of city life pushed or pulled them elsewhere. My social circle has shrunk in recent years. If I were braver, and smarter, I would have seen this coming and started to recruit new friends. But this would have necessitated actual socialising – book clubs, nights out, dinner parties, even *hobbies*. Socialising made heavy calls on my already limited supply of conversation. *And I'm officially terrible at human interactions*, I think, miserably, remembering the 'hiding from living, breathing *people*' behind black drapes backstage at the dentistry conference to avoid awkward encounters.

But if that's true, I think, *then what's this weirdly warm and pleasant sensation I'm experiencing, right now? Almost as though I'm ... content ... in the company of these women, doing something, just for 'fun'?*

'Relaxing, isn't it?' says Margot, chipping away at her wood without looking at what she's doing.

Now she's 'blind-whittling'?!

'It's the dopamine,' she explains. 'A natural antidepressant released when you do something creative and really concentrate. That's why I love joinery.' She holds up her finished product: a staggeringly intricate phoenix, rising from flame-like sawdust curls.

'Bloody hell!' The words escape from my lips before I can stop them. 'Is there anything you're not good at?'

Margot thinks about this for longer than is strictly tactful. She pouts as though forming a word, before changing her mind and settling on: 'Badminton.'

Magnus doesn't just come back with herring – he has mackerel and offers to cook it, too. All we have to do is gather leaves and berries as accompaniments.

Being old hands at foraging now, our contribution to the meal takes us no time at all. I volunteer to take on berries, and together we round up all the foodstuffs the forest feels like bestowing on us, before returning to base to Fill Our Faces. It's still cold. It's still damp. But under a sky the colour of a forgotten sock, we sit around a campfire and eat food that was in the wild just moments ago. And it's ... nice.

Once we're bloated beyond description, we lounge about the fire comparing handcrafted goods and happily full bellies.

'So, a good day, eh, ladies?'

Margot nods. 'Most fun ever!'

I'm not sure I'd go that far, I think, but then struggle to recall a time I've felt as free as this. *I am perilously close to enthusiasm,* I observe.

After dusk falls, Magnus returns home – wherever that may be – leaving us to brave another night in the great outdoors. But this time I'm not scared. Instead, the four of us lie on our backs, feet toasting in the warmth of the fire, and look up at the starry sky.

'Isn't it amazing, to think that there are whole other worlds out there?' Margot is still prodigiously perky. 'Or that people have gone up there, into space!'

'*Pfft.* Space.' Melissa pulls a face as I take a sharp intake of breath.

Here we go ...

'Sorry?'

'Oh, it's just that I'm not really a believer,' is all she says.

'In *space*?' Margot props herself up on her elbows and looks incredulous.

'Melissa thinks the moon landing was a fake,' I say as discreetly as I can. The fact that my sister doesn't believe in space, thanks to a less-than-stellar attendance record at school, isn't something I want to dwell on.

That's the last thing I need, I think, *being shown up in front of Margot …*

'Really? Tell me more!' Tricia has no such reservations about delving a little deeper into this particular treasure trove and rolls onto her side to face Melissa.

'Yeah, I just don't buy all the funny suits and how come we can't all live on Mars if it's all so easy to get to, like, *fifty years ago*!' my sister scoffs.

'Right … well … I suppose we all have our things …' Tricia says darkly.

'What do you mean?'

'Well, I'm the other way. I think space is too close.'

I arch an eyebrow at this, to which she responds, 'Have you seen *Armageddon*? I worry that Bruce Willis is getting a little long in the tooth to save us from an asteroid attack now. Plus Affleck's busy with other things.' She waves a hand to summarise Mr Affleck's preoccupations before concluding, 'I just don't think they'll have time to *fix it*, next time – so I always keep a few extra tins in …'

Margot's eyebrows are now somewhere around her hairline.

They didn't teach her about people like this at her school … And now I'm going to get lumped into 'people like this', thanks to my genetic proximity to the moon-landing-denier. Cheers, Melissa …

'So you stockpile food?' Margot seeks to clarify, 'In case an *asteroid* hits?'

'Not *in case*,' is Tricia's comeback. '*When*!'

'I think we'll be OK … for tonight at least …' I try to bring this conversation back down to earth as delicately as I can.

'That's what "they" want you to think,' Tricia says.

'*Do* they?'

Tricia taps her nose as if to say 'you didn't hear it from me'.

Melissa nods in support of her fellow conspiracy theorist, as I flop back down onto my back in despair.

Margot, sensing that any attempts at scientific conversions are likely to be fruitless this evening, slowly lowers herself back down too, and we stare at the constellations in silence after this.

'You don't see those at home,' Tricia murmurs eventually, to which Melissa replies that you do if you live round her way, in the 'proper countryside'.

'So not Streatham then?' I ask.

'No,' she tells me firmly. 'Sorry.'

I've never had much interest in the natural world before. But being treated to such an extravagant expanse of starry sky, extending forever, I think perhaps Melissa might be on to something with her countryside evangelism.

'That's a bright one!' she nods, vaguely.

'Getting a bit technical there,' I tease and she sticks her tongue out at me. Yawning with a comfortable fatigue, I blink a few times, then a couple more – convinced I've seen a shooting star.

I rub my eyes to check they are to be trusted.

'Did you see it too?' Melissa asks.

'I ... I think so!'

'Make a wish! Quick! All of us.'

And so we do.

Six

Burr-burrr-burrrr!

The blare of a horn starts up: a stirring, rallying call that blends into an alarmingly realistic dream sequence I'm currently immersed in involving the treatment of an impacted third molar.

Burr-burrr-burrrr! The summons continues, for what seems like an age, until I am fully awake and squinting to take in my surroundings.

Burr-burrr-burrrr …

I start to wonder when it will stop.

Burr-burrr-BURRRR!

Will it EVER stop?

The horn gets louder. And louder. Until an imposing figure, clutching an appendage from what must have been a pretty terrifying bull, is looming over us.

'Impressive lung capacity.' A crumpled Tricia emerges from a mass of blankets opposite and rubs her eyes. Margot and Melissa aren't anywhere to be seen, but my sister, at least, I can hear.

'Wake up! It's a beautiful day! The sun is shining, the birds are singing!' she is trilling from beyond the shelter.

'All right, Snow White, keep your bodice on,' I grumble, propping myself up on one elbow then deciding the outside world is far too cold, so slumping back down and burying my hands in my armpits for warmth. After listening to Melissa hum tunelessly, albeit with enthusiasm, for another five minutes, I decide I can't take it any more. I'm going to have to get up. I wriggle a bra on underneath the jumper I've now taken to sleeping in and manage to turn my underwear inside out for a second wear. Yes, it's come to this. And amazingly, I'm coping pretty well.

Maybe I am *a Viking* ...

Margot appears, hands on hips, glowing almost ethereally and with a halo of early-morning sunlight making her caramel mane shine even more than usual. 'Everything always feels better after a run, doesn't it?'

Tricia and I exchange a look along the lines of *'I wouldn't know'*, followed by a telepathically mutual *'give me strength, and, preferably, espresso ...'*

On seeing Magnus, Margot stands a little taller than even her excellent posture usually allows. 'Oh, hi! How are you today?'

But today, Magnus ignores her. Today, there is no time for such social fripperies. Because today, he informs us: 'We are warriors.'

'What about breakfast?' I ask. Me! A woman who eschewed the first meal of the day for more than a decade! *You've changed, Alice,* I think.

'Yes!' Tricia attempts to smooth down bed hair and make herself presentable. 'Isn't there a kind of waking-up ritual for warriors?' She tries to delay the inevitable. 'A warm-up, perhaps?' she suggests, grasping at straws. 'Or a "getting to know your inner warrior" game ... ? Something with quoits, maybe?' I can tell by the look on our leader's face that this isn't going to be a goer. 'No ... ?'

'Come with me,' is all Magnus says, extending a taut bicep to help each of us up, as though we're Marilyn Monroe and Jane Russell in *Gentlemen Prefer Blondes*. I assure him I'm fine, but Tricia accepts, before accidentally-on-purpose brushing past his bare chest.

'Smoother than a freshwater otter,' she murmurs as he hoists her up and out of the hut.

'Waxed,' I whisper. 'There's no way a man with that much facial hair has a body-carpet that stops conveniently at the neck.'

Tricia honks with laughter and it's then I notice that, today, our great leader has styled said facial hair into no fewer than *three* braids.

Like a tripod ...

'Say what you like about manscaping,' Tricia regains her composure. 'There's a reason the woolly mammoth died out ...'

After another decent tramp across scrubland and past the 'craft sheds', we reach a large, chimneyed ... what exactly? Hovel? 'House' seems too grand a term. From inside comes the roar of flames and the hush of bellows, and I cough as my lungs adjust to the air, thick with blue smoke. Once my eyes have stopped watering at the prickling haze of carbon, I make out bare stone walls, wooden beams hung with tools, and what looks like something life-size in the far corner.

'Is there someone in here?' I whisper.

'Oh, yes.' Magnus looks a little irritated. 'He's just helping out.' Then he says something in a language I don't understand but that sounds a lot like he's been drinking.

That, or about to solve a murder in a subtitled show set against drab skies.

The figure bellowing is apparently dismissed and moves past us quickly, a soot-smeared face turned away so that the only lingering impression is that of a smoky, musky smell.

'Mmm.' Melissa breathes it in. 'Reminds me of a farrier.'

I have no idea what this means, but my sister turns a little misty-eyed at the recollection. Tricia translates that a farrier is 'a specialist in equine hoof care – basically, they put shoes on horses' ('I did the third series of *Celebrity Gymkhana* on ITV2,' she explains).

Now, Magnus is taking up the bellows and doing his best to control them with the same ease as their previous operative, telling us that, 'The blacksmith was one of the most important people in Viking times. One king,' he grunts between bangs, 'had his blacksmith's legs chopped off so he couldn't leave the village.'

Unsure as to the appropriate response to this, we say nothing.

'So, this is how you make iron,' he puffs.

'Right. And ... err ... how much of that do we need for a sword?' Melissa asks.

At this, he turns on her sharply. 'You're not making a sword.'

'We're not?'

'No!' He laughs. In her face. Magnus shakes his head as though Melissa's suggestion was simply 'too funny', then offers by way of compromise. 'Most students start by making a nail.'

'A *nail*?' Melissa isn't impressed. 'We're making *a nail*? On 'weaponry day'?'

'Yes. It takes *years* to become an expert sword forger.'

'Right. And how long have you been doing it?'

'*Years*,' he responds.

Melissa adopts her best sulking face and even Margot looks put out. Tricia is busy dodging sparks from what looks like several dozen firecrackers, but I realise that, deep down, I'm also disappointed that we're not getting to fulfil my *Xena: Warrior Princess* fantasy.

'I'm not making this nail on my own you know!' Magnus barks, patting at a small fireball that has landed in his beard.

If there was ever a man in need of a welding mask, it's a hipster, I muse.

Magus grunts and bellows some more. He's in a strange mood this morning and even Tricia's attempts at flattery and Margot's short shorts can't win him around. Making a nail, as warned, appears to take 'a bloody long time' as Tricia puts it and, midway through, she announces that she needs a comfort break. Since we're stopping anyway, an early lunch is declared by mutual consent. At this, Magnus excuses himself and disappears into the woods, with an unusual gait.

We finish eating – salted herring from yesterday and bread that doesn't taste too stale once it's been toasted – then remain in situ, primed for the 'thrills' that lie ahead, when Tricia notes that our leader has been gone rather a long time.

As Melissa is the only one of us to wear a watch, she tells us that we should give him another five minutes ('You can't hurry dump,' she tells us, in an update of Diana Ross's famous refrain).

Oblivious to any external pressures being placed on his bowels, Magnus does not return by the time five minutes are up. But somewhere around the six-minute mark, Melissa informs us, there is a strange, whimpering sound.

Please don't let it be a wild animal, I beg silently. *Don't let Magnus have thought we're all such voracious herring eaters that he's gone and speared a squirrel ... or sacrificed the shitting sheep ... or been attacked by a raccoon dog ... or a wolf ...*

'*Ohhhhhhh*,' the moaning goes up a notch, the timbre of a siren now.

'Magnus?' Margot looks concerned. 'Should we go and look for him?'

'The man's answering the call of nature,' Tricia says. 'I think we can afford him a little privacy—'

'*Arghhhh!*' There is another audible outburst.

'On the other hand ...'

We're just having a whisper-debate about what to do next when Magnus lurches into view, harem pants at half-mast, displaying all that this Viking has to offer. He sways, then slowly leans to one side. We watch, passively, still sure that he's going to right himself until he topples beyond the angle of recovery, whereby we all leap to our feet.

'He's fainting! He's going to faint! Tricia commentates as Melissa makes an admirable stab at running to save him, before being outstripped by a sprinting Margot. She catches him mid fall, just before his head can strike a particularly angular rock ... and he loses control of his bowels.

'Oh my ...' Margot struggles to support him and try to avoid getting covered in excrement ' ... *crumbs*!'

'Crap more like.' Tricia swears on Margot's behalf as we take in the sorry figure of our once-great leader. An angry rash has spread from one cheek to the other, until he looks like a teen troubled by acne, and he is visibly perspiring. Then he vomits. Great pools of viscous liquid, largely mauve in colour, with the odd curl of foraged leaf in there.

Repulsed, yet fearing that this is something a woman with four bags-for-life in her car *should* be able to handle, I say the line I've been rehearsing since I was seventeen. 'Let me through, I'm a medic.'

At which point, Melissa says the line she's been rehearsing since she was fifteen. 'You're not a real doctor, you're a *dentist* ...'

'Dental-care professionals undergo regular training in the management of medical emergencies to a level appropriate to their clinical responsibilities!' I tell her impatiently.

'And in normal person's speak that means what exactly?'

'We learn first aid!' I retort. 'Why, what are you going to do? Horse whisper him better?' This shuts her up.

In truth, other than feeling his brow for a temperature, establishing he's suffering from stomach cramps and confirming that he is too weak to stand, I don't do much. There is, thankfully, no blood in his 'emissions' – from either end. But he's shivering now, and there can be little doubt judging from the berry sick about what's caused this. All eyes are on me. Well, the ones that aren't currently rolled up into the back of our illustrious leader's head.

Shit …

'So what do we do now?' asks Tricia.

I try to think, fast.

What would a woman with four bags-for-life in her car do in this situation? Then I remember. *Survival skill 101: check the rest of the party is all right.*

'Anyone else feeling unwell?'

Heads shake, and other than suffering from nausea on account of the crime-scene investigation tableau in front of me, my stomach is lining is mercifully intact.

'Did he eat the same as us?' Margot asks.

'I think so …'

'Well, he did finish off those berries …'

I start to sweat now. Because having become fairly cocky about this edible plant malarkey, I now begin to worry that I may have inadvertently poisoned Magnus with some rogue fruit from the one tree I wasn't supposed to pick it from.

I'm like Eve in the garden of Eden, I think, *only I haven't even got a sodding snake to blame …*

Luckily, Tricia throws me a lifeline. 'A lot of men have issues at this sort of age,' she says with some authority. 'My ex was always on the loo with something or other. Didn't have the stomach for it. Literally.'

The blame storm is put on hold by the beginnings of rain and the returning bowel grumblings of our sickly Viking.

'I have to go,' he groans. 'Again ...'

Oh Jesus.

'Can you make it over to the bushes?' I ask.

Magnus moans some more.

'Well?'

He shakes his head.

'Right then,' I say, but discover that I can't move either.

What is wrong with me? Why is nothing happening?

'Right.' I have another crack at sounding convincing, but all in vain. I am frozen to the spot.

Please don't have another panic attack, please don't have another panic attack ...

'Get out of first gear!' Melissa berates me. Then she pushes up her sleeves and ducks her head under one of his arms, trying to lift him while still grumbling at me. 'You have kids – you've dealt with human crap before—'

'They were cute tiny babies! Not fifteen stone of Viking!' I find I can't unclench my buttocks as fear flows through my veins. 'Besides, you have animals!' I counter.

'So? So does Tricia! And a son!'

'Your animals are bigger!' I come back. *A little Shih Tzu hardly compares.*

'Err, shows what you know because a) horse poo is mostly hay, b) the rabbits eat theirs, and c) my dogs are very well trained to go in the woods. I don't handle faeces of any kind. It's one of my policies in life.'

'Oh good. It's important to have values.'

Tricia intervenes, looking worried now, her lust for Magnus decreasing with each unpleasant aromatic emission: 'Come on. What we have here is a shit-uation. We can't just leave him here ...'

'We can't. Can't we?' I ask, hopefully.

'No!' The women turn on me.

'We were awful at fishing, the hamper supplies will only last so long, and I don't want another meal of mystery food—' Tricia starts before being cut off.

'And more importantly he needs help.' Margot looks at Tricia, incredulous.

'Yes,' she catches herself. '*That*. Mainly *that*.' But Tricia isn't finished. Because ... what if one of us gets sick next?'

We all look at each other, secretly calculating – in my case, at least – how we'd divvy up further deep-cleaning duties between us.

'Well, I'm steering clear of berries,' says Melissa.

'Oh, thanks very much!' I say. 'What if it was the mussels?'

'They were first-class sea molluscs!'

When she puts it like that, even I want to vomit.

'What were those leaves, you know ... ?' Tricia addresses Margot.

'Wild garlic? The wild garlic was fine,' she responds smartly.

'You're sure?' Tricia asks.

'Yes!' Margot snaps, feeling the pressure. 'Daddy has a book on edible plants in the downstairs loo –' I see Melissa mouth the word 'posh' '– plus I did a course ...'

Surprise, surprise ...

'Let me guess,' I hear myself saying. 'Duke of Edinburgh?'

Margot nods, oblivious to any scorn. 'Platinum.'

'*Platinum*? Does that even exist?'

'Not a lot of people know about it,' she admits.

'You pay enough in school fees, you can have what you like,' Tricia mutters.

'It was probably a yew berry seed,' Margot announces.

Busted ...

'You?' Melissa gets the wrong end of the stick, pointing at me.

'Yew!' three of us bark at her. After this, we eye each other suspiciously until Melissa shakes her head and says, at the precise moment that the heavens open, 'Nature can be a cruel mistress ...'

Magnus groans again and it becomes very clear that he Needs To Go. Now. He doesn't seem able – or inclined – to speak any more so, by a series of mimes, we establish that he's at Critical Code Brown.

Melissa agrees to put her cast iron constitution to good use, even cleaning up afterwards, with the help of Margot and whatever foliage they can find.

Who manages to look pretty while cleaning up poo?

Margot: that's who.

After what Melissa describes as another 'Close Encounter of the Turd Kind', there is an implicit understanding that we're going to need to get help. My sister, who's warming to her role as an Enid Blyton heroine, starts to talk tracking.

'We need to work out where he lives. The house must be nearby. And what about Inge? Shouldn't we tell her what's happened? Take him there?'

'If only we knew where "there" was,' I say.

'Well ...' Melissa thinks. 'When Silas—'

'Silas?'

'One of my dogs. Likes to run off. Randy.'

'Right ... ?'

'So, when Silas runs off, then comes back with evidence of ... recreational activity ... I often have to find out where he's been ... *recreating* ...'

'Do you mean shagging?' Tricia is keen to clarify.

'I do mean shagging,' she confirms. '*The Country Code* dictates that you can't let your dog get another dog in the family way without apologising—' *I'm pretty sure it's a little more nuanced than this* '—so I have to follow his footprints. Of course, rain makes this trickier ...' She scans the sky, then squints at the horizon. 'But Inge came from *this* way yesterday.' She nods, knowingly, then kneels down and touches the earth, allowing a little of it to crumble through her fingers.

Give me strength ...

'And she carried supplies in a sack, which means her gait might have been heavier on one side,' she goes on, with great gravitas. 'The sack could have dragged a bit when she walked ...' She sniffs the air as if following a scent.

All right, Sherlock Holmes ...

'Plus, Magnus has enormous feet so we can tell they're not our prints—'

'You know what they say, big feet, big—' Tricia starts, then Magnus vomits in a bush and even she can't bring herself to continue this line of thinking.

I stare helplessly at the now-mud, unable to see clear footprints in any direction. But Melissa seems certain. 'This way!' she points. Margot doesn't argue, and if there's one person I secretly have faith in to get us out of here alive with some sort of Duke of Edinburgh/posh girl wizardry, it's Margot. *So Melissa must be on the right track. Mustn't she?*

'You're sure?' Tricia asks.

'I'm sure,' says Melissa, sounding not at all sure. Magnus emits a wail that spurs us into action. Melissa, inexplicably, begins getting down on all fours. 'Right, that's it, I'm going to turtle him.'

'What? What are you doing? Is that an official carry-move?'

'Not sure ...'[13] she says, but gives it a go anyway. 'Unnngggg ...' My sister turns softly puce while attempting to heave fifteen stone of floppy, faecal-stained man onto her back. "S'OK ... I can do this ...' she grunts. 'I ... Am ... Strong ... Legs ... Plus I once had to punch an Alsatian in the face. Knocked him clean out.'

'What? Why would you do that?' I ask.

'He'd already taken a tricep out of the gardener and was coming towards us, ears pinned back ... so ... you know ... I love dogs but a girl's gotta do what a girl's gotta ... unngggg ...' She braces herself and lifts again.

'Here, let me help,' Margot takes up his legs, allowing Melissa to slip out from underneath and grab his arms. The younger woman turns out to be superhumanly strong, offending Melissa only slightly ('My muscles are for go, not for show,' she explains). Between them, they toss Magnus up like a ragdoll and start moving in a direction agreed upon by Melissa.

We progress like this for some time, Tricia and I occasionally offering to take over, but finding we can't carry, him for more than a few yards ('Excuse my sister's poor upper-body strength,' Melissa tells Margot. 'She's eighty per cent salad'). We're soon acquitted of our duties and the professionals take over once more.

Margot and Melissa do an admirable job, but after we've covered a considerable distance, even superwomen start to flag.

This isn't working. What are we going to do? I challenge myself.

---

13. Point of order: it is. I checked later.

'Myself' doesn't come up with any bright ideas so I go bad-cop on her.

I said, 'WHAT THE FUCK ARE WE GOING TO DO?' I don't plan on wasting away in the woods, hungry, covered with mud and in charge of a shitting Viking. We need a plan. A PLAN, I TELL YOU! Come on, Alice, THINK!

'Um … perhaps …' I start, hesitantly at first before realising that no one else has any better suggestions and I should just go for it. 'We need a stretcher?' I point at Magnus's sagging body, dangling and moaning between Margot and my sister.

'A stretcher?' Melissa demands. 'And where are we going to get a stretcher from?'

'Well …'

Think, Alice! You're a medic, remember? A life sciences professional! You have a white coat … somewhere. And you wear special clogs to work. You can do this! You've said the thing out loud, now people are relying on you. Say something else. Something good … and fast …

'We can … MAKE one!' I sound … *confident*. 'He'll be easier to carry that way, plus if we had a stretcher, we could take a corner each.'

Margot and Melissa exchange a look as if to confirm assent and Tricia nods along, keen to contribute.

'All right.' Melissa sets the patient down. 'So how do we do this?'

It worked? It worked! My plan has been approved! I resist the urge to high five myself realising that this is where schizzle gets serious: execution.

How to make a stretcher … I think back to old episodes of *Holby City*.

'Well, we should start with two poles,' I say, with as much confidence as I can muster.

'OK then, genius,' says Melissa. 'Where do you suggest we find poles?'

'Err ...' I gesture all around us.

'Those are trees,' she snaps. 'We can't carry whole *trees*!'

'If we look, we should be able to find something more ... streamlined ...' I'm not going to be deterred now. And, miraculously, the troops comply.

We manage to locate a couple of durable-looking but not too hefty branches, reasonably straight, and foliage-free apart from one sprouting end, which we start stripping. This doesn't go brilliantly – in the rain, with fingers near numb from cold, to the soundtrack of a Great Dane with dysentery – but we do our best.

Deciding that our man-giant of a patient may need something fairly substantial to convey him cross-country, Melissa suggests adding a couple of diagonal branches to create a farm gate effect.

'Great idea!' Margot approves. 'The triangle is the strongest shape due to the rigidity of its sides, which allows it to transfer force more evenly along its outline than other shapes!'

'Ye-es ...' says Melissa. 'That's exactly what I meant ...'

'Good old physics A-level!' Margot enthuses, as though this is something we can all bond over. It is not.

'That's right!' I manage brightly. 'Then we just need to bind them together and make a fabric base.' I continue, as Margot is already shedding her outer layer to reveal a contoured, racing-backed technical top, so tight it displays her washboard abs.

'What are you doing?' I ask.

'We'll have to use our clothes, won't we?' she asks, innocently.

'Err, yes,' I try to sound authoritative. 'Come on, everyone! We must all have something we can take off and tie together!' I chivvy the others on.

'Couldn't we go back and get a blanket or something?' Tricia looks around in desperation.

'We've come too far.' Margot shakes her head, then looks to me for reassurance. 'Haven't we?'

'Yes, we have,' I say, hoping this sounds decisive. 'We're better off moving forward now. The house must be close if he made it to us less than an hour after sunrise. We've been walking for, what, half an hour now?' My sister checks her watch and nods. 'So we're more than halfway there!'

On the inside, I'm quaking at my own uncharacteristic Pollyanna-style positivity. On the outside, I'm breezy. *You're nailing this!* I congratulate myself on my cool, calm, four-bags-for-life exterior.

'OK then, come on everyone.' Tricia peels off a layer of designer athleisurewear. 'Let's be having you!' I relinquish my jumper to the rescue-mission, trying not to dwell on the fact that Sweaty Betty's finest is now being used to form a stretcher for a shitting man. 'I feel your pain,' Tricia tells me as she holds up my sweatshirt admiringly before adding it to the war-effort. 'When your face starts to fall apart, you have to buy slightly nicer clothes, don't you? To distract the eye. Otherwise we can start to look a bit homeless, can't we?'

'We'? Does Tricia think I'm the same age as her?! Why does everyone keep assuming I'm older than I am? Do I give out old vibes? Vibes of 'I'm completely knackered with life'? Must work on that ...

'Melissa?' Tricia turns her attention elsewhere. 'Your turn!'

But Melissa wraps her arms protectively around her maroon fleece. For a moment, I wonder whether she's cold, but then I remember that Melissa doesn't get cold; that's my job.

'Please may we have your top, too, Melissa?' Margot asks, patient and polite to a fault.

Melissa mumbles something in barely audible tones.

'Sorry?'

'I said, "No" ...'

'What?'

'It's my lucky fleece!'

Really?

'Not in the *sexual* sense ... ?' Tricia looks aghast at the stained, bobbling garment.

'No,' I answer Tricia on my sister's behalf, with some confidence.

'Oh, you'd be surprised. I do CK.' Melissa raises her eyebrows by way of a challenge. 'I've worn it for nine out of ten of my last dates with a hundred per cent strike rate, *actually*. This fleece equals slamming it.'

'O-kay then ...'

Well, this just got weirder.

Thinking about your little sister having sex – not to mention in a bobbled maroon fleece – is a lot like picturing your parents at it: gross. And somehow against the natural order of things. In my head, she frolics around with dogs and horses and drinks loose-leaf tea out of Kate Middleton commemorative mugs. In my head, she, along with all other family members, is conveniently and hygienically *asexual. Sans* genitalia, even. A lot like Barbie and Action Man. Nowhere in the imagined version of my sister's bucolic life have I got her going on dates with strange men before rutting away in a maroon fleece. I try to shake off the image, banishing it from my head to return to the task at hand.

'I appreciate it may have ... *sentimental* value,' Margot is saying carefully to Melissa while tying the clothes donated so far to the poles with some pretty impressive knot work, 'but I'm afraid we're going to need something else, something substantial, to cover the large surface area of the stretcher –' she breaks off '– no offence ...'

'None taken.' Melissa smooths down the sides of her fleece as though agreeing that it is indeed roomy and made from the highest quality polyester. Reluctantly, she unzips, and I hear a crackle of static electricity as she unsheathes each arm in turn. Underneath, she's wearing her '*Keep calm and think about Cary Grant*' T-shirt, which, I hope, might soften the blow a bit. But she holds on to the fleece tightly and stalls in loosening her grip when handing it over. Margot has to near-wrench the garment away from my sister before she can begin to transform it from 'ugly jumper' to 'emergency medical supply'. It does, as predicted, make an excellent final panel for our makeshift stretcher and I'm sure that The Duke of Edinburgh would be proud.

Once we've loaded on our cargo, we continue apace: Magnus moaning and periodically clasping a hand to his stomach while releasing toxic emissions, the rest of us holding him aloft. It's far easier to carry him this way and with one of us on each corner, we do OK. Or at least, we would were it not for the fact that Melissa is a foot shorter than Margot and me, so that Magnus occasionally slides towards the lowest corner of our ambulatory rectangle.

'You're very long-legged women,' she pants. 'It's difficult to keep up!'

This handicap reveals itself to be especially treacherous when crossing a babbling brook and we nearly lose our leader to a stream, heading out to sea.

Imagine the headlines! I think.

'Viking' dies at hands of four Englishwomen on experimental retreat.
    One of the women, Alice Rat [probably], *dentist and mother of two from Streatham, had recently been involved in a drink-breakfasting incident at a Premier Inn in the Midlands where she had to be asked to leave a family buffet. 'She was a mess,' several onlookers observed.*

Then I remind myself that this isn't all about me – and get my act together. Post stream-gate, we carry on, in a rhythm now, remaining alert to each others' weaknesses ('height' and 'poor strength' mostly), factoring them in so that we move in sync, as one.

We navigate our way through a crag of rocks with a Chuckle Brothers'-esque finesse ('To me!'; 'To you.'), then just when I start feeling as though my arms and legs really can't take any more, Tricia announces dramatically that she has, 'Seen the light!'

Tramping through the driving rain for another few paces, I too spot lights flickering in the distance and a small chimneystack sending up a steady stream of smoke. And there, finally, is a house.

'Bricks! It's made from actual bricks!' Tricia near keels over with delirious excitement. 'And it's got a door! And windows!'

Relief washes over us and I find myself erupting into nervous laughter that soon becomes contagious. My heart pounds – in a good way, for a change – and I feel … elated.

'We did it! We really did it!' I can't quite believe it.

'Who needs sword-forging – we just saved someone's life!' Tricia adds. 'Probably.'

'We are Vikings!' my sister hollers, holding up a fist in victory and nearly dropping her corner of the stretcher in the process.

The resultant commotion and Melissa's prolonged whooping is interrupted by a primitive, screeching noise.

'Bloody hell! What was that?'

'Magnus?'

We set down the stretcher to check whether or not the din is coming from our great leader, but aside from some drooling and more suspicious stains, Magnus looks peaceful, sleeping deeply. *That or he's dead*, I worry. *But for now, let's go with sleeping* ... Either way, it's not him producing the most atrocious pit-of-hell sounds I've ever heard.

'*Reeeeeeeeeer–urghhhhhh!*' someone – or something – cries again. I grab Melissa's arm and hold on tight. Just in case she's frightened ...

'It's OK,' she says. 'It'll be OK ...' She squeezes my hand as a mud-crusted, corpulent creature waddles into view, fat rolls shuddering. 'It's just a pig!'

Oh God. Lord of the Flies. I knew it.

The beast pokes its head through a not-very-reassuringly-robust fence and screeches at us once more – '*Reeeeeeeeeer–urghhhhhh!*' – before returning to the business of rucking up his field and scaring away several chickens, scratching at the earth.

Having now concluded that 'Magnus keeps pigs as well as chickens' we approach the door of the whitewashed house and stand nervously outside.

'Should we knock?' Margot asks.

'Of course we should knock,' I say, then nudge Melissa forward so that she can do the knocking. She raps, putting some welly behind the action, but there is no response. 'Is there a bell?'

There is no bell. So we wait, like polite Brits, occasionally bolstering a now mewling and puking man-bunned Viking.

'OK, let's just try going in,' says Melissa, reaching for the door handle.

'No! We can't!' I object, swatting her hand away.

'Why?'

'It's rude.'

'He's about to shit himself! *That's* rude!'

This is a fair point.

Melissa goes for the heavy wooden door again, just as it swings open.

Inge, it turns out, is no less impressive on second sight: shrink-wrapped in black Lycra, as if working out were a constant possibility.

'Mmm, hi ...' Melissa mumbles, awestruck.

I don't fare much better.

'I like your house,' is my best effort at 'talking like a normal human being'. Fortunately, Inge saves us. She holds up a hand to halt all further blathering, then cranes a swan-like neck around Melissa to take in the sorry sight behind us on the stretcher.

'Is that my husband?'

'Oh, god. Yes!' Tricia declares.

We're all instantly apologetic and filled with remorse that we had temporarily forgotten the reason why we're here.

'He's sick ...' I start, but there's no need, since Magnus obligingly illustrates his ailments at this very moment with a violent purple chunder.

'*Again?*' She appears more irritated than concerned about her husband's wellbeing. 'I *told* him,' Inge continues, riled now. 'I said. "Use flashcards!" I said, "tourists never know anything about foraging and think berries come from a shop!"'

'Ha!' Melissa laughs, keen to get across her countryside credentials and distance herself from the tourist tag. Unfairly, in my view.

'Well, they do, usually—' I start.

'I get them on a two-for-one from the supermarket.' Tricia backs me up.

'What's a two-for-one?' asks Margot, innocently.

Oh, that's just like her. Of course she doesn't shop around for bargains! Probably doesn't even shop! Probably has someone to do it for her! Like a butler ...

Inge, uninterested in our shopping habits, signals for us to get out of the way so that she can get to her ailing husband.

'I'll take him from here.' She hauls Magnus up from a heap on the ground with apparent ease and carries him as though he's a backpack into the house, calling back over her shoulder, 'You'd better come in.'

We follow, over the threshold and into a hallway crammed with outdoor wear in various shapes and sizes. We're led past a room full of footwear and – I spy with some joy – our shoes. A chubby infant is feeding worms to some chicks under an infrared light, crawling over a rusty chainsaw and several pairs of trainers to make sure a couple of the stragglers peck their fill.

Extraordinary ...

The hallway opens out into a warm, predominantly wooden kitchen, where, Inge warns us, any strange sounds can be put down to 'the lamb in the cupboard'.

For a moment I assume this is a euphemism or something that's been lost in translation. *Like Magnus and the windy pelicans*, I think, until I hear a gentle high-pitched bleating and a small, pink nose appears from the cupboard under the sink. A spindly leg follows suit, and then another, until a small woolly face can be seen. Two beady eyes take in the new arrivals, then the creature bleats again, before retreating back into the cupboard. 'Its mother abandoned it so we're keeping it in here for now,' Inge tells us, still lugging her Viking load.

'That's awful!' Tricia says, cooing over the creature.

'It happens, *in the countryside*,' assures Melissa, our resident *Countryfile* correspondent, with an eye to impressing Inge, I can tell. I'm starting to wonder whether Mrs Bad Sheep was my nemesis-ewe ('nem-ewe-sis'?).

The one who tried to put me off my berry foraging and crapped everywhere ...

On the roughly hewn kitchen table is a loaf of bread and a bowl of something white and cloudy-looking.

'Goat's milk,' Inge informs us. 'Fresh this morning. Good for dunking.'

'Oh my ...' says Tricia.

'Are we in the olden days?' I whisper.

'I think we might just be,' she responds in hushed tones.

'You have goats, too?' Melissa is asking.

'Yes.'

'Wow.'

'So you found the house all right?' Inge asks and we nod. 'Did you use the trailer?'

'Trailer? No ... we built a stretcher,' says Margot a little too keen in my view to take credit for the idea.

'You *carried* him? All this way?'

'Yes.'

'Along the road?'

'There's a *road*?' Melissa is stupefied.

Inge shifts Magnus's weight against her to free up an arm and points out of the window. There, next to the worn path we have taken out of the woods is a parallel, perfectly tarmacked road. 'Right there, past the pig,' she says, as though we are idiots.

We are idiots, I think, *or, rather, Melissa is. She made us go that way …*

'Oh! Right. Yes, we saw the pig,' Melissa nods, attempting to wrest back some pride.

'Yes, we just have one now. There were eleven, but we ate them,' Inge says simply before addressing Magnus and saying something that sounds slurred.

'I think it's *Danish*,' whispers Tricia.

'Right.' I nod.

Inge pulls back her husband's eyelids to study his pupils, then examines his tongue before propping him up like a ventriloquist dummy against the wall.

'Well, she doesn't butter her parsnips,' murmurs Tricia, just as I'm admiring her brisk and efficient bedside manner.

She 'wifes' a lot like I 'dentist', I think.

'Will he be OK?' Margot looks concerned.

'Oh, sure. I'll make him the usual,' she says, reaching into cupboards for an assortment of implements and ingredients. She selects a gnarled arthritic hand of ginger from a wooden crate of produce and begins to peel it with the back of a spoon before chopping, expertly and without looking, until it has been thoroughly pulverised. Then she adds a dash of hot water from a pan on the stove, and finishes it off with a sprinkling of something brown.

Melissa sniffs, trying to identify the mystery powder before finally nailing it. 'Smells like tacos!'

'Cumin,' Inge says. 'Helps him sweat it out.' When she's done, Magnus is flopped over her arm like laundry and she carries him out of the kitchen, throwing back an, 'I'll just get this down him, then we can talk. Make yourself at home – coffee's in the pot.'

'*Coffee?*' My ears prick up and I can feel my pulse race and fingertips tingle in anticipation. 'We're allowed coffee?' I half gasp with delight.

'Of course.' Inge shrugs. 'We're Vikings; we're not Amish.'

Good point! Stupid Magnus and his stupid rules, I think, before adding as an afterthought: *Though obviously I hope he's OK ...*

'And help yourself to salted liquorice,' she adds, as though this is a 'thing' we should know about.

'Sorry?'

'You don't have that back home? Good for reviving. Looks like you might need it. Anyway, it's just there, on the table.' Inge gestures at a small glass dish containing dusty pellets I had previously taken for something the lamb had excreted.

Melissa digs in at once, explaining that she's sampled these on her previous adventures in Scandi-land and proclaiming them to be 'delicious'.

I'm not convinced but I gamely pop one in my mouth when the bowl is passed around before instantly wishing I hadn't.

'I think my airways are on fire ...' The taste is revolting. *Like someone is urinating in my mouth ... someone very dehydrated ...*

'Oh yes, salted liquorice originated as a decongestant,' Melissa thinks to mention now.

Expectorant sweets? FFS ...

'Well, my tubes are certainly opening ...' I swallow as fast as I can to get rid of the abomination currently taking my mouth hostage and reach for the coffee, asap. Margot makes 'mmm' noises but her face tells a different story and so Tricia politely declines what she terms 'a piss-sweet'.

Margot winces slightly at this, and I realise I've never heard her swear. *Interesting*, I think, *Sodding perfect, sodding Margot …* Then she begins to choke and I realise it might just be the salted liquorice making her face contort.

'You OK?' Melissa asks. Without waiting for an answer, she thumps her on the back until the offending lozenge is released from Margot's windpipe.

'Thanks.' She nods.

As soon as Inge is out of the room, a flaxen-haired child appears from inside the cupboard that has also been housing the lamb.

'What the …' Tricia is startled, but the child's face melts into a mask of pure mischief, as he scampers towards the kitchen table.

It's the berry puker! I think, affectionately, remembering the little boy who so perfectly cut his father down to size via the medium of regurgitated fruit the other day. *Ahh, good times …*

Berry Puker scales a chair until he's high up enough to reach a box of matches lying next to a Scandi-cool candelabra.

'Is he old enough for those?' Melissa looks doubtful.

'Err, no! *Definitely* "no"!' I'm already on the move to intervene. 'He's about three years old, four at a push.' I edge towards him and hold out a hand in what I hope is international sign language for 'give me the matches you tiny pyromaniac'. But he responds with a look that is international kid language for '*Noooo way!*'

'Children and naked flames, what could go wrong,' Melissa observes.

'Don't just stand there, help!' I demand, as the child strikes two matches in quick succession then runs away, whooping.

'OK, let's do pincer formation!' my sister suggests.

'What even is that?' I don't take my eyes off the Prometheus toddler and wonder on what planet Melissa is on if she thinks now is the time to start referencing obscure military formations.

At this inauspicious moment, another child appears, similarly blond and no more than five – Thomas's age – clutching what appears at first to be a fistful of knives.

'Jesus Christ!' I yelp. Then I see a fork or two glinting in there as well and realise she's merely grasping … cutlery.

OK, so maybe you'd allow an exceptionally mature (?) five-year-old sole charge of silverware but you're still not allowed to give a child matches, are you? Even in Scandinavia …

'Just get those matches!'

'It's like herding hellcats!' Tricia yammers as she and Margot try to round up the pre-schooler packing fire.

'Everything OK?' Inge returns, hands on hips.

'Oh, thank god!' Tricia exhales. 'The kids, they just appeared and then went for matches … and knives … and *forks!*' she adds, somewhat unnecessarily. 'And they move so fast!' She attempts to justify our woeful lack of control over the situation, but Inge looks unfazed.

'I see you've met Villum and Mette,' she says, beckoning over the would-be assassins and making them wave at us.

'Villum'? I think. *'Villain', more like.*

The two children say something we don't recognise in Danish, then Inge moves on. 'And we passed Freja, the youngest, on the way in.'

'There are three … ?' Melissa exclaims, doing the addition in her head. In all the excitement, I'd almost forgotten about the toddler using a chainsaw as a climbing frame.

'Yes.' Inge nods. 'But everyone helps out,' is how she puts it as Berry Puker Villum climbs up onto the table to light the candles and the five-year-old – *Mette, it must be* – lays out knives, forks and spoons. *Shit,* I think, *Thomas couldn't tell me where we KEEP the cutlery. And Charlotte's seven but she can't even be arsed to change a pillowcase …*

Inge retrieves Freja and carries her like a rugby ball, a fluffy yellow chick still clamped in the infant's chubby miniature fist. The child's face and spare hand are presented under the kitchen tap for a cursory 'wash', then she's deposited into a plain wooden high chair.

'We were just about to eat,' she explains, pulling a heavenly-smelling tray of buns out of the oven and setting it down on the table, along with bread and butter. 'Join us?'

'What about Magnus?' Tricia asks, reminding us all of the medical emergency we had been immersed in just five minutes ago.

'Ah—' she waves a hand dismissively '—he'll be fine; just a mild case of neurotoxicological poisoning.'

'Mild' and 'neurotoxicological poisoning' aren't words I've ever used in the same sentence, but Inge appears calm.

'The symptoms will be gone in a few days. He just needs simple food, fluid and rest.' She flings a tea towel over her shoulder, pulls down plates for everyone, and is about to sit when she notices small puddles now forming around our feet. 'Oh, you're wet! Let me get you something to change into.'

And with that she is gone, with three feral, flaxen-haired children in her wake.

'Well, I think we've earned some refreshments,' says Melissa, sitting down and pouring coffee.

'This isn't roughing it at all,' says Tricia, before adding, 'but I like it!'

'Christ … so good,' is my only input as I savour the sharp tang of the first coffee in days on my tongue and inhale the tantalising aroma – appreciating the ebony nectar in a way I've never allowed time for before. It is exquisite. And after the second sip, I feel like a new woman: caffeinated with *life*.

Margot slumps slightly in her chair at the far side of the table and eats ravenously. I realise that for all her Girl Guide survival skills and Little Miss Sunshine tendencies, she has borne the brunt of Magnus's weight for the past few hours. *She must be exhausted*, I think. *No wonder she's starving.*

I catch myself in this unusual manner of thinking. *What is it*, I ponder, *an alien sensation … or at least, a feeling of the sort I normally reserve for Thomas and Charlotte … a sort of … Oh!* And then I realise: *That's it! It's compassion-for-another-adult-human-being-who-is-not-a-blood-relative/the victim of some televisual atrocity, and whom I have no professional obligation to be nice to …*

I see I still have some work to do.

'Here, dry clothes.'

Inge is back, bearing armfuls of fabric in strictly grey or black. 'They should be clean, or as clean as things get with three kids around. They might be a bit … for some of you …' she tails off as we all realise what she's thinking: none of us are built like Amazonian goddesses and it's likely we're going to look a lot like we're playing dress-up here. But we try, Melissa and Tricia stripping off in situ ('What? The kids won't mind … bye bye, Cary Grant, see you later …') while Margot and I take it in turns to do a Mr Ben in the loo. After a seamless sartorial rejig, we're all dressed in Inge's out-sized monochrome cast offs and look a lot like we're in an all-female experimental theatre troupe. But we are warm. And dry. And my fingers and toes tingle with renewed circulation and gratitude (if fingers and toes can experience such emotions, which – I give mine a wriggle – I'm pretty sure mine currently can. So there ...).

Our clothes are freed from indenture as a make-shift stretcher and Melissa gratefully accepts the offer of having her 'lucky' maroon fleece laundered and returned to her as soon as is possible.

We eat, raisin-encrusted buns delicately spiced with cardamom and slathered with butter – even mine. Then Inge asks the children to clear the tea things away and, astonishingly, they do as they're asked.

Are they drugged? I think, watching perfectly poised children stacking plates. *Hypnotised, maybe? How is this happening?*

'Tell them what they can do, then you don't have to spend so much time telling them what they can't do.' Inge appears to read my mind.

She IS magic ... I'm trying to reconcile these feelings of giddy heroine-worship with sensible, *four-bags-for-life* Alice, when Melissa gives me a dead leg and tells me, 'See? I told you this would be an adventure!'

Inge summons our attention by laying both forearms on the table as though she's about to talk business. Which, in fact, she is.

'OK, so you can have full refunds, of course – and we can get on to the airline this afternoon to find out about moving your flights.'

'What for?' Melissa asks, fishing out a rogue raisin from her back teeth.

'Going home,' Inge answers.

'Home'?

It's as though someone's sucked the air out of my lungs.

Melissa swallows hard, trying to take it in, and Margot looks pale. None of us have had time to think this one through. No Viking leader: no Viking training.

It comes as a jolt. Because despite my moaning – to Melissa, Tricia, the universe, anyone who would listen, in fact – the thought of returning to my old life fills me with a sort of sinking feeling.

We've come so far, learned so much. Heck, we've even bonded over a make-shift stretcher and found a way to compensate for our varying physical defects to carry a man four miles across unfamiliar terrain ... I've made a beetle-brooch, for god's sake! We can't leave now!

The idea of going back to my own life now seems impossible. Implausible, almost. I want to shout this, to object in some way. But no one else is speaking. No one else is articulating just how much 'going home' now would be a Very Bad Idea. Indeed.

That's it then, I think. *It's over. Nothing will change.*

I'll get to see the kids sooner, which will be great. I'm already aching for them after four nights away. But it also means going back to work. And to Greg. And – did I mention? – *NOTHING WILL CHANGE ...*

I feel very hot all of a sudden, as though something is bubbling up inside me until ...

'No!' The protest emerges from my mouth quite involuntarily. Four pairs of eyes swivel towards me. 'What I mean is, well, maybe, we should discuss it, first ... between ourselves.'

Melissa's expression alters slowly from despair to something resembling hope/her habitual human Labrador persona. I notice Margot nodding, slowly and even Tricia brightens.

'Would that be OK?' I go on, pleading now.

Inge regards me, perfectly still.

'That would be OK.' She nods. 'I'll give you a moment. I think Freja needs changing anyway.' She seizes her smallest child and sniffs her undercarriage before conveying her to the bathroom like a rugby ball. Once she's out of earshot, we all look at each other, unsure of where to start.

'I like it here,' Margot says, finally. 'There's nothing to go back for ... this week, at least, I mean ...'

Melissa nods. 'The dogs are being fed and walked, some local teens are keeping an eye on the horses, my neighbour's got the rabbits – I'm home and dry.'

'I can honestly say that I've never had so much fun carrying a semi-conscious Viking through unfamiliar woodland,' is Tricia's reasoning. 'I don't even mind that there aren't any available men here! It's been nice, having a bit of a break. Stocking up on lady hormones ... it's like HRT without the bloating!'

'Plus, I really want to build a boat!' Melissa adds.

A feeling of connection passes around the table and I find I'm smiling.

'So we're agreed?'

'I think we might just be.'

When Inge returns, we all look at her with our best imploring faces.

'We'd like to stay,' I tell her, to much enthused nodding around the table. 'Is there anything we could do, to make it work – without Magnus?'

There is an anticipatory silence that crackles, almost, in its intensity – so anxious are we all to know what our future holds.

Finally, Inge speaks. 'Well ... I've done a couple of these now ... when Magnus ... well, you know ...'

'When he should have used flashcards?' Melissa asks, tactfully (for her).

'Exactly. So, I suppose, *I* could teach you some stuff ...'

'What, as well as looking after three children and a lamb in a cupboard and a sick husband?' I want to stay. I really do. But I can barely cope with myself most mornings so want to give Inge the chance to think about what she's signing up for. *Teaching four batshit British women on top of running a child-animal menagerie and tending to a vomiting Viking would be too much for any woman, wouldn't it?*

Margot doesn't give this much consideration.

'That would be amazing!' she beams, and Tricia claps her hands together.

'OK then,' Inge nods, as though the matter is settled, before adding a caveat. 'But I can't be coming over to the shelter every day – not with Magnus and the kids here.'

'Oh, right, yes,' I say. 'Well, we could come to you ... ?' I have absolutely no recollection of the route but now that I know there's a road option, I'm pretty sure at least one of us could remember it.

'Or you could just stay here, in the house,' she says.

'*Could* we?' Tricia's eyes widen. 'Have you got room?'

Mmm, hot running water ... I start to fantasise already: *Sheets ... !*

'Sure,' says Inge, 'the kids usually co-sleep—'

Of course they do ...

'So you can have Mette and Freja's room,' she says. 'I made them bunk beds last weekend.'

'By yourself? From flat pack?' Tricia is impressed.

But Inge looks confused. 'No – from trees ...'

Tricia gulps in the presence of a woman so handy and formidable that she can even extend herself to 'free-style' furniture building.

'Wow, good whittling ...' Melissa murmurs, as Inge gets up and starts checking the vegetable box for supplies for supper.

'Is she for real?' I whisper to Tricia.

'I think so ...'

'Well, this is going to get interesting ...'

Seven

'So where do we start?' Margot asks.

Lousy with oestrogen and still buzzing from having made a collective decision about our continued adventure, we wait with baited breath for the response.

'Start?' Inge looks up, a potato in one hand and a dishcloth in the other. 'Well, we *start* by clearing up. Even Vikings have to load the dishwasher.' She points out where to put our mugs.

'Oh. Yes, sorry ...'

Chairs screech backwards as we leap to our feet and begin clearing the table like women possessed. Inge flings a cloth at each child for them to wipe up before thrusting a dustpan and brush at a confused Margot.

The younger woman looks at this as though it's kryptonite.

'You have seen one of those before, haven't you?' I ask her.

'Yes. Absolutely.' She shakes the two parts of moulded plastic, then tries to prise them apart. Through a process of trial and error, she manages to twist the brush free. Margot hesitates, then has a cursory dab at the floor before being saved from further humiliation by the lamb, emerging from his cupboard to vacuum up the rest of the crumbs.

'Next, we'll get you settled in and prepare the beds.'

This is a boon and I am near vibrating with anticipation at the prospect of a) sleeping in a bed and b) seeing how this magical unicorn of a woman lives.

Although it doesn't quite feel like the 'roughing it' retreat experience that Melissa signed us up for, I think, studying her expression while we walk.

'Is this OK with you?' I ask her. 'Swapping roll matts for bunk beds?'

'Yeah, I think so ...' She sounds more ambiguous than I've ever heard my sister sound before. 'I have a few ulterior motives,' she adds, equally mysteriously.

'Ulterior'? She's never had anything ulterior in her life!

I think that perhaps she's got the wrong word so just smile and keep on walking, satisfied that I seem to have got away with this whole bed ruse, for now.

Result!

'Are you smiling?' Melissa asks, staring at me.

'What, I can't smile?'

'Well, you can ... only it's unnerving.' She mock shudders. I make a sarcastic face back at her in response before noting, with interest, that I do feel something approaching 'happy'.

Weird ...

We're led through the kitchen into a second hallway – a sort of ground floor bungalow-landing equivalent – past a room containing a still-moaning Magnus.

'Should we ... ?' Tricia starts. 'Is he ... ?'

'He'll be fine,' Inge says. 'Bed linen's here ...' She doesn't stop to dwell on her sickly husband but continues the tour, showing us into a room with a washing machine, dryer and chest freezer as well as a repurposed bookcase, laden with crisp, white, folded sheets. 'Arms out,' she instructs and we do as we're told. 'There's a sheet and duvet for each of you, then you can help yourself to pillow cases.'

This must be what it's like in prison, I think, lining up to receive the neatly folded linen, *a really nice prison, but still ...*

'Is that everyone? Right, let's go,' Inge says, and we are shooed out. 'That's the bathroom.' She nods at a large, white, tiled room with a single candle flickering serenely.

What is it with Vikings and fire?

As we move along, I notice a bookcase in the hallway, this time with books on it as well as a basket – hidden in plain view – containing a collection of mobile phones.

'Are those—' I whisper to Tricia.

'Yes,' Inge replies, overhearing. 'But I trust you to leave them there until the end of the week.'

Do you? Have you met me?

I experience an almost uncontrollable urge to reach out and grab the white iPhone that has been an extension of my right arm during all my non-dental practitioning hours for the past God knows how many years. It's intriguing how urgent this impulse is – as though it has nothing to do with me but is just another function my body must perform. Like breathing. Sometimes, I'll ignore my children to look at pictures of my children on my phone. *Which*, I realise now, *probably isn't stellar parenting. And yet ...*

No, Alice. Just. No!

My arm jerks towards the basket, involuntarily.

I've made it this far ... I didn't overcome conversational reticence, survive a near death-experience with a swinging sock, or break my carb ban to crumble now ...

As though reading my mind, Inge begins to run through a few ground rules of the new arrangement.

'You're familiar with the Viking code of conduct by now, right? The nine noble virtues of Viking life: truth, honour, discipline, courage, hospitality, self-reliance, industriousness and perseverance?'

'Nine?' Melissa frowns at her fingers. 'I only counted eight.' She holds up her hands to demonstrate.

'Well, yes. The ninth is fidelity, but, you know – we're pretty liberal in Scandinavia. So let's say there are eight *main ones*. The point is, trust is at the heart of many of them. And honesty. OK?'

'OK.' Melissa nods, marginally less flummoxed.

Goodbye phone. I give it one last, lingering look before being ushered on. *I won't forget you …*

'This is the kids' room,' Inge explains, gesturing to another all-white space with light wooden floors. 'I made bunk beds so it's easier for sleepovers and stuff.'

Sweet Jesus, the woman handles sleepovers too? I've been resisting Charlotte's requests to add to my child-count for years now. I find it challenging enough with two small people running around and demanding things. *But three? Or more?* I feel a migraine coming on just contemplating this.

Perhaps I'm a terrible, mean mother.

Perhaps I just need to learn to relax a bit more.

Perhaps I need to be more Viking …

At speed, Inge and her two eldest strip the beds and bundle their sheets next door, instructing us to make ourselves at home.

'Shall we?' Melissa asks, gesturing to the bed on the far side of a wall, decorated, not with childish scribblings stuck up with sticky tape as at home, but with three vast canvases. Each has been painted, dated and signed by Inge and Magnus's offspring – then elevated to 'art' by their mountings. *Damn it, I should be doing that!* I think. *Memo to self: add this to red colour-coded iPhone calendar 'family to do' list. Once I get my hands on a phone, anyway ...*

'Bagsy top bunk!' Melissa is already scrambling up the ladder and positioning herself, corpse-like, to try out the mattress. 'Not bad,' she says, before starting to bounce.

'Err ... I'm not sure that's wise ... They were built for kids ...'

I haven't shared a bunk bed with Melissa since I was eleven, when, apparently, I insisted I needed privacy and moved into the spare room. I remember none of this until I'm reminded by an over-excited little sister testing the strength of Inge's self-whittled wooden slats.

'It'll be just like old times!' she declares, before appearing upside down, blood rushing to her head and hair hanging like a curtain. 'But don't fart in the night because hot air rises and it'll come right up to me ...'

'I don't far—' I start, then realise that I'm playing into her hands. *She wants me to regress to my eleven-year-old self!* 'I don't ... *do* that ...'

In fact, a largely vegetarian diet combined with more worthy pulses than you can shake a stick at, means that I probably do more of *that* than your average woman.

But I'm not letting her know this ... Besides, I must be nicely clogged up with baked goods by now ...

Margot stands by the other bunk shyly, clutching her sheet bundle to her chest and not wanting to seem presumptuous, I suspect, after dustpan-gate. Fortunately, Tricia has no such reserve.

'Mind if I take the bottom one? I always need to pee in the night and you risk a foot in the face otherwise,' she tells Margot, who acquiesces immediately.

After this, we return to the kitchen to find the lamb having a snooze in front of the wood-burning stove and children juggling chicks as Inge stirs something on the hob. She licks a wooden spoon appreciatively, sets a lid on her creation, then turns down the heat before checking where we are on the Viking curriculum.

'So, Magnus says you've done shelter, foraging, handicrafts and half of weaponry, is that right?'

We nod.

'Have you had the talk about monkeys and gym rats bla bla bla? Yes? OK then. I'll just finish this stew, then we can start on sword-forging ...'

Melissa's eyes light up and a smile plays on her lips, as though she's eight years old and has just conned her way into staying up past bedtime. Her dimples threaten to give us away, but Margot gets in there first. 'Magnus said we weren't allowed to make a sword!'

Why can't that girl keep her mouth shut?

'Snitches get stitches ...' Melissa mutters and Inge arches an eyebrow.

'He said you "weren't allowed", did he?' she asks. Margot nods. 'Well, Magnus is busy puking in a pot. So we're *making a sword.*'

'Yesss!' Melissa treats herself to a small air punch.

'In one afternoon?' Tricia marvels, echoing my thought process. 'Can we?'

'Of course.' Inge shrugs, turning off the hob and making for the door. 'Aim high. Declare victory before you see it.'

'Is that a meme ... ?' Tricia asks, struggling to keep up with Inge's long strides. 'Like one of those *Keep Calm* ones?'

'It's about having such unwavering belief in what you do that there is no other outcome but to win,' says Inge. 'It's a Viking saying.'

Blimey, I think. *You don't get that at Not On The High Street* ...

'Everyone ready?'

After exchanging a final look of solidarity, we nod: we're ready. We set off, the youngest child strapped into a huge Silver Cross perambulator and left outside to sleep ('fresh air's good for the lungs, plus no one steals babies in Scandinavia,' Inge assures us) and the other two instructed to 'get dirty and have an adventure'.

I feel I've lived a thousand lifetimes since we were here last in the smoky outhouse, but for the second time today, we aren't its only occupants.

'*Hi!*' Inge shouts as soon as we step inside. A large man emerges from the far end, sporting a beard, a plaid shirt and what look a lot like dungarees, the kind I regularly dressed Thomas in before he, aged three, told me that they were 'for babies'.

Well, more fool you, kiddo, because it turns out strapping Vikings wear 'em, too ...

As the man comes closer, I notice that he also has big brown cow-eyes, fringed with lashes.

'Who's this long cool drink of water?' Tricia asks in a voice like hot chocolate.

'This is Otto,' says Inge. 'My cousin. Otto? Come say hello – we have visitors!'

'I could pop him open like a pistachio ...' Tricia sighs.

The bear-like man ambles over and extends a large, sooty hand to whichever of us is willing to take it first. Tricia immediately volunteers, then has to be encouraged to release him so that the rest of us can have a turn.

'Did we see you earlier?' Melissa asks.

'Yes, that was me.'

'You left without saying hello!'

'Yes,' is all he responds, leaving Inge to explain.

'Otto tends to work when he knows Magnus isn't around.'

'Why?' Melissa asks, directly. 'Don't you two don't get on?'

How does she do that? I wonder how my sister became so adept at cutting to the chase.

'Oh, he's never done anything to me, personally,' Otto says. 'It's just ... how would you say it in English ...' He opens his palms and thinks for a while, before landing on the perfect translation. 'I think he's kind of an arsehole.'

Hear, hear ...

'Now then ...' Inge makes a half-hearted attempt to chastise him while also suppressing a smile. 'Otto's a fellow Icelander,' she adds, 'so we're the original Vikings, right?'

'Right.' He smiles.

'And sometimes Magnus can be a bit ...' She stops to search for the word. 'Well ... *Magnus.*'

'Mmm.' I find myself agreeing, then feel compelled to say 'sorry' immediately and repeatedly – as a flush creeps up my neck.

'Never apologise,' Inge tells me, firmly.

'No. OK. Sorry. Not sorry ...' *Shit, I should shut up again now*, I decide.

'Anyway,' she goes on, 'this afternoon's not about him. It's about you, becoming Vikings. The sword we make together won't be perfect. It won't be beautiful, but it will be yours and you will have made it with your own hands.'

I glance at Margot's flawless plastic-model hands – *Ha! Good luck doing metalwork with those* – but when I look up I notice that Inge is also studying Margot, sizing her up.

'What first?' the girl herself bounces, eager to get started. A wry smile plays on Inge's lips that she soon shakes off and gets down to business.

'First you take the iron, hammer it into a bar, then hit it. Hard. We make a blade with steel, using lots of layers. Then you flatten it out, fold it over and do the same again.'

'Like filo pastry,' Otto interjects, helpfully.

I knew my years of watching Bake Off *while doing laundry and getting my carb hit vicariously would pay off,* I think, pleased.

We try – and I'm impressed to find I have seemingly acquired some Viking-style strength since this morning. Tricia has no such luck. Again. And when Inge ducks out to check on a fretting Freja, Tricia enlists Otto to give the sword a few bashes on her behalf and use up her 'turn'. Inge comes back in to catch Otto hard at it – and she isn't impressed.

'Vikings help *themselves*,' she chastises Tricia. ('You're not some maiden who needs to be saved from a dragon; you *are* the dragon'). Tricia promises to woman-up, and I seriously consider getting Inge's aphorisms made into motivational mugs for the surgery.

Inge proves to be an excellent teacher, manipulating red-hot steel, then grinding it to make a sharp edge. She finishes off the sword effortlessly, producing a prototype blade as we watch, slack-jawed. The final weapon is an awe-inspiring creation.

Its weight makes me sink into my heels, grounding me, but I manage to raise it above my head, sending several doves flapping from the rafters, and feel my shoulder blades pull back and down, triceps tautening. *I really am a Viking!* I think, *Not bad for a dentist from Streatham ...*

'Right, who's up for an axe next?' Inge asks.

Well, when she puts it like that ... Even I'm excited.

We 'whip one up', as Melissa puts it, by grinding an 'axe-y sort of shape' (again: her words) then sprinkling molten steel on top to make the blade sharp.

I know! Smell me! Just casually 'sprinkling molten steel' as if it were cocoa on top of a full-fat cow-juice cappuccino! (which I definitely do not indulge in. Except when I do ...)

Once we've smoothed it down and dunked it into the murky depths of a tank of cold water next to the furnace to cool, we learn how to lob it (technical term).

We take turns to carry the axe until we're well clear of the outhouse, then Inge explains the basics of axe-throwing.

'We'll use ... *that* tree as the target.' Inge points to a fir in the middle distance. 'Then you just stand with one foot forward, swing it up like you're throwing a ball overarm, release, and let your arm follow through.'

She demonstrates and the axe twirls balletically through the air before hitting the right-hand side of the tree trunk target with a *crack!*

Inge retrieves the axe and sets it down, explaining. 'The aim is to rotate the axe three-sixty degrees so that the sharpened head hits the target. This can be hard for a beginner, but see how you get on—'

She is cut off by an almighty *THWACK*, as our axe is lodged in a perfect 'bull's-eye'.

Inge turns to find a red-faced Margot, looking shifty now.

'I ... I got carried away ...' the younger woman apologises.

'You were supposed to wait until I said "go" ...' Inge stares at Margot.

'Yes. But did I do it right?' she asks, innocently.

'Yes.' Inge narrows her eyes, then nods. 'Yes, you did.'

Melissa takes up arms next and fares pretty well – her hand-eye coordination having always been better than mine at long range.

This is because I deal in the details, I console myself, *whereas she deals in livestock. And ... fields and things ...*

I hit precisely nothing, but it's a satisfying 'lob' nonetheless. Bringing up the rear is Tricia, who, as suspected, has trouble. This time it's with her overarm technique.

'I think my boobs get in the way.' She tries to readjust each in turn and experiments with different angles to allow her throwing arm free reign.

Melissa sympathises. 'No wonder it's tricky. Those are some serious sweater puppies ...' – at which I blush. On everyone's behalf.

We are not related, we are not related, we are not related ...

Tricia nods. 'I should have packed a sports bra. Anything to keep them out of trouble ...'

Margot pipes up. 'I quite often don't wear a bra.'

We all look at her.

Oh shit off, Margot! I think-shout, resenting her youthfully *perky-yet-pleasantly-full-B-cup*s that DON'T NEED SCAFFOLDING!

Eventually, Tricia manages to hit a tree. It's not the right tree, and, rather than lodge itself in there, the axe merely bounces off again and nearly kills a bemused squirrel. But Inge agrees that it's an 'A' for effort

'And we made the thing ourselves! As well as a sword! *And* saving Magnus's life!' Tricia brags now. 'What a day! Early bath for all of us!'

'There are baths?' Margot looks hopeful.

'No, we mostly shower in Scandinavia,' Inge clarifies.

'It's *just a saying*.' Tricia tries to mollify all parties. But in truth, a shower will be almost as welcome and I can't wait.

First, we're roped in to helping with 'life on the homestead' as I believe the scriptwriters of *Little House on the Prairie* referred to it.

'The pig can have scraps from the bucket under the kitchen sink,' Inge instructs us, pushing the tank of a pram over bumpy terrain back to the house. 'The chickens just need a scoop of grain from a barrel by the back door, the horses look after themselves—'

'Horses too?' Melissa looks delighted.

'Icelandic horses,' Inge corrects her.

Bloody hell, even the horses are Vikings round here!

'The goats eat anything.' Inge runs through the rest of her checklist. 'And I'll do the others.'

'There are *others*?' Melissa asks, thrilled to be in the company of a woman as *Dr Doolittle* as she is.

'Just a couple of cats and the lamb. And the kids of course. And Magnus.'

'Oh, right. Yes.'

What happens next could easily pass as an out-take from an all-female remake of *Rocky II* – because even though we're not trying to catch the chickens, we hadn't banked on them attempting to escape. Along with the – frankly terrifying – pig.

'Chase it!'

'*You* chase it!' Melissa and I shout at each other to be heard above the din as Tricia laughs and Margot tries to 'mark' the pig as though it's an elaborate game of netball.

The *Lord of the Flies* extra eventually plays ball and rolls in a patch of fresh mud instead while we round up the chickens.

'This is hard!' I protest, mid pounce, trying to catch a winged creature.

'Isn't it?' Tricia pants. 'Bloody good workout though.' She gasps, taking a break from any pretence of chasing to do a few squats. 'My bottom's going to look better than after Ibiza boot camp at this rate. Buns. Of. Steel ...'

It's at this point that I realise Inge is watching and she looks disapproving. 'It's not about looking great,' she corrects

Tricia. 'It's about *being* great.' She glances at her eldest daughter to check she's listening – a limited grasp of English apparently no barrier to an early lesson in gender equality. 'Your biggest assets should be in your head and your heart. Not what you sit on.' *It's all right for her*, I think, admiring Inge's Lycra-d curves as she starts back towards the house, brood in tow. 'The brain is the new ass!' she shouts over her shoulder.

I get my head down and carry on chicken chasing as Tricia mutters, 'Yeah, but what an ass! If I had a bottom like hers I think I'd wear assless chaps the whole time. Like a biker. Or Christina Aguilera ...'[14]

'Yeah!' Melissa laughs along.

'Are you familiar with the work of Christina Aguilera?' I can't help asking.

'Shut your face,' she tells me, with what I'm choosing to interpret as sisterly affection.

'Then again, can you even get chaps that aren't assless?' Tricia ponders.

This is a good question and one we contemplate for a moment.

'That's the thing about a life without Google,' says Tricia. 'It really forces you to think ...'

Back in the house we're greeted with the beatific sight of Inge, hair swept back, now nestled in an outsized woollen jumper, cradling the lamb and feeding it milk from a baby's bottle.

It's like an Athena poster! I marvel.

'We'll start weaning next week but for now it's the teat,' she explains.

[14.] Circa her 2002 album, *Stripped*. Worth a listen.

We nod, largely dumbfounded.

'Can we do anything?' Melissa asks.

'Yes, what now?' Margot adds, keen to sound helpful.

'Now, I need to do some work,' Inge says.

'This isn't work?' Tricia flops in a chair. 'I'm exhausted.'

'There's more coffee in the pot,' is her response.

Coffee: always the answer.

'But no, this isn't work – this is just *life*.'

'Oh. Right. So, what else do you do?' Margot is intrigued.

Inge burps the lamb, sets it down to sleep in its cupboard, reaches to the top of the dresser for a white lever arch file and a laptop, then tells us, 'I study.' I presume she's going to say something like 'to be a part-time yoga teacher' or 'personal trainer' (because: that arse), but what actually comes out is, 'Psychology. At the moment I'm doing my PhD thesis.'

I hadn't expected this.

'As well as all—' Melissa waves a hand at a couple of feral children whizzing past ' – *this*?'

'Yes.'

'Wow.'

'And, what's your thesis on?' Margot asks, wide-eyed.

Even Margot hasn't got a PhD …

Inge looks her squarely in the face and says, 'The psychology of over-achievers.'

Margot swallows hard as she takes this on board, torn between curiosity and a mounting suspicion that perhaps she's being observed as part of a scientific experiment.

At least, that's how I'm feeling, so I'm magnifying this (because: Margot …).

'So now, I'm going to take myself off for an hour,' Inge declares. My sister looks bowel-looseningly alarmed at the prospect of being left in charge of three children for the second time in a single afternoon. Fun Aunt Melissa's duties don't normally extend beyond an initial wrestle and then doling out chocolate until the kids are suitably hyper, before handing them back after ten minutes with an air of, 'not my circus, not my monkeys ...'.

And there are only two of mine! Maybe my sister really doesn't want a family, I think. *Interesting.*

Inge hasn't asked if any of us have children. Or indeed have a clue what to do with the three mini Vikings currently weaving in and out of the table legs.

'Will you be OK?' she adds as an afterthought, preparing to leave the room.

'They'll be fine,' I say, hoping to reassure her that I'm a capable childcare provider – the kind of woman with four bags-for-life in her car.

'I meant *you* lot ... ?'

'Oh.' *Well, this is embarrassing.* 'Yes. Thanks.' I nod.

'Well, help yourself to showers – towels are on your beds.' And with that she is gone.

Despite having been assured that the children – even the toddler – are self-sufficient, all three now look at us expectantly. That or challenging us. I can't be sure.

'And there's no TV?' Tricia checks, sounding concerned. '*T-V?*' she asks again, louder this time and with raised eyebrows in the universal code for, 'I don't speak your language because I'm bloody British but I'm asking A Question now. Loudly.'

Fortunately, it seems 'TV' is the same in *Viking* as all the children catch her drift and shake their heads in response.

'No iPads?' I try, but heads cock to one side like a pack of confused terriers.

'I think that's a "no",' says Margot.

'Right then, time to get Poppins on their ass.' Melissa slaps her hands on her knees and pushes herself up to standing.

'I don't think Mary Poppins is a realistic role model for the current situation—' I start, but Melissa cuts me off, holding up a hand as though I've overstepped a line.

'What?'

'You mess with Poppins you mess with me.'

'Oh, come on!'

'Or Maria Von Trap.' She explains to Tricia: 'Another of my idols.'

'Do you feel this way about all Julie Andrews characters?' Tricia asks, curious.

Melissa shrugs. 'I can take or leave Victor Victoria.'

'What about the one she plays in *The Princess Diaries*?' Margot chimes in.

'What?'

I'm forced to explain that Melissa stopped watching anything made after 1997 as a one-woman protest at *Soldier Soldier* being axed from ITV.

As it happens, we do not 'Poppins it'. After a few minutes of rectal clenching, Melissa observes that the children seem to be 'totally nailing fly-a-kite era Jane and Michael'. Taking Inge's recommendation of healthy neglect to heart, she straddles a chair backwards and announces that we should all 'just relax' instead. And so, after hiding the knives, at my insistence, we do. We drink coffee, chat, have showers in turns and eat *more* buns and feel ridiculously decadent (on my part, anyway) for lounging around at 4pm on a Thursday, merely observing as a child occasionally streaks past. Sometimes with an animal in tow, sometimes clutching the hair of a sibling, sometimes not. And no one dies. Or complains. An *in loco parentis* 'win'.

I haven't sat still and done nothing ... ever ... *I must have once, mustn't I?* I frown, trying to remember. *Maybe some time in the late 1980s when I had pneumonia one half-term ...* Or the time I broke my leg. Either way, this feels ... nice. I run my hands over the surface of the wooden table top, tracing the worn patterns of rings from the tree. It feels lived-in and loved – quite unlike the permanently disinfected grey granite slab back in my own kitchen.

This, I think, *is like the table we had growing up.*

I look over at Melissa, positioned on the other side of it, just as she used to be across the family kitchen table. There was hot competition for who got to sit at the end by the drawer filled with placemats. She never knew why I wanted to sit there but the fact that I did made this seat infinitely more desirable than any of the others. I would watch her eating dumplings, or toad-in-the-hole, or suet pudding from Portmeirion plates – holding her knife like a pen and speaking through mouthfuls of home-cooked, stodgy fare with pure, unalloyed pleasure; at least she did in the days before the Obesity Clinic and before Mum halved her carbohydrate quota. We would have competitions to see who could mash the most mayonnaise into their jacket potato or who could load the most butter on their toast. Then, if I had the drawer seat, I would carefully convey my food into the drawer to be disposed of later, when no one else was around.

At first I just skipped breakfast. No one minded that. It was one less thing to worry about in the morning and Mum used to thank me for taking care of Melissa and cleaning up after the rest of the family's soft boiled eggs. After she left us, 'mealtimes' stopped meaning much. We ate in ever more divergent ways – so that no one blinked if Melissa sat down with a whole rotisserie chicken at 3pm, or Dad had cereal for dinner. And no one noticed what I ate. Or didn't. Melissa's healthy appetite was celebrated once Mum was gone. Bye bye, Hay Diet; hello, all manner of sweet treats and goodies brought around by well-meaning neighbours and relatives keen to do all they could for the 'poor widower'. It made them feel better somehow – dropping off a lasagne on the doorstep then legging it for fear that they would have to say something if we caught them in the act. And no one ever knew what to say. So the anonymous food parcels kept coming. We had so many lasagnes one month, I seem to recall now, that Melissa drew up a chart to rank them, scoring them out of ten. Dad joined in, and it made him feel better, too, somehow. Everyone desperately needed someone to nurture and feed, so Melissa stepped up to the plate. *More than once*, I think, looking back now. I remember feeling pleased when someone described my legs as looking like 'snowdrop stems', extending out of my shorts one summer. And so it continued.

I once read that meerkat sisters use food as a form of competition, with the 'alpha' sister eating more and attempting to gain weight to reinforce her position. For us, it worked the other way around. But there was still something there. Something basic. As I got thinner, I was 'winning'. As I got thinner, I was in control.

I left home as soon as the ink was dry on my A-Levels, before my eighteenth birthday, even. And I haven't been back since.[15]

[15.] For younger readers: this was possible at the time thanks to university grants (see 'old'). Plus I had a waitressing job where I excelled at paper napkin folding and condiment management. Dentistry's gain was the Plymouth branch of Pizza Express's loss …

I could tell that my sister was unhappy, just as I was, but I couldn't reach out to her – or rather I didn't dare. Lest I'd get dragged back down there into a pit of sadness with Dad and Melissa, never to emerge.

'Another bun?' Tricia extends a plate in my direction, hair wrapped up in a towel turban now, post-shower, so that she looks a little like a classic Hollywood film star snapped in St Tropez.

'No thanks, I'm fine,' I respond – but not, I note with interest, out of any fear about what it will do to my thighs (i.e. un-Margot them). I decline because the aromas from the stew simmering gently on the stove are making my mouth water in anticipation of what's to come. 'You have mine,' I tell Tricia, and she doesn't refuse.

My muscles ache, as though I've used them well and as nature intended. I feel like a new woman after a good wash and then Inge returns and announces that her studying time is up and asks if we'd all like a beer before supper.

Normally, I don't drink beer (*at 200 calories and up to eighteen grams of carbohydrates a go? Hardly…*), but this evening, I think, *Fuck it*.

Melissa opens the bottles with her teeth, just to annoy me (*'I wish you wouldn't do that! It's the worst thing you could possibly be doing! Even worse than the impact on your enamel of tearing Sellotape!'* You can see how scintillating my small talk is. It's no wonder I seldom bother …). But from the first taste, I forget my irritation, because it is *sublime*.

Mmm … beer … If this is wrong, I don't want to be right.

Effervescing with a cold, slightly bitter note, it makes me feel a little loose and loopy from the first mouthful before sitting heavily on my stomach, like a large, beery man-hug.

Another large beery man-hug appears shortly after this with further supplies of local brew and baked goods.

'Otto! Beer *and* cake? You're really spoiling us!' Tricia coos.

'All right, Ambassador,' I quip, and she laughs. Margot looks mystified.

Otto probably doesn't look anything like the ambassadors she usually meet ...

'We just thought you might like a good feed.' Otto grins amiably, oblivious to any 1980s Ferrero Rocher references.

'There's a saying in the *Hávamál* saga,' Inge goes on, giving the stew a final stir before setting it on the table. 'If guests are coming, you have to prepare. So that's what we do. It's how we are.'

The only saga I have ever read was the Sweet Valley High series (*The Wakefield Legacy*, FYI) – a tome found wanting in the way of deep and meaningful moral coda or life lessons. *Other than 'always wear ChapStick'*, I think, touching my dry, cracked lips now. *That one was pretty smart ...*

'The Sagas are a set of stories that Vikings lived by,' Inge clarifies as she sets the table.

'Like the Nine Noble Virtues?' Margot asks, standing up and trying to look useful.

'No,' says Inge. 'They were made up by Americans who wanted a shortcut and couldn't be bothered to read the Sagas—'

'Americans *and* Magnus?' Otto jokes, opening a beer with the back of his hand against the roughly hewn table, much to Melissa's admiration.

Inge ignores this, going on to explain. 'But I'm more about Ásatrú, anyway – the ancient Norse faith. I'm a *Völva*.'

She pronounces the word as though it rhymes with the first two syllables of '*pulver*ise'. As though she's referring to the outer part of the female genitalia – or Tricia's semi-successful handicraft project. I can only presume that this is another example of Scandinavian empowerment and their famously liberal approach to sex and the body.

Is this what fourth-wave feminism looks like now? Is this the Nordic version of Pussy Power?

I worry that I am horribly out of touch as Tricia seeks further clarification.

'You're a *vulva*?' she asks. 'You mean you *have* a vulva, right?'

'No, I am one,' Inge says simply.

'A "vulva"?'

'A *"Völva"* – v-ö-l-v-a.'

'There's a difference?' Tricia appeals to Otto for help here.

'The ö has dots over the top,' he says, as though this will illuminate us.

'Basically we believe in Thor and Odin and everyone but we don't rely on them to fix our problems – because, why should they care?' Inge says, taking a gulp of beer. 'Völva don't wait around for a miracle ...'

Jesus ... Mary, Joseph and all their carpenter friends are getting some shade thrown at them here ...

'We're more about making our own luck – and *hospitality*,' she says. 'So if I went into a room and there was no coffee, no beer, no cake – that would be bad form.'

Melissa looks a little dreamy-eyed and murmurs, 'I think I might be a Völva ...'

'Being a true Viking isn't about raiding or pillaging, either—'

'Unless it's the fridge!' Melissa jokes but Inge ignores her.

'It's about being able to face yourself every morning. It's about being a decent person who tells the truth, treats people fairly, and behaves well.'

Tricia shifts slightly in her seat.

Odd ... I try to catch her eye but she won't meet my gaze.

'You must know that your actions always affect someone or something else – like nature or society or another person. What you send out comes back. It's not about your qualifications, how many hours you work or what your job title is.'

Cannot compute ...

I struggle to process this as all the things I've ever striven towards are dismissed in one swipe of Thor's hammer. 'Vikings *earn* respect through their behaviour. You start over, with everyone you meet. You inherit nothing. It's not about money or social standing. Even if you're born to status, you have to live up to it.'

Now it's Margot's turn to look uncomfortable. Only Melissa appears unruffled.

The children materialise and sit in their places around the table, with Otto lifting the littlest up and into her high chair as though she were a balloon, and then we're invited to a feast of chicken and vegetable stew. A meal that Inge has apparently whipped up while simultaneously solo-parenting three children, sword-forging, axe-throwing, lamb-rearing and dispensing Viking gems.

She is my idol ...

I begin to load my plate with stew, carefully eschewing the poultry on offer, before Otto notices and pushes the dish of chicken in my direction.

'Oh, no thanks, I'm vegetarian,' I tell him, as Melissa pulls a face.

'But it's chicken?' He looks quizzical.

'Yes.'

'Does that *count*?' Otto appeals around the table.

Inge shrugs.

It's my turn to look around the table, in case I'm missing something here. *No? Just me then?*

'Chicken is definitely still meat,' I clarify for anyone who may be in doubt.

'Oh. OK.' Otto shrugs in an 'it's your loss' sort of way, before adding, 'But it's dead anyway.' He picks up the dish and jiggles it to demonstrate its contents are unlikely to fly off any time soon. 'So, you know … might as well eat it.'

'We don't get too many vegetarian Vikings,' Inge explains. 'Though of course you're welcome to eat what you like.'

Otto moves to set down the dish and I'm about to say, 'Thanks, I will,' when I catch a whiff of warm, succulent, bird.

Sweet Jesus, that smells good …

'Fill your boots,' Melissa adds mid-mouthful, boots decidedly full.

'Would it help if we all looked the other way?' Tricia asks. She does, just in case it would, while Melissa seizes a drumstick and drops it on my plate.

Childish, I think. *But also … well, it's there now …*

I eat it. And it's divine.

I am a very bad vegetarian indeed, I reprimand myself, looking around for a distraction to stave off the low-rent Greek chorus of *'you suck, Alice Ray …'*

Despite having set the table beautifully and behaved like alarmingly perfect Viking-angels, I'm gratified to see Inge's children go to eat the chicken with their hands.

Ha! At least they haven't got impeccable table manners, too!

But then our Viking leader catches me looking (aka 'judging') and nods at the scene ahead.

'Viking etiquette,' she explains mid-poultry. 'Anything that flies can be eaten with your fingers.' With faultless timing, the children take up their cutlery to skewer vegetables … and my 'smug-parent' bubble is burst, too.

Mette, Villum and Freja eat well, with no complaints and no requests for fish fingers or ketchup.

Magic, I think. *Definitely magic.*

Melissa tucks in appreciatively before coming back for more. 'Seconds? *Thirds?*' I note. She fixes me with a stony look. 'I'm in training,' she tells me through a mouthful of chicken, 'for the berserking.' My face clearly isn't buying this. 'What? I'm skinny in Texas,' she adds, tearing flesh from a drumstick. I half expect her to throw it over her shoulder so am relieved (*or am I disappointed?*) when she places it neatly on the side of her plate.

'Right. Good ...'

After supper, Otto offers to supervise children's teeth brushing and see them off to bed before taking his leave, enabling the rest of us to, as Tricia puts it, 'get stuck in to the lady petrol'.

'I thought you said that was gin?' Margot asks innocently.

'Gin, cava, beer – they all work,' Tricia clarifies.

'Oh.'

By my third bottle of locally brewed pilsner, I'm a little light-headed and find myself asking Inge, very seriously, 'how she does it'.

This is a lie.

What I actually slur is something along the lines of, 'I mean, I'm jus' so *tired*! All the time! And I complain. A lot. And you manage to do all the stay-at-home parenting and the PhD and all the animals and the cooking and the sword-forging and axe-throwing and animal rearing and the being so *pretty* all the time ...'

Inge is modest enough to ignore the last observation and merely looks at me intently, asking, 'Are you crazy?'

Yes! Very probably! I want to tell her: *You should have seen me last month at the Premier Inn with the hands-free wine! I eat*

Big Macs in my Renault Espace and tell myself it's not a 'drive thru', it's a 'car picnic'! Of course I'm crazy!

Fortunately, Inge's question proves rhetorical.

'The kids are only home because day care's closed this week,' Inge explains. 'Some religious festival no one celebrates any more when everything shuts and we eat special cakes. We have a lot of those – days off and cakes. I wouldn't want them here all the time!' Then she adds as an afterthought, 'Plus it's good for them to socialise. School doesn't start for ages so they learn through playing with other kids. Other than that ... I *like* animals, I don't mind cooking, and I do the PhD just for me. That's the important thing. We have a saying here: you have to put your own oxygen mask on first.'

'Is that a traditional Viking saying?' my mouth asks before my brain can get in gear.

'No: traditional Vikings didn't have much use for oxygen masks. In fact they rarely flew anywhere,' she replies patiently as I facepalm. 'It's a *modern* Viking saying. It means you have to look after yourself before you can look after anyone else.'

There is a strange, fleeting stillness all around as I take this in.

'*That's it?*' I ask, finally, sceptical. 'That's the key to all ... all this?'

'That's it,' she tells me.

'You're not perfect ... ?' I slur. Like an idiot.

'I'm not perfect. No one is, in the real world.' She takes another swig of beer, sizing me up. 'Listen, I'm not going to tell you that it's easy – but I can tell you that it's worth it. Really living, I mean.' At this, she stands and pulls down the side of her Lycra leggings. 'Look.'

Oh my! I wasn't expecting this.

'See? Here?' She points to a filigree of silver-white lines festooning her upper thigh.

'Wow, you have stretch marks ...'

'No, I have battle scars,' she corrects me, running her fingers affectionately over the intricate birch tree patterns she carries with her always. 'Battle scars from *living*. That's what it's all about.'

I think I love her ...

I worry that I might not remember all this by morning in my current state. *I wonder if she could put it all in an email for me ...*

The candle in front of us starts spitting and Inge, without breaking my gaze, reaches out a hand, snuffs out the errant flame with a flat palm.

She's like a badass Viking pegacorn ...[16]

Then she pulls up her trousers, pours the rest of her beer into a glass and downs the lot, adding with a nod to the bottle, 'Remember: put your own oxygen mask on first.'

I want to. I do. But as a woman exhausted from producing a version of herself for other people for the past quarter of a century, I'm not entirely sure *how* to look after myself.

But I might just be in the best place to learn ...

I decide, there and then, that I am going to soak up every pearl of wisdom this woman has to offer.

'Who's for dessert?' she asks next.

Remembering Magnus and the berries, the four of us squirm slightly at the thought of our last foray into 'afters', until Inge reassures us that no berries have been plucked in the making of this pudding. 'Otto made a tart!'

'He bakes, too?' Tricia claps a hand to her décolletage and then adds, 'I'll just let the hairs on my arms settle ...'

[16.] A cross between a unicorn and a Pegasus. Obviously ...

'It's got a sea salt and chocolate on top and he's experimenting with some orange zest in there too,' Inge adds, setting it down on the table.

The results are good. Really good. And only slightly remind me of the whole Terry's Chocolate Orange I ate to myself, through sobs, in the loo one Christmas. I have a sense memory of a combination of salty tears, cheap chocolate and synthetic orange. Mum had just told me that this would be her last Christmas but that I had to be strong – that we were to carry on as normal and I wasn't to tell Melissa anything. So I communed with confectionary instead.

Ding-dong merrily on high …

I remember the incident vividly, in a way that I don't often remember anything from this period. Or before. Or after, usually.

I was sad, I realise, *really, really sad. And I had no one to talk to.*

If Charlotte had to go through that in a few years' time, I would want to scoop her up in my arms and tell her that everything was going to be OK. That I would make it OK. But back then, no one did. No one came.

On the plus side, I think, as I swallow a lump in my throat, taking the last of the Proustian tart with it, *half an hour's hardcore crying and a solid 175 gram orb of chocolate mean that, technically, I invented the whole salted chocolate thing a good twenty years before anyone else …*

There is a lull in conversation as we all digest, so Tricia, with an allergy to silence, starts giving Inge potted biographies of the assembled party.

'Melissa and Alice are sisters,' she's telling Inge as I do some blinking in an attempt to compose myself. *Don't cry, don't cry, don't cry …* 'So what were the two of you like growing up?' Tricia is asking me.

'Oh, you know,' I mumble so as not to catch my throat.

'No, I don't ... ?'

'Do *you* know?' Melissa looks at me closely. 'Alice has a mental block up until the age of eighteen,' she tells the rest of the group.

'That's not quite true ...' I object.

'Really? Prove it!'

I'd like to. I'd like to find a way to tell my sister everything I could never say before. But I don't know how.

It's been so long and it feels so alien and I don't have the words ... and it's likely that I'm only feeling this way because of the beer ... I look at the bottle in my hand and try to keep my brain from becoming woolly. Or at least, woollier. *So I ... just ... can't ...* Instead, I attempt to wrestle back control of the situation by reciting the physiological processes currently taking place in my body (because dentists = medics. Fact ...).

... the beer is now travelling to my stomach and the alcohol is hitting my bloodstream – more quickly than usual because of the bubbles, increasing the pressure in my stomach ...

I take another swig as Melissa offers up her version of our childhood.

'And then there was the time I found a stray cat and brought it home, but Alice told Mum and I had to let it go again ...' Melissa says, looking at me like I'm some sort of child-catcher. So I drink again, automatically.

Damnit!

... my liver's now converting the alcohol into different chemicals to break down the poison ... with ... with ... I can't quite remember. *Oh great, now I'm losing my adult memory too ...* then I light on it. 'Enzymes!' I say out loud, delighted. 'Sorry ...'

'I wouldn't mind so much but she'd already said I couldn't keep the stoat because of her "allergies",' Melissa goes on. This,

I remember. 'I asked Mum if Alice could move out instead, but she said no.' My sister sniffs at the recollection. 'I cried for days.'

'Yeah, Daddy shot my first pony,' Margot slurs. Tricia and Melissa look horrified. 'By accident,' she clarifies. 'He got out of his field during grouse season. The pony, not my father ...'

'Whoa there, Nelly!' Melissa slams down her beer and extends an arm to Margot. 'Were you OK?'

'Sad, of course.' She nods, thanking my sister for her support. 'But he got me another one.'

Inge looks bemused, but then becomes distracted by the lamb emerging sleepily from its cupboard. He nuzzles to get up on her lap and she acquiesces.

'Yeah, I killed a cow once,' Tricia adds.

'What?' Melissa turns on her. 'How?'

'Well, what it *was*, was, as you may or may not know, the Range Rover Sport has a fridge between the driver and passenger seat,' Tricia says this as though fridges and Friesians are inextricably linked. 'Glorious four by four, that one.' She shakes her head.

'So ... ?' Melissa attempts to bring her back on point.

'Oh, well, I like to go fast,' says Tricia. 'Or rather, I *liked* to go fast. And I was just getting something out of the fridge. I only looked down for a *millisecond* – but then I went through a five-bar gate. And I didn't open it. That was the main problem,' she clarifies. 'I don't drive any more.'

'Wow. No ...' Melissa is wide-eyed as I try to refocus my swimming mind.

My liver's now using an enzyme called ... called ... I rifle through the filing cabinets in my head but I can't find the word ... *using something to convert the alcohol into ... something beginning with an 'a'? Or perhaps it's an 'e' ... Bugger it!*

I draw a blank so go to have another swig of beer and am surprised to find the bottle empty. Inge, who has been observing the scene with some amusement, now pushes back her chair and makes to retrieve milk for the lamb and more beer for us. She throws a bottle of the latter at me and I catch it. Just.

'What about you?' Tricia is asking me now.

'What about me?'

'Well, Vikings are all about honesty and sharing, aren't they?' She looks to Inge for approval, who nods, ever so slightly. 'So, tell us something no one else knows about!'

'Well, that'll be easy. We only met a few days ago.' Melissa laughs. 'And this is my sister "Closed-Book Alice" that we're talking about!'

'Just 'cos you're a massive oversharer!' I say this in an attempt to match my sister's jocular tone but it comes out awkwardly and a tremor of hurt emanates from across the stretch of oak.

Tricia, apparently, doesn't notice and perseveres. 'But you two have known each other since *birth*!'

'Barely!' my sister snorts.

'Come on then, spill! It'll be fun!' Tricia claps her hands.

It won't, I feel with a degree of certainty.

'Someone else go first,' is all I can manage.

'OK then. Inge?' She turns to our illustrious host.

An unfazed Inge reveals that her firstborn was conceived on a Viking longship, which seems entirely appropriate. She also shares with us that she speaks five languages and is a trained scuba-diving instructor.

Overachiever, I nod, sagely. *Must up my Mandarin Duolingo time. And learn Spanish one day – when the kids go to university, maybe ...*

We also learn that Tricia once had a threesome (a revelation that surprises me not one iota but that sparks a myriad of questions) and that Margot is 'allergic to ibuprofen'.

That's it? That's all she's got? God, perfect people are boring.

Melissa 'wins' by announcing that she was, briefly, the front woman in a pro-monarchist punk band called 'Regal Gristle' after her A-Levels ('We sang 'God Save The Queen' non-ironically …').

I did not know this.

'But you can't sing!' I blurt out, as another tremor undulates through the floor.

'Well, neither can you, but at least I know it!' This is a low blow: my own singing career was put on hold when my sister caught me doing my best Whitney Houston in the shower, aged twelve, and told everyone at school that I 'warbled'. I'd been a regular shower songbird up until this point but I haven't sung a note since. 'Anyway, it was punk. No one cared what we sounded like – though, to be fair, it sounded a lot as though someone was building a shed …' she adds as an aside. 'But mainly, they let me be the leader because I had this great floor-length black leather coat—'

'That was *my* black leather coat!' I turn on her.

'You'd already left home! You didn't miss it!' This is true. But now she's reminded me, I'm furious. Melissa glares as if challenging me to a duel. 'Just because *you* never did anything fun …'

'Ouch!' Tricia feigns outrage, then adds. 'Sorry – I only had a brother and he was a clod, so this is new for me. Carry on, carry on …' she ushers.

But I don't know where to start. Because apart from the sad bits, most of what I recall is me wanting to grow up as fast as I could to *get out* there. Or rather, get out *of* there.

Melissa loses patience and speaks for me. 'Basically, Alice married too young and should have slept with more people first.' A cutting précis of my adult life. 'But her husband's an idiot and she's miserable.'

What? This isn't fair! How does SHE get to share a story about a school band while I get to have my marriage dissected in front of strangers?!

'Just look at the bags under her eyes,' Melissa directs her audience's attention to my dark circles now. 'He's taken the best years of her life.'

'You're unhappy in your relationship.' Inge nods before I have the chance to defend myself, as though there's no point contesting this notion that's evident for all to see. 'So why don't you split up?'

Because it doesn't work like that! Because our roots are too tangled together by now! Because we're due to have an extension next year! Because my family is the first thing I've ever put all my chips on and I'm afraid of losing. Because that would mean admitting I'd made a mistake ...

This is what I think.

What I say, is, 'It isn't that bad. It's just ... not like an exciting, new relationship.'

'What is it then?' Tricia asks.

I think about this. 'It's ... the saggy middle bit ...'

Tricia nods, knowingly.

'Do you do anything to keep the romance alive?' she asks. 'Send each other sext-messages during the day?'

I look at her as though she is deranged 'No, we're married. We only message each other when we need something from the shops.'

'Ah, *that* stage ...' Tricia says nostalgically.

'How do you feel when you think about your husband?' Inge addresses me head on.

I hesitate as the alcohol catches up with me before testing my voice with a, 'Well ... I feel ...' I stall to avoid letting slip what I'm really thinking, which is: *Trapped! Shackled! Like I want to climb out of a VERY HIGH window!*

'He can be a bit annoying, at times,' I say finally. 'You know, when he snores. I hate that. And the way he dribbles toothpaste spit around the sink and just leaves it there. And the way the gap in his teeth makes him sort of whistle some-times. And I hate the way he chews—'

'Basically, you hate him?' Tricia asks as I pause to draw breath.

'No!' *I don't hate him. I just fantasise about him dying ... regularly.*

'Yeah, it shouldn't be like that,' says Inge as though mind reading. *Again.*

'But we have two children!' I tell her, as though this is all the justification I need.

'You'll still have two children if you split up,' says Inge, matter of factly. 'You don't have to be best friends after – I mean, you can be – but as long as you're friendly enough to coexist in the Venn diagram of parenting, you'll be fine. Whoever you choose to share your life with will drive you crazy, so you choose the best you can. But if you get it wrong, you get it wrong.' She shrugs, then explains, 'There's no stigma to splitting up here. Viking wives could divorce husbands for reasons as small as "showing too much chest hair".'

'Hear, hear!' Tricia slurs as Inge goes on.

'We have this saying here: "you marry first for kids, second for love".'

'Oh, that's tremendous!' Tricia claps her hands. 'I love a second wedding! Man looking nervous? Wife in a cream trouser suit? Teenage children looking on, sulking? Everyone drinking to overcompensate for the awkwardness? Lovely!'

Inge permits herself a smile, as though getting to grips with British humour.

'So you and Magnus ... ?' Melissa stomps in with both feet. *Bloody hell, she's brave ...*

'Another couple of years, tops,' is all Inge says, in a tone that is both calm and assured. As though this isn't a disaster, it's a plan. 'And next time, I'll choose a man who eats quietly and doesn't feel the need to rearrange his genitals quite so often ...' she adds, as though these grievances have been the deal-breakers.

Tricia runs a tongue over her top teeth, before adding. 'Oh, I hear you there – much better to split up than let things fester. My *ex* ex and I stuck it out until Ed left home – you know, separate bedrooms, conversations via email written entirely in caps lock. But if we'd broken up before we wanted to gouge each other's eyes out, we could have moved on – gone from being a crappily married couple to two people with manageable part-time childrearing duties. *Et voilà!*'

I don't know how to explain to Tricia in a tactful way that I don't just want to 'rear' Thomas and Charlotte – I want to love them and be there for them. So instead, I try to convey how I don't think I'd be much cop at the whole shared parenting lark.

'I think I'd miss them too much.' I shake my head.

The love I have for my children has only ever gone in one direction: up – throwing into relief anything that came before. *I didn't love Greg*, I realise now. *Ever.* He was just there. Conveniently. Around about the time I'd had my fingers burned by the one before and my newly active ovaries were screaming at me to have babies, with someone.

Anyone, really ... But it's been worth it, hasn't it? For Charlotte and Thomas?

'I love spending time with my kids,' is the best way I can think of to communicate this, before adding the qualifier, '*Mostly* ... except when they're being little shits.' I blush instantaneously at this admission. 'Sorry.'

'Never apologise!' Inge commands. 'It's OK to feel like that.'

'Course it is!' Tricia stammers. 'Can't always be Mary bloody Poppins!'

'I told you before: leave Poppins out of it!' Melissa may share Tricia's sentiments on Greg, but she's not letting Julie Andrews hate-speak slide.

Tricia holds her hands up before continuing, 'I just mean, parenting is hard!' Inge nods. 'And admitting this doesn't make you a bad person. Before they can look after themselves – you know, switch the coffee machine on and vote and stuff – it's knackering! Boring, too, a lot of the time. They take bloody ages to put their shoes on, their conversation is *basic*, at best, and standing there, watching a child on a swing?' Tricia appeals to Melissa and Margot here. 'Dull! No one ever tells you that, but it's *desperately* dull! It's either forward or back. Where's the drama? Where's the suspense?'

Melissa gives an 'I hear you' nod.

'They're not like animals,' Tricia says, addressing my sister. 'With the dogs, I could go away for a couple of days, come back, give them a biscuit and they'd be delighted to see me, wagging their tails all over the place – but kids get *sulky*. My son was always going on about how he had to make his own packed lunch for school ...' Tricia shakes her head as if to say, *kids, eh?* 'And the noise!' she goes on. 'They never warn you about the noise! And that was just with one – I don't know how you do it with two!' Here she looks at me. 'Or three!' she near-shrieks at Inge. 'I spent the entirety of Ed's sixth birthday party wearing industrial ear defenders I'd 'liberated' from Anneka Rice's house.[17] But for all of that, you do your best – and then they go. They're not *yours*. Never have been. And if you're stuck with someone you hate after that then, well, it's pretty bloody miserable. My ex ex and I used to watch TV in evening to avoid rowing. But once it was just the two of us, we couldn't even agree on what TV programmes to watch any more. So we divorced.'

I adopt my best 'I'm so sorry' look, but Tricia bursts out laughing. 'No, no sad faces. I wish we'd done it earlier. Things might have been better with Ed if we had. Divorcing his father was the best twenty grand I've ever spent ...'

'Right. Good for you,' I say, rearranging my features.

'You're in the eye of the storm right now – but you'll be OK,' Inge tells me.

But how do you know? I want to shout. *I'm not like you! I can't be single again ... I'd have to wax, wouldn't I? Or have I caught a break and the seventies bush is back?*

Bigger than the bush problem is this: divorce would mean failure. And I don't do failure ...

'Greg and I are fine,' I insist, fooling precisely no one.

'That's my sister, always "fine",' slurs Melissa. 'Even when she's not. Just call her Robo-Alice.'

I choose to take this as a compliment.

'Never let anyone in, never show a chink of weakness. Always keep up appearances – even when your husband pisses sitting down and leaves skid marks in his pants—'

[17.] *Challenge Anneka* aired on BBC1 from 1989 until 1995 when it was cruelly cut from the schedule and Anneke choppered her way to her very last lion sanctuary. Sad times. She hasn't had much use for the ear defenders of flammable jumpsuits since, and so presumably hasn't missed them. Yet ...

'Skid-what?' Margot asks, puzzled.

'Nothing!' I fume, attempting to cut off this line of conversation.

But Melissa will not be stopped. 'Robo-Alice, always the straight one, always doing the right thing.'

'Not *always*!' I correct her.

'Oh yeah? When have you done anything wrong? *Ever*?'

I want to laugh out loud at this, because lately, it's felt as though everything I do is wrong. As though I'm not succeeding at anything – parenting, work, being a good sister, friendship, 'actual social interactions', or even getting to grips with the basic tenets of Viking life. Whereas Melissa seems to be, in her words, 'slamming it', with a work-life balance I scarcely dare contemplate, people skills I can only dream of, and a positive outlook I've never really believed was possible without the aid of nitrous oxide (aka 'laughing gas' – the dental practitioner's best friend).

'I do things wrong!' I protest. 'I make a mess of things ...' I insist, adding lamely. 'Loads!'

'Like when?'

'Like, recently ...'

'*Really*?' Melissa challenges.

'Really?' Tricia echoes her, eyes widening in excitement. 'Go on!' she urges.

'It is your turn,' Inge confirms, with paired back Scandinavian logic.

By now, my muscles feel wonderfully slack and my head is all swimmy after the beer, so I do.

'Well ...' I ramp up to my admission, extending the word for as long as possible to buy myself time. A stay of execution, if you will. Then I take the biggest breath that my lungs can manage and start. 'You know when you picked me

up from the Premier Inn after that dentistry conference last
month—'

'The one where you puked?' Melissa clarifies.

'Yes, thank you, the one where I puked. And you know how
I told you I got drunk with a friend?'

'Yes?' Melissa still looks sceptical at this.

'Well, it wasn't exactly a friend. There was this dentist there—'

'What? At a dentistry conference? You do surprise me ...'
Melissa has another swig of beer, losing patience with my
non-story.

'And I think ... maybe ... I slept with him ...'

As soon as I have unravelled myself, I immediately wish I
could spool the confession back in.

There is silence, all around the table. Melissa's expression
shifts and I feel all my muscles tense up.

'You did *what*?' she says, finally. 'Are you mental?' She looks
appalled.

'No!' I say, defensive, now. *Maybe ... Yes ...*

'Well? How was it?' Tricia wants details.

'I ... I ...' I falter. 'I can't remember ...'

'What were you *thinking*?' Melissa demands.

'I wasn't! That's the point ...' I glance around for support.

'What is the matter with you?' my sister continues.

This isn't how I thought the conversation would go.

So Tricia is allowed to have a threesome and I'm not allowed one
minor/medium indiscretion in twelve years of dutiful wifely service?

I realise too late that I have misjudged the tone of this
'girly chat'.

This is why you don't do 'girly chats', I censure myself. *Idiot!*
You're out of your depth!

'Big? Was he?' Tricia goes on, oblivious to the simmering
undercurrent of sibling disharmony.

'I-I don't know ...'

'Of all the—' Melissa stops herself and shakes her head instead. 'I just can't believe it.' I hadn't expected Melissa to take it this hard. Or to have the jagged seams of our relationship exposed quite so publically. 'Since when did you become such a prude?' I retaliate, moving into unfamiliar territory. 'You never liked Greg anyway—'

'Oh *Greg*.' She makes the name sound as though it's a made-up word. '*Greg*. No one likes *Greg*.'

'Excuse me?'

'Dad doesn't.'

'Oh *really* ...'

'Called him a prick last Christmas.'

'Did he now? How very gentlemanly ...'

'Greg *is* a prick.'

'That's not the point!' I yell, now.

'No, *Greg's* not the point!'

'Is Greg her husband?' Inge frowns trying to keep up.

'I think so,' Margot whispers, too loudly to really qualify as a whisper.

'Yes,' Melissa confirms. 'And he's a bell hop ...'

'At a hotel?' Margot asks – convinced by now, I am sure, that the rest of us are mere serfs. *Stagehands and servants in the lives of her and her kinsfolk,* I muse, bitterly.

'No!' Melissa clarifies. 'I'm using the phrase as a term of abuse. His idea of a good time is sitting in a darkened room with only Fiona Bruce and some stones for company. He thinks childcare means parking kids in front of an iPad.'

'You don't get to judge his parenting skills!' I am doubly outraged at this because a) it's not her place to criticise and b) she's right. Which I hate.

'I told you! Greg's not the point!' Melissa fires back.

'Well, if it's not about Greg, then what's your problem?' I ask, baffled. 'Why are you being so judgey?'

'*Me* judgey?' Melissa looks disbelieving. 'Coming from you, Judge Judy?'[18]

'That's not my name—'

'It *should* be—'

'Now now, let's save the handbags until dawn.' Tricia attempts to broker peace but fails.

'You talk about family life,' Melissa persists, 'but never make *any* effort to see Dad ...'

'Were you *very* drunk? At the dentistry conference?' Margot asks, not knowing quite how to pitch the tone of her enquiry, or whose side she's on, but keen to join in.

'What?' I turn to her, feeling confused now and shaking my head slightly. 'No. I mean, yes.'

'*Hypocrite.*' Melissa relishes the word, annunciating every consonant.

I'm open-mouthed in shock for a second. 'Why do you care so much?'

Melissa narrows her eyes at me before she speaks. 'I "care" because you've spent years – for as long as I can remember – on this huge, enormous, horse—'

'Do you mean a high horse?' Margot asks, helpfully.

'That's what I said!' Melissa raises her voice now. 'And I've been scared to tell you stuff in case you went all Judgey Mc Judge Face—'

'Again: not my name—'

'And all along, you criticise and give everyone those looks—'

'What looks?'

[18.] Star of the self-titled long-running American reality court show and author of *Don't Pee on My Leg and Tell Me It's Raining.* Wise words ...

'That one! You're doing it right now! Isn't she?' Melissa appeals to Tricia.

'You do have a pretty fierce face on you,' Tricia admits carefully. I rotate my body to give her the full benefit of my fierce face. 'Yep, that's the one.' Tricia nods, shielding her eyes theatrically. 'Ooh, I can *feel* it! It's the look of a woman who could kill. *Again* ...' She turns to Melissa. 'Is this the gale force ten you warned me about?' My sister sucks her teeth and nods.

'You've been talking about me?'

I'm hurt. I'd thought that Tricia was my ally here. My comrade in crap Viking skills. *And all the while, she's been Judas-ing me with Melissa?* 'The two of you have been discussing my *"faces"*?'

'Don't flatter yourself ...' Melissa starts, at the same time as Tricia says, 'Only briefly ...'

'They haven't with me—' Margot adds, by way of consolation.

'Oh, SOD OFF MARGOT!' I intended to convey this with a facial expression but find that the words have slipped out of my mouth.

There is another tremor as the pressure builds and I feel the tectonic plates shift.

I try to laugh this off but it comes out flat. Nobody speaks – or even breathes, it seems – for a beat.

'You know, for someone who cares so much about being liked, you'd think you'd have worked out a way of being less of a cow by now.' Melissa shakes her head and looks genuinely disappointed in me. Some crisps have magically materialised on the table, so I stuff them in my mouth to keep from saying anything else I might later regret. But Melissa persists. 'Well? Aren't you going to apologise?'

I'm so tired. And drunk. And full of crisps ...

'We're waiting ...' Melissa is still talking.

'You can bog off, too!' I splutter through a mouthful of semi-masticated potato.

'I rest my case,' says Melissa, leaning back in her chair, before deciding that her 'case' has a second wind. 'Do you know—' she pitches forward, finger jabbing, '—I *knew* something was up when I collected you from that conference and you smelled like a dead badger ... And you gave me a hard time for ... well ... everything. As usual. Unbelievable! Do you *ever* think about how other people feel?'

'Are you serious?' I near splutter. 'I'm *always* thinking about other people!' I wonder whether now might be an apposite time to mention the four bags-for-life. *Not to mention the spare dental masks I usually keep with me to distribute to patients/ supermarket workers/teachers/other parents at the children's school if they have a cold ...* 'I look after *everyone*! I have a direct debit to Dentaid! "Improving the world's oral health one smile at a time"! I run the PTA! I always pay and display! I'm never late! If anything, I'm usually early—'

'You're not early for everything because you care!' Melissa fires back. 'Your timekeeping is an act of military aggression! You just want the upper hand. You *have to* have the upper hand!'

I look around for support. *Is this happening? Are we having a row? Like on reality TV shows?* I wonder, hazily. I don't know how to do rows. Never have. Melissa would shout and rage as a child (and kick, too, as I recall now ...) while Dad would occasionally raise his voice at the cricket. Mum and I stayed silent and observed. Melissa always used to say this was worse – why couldn't' we just 'let it all out' and then get on with things? But that was never our style. Bottle it. Zip it up. Concede nothing. Even with Greg, even at our worst, we've always maintained a sort of quiet loathing. A sanitised, simmering resentment. But losing it? Never. *Because if you lose it, you might not get it back,* I remind myself. And yet here I am, gesticulating wildly and hurling abuse like some sort of batshit banshee.

'It's the quiet ones you want to look out for,' Tricia is joking now, trying, I suspect, to make light of the situation. But I'm not in the mood.

'That coming from a lush who bangs on about gin and tonic all the time!' It comes out of me, from nowhere, and I clasp a hand over my mouth to try to stuff it back in.

Tricia bristles for a moment and there is a sudden intake of breath from Melissa. A look passes between them before my sister shakes her head slightly. At this, Tricia relaxes and shrugs. 'I'm very worried about malaria ...'

Does Melissa know something I don't?

A feeling that I'm being ganged up on – or at least left out of *something* – grows and gnaws at me. This escalates with each wave of now-drunken paranoia.

Margot is still giggling at the malaria comment, so I turn on her next. 'And you, with your perfect cat-face, and plastic mannequin-hands that have never done a day's work in their life – whereas I've been removing stubborn plaque for *decades*!' This isn't strictly true – one and a half decades would be more accurate but it doesn't have the same ring to it.

'That's enough!' Melissa demands.

'Says you!' I blurt in response.

'Just shut it!' she tells me.

But I don't.

Instead, I fight back.

'You don't get to tell me what to do! What do you know about anything? Your life's a fucking teddy bear's tea party!

We can't all fanny about playing toy farms all day – some of us have to work in the real world to earn money and keep things going. Like a grown-up ...'

Even as I'm speaking, I'm aware that I'm making a mess of things.

'Relax', everyone tells me. 'Let your hair down once in a while,' they say.

Well, I have. And what's happened? My sister is currently incandescent with rage and on the verge of tears. I'm behaving like a cornered animal and yet, curiously, I can't seem to stop myself.

'You don't know what my life's like,' Melissa says in an uncharacteristically measured, stony voice now. 'You have no idea.'

This is it, I think. This is the moment when I could apologise and try to make it right again. That's what I should do. That's what a normal person would do. But I feel punchy with fear and adrenaline. *People don't speak to me like this as an adult. No one has spoken to me like this since ... well, since Melissa. At home. The night I left.*

So instead of apologising, I come out swinging.

'Are you joking? You barely live in the real world – post 1950s, anyway. I mean, who doesn't have a smartphone? Or Wi-Fi? Or pyramid-tossing-teabags?! It's like you're just doing it for the attention! You're a total drama queen! Always have been!'

'Well, you're cold and stuck up,' she chokes back, holding a hand to her jaw in what I know is an attempt to nurse her aching wisdom tooth that she *still* hasn't had seen to.

'Well,' I start, blazing like wildfire now, 'I'd rather *that* than emotionally incontinent! Take a look in the mirror and sort yourself out before you start on me! And maybe invest in an electric toothbrush! You big ... *baby!*'

With this, Melissa skids her chair back and storms out of the room with an impressive, room-shaking door-slam.

'See what I mean?' I address the table of thunderstruck remaining Vikings. 'No regard at all for the fact that there are children sleeping and a man currently in bed with food poi—' I stop myself in case this acts as an admission of guilt. *'Poisoning' is a strong word*, I reason. I fear I'm losing my audience anyway without bringing up berry-gate again, so I rephrase '—a very sick man,' I offer, instead.

See, I'm not cold and heartless, am I? I want to shake each of them in turn and demand confirmation: *I'm practical. I'm a good person to have on side. I'm a good person, full stop. Aren't I?*

The door bangs again. It's Melissa.

'I haven't calmed down – I just came back for my sex-fleece,' she announces, seizing the newly laundered maroon monstrosity from the back of her chair and flinging it around her shoulders, like a poor woman's superhero cape. As an afterthought, she picks up her half empty bottle of beer to take with her, before stomping out once more.

Eight

'Egg? I had you down for an egg. Want one?' Tricia is asking as I rub sleep from my eyes. She's wearing her hair in a 1960s' film-star turban again with a slotted spoon in one hand and what looks a lot like a Bloody Mary in the other, but I'm so relieved that she's still speaking to me, I keep all observations to myself.

'Mmm, thanks,' I reply sheepishly.

My limbs feel like lead and everything aches; whether through exertion, alcohol, or a combination of the two, I can't be sure. Though the pounding head and tacky mouth are a testament to the fact that 'beer' may have played a significant part.

Margot is stretching her quads against the wall and appears run-fresh, which only makes me feel less 'fresh'. Inge has a child clamped to each leg and one hanging on for dear life around her neck, piggybacking a ride. She picks up the lamb in one hand and a butter dish with the other, depositing the latter on the table before shaking off her progeny and telling them to help with breakfast. They obey, dutifully, without a murmur of dissent, while she gives the lamb its bottle.

The psychology of overachievers. I try turning the phrase over in my mind, but find the effort hurts, so instead I slump in a chair and wait gratefully for my egg.

'Laid this morning!' Margot beams. 'I collected them, didn't I?' She looks to Inge for approval but gets nothing. So she adds, 'Still *steaming*, they were!'

If I'm honest, the image of my soft-boiled squeezing out of the intimate area of a scratchy chicken just an hour or so earlier puts me off slightly. *Stop. Being. A. Wuss*, I scold myself for my squeamishness and, unwilling to lose face in front of either Margot or Inge, smile and crack the shell. As quietly as possible. The candles have already been lit – a while ago if their current height is anything to go by – and I marvel that Vikings seem incapable of getting through a single mealtime/coffee break/ opportunity for a sit down without a naked flame nearby.

You'd think electricity had never been invented ...

'Do you always breakfast by candlelight?' I ask Inge.

'Yes,' she tells me plainly, before adding, 'have you heard of *hygge*?'

'Hasn't everyone by now?' I mean to say this in my head but can tell by Inge's amused expression that I've said it out loud.

'It's not just about candles, but they're a good start,' she says. 'The rest, you have to feel. You will, by the time the week's through.'

Despite my splitting headache, somehow, I believe her.

A child (*Villum, is it?*) thumps a brick of rye bread down in front of me along with a large, serrated knife. Because knives and children are evidently an acceptable Viking combination, I've learned. I saw through the block for about five minutes before a slice is liberated, then spend another eternity axing it into soldiers before I can dip it into the fire-coloured yolk. But the taste is worth it and I wolf the lot.

Rye bread is barely even a carb, I tell myself: *it's good for me ... probably.*

'How's Magnus this morning?' I manage through a claggy mouthful.

'Oh, you know ... Magnus-y,' Inge replies. 'A couple more rounds of cumin juice and he'll be fine.' I nod.

'And ... where's Melissa?' The top bunk was empty this morning when I finally plucked up the courage to look. I'd assumed she was already up, like everyone else. *Like I am, normally*, I think, with a hint of shame tinged with rebellion: *Screw you, 'old me'! The new Alice drinks beer and sleeps in until ...* I consult the kitchen clock. *Oh, it's still only 7.15am. Rock and indeed roll.*

'Melissa?' Tricia looks up. 'You don't know?'

'No?'

'Neither do we!' Margot does a few lunges to prolong her post-run flush. She looks hellishly beautiful and a little too happy to be involved in the unfolding drama.

'I didn't hear her come back last night,' Inge confirms, as a kernel of dread lodges itself inside me.

Shit ...

Melissa had been angry when she left but I had presumed she'd cool off after a few minutes. Literally, if the post-dusk temperatures of the last few days are anything to go by. *I hope she hasn't done anything daft*, I think. Because my sister has form in this area.

There was a night just before her mock GCSEs when Melissa was in self-destruct mode and disappeared with two litres of Dad's home-brew cider disguised in a Fanta bottle. I had to scour the local parks, dodging tramps and other teenage drunks (we grew up in a town dedicated to underage drinking) until I found her sobbing under a slide in the kids' playground. I dragged her home and made her drink a pint of water before putting her to bed, quietly so

Dad wouldn't notice she'd been gone. *As if he needed anything else to worry about!*

It occurs to me now that I never asked Melissa why she was crying. I'd assumed it was the pressure of exams. *But now I'm not so sure.* Or the time she played truant from school and I had to go and see the headmaster and apologise. *As if Dad needed the extra stress!*

I did some sleuth work (aka diary reading – a course of action that was, I felt certain, entirely justified and to my credit). I found out she was volunteering at a donkey sanctuary instead of doing double Geography, so I threatened to take away her Charles and Di commemorative cup and saucer unless she improved her attendance record. A ploy that worked, for a while.

But I've never had to deal with her impromptu excursions in a foreign country before. Or in front of strangers. And her disappearances have never *whispers it* been *my fault* up until now ... have they?

'I thought maybe she'd gone for a run, like me,' Margot goes on, 'but then, that was hours ago. You know what they say, "The early bird catches the worm".'

The early bird can bog off, I think, unkindly.

'So if Melissa's still out running, well ... she's putting me to shame!'

We both know that this is unlikely. I manage a tight smile and say nothing, allowing myself an eye roll in Tricia's direction while Margot busies herself with a hamstring stretch.

'Your sister will be totally safe here,' Inge assures me, resting an arm on my shoulder. Her long hair is still damp from the shower and she smells of clean clothes and hope. 'I once lost Mette for a whole day when we first moved.'

I should be reassured by this, but I'm not.

Just as we're preparing to leave the house for day five's 'Introduction to Boatbuilding', the door swings open like a saloon in a Western and Melissa stands there – the pink morning sky giving her a rosy glow. Her hair is dishevelled, accessorised with what looks a lot like straw. Her trousers are rolled up unevenly, one a mere turn-up and the other suggesting she's selling drugs of some description. And her maroon sex fleece is flung jauntily over one shoulder. But she looks ... radiant.

If I didn't know better I'd think she HAD been on a run, or ... or something else ...

'Right then, are we off?' is all she says, directing her question at Inge.

'Don't you want breakfast?' She gestures at the table, still laden with condiments, buns and the rye bread that Freja is now tunnelling into with bare, chubby fists. *Viking skills,* I think.

'No, thanks.'

'You don't want breakfast?' Even Tricia's mouth drops at this.

'There are cinnamon buns!' I protest. 'You love cinnamon buns!'

'I'll be fine.' She shoots me a lemon-sucking look that silences and scares me simultaneously.

Things must be bad, I deduce.

'Listen,' I start, hurrying towards the door to catch a moment with Melissa on her own, 'I'm sorry. About last night, I mean ...'

But she blanks me. *She actually blanks me!* I can't quite believe it. *Are we tweenagers again? Perhaps she didn't hear.* 'I'm sorry we fought,' I try again. *If that's what we did ...*

'You're sorry we fought?' She stops now and looks at me.

'Yes.'

'You're not sorry about what you said?' Her mouth turns slack.

Ah ... now ... what was that, exactly? I run a furry tongue around my still-furry-despite-ten-minutes-of-sustained-brushing teeth. 'We probably both said things we regret—' I say, but am cut off.

'Forget it.' Melissa shakes her head and turns away from me to begin her tramp towards the coast to where the boat yard is located.

I stand on the threshold, feeling helpless, and watch her leave. It's rained again overnight and trees twinkle with droplets of water in the morning sun. The place smells fresh – restorative, even. And not at all how I remember it from yesterday's molten metal-fest and livestock wrangling.

It'll all be OK, I think, taking in the fortifying view. *Won't it?* I don't know who I'm asking any more.

'You're still worried.' Inge is packing a picnic hamper – or rather, a picnic grey-hessian-sack. She follows my gaze to the image of Melissa trudging across fields, towards the sea, with Tricia now trotting to catch up with her. *My closest ally and my sister,* I think. *Great ...*

'It'll be good for you to keep active today,' Inge asserts, tipping a bowl full of apples into her bag.

'Ye-es,' I say in a voice that comes out much smaller than intended. I have another go and try to sound upbeat. 'I like to keep busy ...'

'Not "busy",' Inge corrects me. 'Active.'

'There's a difference?'

'You'll see,' she says, then noticing that my neck is beginning to colour and that my eyes are watering up, she relents and gives me a little more to go on. 'When you were learning a new skill – working with your hands over the last couple of days, you weren't thinking about home or how much you miss your kids so much, right?'

'Right ... ?'

'You had no time for the – how do you say – winding up of your mind?'

'Whirring?' Margot offers, in earshot now.

Sodding Margot ...

'Sure.' Inge shrugs as though such pedantry is missing the point. 'So, the thing to remember today about boatbuilding—' she says as she swings Villum up onto her back and deposits Freja in her pram, leaving Mette to trip alongside us '—is that it's *not about* the boatbuilding.'

'It's not?'

'No.'

'Oh.' I don't mean to be obtuse, but I'm not sure I get it. If it's not about the boat, then, err, what *is* it about?'

'*Doing* something. *Anything.*' Inge sounds as close to exasperated as I expect she's ever likely to get (i.e. still preternaturally high on the patience scale in my book). 'You've heard of walking therapy?' she goes on. I haven't.

'Yes,' I lie, unwilling to lose face.

'And there's dance therapy, even horse therapy ...'

WTF? I try to process this. *Melissa was RIGHT? With her mad idea about painting on ponies?!* I can just imagine her cracking her knuckles in triumph when she hears of this vindication ...

'Horse therapy?' I ask Inge, tentatively.

'Yes – you can tell a lot about someone by the way they react to a horse.'

Okay, so we're not painting on ponies ...

'Animal therapy a technique we use in psychology a lot,' she says.

'Is that ... ? Are we ... ?' I try to dismiss the idea before it can even form in my mind, but when Inge is side-tracked by one of the children needing a wee, Margot looks at me with her big old cat-eyes and I wonder whether she's thinking what I'm thinking. So I ask, 'Is Inge psychologist-ing us?'

Margot begins to blush and doesn't even correct my poor grammar. I've clearly struck a nerve.

'I think she might be ...' she says.

I flatter myself for a millisecond that perhaps I'm under scrutiny as a case study for her PhD thesis but then I note that Margot has now turned practically purple. *If anyone's being observed as an overachiever, it's sodding Margot,* I rationalise. This results in mixed emotions. Obviously, I'm glad not to be under the spotlight. Obviously. *Although ...*

Wasn't I a high achiever once, too? Dentistry conference panel discussions aside? I've got a feeling I've been so busy and tired over the past ten years that I wouldn't have been able to remember either way. But Margot is visibly rattled.

'Is that why you don't mind teaching us?' Margot asks Inge anxiously when she's back in view, children fully relieved. 'The rest of the Viking skills, I mean?' Margot goes on.

'What gave you that idea?' Inge replies, her face betraying nothing. 'I want to you to experience *Viking culture,*' she says, simply. 'Just like Magnus does, or at least, he will once he's finished off-gassing ...' Here we wrinkle our noses collectively and agree Never To Speak Again of the alarming smells that have been emanating from the master bedroom's en suite of late.

'How is Magnus doing?' I ask tentatively.

'Anyway, as I was saying—' she's keen to move us on '—there's also a value in focusing on something, in switching off the "whirring" and using your hands. Everyone needs to know how to be the captain of their own ship. And if you know how to sail, you're not afraid of the storms.'

God, she's good, I think, *she's boat metaphor-ing us into learning something!*

'You become aware of your strengths and weaknesses,' Inge goes on, 'of the factors that can be controlled and those that are beyond your control. Like water. And winds.' At this she sets off, with Freja in her tank-pram, Villum on her back and Mette struggling to keep up. She's going at such a clip that even Margot and I have to skip slightly every few paces, keen not to miss any of this prize *Völva* intel.

'Sometimes you can be floating in one place, bobbing on the waves,' Inge continues, and I notice Mette rolling her eyes, as though it's a talk she's been subjected to before, in duplicate languages. 'Sometimes all you can see is a leaking boat – taking on water. Sometimes you'll be afraid that your boat won't withstand stormy weather.' Here Inge looks pointedly at me.

Jesus – if even handle-it-all Inge thinks I'm in stormy weather, perhaps my life really is car-crash-shit …

I wonder how much further she can stretch the boat metaphor.

'You need to question: what aspect of my boat has the highest priority at the moment?'

Oh: still going …

'You have to consider the options,' Inge continues. 'Like, what do I want my boat to look like? What kind of destination do I want to reach with my boat? In a boat – as in life – sometimes the waves will wash over you and you'll get wet feet. And when you've got wet feet, you need to start bailing.'

'Right …' I'm not sure I buy it all, but part of me wishes I'd been taking notes. Margot is also frowning, trying to absorb all the new ideas.

'Magnus never mentioned any of this ...' she says now.

'Well, no.' Inge sighs. 'For Magnus, it pretty much is *all about the boat*. He likes the exertion. Plus it's hot work so he gets to take his top off a lot. Which, as you may have noticed, he loves to do. Also, I think he might be addicted to tar fumes ...' She frowns.

I make a mental note not to mention the Sharpie-sniffing and shoot Margot my best 'drop it!' look to encourage her to do the same. She nods, knowingly.

Have I just built a rapport with my arch cat-enemy? Arch-cat-emy, if you will? I feel strangely pleased – as though I can't possibly be such a terrible person, after all. Even if Tricia has also abandoned me. There's a skip in my walk the rest of the way across the stunning vista, with me occasionally pausing to take pity on Mette and give her a piggyback when I think her mother's too far ahead to notice ('Viking children *walk*,' Inge tells us of the five-kilometre hike she's currently subjecting her daughter to).

When we reach the coast, Melissa and Tricia are already there – shrieking with laughter and then speaking in huddled confidences as though they're the oldest of friends. I see Melissa give her a friendly wallop on the back. *I'll bet that hurts*, I think, wondering whether Tricia had braced herself for one of Melissa's 'affectionate' punches.

Just before the sand trails down to the sea, poking up above bulrushes and the long grass, is a support frame, already in place, with the skeleton of a wooden, almond-shaped boat on it.

'Aren't we building the whole boat?' Margot sounds disappointed.

'No,' Inge tells her. 'Even the smallest boats take about two weeks to make – ten days, at a push, if I haven't got kids with me.' It dawns on me now that she means single-handed.

Overachiever #101. 'But there's still lots to do,' she tells us as we reach Melissa and Tricia. The women swiftly disengage and listen up. 'We need to check the planks are overlapping, stuff wool in any gaps.' She gestures towards the 'three bags full' – presumably from my ewe-nemesis and her kinfolk – in hessian sacks a few yards away. 'Then we smear everything with tar to keep the water out.'

'That's the stuff that Magnus likes?' Margot asks. *She may be a genetically gifted superhuman, but she doesn't half lack tact …*

'What?' Melissa looks nonplussed.

'Yes, that's right.' Inge sighs. 'The stuff Magnus likes. Anyway, you make the tar by cutting up pine or birch, covering it with grass then setting it on fire—'

'Is it just me or do a lot of things in Viking culture involve fire?' Tricia asks.

'Yes.' Inge feels no need to defend this fact. Instead, she nods towards a large oil drum with the embers of a fire underneath and says, 'Here's some tar I made earlier', at which we all snigger.

I'm in an episode of Blue Peter …

'So, err, will we all fit in the boat when it's finished?' Tricia asks.

I'd been wondering this, too. *It does look a little on the small side …*

'Officially?' Inge replies. 'It takes two people. But that's Viking men. You lot—' she sizes us up '—I'd say we can fit three in. We won't all go out in it together. You need some ballast, of course, but the water should be no higher than two fingers below the top plank.' She demonstrates an imaginary line just beyond where the uppermost plank ends. 'I always recommend two oarswomen and a steerswoman who's also the navigator or sub, like in football.'

'Oh.'

'The substitute person can also be the bailer, if needed. And there's a plug in the bottom of the boat to let the water out,' Inge instructs us.

'A plug?' Melissa asks. 'Doesn't that let the water *in*?'

'No.'

'Are you sure?' Margot asks, helpfully.

'Am I speaking?' Inge fires back.

'Y-es ... ?' Margot doesn't sound quite so confident now.

'Then I'm sure,' says Inge.

That's us told ...

She points down at the rubber stopper in the base of the boat and speaks slowly, as though we are morons. 'The *plug* is for when the boat is *out* of the water, to let out any rain. When the boat's at sea you should never pull the plug. Obviously.'

'Right!' Melissa looks relieved.

'And do we need an anchor or something?' Margot asks, still keen.

'Vikings didn't bother for boats like this − we just make them light enough to drag on land.' Inge demonstrates this by lifting the boat and giving it a gentle toss in the air. Margot does the same, to reassure herself. I try, and it moves not an inch.

Stupid upper body strength! Stupid Margot with her Michelle Obama-arms. Just because she and Inge hit the DNA jackpot ...

The section of the boat that's already been tarred (a term to which I struggle not to add '*and feathered*' to) feels like metal to the touch − warmed by the sun, oxidised and scaly, almost. Melissa also has a go, tracing her fingers along the tactile surface.

'Like a dragon ...' she murmurs to herself

'You do know they're not real, right?' The quip slips out of my mouth before I can think better of it.

'Yes!' Melissa snaps, but looks disappointed.

Oh brilliant, I think, *Space: no, but dragons? Sure ...*[19]

'OK,' Inge calls out. 'Time for action.' She looks at me here. 'We need to finish tar-ing up, then we can do seats, oars, oar locks, and a rudder frame – plenty to be getting on with!' We're each given a task and, first up, I use my less-than-impressive might to shift ropes, stiffened with seawater.

I want Melissa to speak to me again after my outburst last night, but my misguided dragon comment hasn't helped. She's happily chatting and laughing away with Tricia and Inge – even Margot. But she won't even look at me. I am frozen out of all conversation.

Talk to me! I will her, arms full of salty hemp coils. *Me!* Only it appears that my reserves of sisterly telepathy are spent.

My spirits are lifted slightly by a cameo from the sun – a hot white orb burning west across the sky as we work. Hard. The labour is so physical that often there's silence all around. Our collective energy is used up by the sheer endeavour of lugging planks of wood, nailing them, stuffing gaps with fist-fuls of wool, then conveying leaden, lava-hot tar in buckets from the oil drum to our painting positions surrounding the boat. The children play in the long grass, occasionally fetching food for us or tucking into the picnic-rucksack and gorging on apples until Inge commands the youngest to stop ('I can't cope with a toddler and a husband both shitting liquids,' is how she puts it, eloquently). Finally, once I'm convinced that

---

[19] Yes: I know I compared Inge to a pegacorn. But I was DRUNK at the time. MAGGOT DRUNK, I tell you ...

I can't do any more without dropping or at least finding somewhere to hide in the bulrushes for a power nap, Inge says, 'Well then. Let's give it a go.'

Translation: Let's watch it go wrong together ...

'Should we wear life jackets?' I ask, not entirely trusting our own creation. Inge looks at me as though I've just suggested defecating on her firstborn. I take this as a 'no' and remember Magnus's insistence that Vikings don't do health and safety. I'm not, however, the only one with reservations.

'If we fall in the water, will we get Weil's Disease?' Tricia is asking in all seriousness, as she pushes back hair from her face with tar-stained hands.

Inge looks puzzled.

'Maybe you don't call it that here.' Tricia appeals to the rest of us for help, but sadly my medical knowledge doesn't extend to translating urine-born bacterial infections usually carried by rodents. 'Rat syphilis?' Tricia tries again. 'Do you have that?'

Inge allows herself two raised eyebrows at this. 'Me? No, I do not have rat syphilis ...'

'No, not *you* – I mean the water! Is it clean? If we fall in while out at sea?' Tricia looks anxiously from the boat to the sea and back again. 'Or ... sink?'

'Of course it's clean,' is the response. 'This is *Scandinavia*.'

'Fair enough.' Melissa sniffs and begins to lug the boat towards the water, single-handed.

Even at her most irritating, my sister can be very impressive, I think, a little proudly.

We take it in turns, two mere mortals and an Inge, for each 'go', so that we don't sink our cherished creation on its maiden voyage. Melissa elects to go out with Tricia, which stings. So I'm left with Margot. Again.

My sister's party heads out first with whoops of excitement (hers) and even from my station on the shore I can see that Melissa's having the time of her life.

'I'm the King of the World!' I hear her calling out as she stands, wobbles, and is swiftly pulled back into her seat by Inge. 'Sorry,' she shouts back. 'I mean "Queen". Or rather, "Viking"!'

'My sister is no Leonardo DiCaprio,' I mutter.

'Oh, I know him! A girl in my class went out with him for a while. She met him doing some modelling,' Margot pipes up, mid-apple.

Of course Margot went to school with models who date Hollywood A-listers!

The biggest celebrity link our school ever had was Geoff Capes, the shot-putter, coming to open the summer fete one year. *That and Jamie McMahon getting two girls in the year above pregnant before their A-Levels*, I remember now.

I leave the Leo line hanging and am already paddling out to meet the boat and help heave it out by the time Tricia and Melissa come back at the end of their turn.

'That. Was. Amazing!' Tricia gushes. 'And to think, we built it! Almost!'

I hadn't expected this. Axe-throwing enthusiasm aside, my dealings with Tricia to date have involved the two of us, unified by our poor attempts at mastering the hallowed Viking skills. *But one morning with my sister and now she's apparently a new Viking woman ... ?*

I feel my mouth become pinched with envy.

Melissa and Tricia proceed to high five, and even offer Margot one as she wades past to gracefully vault aboard. But me? Nothing.

'That looked like fun!' I try, but Melissa ignores me and just holds the boat steady while I clamber not-at-all-gracefully on board.

Inge instructs us on where to sit and heaving at heavy, freshly sanded oars, we set off.

It's nothing like the rowing I used to do at the gym, back in the days when I had time to go to the gym. It's real. And scary. And yet ...

We built this! I tell myself, with every stroke. Despite my trepidation at leaving dry land and mild queasiness at the buck and quell of the sea, there are some distinct pros to this boat business. I quite enjoy the cool breeze in my hair and the fresh, salty spray occasionally giving me a facial spritz. There is a sail, too, I learn, as Inge points out the 'big white thing wrapped around a pole' sticking up from the centre of the boat. But this, apparently, is for tomorrow. We aren't going far enough today to warrant such further excitements, and although Margot looks disappointed, I find I'm beaming like a deranged woman in appreciation of the whole exercise in general.

I like this! I could do more of this! I think, and feel a little sad when Inge announces that it's time to return to shore.

'I can see Mette trying to wipe Villum's butt with a bulrush again. She thinks she's being helpful but I just end up with a kid covered in crap *and* bulrush. She does tend to think outside the cube ...' Inge explains. I wonder whether she means 'box' but don't mention this. And either way, we return, jubilant.

I am now a sea-faring Viking! Hear me roar!

Once we're back on terra firma, I'm feeling more optimistic about everything. Invigorated, even. *I can see why there was high-fiving before,* I think now, *and why Tricia loved it so much.* She and Melissa have already started walking home by the time Margot and I (mostly Margot) heave the boat up on shore. Inge takes the younger children in hand and Margot offers to give Mette a piggyback, usurping my previous role.

With Inge up ahead and Margot wowing Mette by pretending to be a horse (something she was always going to be better at than me on account of actually *owning* several ...), the rest of the walk passes slowly. And alone.

After the adrenaline of the boat trip, a wave of fatigue washes over me. I feel as though I've used up a lot of energy trying to put in command performances today, failing at every turn. *Contrition isn't my forte,* I think, *and Melissa's still mad as hell ... Bugger ...*

I want to get home, slide off to the bedroom and feel the wave of relief that I know simply closing my eyes will bring. Getting up again might require a more heroic effort than I currently have in me, I reason. *But I'll do my best. I always do. Don't I?*

I finally make it back and while the rest of our party are showering or refuelling, I head to our room for a lie down – just for a while. But on the way, having tip-toed past the master bedroom to avoid any awkward confrontations with Magnus over rogue berries, I brush up against the bookshelf in the hallway. So close that my elbow catches on something, wicker spikes hooking themselves into the fabric of my jumper. There's a clattering sound and I realise that whatever it was has fallen off the shelf, scattering its contents over the wooden floor. I stoop, meaning to right the accident before anyone sees, but soon find myself face to face with ... my phone.

Looking around to check no one is watching, I pick it up. Instinctively, I turn it on. Breath quickening and heart hammering, I unlock the screen and am rewarded with their faces: Charlotte and Thomas, grinning up at me. A quake disturbs something inside me; plates scrape over each other and I realise that the very *core* of me has missed them.

I only planned to have a quick look at their picture, but I find I can't put them down.

I can't *not* look at this, at them, a moment longer. The soft, fleshy faces of these two extraordinary human beings I was mostly responsible for bringing into the world.[20]

I stuff the phone up my sleeve, drop the rest of the devices back in their basket and scuttle off to our room to try calling, or at least do some elicit scrolling through pictures of them under the covers. Much like my experience of reading the *Sweet Valley High* saga by torch after lights out as a child. *So, you know, it's at least Viking-saga-related*, I think, conveniently overlooking the fact that I am now breaking Inge's overarching Noble Virtue and her lynchpin for Viking and Völva life: honesty.

But I tried honesty last night and look where that got me. Here goes nothing …

---

20. Yes 'mostly' responsible: all Greg had to do was stop thinking about employment legislation in the Czech Republic or parking restrictions in Brent, for ten minutes. Twice. I've done the rest …

Nine

I try calling Greg first. Not through any huge desire to speak to my husband but in the hope that he can put the kids on the phone.

I can check whether Charlotte's lost her upper central incisor[21] *and find out whether Thomas got on OK at assembly ...*[22]

But there's no response on the mobile. Or on Facetime. Or Skype. Greg and I have a tendency toward muteness in common (along with low-level mutual contempt ...) so I'm not hugely surprised by this. It's not our habit to contribute unnecessarily to conversation, let alone initiate one. I also told him in no uncertain terms that this was my 'week off' – 'off' childcare, wifeliness, dentistry, everything. And Melissa warned him that there might not be adequate 'telephone reception waves' for calling home at our retreat destination. *So really, I've made my own no-contact-with-the-kids bed,* I think now, wretchedly. But I try. Again. And again. Until the gloom of having to assess my own face, for an age, like in the hairdresser's mirror, for another round of fruitless *blob blob blob* video dialling proves too much. I hang up, feeling dejected.

---

[21] The wobbly top tooth that was loose last week

[22] A class presentation on dinosaurs = a Big Deal

Greg's probably mired down in a busy day of News 24 and toast ...

I send him a text instead and it occurs to me how much I've missed the boo-wip sound of a message shooting off into the ether.

Not as much as my children, OBVIOUSLY ... but a bit.

I've missed seeing those little bubbles come up underneath my blue messages that tell me someone's composing a reply. And then ...

I have bubbles!

Greg appears to be responding. The bubbles keep bubbling as he types ... but then, nothing. Just my message, hanging there, suspended in nothingness.

This is bad, I think. *Really bad ... But we can't split up,* I'm still trying to persuade myself. *We've got two kids! Who's going to want me with two kids?*

I look back at my phone, doing precisely nothing. No bubble. No reply.

Who'll want me? Not Greg, clearly ...

Dear Greg, I want to write: *Don't start something you're not willing to finish* ... But then I realise a more grown-up approach as befits a professional mother of two with four bags-for-life in her car would be *not* to enter into a passive aggressive SMS exchange. *When they go low, you go high ... or something.* Taking a deep breath, I call. Again. But there's no reply. Again.

He doesn't want to speak to me. Which means I don't get to speak to Thomas and Charlotte ... A scenario that is partially of my own making. This makes me feel very low indeed and the Greek chorus warms up for an encore. So instead, I distract myself by making the most of my contraband phone access.

Ta da! Bad feelings: buried.

A few texts from work give me a rush of importance and validation, notwithstanding the fact that they are predominantly '*where ARE you?*' variants from colleagues who've forgotten I'm on leave. But aside from the office, no one has missed me.

No one? I think, a little wounded. Of course, I'm relieved to see there's nothing from the anonymous number that I am now 99 per cent sure was Mr Teeth. *But really ... no one? No friends? Nada ... ?* I realise, again, that I may have let my social life slide in recent years.

In lieu of a life outside of work and my immediate family, I scroll through the collection of photographs I keep of Charlotte and Thomas on my phone. My mood lifts as unconditional love takes my face hostage. I see my children dressed for the first day of school; in the garden against a wash of blue sky; playing in the snow last winter.[23]

There's no response to another round of calling, so I diversify, dipping into various other apps. I check LinkedIn for a digital reward pellet (*Another new endorsement! Does Alice Ray know about Veneers? Does she heck!*), dismiss a few emails from the surgery that can wait, and flag up the others to respond to when I'm back. Because, I recognise now with the perspective of a few days away, nothing is really as urgent as an email marked '*URGENT*' makes things out to be.

Except for Mrs White's filling. That does need replacing asap ...

I forward the request on to reception with an angry red exclamation mark to signal that it's high priority. Then I have a browse around, taking full advantage of the password-free WiFi access.[24] And before I know it, I'm three years deep into

---

[23.] I like snow. It's very *clean* ...

[24.] See 'trusting hosts'

an old school friend's Facebook photos, envying her picture-perfect home and feeling a twinge of the RSI I regularly suffer from. *That's not good,* I remind myself. *Stop it. Stop scrolling, now.* Just as I'm about to close the app, I notice that Steve from the surgery has posted a '*LOL*' video that has apparently been shared several hundred thousand times called 'Woman Goes Crazy at Work', accompanied by the hashtag #*thatss-howbusiness.* Steve has added his own comment. '*MUST watch – feel better about my job already … !;)*' to which Beverley from reception has oh-so wittily replied. '*You don't have to be crazy to work here, but it helps!*'

Without thinking, I click.

The link takes me through to one of those websites where I can also see long-range pap shots of women in bikinis, swarthy-looking men looking a bit shifty, and a piece about how Belgian drag acts are morally corrupting our youth at British tax payers' expense. I wrinkle my nose and am preparing to click away, vowing to be higher minded than this, when the video starts playing automatically.

Oh well then, not my fault, I think. And watch.

At first, it appears to be a mistake – just footage of some-one's shoes against grubby blue carpet tiles, as though someone's pressed record on the video function of their phone without realising it. I lean in, to check I'm not missing something, and make out a muffled audio. So I turn the volume up, until a woman's voice can be heard. She sounds upset. Irate, even.

'Why do I *bother?*' she's asking. 'Why *do* I bother?' she repeats, changing the inflection. 'Tell me? Why? I'm surrounded by people who haven't seen a hairbrush in years, who all look as though they need a good going over with a hot flannel, who weren't even *born* when I did my first celebrity telethon, but do I complain?' She doesn't wait for an answer. 'I do not.'

The camera tilts upwards at this point, shakily and in the style of *The Cook Report*,[25] as though the videographer is growing in confidence – filming without the protagonist's knowledge but determined to get a better shot of the action. I can make out a pair of court shoes from which a woman's slender, nut-brown legs emerge. She's standing by a water-cooler, undulating slightly and occasionally prodding a second figure – a man wearing jeans and a hoodie. The camera moves so much that the faces on my tiny screen are blurry, but, between sentences, the woman appears to swig from a white, branded mug.

'The one thing – the *one thing* – I expect is a little loyalty. But no. I have to learn second-hand – *second-hand* – that that ... *embryo* ... has been given my show!'

'They just said they were going for a younger vibe,' Hoodie Man tries to explain.

'Why not one of the others? They want youth, they should try shunting Marcus. Or Nigel. Or Doug. What about DOUG!' she says, with a prod. 'I mean, this is *radio*! It's a sad day when you can't have a woman over fifty—' she stops to correct herself '—*forty-five*, even, on bloody radio!' She takes a swig from her mug. 'Well, let me tell you, I have had *enough*! ENOUGH! You hear me? I don't have to put up with this! I've done *Celebrity Shark Bait*! I was lowered into the sea by a woman with three fingers! These thighs?' She points. 'In a wetsuit? The shark thought I was a seal in distress! Went right for me and I STILL went on air and did my show the next morning. *That's* show business!'

Hoodie Man proffers a plastic cup of water, but Mug Woman, who sounds strangely familiar, bats it away and goes

---

[25.] Current affairs show majoring on investigations with hidden cameras that wobbled, consistently. Excellent journalism: sure-fire nausea. Good times.

on. 'I've jogged out of helicopters to hospitality tents and drunk champagne with the cast of *Casualty*! I've worn a shell suit and eaten lobster for a spread in the *Sunday Times*!'

The camera jiggles a little at this and I realise its owner must be chuckling.

'Is that ... ?' Mug Woman turns and looks in the camera's direction. 'Are you *filming* me ... ?'

'No ...' a man's voice mumbles to reassure her/lie as the camera pans away to a row of grey plastic chairs occupied by a courier, motorbike helmet dutifully in hand, a few Brownie Guides giggling nervously, accompanied by a matronly looking woman, and a couple of beardy types clutching postcards. Two more women enter through a revolving door, shaking off umbrellas. One is clutching a Boots Meal Deal bag but both fall silent when they see who's there – and the camera trains back on to Mug Woman's face.

It's not ... is it? I wonder ...

Something about the overly teased blonde hair and Mug Woman's mannerisms ring a bell. I know I should stop watching. I want to. Really. At least, the good part of me does (essentially: Kylie). But I find I can't.

I can't stop watching. I have to see how this ends ... I have to see if this is who I think it is ...

'Well, would you look who it is!' The protagonist in the video greets the woman with the Boots Meal Deal, who blushes vermilion and appears flustered. Mug Woman takes another swig of something then leans against a wall next to a rack of what looks like leaflets and postcards. I make out tiny head-shots, pictures of men and a few women, grinning inanely. Unfortunately, Mug Woman overestimates the gap between herself and the wall and shunts it hard, disrupting the rack and scattering its contents over the blue carpet-tiled floor.

Boots Meal Deal stoops to pick up the postcards.

'Oh, don't bother,' Mug Woman commands, pinning down a picture of a bearded man with her court shoe. '*Doug* deserves it!' She spots a few postcards still clinging to the rack and flicks them out, laughing maniacally as they cascade to the floor. 'And Nigel! And *Marcus*! And *you*, soon enough!' she tells Boots Meal Deal. 'I was like you once! When I started out, I was so young I looked like a scrubbed knee ... ! All those critics and men with fat backs gave me hell over the years, but I kept going! Even when high definition TV came in and every flaw was magnified and most of us looked like we were auditioning for the London Dungeons – and *of course* I don't make the cut on *The One Show* sofa any more – not like Giles *bloody* Brandreth on account of his having a *COCK*—'

The camera pans to take in the shocked faces of several Brownies, two of whom are now crying.

'But they get you in the end!' The white mug is now being waggled at the younger woman, sloshing clear liquid over its sides in the process. 'I had it all, once!' Mug Woman goes on. 'I mean,' she slurs slightly, 'I've played *Pictionary* with Robert Plant! I had coq au vin with Phil Collins! *That's* show business!' More liquid is spilled.

It IS her! It's ... Tricia!

I wonder what on earth I've stumbled upon – and whether this explains a lot about why the former *It's a Royal Knockout* sub-bencher is currently slumming it in deepest darkest Scandinavia, as the drama continues to unfold on the tiny screen in front of me.

'OK, let's all just, like, *chill out*—' Hoodie Man is starting to say, just as Mug Woman – sorry, *Tricia* – hurls the rest of her beverage down his trousers.

'*Chill?* You want me to "*chill*"? *Like*, just, "*chill, man*"?' Tricia is keeling to one side, doing what I can only assume is intended as an impersonation of youth. 'Well, you can, *like*, PISS OFF!'

'This is outrageous!' Brown Owl is harrumphing as the camera swings around. 'Excuse me, can you call someone please?' she asks a receptionist with too-long turquoise talons who executes a theatrical eye roll before picking up the phone and dialling, slowly.

'You have to admit, the show hasn't been going brilliantly lately—' Hoodie Man continues, bravely, ignoring his now-soaked crotch.

'So what if I was on the radio eating cashews? I like cashews!'

'It's not about the cashews, Tricia ...' Hoodie Man counters.

'Oh, OK, so I had ONE big night!' she screeches in response. '*Two*, max! So I forgot "the news" a couple of times ...' She mimes bunny ears around these words as though she's not entirely sure she believes in the concept. 'James Naughtie dropped the C-bomb on the *Today* show and he got away with it! Tony Blackburn played Chicago's 'If You Leave Me Now' on loop and he didn't get this sort of abuse!'

'I think he did, actually,' another voice sounds out from off-screen.

'Shut up, patriarchy!' Tricia retaliates.

'That was Sheila ...' Boots Meal Deal hisses.

'Oh, sorry Sheila. Hope the thyroid works itself out ...'

'Karen from HR is on her way,' the bored, blue-talonned receptionist drones.

'Karen from HR is a snide bitch who's wanted this from day one!' Tricia isn't stopping now. 'And you all know she used to *shag* Doug too, right?' The motorcycle courier to the far left shakes his head to indicate that this is news to him.

'OK, OK – let's not have a meltdown in the studio,' Hoodie Man goes on.

'You think THIS is a meltdown?' There are some murmurs of agreement, so Tricia throws her head back and laughs a large 'Ha!' in a way I've seen before. 'You haven't LIVED! This is nothing! I'm not telling everyone I've got "Tiger Blood"! I haven't thrown a phone at anyone! I'm not shaving my head or smuggling a pet monkey into Germany, damn it ... I'M NOT TWERKING!'

Only then, it appears, she is. Attempting to, anyway.

'Is this what you want? You want me to twerk for you? Do a special dance so I'm like the YOUNG presenters? Start a Snapchat account? Take up an extreme sport? I'll show you extreme sport ...'

A woman with a stiff perm who I can only assume is Karen from HR can be seen marching into reception. She pushes round-rimmed spectacles up the bridge of her nose with an index finger to indicate that she means business and smooths down her blouse for battle, just as Tricia disappears into a glass-fronted cubicle, emerging with a couple of ancient reel-to-reel audio tapes.

'That's enough, Patricia,' Karen from HR says, trying to quell the commotion.

'*Is it* Karen? Is it enough? Don't you want to see just how young my "vibe" can be?' Tricia replies, eyes blazing. She drops the mug, takes a reel in her right hand, draws her arm back and hurls the disc against the wall, thin brown film trailing behind like jellyfish fronds in its wake. 'See, ultimate Frisbee!' She flings the other one at the far wall, narrowly missing a Brownie. 'How d'you like them apples!"

'Do something!' Karen from HR is shouting at a large man in lapels who has ambled into view. He adjusts his bulk, takes a long time to fish synthetic-looking trousers out from around his testicles, then takes Tricia by the arm and escorts her towards the revolving door.

'Get your hands off me!' She struggles, thrashing limbs and losing a court shoe in the process.

'Leave it, love. He's not worth it!' One of the bearded autograph hunters calls out, lending her moral support.

'Yeah – you got more class than all of 'em, Tricia,' offers another.

'Thanks, chaps,' she says to them before turning back to her adversaries. 'See? See? I've still got *FANS*! You better get ready to lawyer up!' Tricia is now yelling.

'You what?' the security guard grunts in response.

'It means "get a solicitor" in American!' she yells, before being bundled out of the building. 'This isn't over! I've got friends in high places! Did I mention I know Phil Collins? PHIL *"THE FAX MACHINE"* COLLINS! *That's show business!*' is her final retort before the screen goes blank – and yet, somehow, I can still *hear* her.

'What the hell?' the voice continues to sound out. I stare, hard at the screen, turning up the volume and pressing a few buttons, wondering what's happened.

The video reappears and starts again, from the beginning: '*Why do I* bother? *Why* do *I bother?*'

'Alice? What are you doing?' It's the same voice but it's not coming from my phone any more.

I glance up, startled. And that's when I see her. Her bare feet on soft pine floors announced no arrival, and I've been so absorbed that I've been totally oblivious to my surroundings. And the fact that I should never have been watching this in the first place. And the fact that the video's star is standing in front of me.

'Tricia! Hi!' I try to sound bright and shove my phone behind my back at the arrival of the real-life version. But pressing buttons willy-nilly doesn't turn out to be the *best* idea I've ever had.

'I'M SURROUNDED BY PEOPLE WHO HAVEN'T SEEN A HAIRBRUSH IN YEARS!'

'Oh shit, oh shit, oh shit ...' I fumble to retrieve my phone, realising all I've *actually* done is turn the volume up.

'Is that ...' Tricia frowns. Or rather, tries to.

'WHO WEREN'T EVEN BORN WHEN I DID MY FIRST CELEBRITY TELETHON,' the voice on the video continues as I experience a hot wave of shame.

'Where did you find that?' Tricia demands, lunging towards me. There is a short, inexpert scrap, as virtual Tricia belts out something about 'embryos' and real-life Tricia tries to wrestle the phone from me.

'I'VE DONE CELEBRITY SHARK BAIT!' video-Tricia begins to yowl now.

'I'm sorry,' I start, 'I never meant to—'

'Give me that!' Tricia tears the phone out of my hand and stares at it in horror just as I hear. *'THAT'S SHOW BUSINESS!'*

'I had no idea it was you, well, until—'

'YOU GOT MORE CLASS THAN ALL OF 'EM, TRICIA—'

Real-life Tricia looks up at me now, her face a mask of horror.

'Well,' I go on. 'Until then, really. I mean, I thought there were similarities before but, you know.' I'm rambling now, embarrassment clawing at my face.

'I knew the footage was out there but I had no idea it was this bad,' Tricia says quietly now, looking pale. 'Or that people would be searching for it.' She looks at me, and I feel as though

I'm in the headmaster's office apologising for some misdemeanour or other (usually committed by Melissa). 'Well, I'm sure you've had a good laugh at my expense,' she says, her voice quivering with emotion. 'Welcome to my meltdown.'

'I'm so sorry,' I mumble, again.

'It says here—' she points at the screen, doubtless now emblazoned with other bikini-clad lovelies '—*"that's show business"* is now a top trending term on Twitter—'

'But these things change so quickly,' I try, on my feet now to prise the phone out of her hands.

'And the comments!' She gasps, one hand rushing to her mouth as the other scrolls down.

Never scroll down! Even I know not to read below the line!

'"*Man, that chick sure is hammered!*"' Tricia reads out a few of the more astute observations. 'And then this one says. "*Doug clearly dumped her.*" Well, yes, Poirot, well done – oh. "*Forget Doug – id do you hotass.*" Well, the spelling leaves a lot to be desired but still ...' She drifts off slightly before returning to focus on the current situation with a vengeance. 'You shouldn't have been looking!'

'I'm so sorry. I know, I should never have switched the thing on, let alone clicked—'

'You and the rest of the world – it says it's been watched three hundred and fifty THOUSAND times ...'

'Has it? Well, I wouldn't worry about it. Most people probably turned it off halfway through—'

'Like you did, you mean?'

'Errr ... no.' I have nothing left with which to defend myself.

'I thought you were my friend,' she says in a small voice.

'I am your friend!' I protest.

'That's not what friends do.'

'No.'

'Well, thanks a lot for making the total viewing figures for my public humiliation thirty-five thousand and one,' Tricia says. 'Melissa warned me you were a snooper—'

'I'm not a snooper!' I attempt to defend myself.

'Oh no? You never read her diaries?' I say nothing. 'And out of the whole of the Internet, you just happened to stumble across a video, of me?'

'Ye-es,' I realise this doesn't look good.

'Your sister's right, you are your own worst enemy.' She passes the phone back to me and walks out. Approximately thirty seconds later, I hear gasps from the kitchen as my faux pas (can I pass it off as this? I wonder) is presumably revealed. If Melissa wasn't speaking to me before, I've got a fair idea things are going to get a whole lot worse.

Ten

'I *told* them,' Tricia's voice sounds out, spluttering between sobs. 'I said to them, I said, "*You'd* drink gin in a mug at noon, too, if you had to present phone-ins on 'the best motorway service stations in Britain' or 'funniest pet names'." I should have gone for vodka – wouldn't have smelled of anything. That's how the rumours got started.' I hear a loud nose blow and murmurs of consolation. 'It was inevitable, really,' Tricia goes on. 'A miracle I didn't hit the wall sooner. I'm just livid that someone captured the whole bloody gin-cident on camera. And that people watched it. And shared it ... *Bastards* ...'

I loiter in the doorway, feeling the temperature in the room drop from 'chilly' to 'Siberia' as soon as they notice me.

'I said I was sorry,' I try, feebly. But the look Melissa gives me is like nothing I've ever encountered before.

It's as though she hates me. As though she's given up on me ...

I wonder whether that's what my 'looks' are like. I pull my sleeves down over my hands before wrapping them around my body for protection. Or a makeshift straightjacket. *Either would probably help*, I reason.

'What happened to Viking trust?' Melissa almost spits the words. 'What were you even doing with a mobile anyway? Couldn't stay away from one of your *devices* for even a week ...' She shakes her head and I lower mine in shame.

Chairs scrape away from me, eyes are angled to the ceiling or the floor, and conversation is stilted as we sit down for dinner.

'I trust that you'll return your phone to its proper place,' Inge says, emphasising the word 'trust' and looking at me pointedly after what feels like an eternity of silence. I nod ever so slightly but don't make eye-contact.

Chunks of potato lodge in my throat when I try to swallow, doing battle with the lump that has taken up residence there. So I knock back as much wine as my gullet can handle to numb the pain and after a subdued supper, I take to my bed. Again. But I don't put the phone back. *You're all I've got left*, I think, as I stare at pictures of Charlotte and Thomas and wish I were with them now. I send a single text message – one I should have sent weeks ago – then do my very best to forget all about it and turn the device off to conserve battery life.

When I hear the sounds of teeth brushing and the bedroom door open and close to indicate that the others are coming to bed, I pretend I'm already asleep – unable to face another showdown tonight. Instead I bury my head into my pillow and do some silent crying – only this time, there's no one to slip a hand into mine.

By morning, Melissa's bunk is empty once again and Tricia is distant, despite further apologies. She also looks a little worse for wear and I'm wondering how much more alcohol was consumed after I left the rest of the party last night. I cook my own egg and even Margot can only bring herself to give me the briefest of awkward smiles.

Inge isn't to be trifled with, either, having been kept awake much of the previous twelve hours, she tells us, by a teething Freja, a partially potty-trained Villum staging a dirty-protest at 3am, and a 'still moaning' Magnus. 'Even Vikings have bad nights,' is how Inge sums up what sounds like a stint of parenting hell. Then Mette fetches her mother coffee (*must teach Charlotte how to use our machine ...*) and her mood improves somewhat. But I wonder whether Inge's regretting the decision to keep the retreat going with only our eclectic cast of characters for company.

'OK, let's do this,' she says, draining her cup and indicating to her eldest that a refill would not be unwelcome. Mette obliges. 'Today is all about where you're going and how to get there,' Inge continues between gulps of jet-black battery fuel. 'So eat well, drink up, and get ready to concentrate: because this shit matters.' Margot flinches at the expletive and Tricia fixes the floor with a steely glare. 'Right then, where's Melissa?' Inge addresses me.

I shrug then reprimand myself. *Very mature, Alice.*

'Well, if she's not here soon, she'll have to find us,' says Inge.

'She'll have to *navigate* her way!' Margot looks pleased with her pun.

I roll my eyes, then realise I haven't got many allies left. *I'd better play nice*, I think. So I give a half-hearted nasal exhalation in lieu of laughter.

It's a later start than usual, but Melissa arrives just as we're preparing to leave, cheeks flushed and her T-shirt on inside out, the label showing (Fruit of the Loom's finest).

On seeing her confidante, Tricia crams a final triangle of toast in her mouth and shoves an arm in her cardigan. She pushes her chair back and hurries towards Melissa, grinning and linking an arm through hers as the pair head outside, whispering.

'It hurts, doesn't it?' Inge speaks sotto voce.

'Yes,' I whisper, before I can think or calibrate my face into an expression that conveys 'nonchalance'.

'Sometimes—' she starts.

'Yes?' I'm hoping she's going to dispense some sage advice or offer me a modicum of comforting consolation. But this, apparently, isn't how Vikings roll.

'Life's a bit shit,' she finishes her coffee with a large swill. 'You just need to get on with things.'

'Right. Thanks. Great.'

Or, I could just slam my head against this oak table, I muse, fingering the woody knots. *Knock myself out, and make this particular 'shit' be over.* That's right, I may finally be losing my four-bags-for-life marbles. Here, in a Scandi-style bungalow, somewhere in rural Denmark, surrounded by overachievers, an estranged sibling, and a sunbed-addict who drinks gin from a mug at noon.

'Come on, let's get you navigating.' Inge stands and gives me a 'pat' on the arm, so hearty it nearly dislocates my shoulder.

Jesus, has she been taking lessons from Melissa? Must. Get. Stronger.

'It's a new day and this is a new skill for everyone, so it's a level playing field. None of you sail or row normally, do you?' Inge asks, loading her bowl and spoon into the dishwasher. Margot looks shifty. '*Do* you?'

'It's just that, I ran a sailing camp one summer,' Margot starts, 'and Dad owns a boat. And I rowed at school ...' she tails off.

Inge takes a deep breath. 'Well, for the rest of us, then, it's about tuning in to our senses—'

'Oh, we didn't do *that* ...' Margot says.

'Right ...'

'We read a lot of books. Did coursework, plotted routes, drew maps—'

'Yeah, we're not going to need maps.'

'We're not?' Margot looks anxious.

'No,' Inge says firmly. She holds open the door and ushers a now unsettled Margot out and into the fresh air. 'Shall we?'

Magnus has now apparently been deemed well enough to take responsibility for his offspring and I notice that Inge moves differently when unencumbered by a child on each limb, or by having to push a tank-pram across scrubland. She strides, purposefully, but there's a lightness about her, too – like a natural athlete. I hasten my pace so as not to fall behind. We catch up with Melissa and Tricia as they near the coast and Inge explains what's in store.

'Viking navigation is a bodily thing,' she says, 'based on feelings and intuition.' Margot and I are none the wiser, so Inge elaborates. 'It's like when you craft or work with wood or metal – you can't read books about it then go and do it properly – you just need to *do it*. Well, it's the same with navigation: you have to feel the sensations. I feel it here—' she wriggles her fingers '—and also feel it here.' She points to her toes.

I can't help smiling at this and notice that Melissa is also sniggering. I catch her eye and, for a moment, I wonder whether a *Wet Wet Wet*-shaped rope bridge can be thrown across the chasm that has opened up between us.

'What's so funny?' demands Inge.

'Nothing.' Melissa shakes her head.

'Why are you laughing?'

'It's nothing. Sorry, that was just a lot like the song ...'

'What song?'

'It doesn't matter,' I join in, still smiling.

Are we ... bonding? Over a Marti Pellow pop classic? I'm hopeful, but Melissa has already moved on.

'So, if it's instinctive,' my sister asks, composing herself, 'does that mean you never get lost?'

'Never,' Inge says with complete certainty. I look at her in awe. *I haven't sounded that certain ... well ... ever.* 'I know my way, she goes on, 'and if I'm ever in doubt, I just let go of my head and remember to be in my body instead.'

I let this sink in.

It takes a while.

The rest of the walk, in fact.

We arrive at the sea and stand in silence for a few moments contemplating the empty beach in front of us.

'So, what now?' Margot asks, taking the opportunity to do a few squats.

'Now, we are *still*,' Inge replies.

'Don't we need to fetch anything?' Margot is gesturing at the hut further up the coast, prone, like a tightly coiled spring, ready and willing to run errands. 'Any equipment?' she asks.

Inge says nothing but points, very slowly, to her eyes. Then, she points to her ears. Before finally, holding out her hands.

Margot looks disappointed. 'No compass?'

Inge shakes her head.

'GPS Plotters?' Margot goes on, hopefully, only to be met with another headshake. 'Dividers?' she tries again. 'Cinometers?' Her voice becomes more desperate with each disregarded crutch. '*Chinagraphic Pencils?*' Finally, she half gasps, 'a whistle?', before slumping, spent. 'No ... *stuff?* At all?'

'No stuff,' Inge confirms. 'People today use all this equipment to get around – like cell phones and Google maps.'

I feel my smartphone burning in my pocket at this. *No one else was talking to me,* I mentally run through my defence: *It was the only company I had, your honour ... my surrogate friend. So what if I spent the night 'liking' old classmate's holiday snaps/kids/lives?*

'Vikings, however, are aware of their surroundings. They know how to read the waves – they can think "are the waves still at the same angle to the boat as they were an hour ago?", or "Is the wind blowing in the same direction?" When you're near the shore, you can look at the water and judge how flat or choppy it is to work out how shallow the sea is. Then, of course, there are swans ...'

'*Swans?*' I wonder whether I've misheard.

'Yes, I often navigate by swan,' says Inge. Four blank faces stare back at her. She sighs, as if tired of dealing with half-wits, then relents and enlightens us. 'So swan necks are around forty centimetres long—'

Melissa looks impressed. 'Good fact!'

'And many boats extend to forty centimetres below the water,' Inge continues. 'So if there are swans around and they've got their arses in the air, you know the water's deep enough for a boat. If the body is visible and the swans are just poking their heads under to fish, it means it's too shallow and your boat will get grounded. Other birds can help out, too – most fly towards land for sunset and you can always pack a raven to be on the safe side.' She throws this out there casually, as if she'd just mentioned she was going to pack snacks for a long journey. 'Ravens fly really high and they don't like being out at sea, so if you set one free from a boat, it'll fly up and up until it can see land. Then it will head straight for it and you can basically follow. If it can't see land, it'll come back again to the boat.'

'And then?' I ask.

'Then you're fucked,' she says, simply.

Ahh, the relaxed Scandinavian approach to swearing, I think, as Margot stiffens at the profanity.

'You can use clouds, too,' Inge goes on. 'Look up.' We all turn our faces skywards. 'What do you see?' We remain silent. 'I know: "*clouds*",' she answers for us. 'But keep trying.'

'OK ... umm ...' Tricia squints upwards as Melissa holds a hand over her eyes and arches her back, legs askance.

'Well, that one looks a bit like a dragon,' is the best she can come up with.

My sister: always with the dragons ...

Finally, Inge takes pity on us. 'You're looking for volume. There are always more clouds over land than there are at sea.'

'Ah! Yes.' Melissa nods as though she knew this all along.

'It's also good to look up and get some perspective,' she goes on. 'Look at nature and feel insignificant.'

I don't know how to tell her that I already feel insignificant in numerous different environments – outdoors, at work; even in my own home ...

'You need to listen, too,' adds Inge. 'You can *hear* land. In Viking times you could make out a blacksmith very far out to sea, or even a dog, barking. And then there are smells – usually bonfires and excrement.'

Lovely ...

'Navigating is about tuning in to all your senses. You're waiting for that meditative feeling,' Inge explains. 'Try it!'

So I try.

Nothing.

I look around. Melissa, Tricia and Margot look similarly lost, and so eventually Inge concedes. 'OK, well let's get you in the water. Maybe you'll get the hang of it that way.'

The rest of the morning is spent readying the boat for another voyage then breaking for a simple meal of bread and cheese. The stonewalling continues past lunchtime, when Inge splits us into pairs. Since Melissa and Tricia now appear fused at the hip, I get Margot. Again. And we're first up.

Margot and Inge bear the brunt of heaving our Viking vessel into the water while I trot behind, pushing the *pointy-bit-at-the-end-that-I-still-can't-remember-the-name-of*.

Once we're in and bobbing along nicely, I concentrate on overcoming the initial panic of not having dry land under my feet and remind myself how much I enjoyed the plain, simple 'rowing' part yesterday. And soon, I feel *o-kay*.

Once we're clear of the shore and the water gets choppier, Inge unties the knot that binds the ream of white fabric to our mast and with a swift, violent unravelling, the sail lashes outwards. It whips and cracks as it fills with air and we lurch forward. My heart starts to pound and the cool breeze now blasting my face makes me feel alive. So much so that, for a smudge of time, I forget that I'm *me*. Which is nice.

Inge pauses, tasting the air, then addresses Margot. 'I don't know what you've been taught elsewhere, but I always say, you need to sail by your butt.'

'Sorry?' Margot looks concerned.

'There's a feeling in my butt when I'm not on the right course,' Inge goes on, half-shouting now to be heard above the racket. 'It's about sensing with your body whether the boat is balanced or whether there's too much weight in the front or on one side. You can use your head, too, of course, but it's not about thinking. It's about moving a little until you can feel the wind blowing evenly on both of your ears. Vikings never relied on just one thing to find their way – you need a constant awareness of the world around you.'

Still feeling a little silly, I adjust my head until I can sense the wind whipping around each ear. I notice that the waves are coming right at us, threatening to engulf our vessel, just before Inge signals to the rudder and shifts the sail so that we turn, changing course ('This is tacking,' Margot tells me with authority).

The boat travels fast, cutting through the water effortlessly. Minutes (hours? Days?) pass as we soar like a rocket, repeating the manoeuvre several times before executing what I'm reliably informed is a 'jibe' and heading back to land.

'How was that for you?' Inge asks finally.

'Actually ... OK!' I manage. 'Thank you.'

'Really?' she says, hinting at something I don't seem to understand.

Are we still talking about boats, here? Or am I being psychologist-ed?

She moves closer so that she can speak without Margot hearing. 'There isn't a "safe" way to do any of this, you know – you just have to do it.'

I AM being psychologist-ed!

'Do you know what the matter is with you?' Inge goes on.

This isn't what psychologists are supposed to do, is it? It's not what that woman did in The Sopranos ...

'Isn't it up to me to "find out"?' I ask her.

'Normally?' she says. 'Yes. But it's your last day tomorrow and you don't seem to be getting it. Plus you're probably thinking of American psychoanalysts like you see on TV. We prefer to tell it like it is in Scandinavia.'

You don't say ...

'So you're being "cruel to be kind"?'

'I prefer, being "honest to be honest",' she says.

You may well prefer that, but it's not a phrase, I want to respond. But don't. Because I'm all at sea – literally – with a Viking psychologist and a model-esque overachiever (or two).

'You've got anger issues,' Inge tells me now.

WTF? 'Me?' I splutter in disbelief. *Cool and calm Robo-Alice?* 'I never lose it!' *Well, apart from the other night ... but in general ...* 'I pride myself on keeping a lid on it—' I say in my defence.

'That's the worst kind,' Inge tells me now. '*Suppressed* anger. It has to go somewhere so it turns inwards.'

What, so I can't even fume inwardly now?

'You can't deny your feelings: you have to face them. Same with the past. It's done; it's happened. But you have to make peace with it before you can move on. I come from a strong seafaring tradition—' she goes on, as I begin to wish that I too had gin in a mug to look forward to.

Oh god, more boat metaphors ...

'And there has long been a tension in the Viking tempera-ment between staying and leaving – yearning for something better that might come along and grief for what we leave behind.' She looks in the direction of Melissa and I see my sister and Tricia sprawled out across each other on the shore, basking in the sun and laughing like drains. 'Many things are out of your control – like the weather, the water, other boats,' she goes on, 'so we need to learn to be still and observe when something's going wrong.'

'*Be still when something's wrong*', *did she say*? I try to take this in, a concept that's met with a small software malfunc-tion: *Surely when 'something's wrong', you just keep busy and try to forget about it?* More work, more stuff – more of *something*, at least – until the sensation has passed. Or been numbed. Or you're so frazzled that you no longer notice the initial stressor. *Isn't that the way to deal with niggling sensations that 'something's wrong'?*

'You need to be open to the signs and learn how to read them,' Inge counsels.

Or, I think, *you can ignore them*!

This has been my modus operandi for as long as I can remember and it's served me, if not 'well', then certainly 'adequately'. Hasn't it?

An eye twitch? Ignore it! Stress knot in your stomach? Take no notice and try chewing sugar-free gum! Carpel tunnel syndrome? Give your wrist a shake and get on with things! Tension headache? Localised alopecia? Nervous breakdown at a dentistry conference at a Premier Inn in the Midlands? Bury it! Deep down! Then run away on a Viking retreat with your sister and try to forget about it! Easy, right? Oh ... Oh wait ...

It's here that I realise my time-honoured coping mechanism has stalled.

Inge moves away to help Margot 'reef in' the sail (*look at me! Learning all the lingo!*) and prepares to take us back to dry land. I watch her calm, dextrous hands doing complicated things with ropes, all the while instructing her pupil on what to do next. *I wish she could tell me what to do*, I think, *always*. But I don't know how to ask. And I have a feeling she'd say 'no' – that, maybe, just maybe, she's got enough on her plate already, what with a retreat, a PhD, three children and a Magnus in tow. The woman must be five years – *a decade, even?* – younger than me, but I can't help wishing that, no matter how much I worshipped my own, Inge had been my mother. *I'd have got the genes for that ass for one thing ...*

As the water becomes shallower and turns a startling turquoise, Margot rolls her trousers up, ready to leap out and drag us onto the sand. Before I disembark to do the same, Inge places a hand on mine and instructs me, in a low voice to, 'Take a walk. Have a think about what you want. Then come back and make your peace.'

So I do as I'm told. As a still-giggling Melissa and Tricia board the boat for their turn at sea, I set off as prescribed, trudging up the hill until I come to a leafy glade. I have no idea where I am, but from my elevated position I can at least see smoke rising from the chimneystack of the house. *So I can't get too lost*, I reason – even with my negligible navigation skills ...

I sit on a rock and watch the boat making its way out to sea, holding my breath for the moment the sail is unleashed and the vessel jolts into a life of its own.

'Beautiful ...' I murmur. 'Just ... beautiful ...'

Baaa! Another sound disturbs the peace.

'What the?'

Baaaaaa! The ensuing vibrations tremble through the air around me, interrupting my trance. There's a shuffling in the bushes, and a pair of black, beady eyes glint amidst the foliage. A few flies start buzzing and a beast shuffles forward – a large, woolly body perched atop bony legs.

You! I think. Or, more accurately: *ewe*.

The creature studies me, unblinking, with eyes that have clearly seen *a lot* in their time. So I stare back. Braver, now, having bested it during my previous encounter.

How long ago that seems ...

My sheep-nemesis lowers her neck and pulls off great mouthfuls of grass, breathing hard through her nose. She chews the cud, mechanically – her mouth arching and stretching into speech-like movements. As though if I could lip-read 'sheep', she might be trying to tell me something ...

I pay attention. Just in case. But nothing happens.

I wait some more.

Come on, sheep! I try telepathy: *Are you attempting to warn me that I'll be wrestling you this time tomorrow during our berserking session? Because if so, I could probably do with a trial run ...* I'm still not clear on exactly what the activity entails, so I'm keen to be prepared for anything. *Or have I eaten something funny and this is all part of some long-game shamanistic ritual? I can handle that: see* Lord of the Flies. *Is this the part where you or one of your livestock friends tells me I can 'never escape myself' or something – and then I get all flustered and faint? At least, that's what that boy did ... Simon, wasn't it?* I congratulate myself on remembering. Then I get riled. *Bloody Simon: typical male! You wouldn't catch a woman losing it in the middle of the jungle just because she was overtired and there was some offal on show. I've got too much on to go around fainting all over the place.*

A gnat lands just above my left wrist and I smack it flat with my right hand, impressed and alarmed in equal measure by my own accuracy and the tangle of fly-guts now adorning my forearm. I take three deep breaths, trying to quell the queasiness. Then I shift my position on the hard rock, my body stiff from a week of unfamiliar exercise, and realise that if the sheep's not going to play ball, I'm going to have to handle this myself. Without wine. Or Kylie. Or any of my usual crutches. *Cheers, world ...*

OK, I start, thinking about Inge's assignment: *so what do I want?*

Me #1 waits for a response but then remembers that this too is going to have to come from . . err ... *me.*

'Oh, bloody hell, it's exhausting .. ' I whimper as the sheep *baa*-s at me to get the flock on with it.

Come on, Alice, think about it: what do you want?

Me #2: I don't know, OK? Stop hassling me!

Me #1: You're not getting out of it that easily! WHY don't you know?

Me #2: *shrugs like a petulant teenager/Thomas, aged five* *I've never thought about it …*

Me #1: What are you, an idiot?

Me #2: Why do you have to be so mean all the time?

Me #1: I'm not mean! I'm … efficient …

Me #2: Is THAT what you call it?!

Me #3: *enters stage left, making a time-out sign with her hands and attempting to mediate* *Whoa there! This isn't helping anyone—*

Me #1: Yeah, but she can be a fucking tool sometimes.

Me #3: I know she can. Jeeze, do I know … *executes eye roll* *But we have to help her.*

Me #1: I can HEAR you both, you know?

Me #2 and #3: *mumbles* *sorry.*

Me #1: This isn't working for me; you're both fired.

Me #2 and #3: You can't fire us!

Me #1: Watch me.

I pinch myself on the fleshy part of my hand to bring myself around, lest I disappear into swooning-Simon territory. *Woman-up*, I tell myself. *And think.*

I don't know where I'm going.

I'm not sure I've ever known.

But do I know what I want?

Actually, yes.

I want a relationship with my sister. I want my kids to be happy and healthy. And Greg … ? Nothing. I feel *nothing*. If pushed, I could probably summon mild irritation as a requisite emotion here. But, at the same time, I'm aware that I can't really blame him for things falling apart lately. I chose all this. And, deep down, haven't I always known what I was getting into?

For a while, I enjoyed being the serious, more successful half of the couple. The one who had it all together. But then it stopped being so funny any more. Especially once the kids were born. Greg wasn't the antidote to my life up until the point I married him; he was a continuation of it. It's like when we got the bathroom done and then I looked around and realised the problem wasn't really the bathroom after all.

The only reason I am with Greg is because of Charlotte and Thomas, I can now admit, *but perhaps they really would be better off having two parents who love them and live apart, rather than a mum and dad simmering with resentment under the same roof?* That part, it seems now, is relatively simple.

What's trickier is Melissa.

I had thought that I wanted to come away to escape Greg and my life back home. But what if what I actually needed was time with my sister?

These are unchartered waters and I'm not entirely sure how to cross them (and by 'entirely' I mean 'at all'). I watch the sun complete its arc across the sky and begin to make its descent as I try to untangle this particular dilemma.

She brought me here, I think, *this was something she wanted. So perhaps the least I can do is make it up to her and play nicely. Throw myself into it, setting aside my usual reluctance and considering the next forty-eight hours a sort of . . . Viking holiday. From a lifetime of scepticism.*

The task feels Herculean. But I have to try. I stand up and plant my feet firmly, stretching my eyes to the sun.

'I want to be more Viking, in all its facets,' I say out loud now, with as much gravity as a woman with only sheep for company can muster. 'Starting now. Or at least in a second . . .'

I draw out the rectangular, metal object that has been warmed by my body and run my fingers over its smooth surface in an attempt to memorise its every seductive curve.

This has to go back, I know now. But there's one thing I need to check first.

I take a deep breath and power it up before waiting – hoping – for a vibration. After a few breathless moments, it comes. It's been waiting for me: the answer to the question I put off asking for weeks. And the message reads:

'No such luck ;)'

I exhale with relief, telling the sheep. 'I didn't do it!'

Baaa! she responds, by way of congratulations.

'I didn't sleep with Mr Teeth!'

Baaa?

A second message buzzes through and I read.

Oh FFS ...

'OK, so it got a bit *handsy*,' I confess to the ewe. 'What does "second base" even mean anyway?'

Baaa.

'Really? God ... Well, the point is, there definitely wasn't "full-blown"—'

Baaa!

'I know, I know, it shouldn't have happened at all. I should never have got myself in a position where it *could* have happened. I'm an idiot. But still. Phew ...'

Baaa.

'Thanks. You too.'

At this, I power down. *Goodbye, smartphone,* I whisper. *You're going back where you came from. Just for a while ...*

I look out at the soul-lifting sweep of blue ahead and see the boat, white sail taut, approaching the shore.

If I'm quick, I could make it to the house, return the phone and get back, before anyone notices. I estimate this by taking into account how long it took us to walk to the beach, how far the tiny smoke stack appears to be away from my current position, and dividing it by two. *Because,* I reason, *I will be powered by both renewed determination and adrenaline, the hormone secreted by the adrenal medulla in response to stress that increases heart rate, pulse rate, and blood pressure, and raises the blood levels of glucose and lipids, all of which can improve performance ...*

Then I realise that I'm wasting precious time and so get going. Thanking the sheep for her counsel, I sprint downhill towards the house making this sort of a sound:

'FUUUUUUCK!'

Just so you know, running, barefoot, on unfamiliar scrubland that's been booby-trapped with razor-sharp flint is quite *extremely* painful.

But I don't stop. Because now, I'm a woman on a mission. And my plan is thus: *put the phone back; apologise to Melissa, get back to the rest of the gang before sunset, live happily ever after.* I repeat the mantra – partially to distract from the throbbing pain now coursing through my right foot and partly to stay motivated.

If I'm quick, no one will notice. If I'm quick, Inge will just think I'm doing more soul-searching on a hill. If I'm quick, I reason, trying to ignore the slicing sensation creeping up my ankle, *there might be an opportunity to have a hunt around for some paracetamol. And perhaps a plaster. And maybe, even, shoes ahead of the 'berserking'* ...[26]

Limping now – my right foot a boot of pure agony, caked-on blood, and mud – I make it to the house. I use a tea towel as a makeshift sock to prevent further bleeding on the pine

---

[26.] Listen: no judging ... baby Viking steps. You can't part a woman from her smartphone AND tell her she'll never see shoes again (at least for a day and a half) all in the same half-hour timeframe ...

wood floor, holding it in place with an elasticated hair band. It's a little tight, but I rationalise that compression can only be a good thing, since I'm unlikely to have the chance for much elevation or ice for a while (Day #1 of basic first aid: ICE. Ice, compression, elevation – this stuff saves lives ...). Tea towel sock in place, I limp along the hall and deposit my phone in the wicker basket, still left on show by our trusting hosts.

As soon as it's out of my hands, I feel free somehow. And slightly smug that I have, finally, Done The Right Thing.

I'm a good person! I knew I was!

I'm just heading back out again, when I hear Magnus and the children coming in from outside.

I don't want to have to explain what I've been doing and I can't leave out of the front door unnoticed now. *I'll have to wait,* I rationalise, *until one of them goes for a wee or something.* I slip into the utility room that the chicks and the chainsaws also call home as well as *drumroll* the shoes ...

I look around with delight at an array of children's footwear along with some stylish ankle boots that I presume belong to Inge and a jumble of trainers. Including ... *mine!* I rush to them, trying not to inhale as I manoeuvre Melissa's stinky plimsolls out of the way and take up my own still-remarkably-white pair of Nike running shoes.

There you are!

It's an emotional reunion as I hold them close to my chest in a warm embrace.

If I put you somewhere safe, I mentally address my footwear, *and find a sock of some confection, I can wear you tomorrow! As long as the swelling's gone down ...*

It's not long before the scamper of small people can be heard. The fridge door goes, a lamb bleats and I deduce that refreshments are being enjoyed by all. Inevitably, after a few moments, there is whining – in a tone universally acknowledged as 'toddler needing a wee really quite urgently now' and I hear the party shuffle out down the corridor towards the bathroom.

Phew!

I press myself up close to the door in an attempt to open it without a 'click' until I'm eye-to-eye with the cubbyholes holding various flotsam and jetsam of family life. Several sets of keys, a block of Lego and a single mitten occupy the first couple of rectangles with two stacks of unopened mail below. The first holds franked, postmarked letters bearing wonderfully exotic monikers including Stine Storm and Lone Wolf (*They sound like Viking wrestlers!* I rejoice. Yes, I'm nosy – but with names like that, wouldn't you be?). The other administrative cubbyhole contains addressed envelopes yet to be stamped. I'm just admiring this as a system and wondering whether to implement something similar at home when I notice an envelope in the 'outgoing' pile bearing my own address.

Examining it more closely in the fading light, I recognise it as the letter I wrote to myself on the first day – the one intended to be read six months from now. *Should I read it now?* I prepare to cringe – to be mortified by my former self. *Can I even remember what's in it?* I think back almost fondly to those first few hours of 'Viking training' and how alien it all seemed. *I'd never even tried rye bread before! Or made a stretcher out of trees and a sex fleece! Or learnt to forage, or build boats, or navigate via my arse! And now I've done it all ... thanks to Melissa,* I realise, making a mental note to thank her. And apologise. Again. Properly this time.

I put the letter back, prepared to be patient – for the first time in my life – and wait.

It hasn't been too bad, I can appreciate now – *any of it. Even Margot may not be so terrible really. Even though she looks far too pretty post-exercise and is hideously privileged ...*

Despite having chastised Melissa for being overly impressed by posh people, something in me is fascinated by the seemingly rarefied life that Margot apparently leads.

I wonder what her parents do? I wonder where she lives?

Realising that there's a very simple way to sate my curiosity for the latter question, I pick up the sheaf of remaining letters and flick through, scanning the envelopes. Tricia lives near Brighton, I see, although this, I think, we knew ... And Margot? I clock a Kensington postcode (*Of course she lives in sodding Kensington!*). I'm just preparing to put the stack back when I do a double take.

Hang on ...

I set down two of the envelopes then rifle around in the cubbyhole in case there are any more lurking.

Nothing ... that's odd ...

I study the remaining pair: both have my name on them. But while one is in my hand, the other is a large, cursive scrawl I've secretly admired for the past thirty years: Melissa's.

The envelope is marked '*Alice Ray, c/o*' followed by my sister's address. At first, I presume that she misunderstood the exercise. *But then, why send it to her home address? Had she forgotten mine?*

I'm not proud of what happens next. And I think perhaps that Melissa and Tricia might be right. *Maybe I am a snooper ... Although the envelope is addressed to me. So, technically, it's mine. But then, so was the phone, and look at the trouble that landed me in ...*

A mere fifteen minutes after my vow to be more Viking and embrace the ethos and all its traits – you know, honesty, truth, not being a massive sneaking-around-snooper – I find myself prising open the envelope and unfurling the crisp white pages within. Hardly daring to breathe, I read.

'*Dear Alice ...*'

Eleven

Dear Alice,

The bad news is, if you're reading this, I'm not around any more. Either that, or I'm in such crap shape that they're making you clear up my stuff and walk the dogs. Alternatively, I've got so used to all the grapes and those cool hospital beds (the ones that let you sit up at the touch of a button), that I'm staging a sit in (or a 'lie-in'?). In any case: sorry.

I break off, turning over the sheet to check it's not a joke – some prank designed to further rile 'uptight Alice'. *What is she on about?* Finding no clue, on either side of the sheet of paper, I continue:

If it's option one, I hope the funeral was a blast and everyone ran up a really big bar bill. And that they played The Clash. And that Dad got hammered and Aunty Jill did a lot of tutting. Some things should never change. But some, I've realised, should.

I'm writing this to you after the first night in our very own Viking shelter. We're watching the sun rise from the beach and you're about five feet away from me, scowling, scrunching up your forehead and huffing loudly the way you do when you're concentrating (Did you know you did that? I bet your patients do ... !). I know I dragged you out of your comfort zone by kidnapping you and whisking you away to Nordic no-woman's-land, but it was

the only way I could think of to spend time with you. The real
you – the 'not knowing' you. I didn't want you to feel sorry for
me or put on that 'sympathy face' that I keep seeing in the people
I've told about the cancer so far—

I reach out a hand to steady myself against the wall as my
stomach twists.

What's happening here … ? Please tell me this is a horrible,
horrible joke …

    I didn't want to be another obligation in your life. You're always
telling me how many of these you have – and I believe you – so I
didn't want to burden you with any of it. You think I enjoy being
another thing on your 'to do' list? I don't. So I'm trying to do this
on my own. I'm trying to be more like you. I may tease you, but
all I've ever wanted is to have my big sister back and hang out
with her more. I miss you.

    I hoped that time with you – a holiday – before surgery, would
help bring us closer. They told me the lump shouldn't get any bigger
by waiting another week, so I wanted to live like normal for a
while.

    Sorry I didn't tell you sooner, but for what it's worth – in the
spirit of full disclosure and in case I never get the chance to say
it – I found a lump at Easter. It was like a pea, below the skin –
then my nipple started turning in slightly, as though it was shy
(and there's normally nothing shy about either of them!). I was
going to leave it – I had a lot on, and I thought 'What harm can
a pea do?' But then I thought WWAD? ('What Would Alice Do?')
So I went to get tested – yes, I braved a medical professional. Are
you proud of me?

    Apparently, I've got very dense breasts, the woman who did the
mammogram told me. I asked her if this was a good thing and she
said 'no' – just meant she had to squish them harder to get a proper

look (which really hurt, FYI). Anyway, to cut a long story short, there were needles, cups of sweet tea in waiting rooms, and then a consultant said lots of words I didn't understand. He offered to spell them for me but my head was too scrambled to tell him I wasn't hot on speling [sic], either. So I just said thank you and shook his hand. I'd gone in there with just my wallet and car keys. But I'd come out with 'cancer'.

The words become blurred at this point as the ink has blended with tears. Hers or mine, I can't tell.

I don't feel 'ill'. I feel great. But it means I'll have to have an operation when we get back and then chemo for three to six months. They've said I can expect hair loss, mouth sores, loss of appetite (we'll see . . .), nausea, bruising, serious tiredness, and the shits. Oh, and my periods will probably stop (like yours!)

I had no idea she knew about that ...

Best-case scenario is that you never get this letter, it all goes OK, and I'm on hormone therapy in six months' time. I'll just have disappeared for a while. It might all be fine. Or I might be diag-nosed with secondary cancer, which has spread to my bones, and when it's in your bones, you're basically buggered.

I'll try everything I can to make it go away – mastectomy, chemo, hormone therapy – but I'm drawing the line at veganism. Bollocks to that. Mum made herself miserable by the end and she didn't make it, did she? So what hope have I got?

I'll be honest; I'm not feeling great about my chances, Al—

This line sinks a hook into my heart. *She hasn't called me Al since we were kids*, I realise with a lump in my throat.

—and I'm scared. But scared's OK, right? You just have to do more of the 'coping'. You just have to keep going.

From what I've seen in the films, a letter like this is where I'm supposed to pass on some wisdom from beyond the grave – so don't laugh, because I'm giving it a go. First up: try to have a bit more fun. Leave Greg or don't leave Greg, but get happier. Somehow. It kills me (no pun intended) to see you like this. I know you don't want to live like I do – and that's fine – but I've always had the feeling you're not really living your way either. So maybe give 'fun' a go. You're always telling me about how you should be cutting out carbs/getting promoted/decluttering/deep cleaning something or other. But sod that. You're too hard on yourself – you always were. Live a little instead. None of us have any control over our future, really, but the one thing we can control is how we live now. I've learned that, just lately. And life's pretty brilliant – I'd like more of it. But generally I've lived to the full and I'm happier about the things I have done than I am worried about the things I haven't. I never wanted kids – I know you don't believe me, but it's true. And I'm happy.

I've never been much good at planning in advance – and now I don't want to tempt fate. So I'm trying to enjoy every 'new' thing I try. The other day I had sushi – and it was surprisingly good! I bet you'd like it.

People spend their whole lives thinking about what they haven't got, rather than how lucky they actually are. I have great friends, a nice life, I can get up every day and have a fried egg sandwich if I want (so could you). So I'm not doing too badly. I know what makes me feel good, and it's not being able to squeeze into tiny-doll-sized-child-clothes (see: Charlotte's Pants – the weird sequel to Charlotte's Web?!). It's walking the dogs and spending time with friends – and you, when you're not being a mardy cow. It's the small things that I might not be able to do for a while. Or ever again. Having a really small bottom or a really big house (why is it never the other way around? You'd save a fortune on furniture...) wouldn't change that.

Maybe it's easier for me to say this because I've had a kick up the arse to get to this point. Shit happens – but that's life. And I don't intend to waste a minute of it feeling sad. Neither should you.

I plan to haunt you daily so this isn't 'goodbye' – just a 'see-you-later'. But I wanted to say this now in case I'm crap at the whole bothering-you-from-beyond-the-grave thing (you can never tell how good ghosts are going to be at getting their message across, can you? Patrick Swayze: crystal clear after a bit of help from ~~Whoopy Whoopeee~~ Whoopi (?) Goldberg. But Scooby Doo ghosts with a white sheet over their head? Vague as hell ...).

I know you think I've always been a drama queen. 'Overly emotional'. So I'm trying, really trying to do this on my own. To hold it in – keep a lid on it and look after myself. To cope. Like you do. I'm only writing this so that hopefully you'll understand when/if it's all over, how much you mean to me. And how I hope I measure up as the kind of sister you wanted, in the end.

Love, always,

Melissa x

Shaking, now, I try to remember to breathe as I fling open the door, not caring who hears me, and bolt outside.

How to tell her I was wrong? That I've been wrong for years? That a lifetime of 'keeping a lid on it' and bottling up my emotions has created an unhappy – if not certifiably crazy – woman? Who talks to sheep?

I need to tell my sister that I want to be there for her. That I want to look after her. That I can't lose her and never want her to have to go through a single moment of pain without my help – if she still wants it – ever again.

I have to tell my sister that I'm sorry.

Twelve

Hair lifts from the back of my neck as I run, at furious speed – heart going like a strobe light. *Must get that seen to* ... I think. My foot is also throbbing, but this doesn't matter now. Dusk has come and gone and the darkness is settling in as I hear a fluttering, blundering sound. Something flaps, close to my head. *A bat? An owl? Bloody nature* .. I curse, but keep going.

I can just make out figures on the horizon and my chest leaps at the hope that Melissa will be there among them.

I'll get her on her own, then I'll apologise. I recite my plan over and over to match the rhythm of my run. But as I get closer, I see that none of the forms are Melissa-shaped. Instead, Inge and Margot round the hill, taking the scenic route home, with a blonde, Tricia-sized figure a little behind.

Melissa isn't there.

I hope she's all right, I think, torturing myself with the recollection of all the times I've let her down. The time she clung to my arms until they were sticky with sweat and tears because she didn't want me to move out, until in the end, I had to peel her off. The family Christmases after Mum died that I weaselled out of, preferring to spend the day with friends or boyfriends or – once – alone. Anything to avoid being home and facing what had happened. You never doubt your parents' immortality as a child. But I had to grow up, quickly, once

Mum was gone. Emotions, I decided, were dangerous. The only feelings I ever had were feelings of fear and sadness – a lot like nausea. So better not to feel anything at all. A peculiar sort of hardening happened inside me – a calcification – and that was that. I could never risk allowing myself to soften again, or let my defences down, because if I did, I might just drift away.

I didn't think of Melissa once, I recognise now, ashamed.

There were times she'd call the hall phone at university and say she could really do with a chat. So I did what any normal, caring sister would do: I put her on speaker phone and got on with my coursework, cross-legged in the hallway, adding in the odd 'U-huh' or 'Really?' to pretend I was listening. Or left her to chat with whichever passer-by happened to pick up. Or just *left* her, saying 'I have to go'. Explaining that I was in a rush. Which I always was, somehow.

In recent years, I've found excuses to avoid visiting her on the 'Animal Farm' in the Midlands. I've often referred to is as this, too – as though it were somewhere spectacularly alien – a remote island that I'd have to have inconvenient, unpleasant immunisations for several months in advance.

I'm a terrible human being, I tell myself, again, as it starts to rain. Again. *What is it with this country?!*

Melissa has barely spent any time with the kids, I realise now. It's a miracle they're so at ease around her and fond of her, based on the scarcity of visits. My fault, again – I never invite her over. And they never visit her. Because *I* never visit her. I hardly make the effort remotely, either. Even on Melissa's birthday, the expensive gifts I've occasionally lavished on her – out of guilt, more than anything – have been things that I thought she *should* have. Never things she's actually wanted. How could I know what she wanted? I never asked.

I cast my mind back and realise I can't remember a single time I've failed in my apparent life's mission to be ungenerous towards my sister. That, or judgemental. Or just absent.

In many respects, my sister and I are strangers.

That's not what I want, I limp forward, blinking through a combination of rain and tears. *I want to spend more time together.* I want to get to know her, properly – as an adult – just like she said in her letter. I want to have time for sisterly habits – like siblings in story books have. I want to be able to say things like, 'Oh, that? That's just typical of my sister!' Or 'my sister always likes to ... [insert preferred activity or mannerism as appropriate]' – followed by peals of easy laughter. I want us to have traditions together and experience that scrum of emotional safety that Charlotte and Thomas already have. Because if they ended up the way Melissa and I are, right now ... I'd be really, really sad about it.

Water tips down from nowhere, with no clouds visible in the now inky sky.

'Bloody Scandinavian, bloody changeable, bloody *crap* weather,' I curse.

The wind also appears to be picking up, plastering my hair across my cheeks as I run to the dock. I'm presuming she's still here. Hoping, at least. *Otherwise*, I wince as the pain in my foot redoubles. *It's going to be a long circuit of all the other outbuildings and the rest of the island.* Mercifully, my hunch is rewarded.

I lurch to a stop just before the bulrushes give way to sand by the coast. A short figure, barely visible by a sliver of moonlight, is trying to push the boat towards a swiftly retreating tide.

I watch her for a few moments as the earth bubbles over with wet, making miniature ponds between my toes. I say nothing, but Melissa seems to sense me there and stops what she's doing to look up.

'Alice?' she calls out. 'Is that you?' My blinking, frightened face must register, because she repeats my name. 'Alice?' Sorrow locks up my throat and I find I can't speak. It's not that I don't want to, like usual. I just … can't. 'If you're looking for Tricia to apologise again, you've missed her—'

'No, it was you I wanted—'

'Me?' She points at herself. 'Lucky *me*. Are you going to try and "fix" me? Because I'm a bit busy right now.' She gestures theatrically to the length of the boat. 'Stuff to do, places to be, no time for a lecture—'

'I didn't come here to lecture you,' I approach tentatively. 'It wasn't that. I … I …' I speak all on the inhale, tripping over myself to get the words out. 'I read your letter; I know you're ill. I'm sorry. So sorry. And I want to help—'

She sets down the oar that was in her hand and turns to face me, square on. 'What? That letter was private!'

'It was addressed to me …'

'For six months' time!' Melissa looks angry.

'Well, yes, but—'

'What is your *problem*?' Melissa asks again, shaking her head now. 'Snoopy Mc-Snoop-face …'

'Oh right, as well as "Judgey Mc-Judge-face"?' This slips out. I can't help it.

'*Yes!*'

'I can't believe you didn't tell me,' I say, quietly.

'I don't want to talk about it,' she snaps.

'You've got *cancer*—'

'Yes, thank you, Dr Quinn Medicine Woman. I *said*, "I don't want to talk about it"!' Melissa looks upset.

'But the letter—'

'You weren't supposed to read that yet,' she's yelling now.

'Well, I'm glad I did!' I shout back, then mollify my tone. 'Look, I came to say I'm sorry, OK? For everything. I'll keep saying it every day for as long as I have to—'

Melissa waves a hand at this. 'It's too late. What I said in the letter, just forget it.'

'What?'

'I wanted to spend time with you during this trip but you know what? You're bloody hard work. All you've done is moan! You're always making out that you're the only one who's got it all sorted, you spend most of your time sneering at the rest of us – don't pretend you don't, I see those eye rolls – and you have a real knack for upsetting people—'

'That's not fair—' I start, before remembering my catalogue of complaints and Tricia's tears from last night. I haven't exactly embraced Margot with open arms, either.

Oh ...

'But I'm your sister ...' is all I can think of to say.

'Well, you've been relieved of your duties,' is her response. This hurts. But I won't leave. I'm not going away.

Nevertheless she persisted ...

'I know I can't mend this with one big rain-soaked apology. I know it'll take time and lots of little conversations and thought and effort. But I'm going to try,' I tell her.

She wears a fixed expression, lips pressed tight.

'Just go. OK?' she tells me, finally.

'N-no ...' the word comes out shakily.

'What?' Melissa looks surprised. I move towards her, pedalling now, furiously, to gain traction – purchase – on anything that will get my sister to let me in. '*What* did you say?' She stares, eyes narrowing.

'I've been a shitty sister, I know it – but believe me, I don't think that "my way" is best. I don't think I've got any of it sorted.'

If only she knew! If only I'd told her ... Or let her see the girl who's spent years repeatedly sticking her hands under the drier in the loos at work or at social events to drown out the sound of crying ...

'I feel completely inadequate—'

'Do you?' She sounds suspicious.

'*Most* of the time! But you ... you're amazing.' I mean it. 'You get on with everyone. You can talk to anyone. Whereas I—' I tug at my now straggly rat's-tail hair in an effort to drag out the right thing to say before lighting on '—I can't even go to the hairdresser's—'

'I thought it was a bit long, for an almost forty-year-old ...'

'Yes, thank you ...' I deserved that. And she's right. Because aside from the snip of scissors, I find the total silence once we've covered all the usual bases – hair, weekend plans, where I'm going on holiday – utterly unbearable. As soon as I've used up my quotas of 'mmms' and 'really?'s, I'm screwed until the nice no-talking bit with the hairdryer. 'But you can set anyone at ease,' I tell Melissa. 'I've always admired that ... and ... and loads of things ... and I'd love for us to be closer.' She looks doubtful. 'I mean it! I want to be there for you!' I feel a wrench just looking at her but can't break eye contact.

Finally, she looks away and wipes her hands on her trousers in a futile attempt to dry them. 'Please stop talking to me.' She sounds tired, almost sighing out her words, before turning her attention back to the boat.

'No.'

'What?'

'I won't stop talking to you,' I say to her, 'ever.'

I've given up on a lot of things in my life so far – things that have been too painful or felt too hard. I've spent years in perpetual motion: always moving, always changing to strive towards the next goal in an attempt to busy myself and dodge anything scary. Well, not this time.

'I'll wait,' I tell her. 'As long as it takes.'

Unsure as to how best to play this, I hobble over and lay my hands on the cold, wet wood of our Viking not-very-longship. Melissa tries to ignore me and shift the thing on her own, but it isn't budging in the wet sand. Plus, I realise I'm holding on to the thing very, very tightly.

Melissa gives it a shove in frustration, then says, 'Well, you can wait all you like. I'm going.'

Shit. Your move, Alice …

'OK then, I'm coming with you,' I say.

She makes a non-committal grunting noise to show she's heard me then gives the boat an almighty shunt as I oscillate with anxiety.

'I mean, I'm pretty sure a storm is brewing,' I try, looking up, doubtfully. 'And it's very dark … you're sure we should go out *right* now?'

'Oh, I'm going,' she tells me, wresting the vessel free from my grasp with a renewed surge of strength. '*Now.*' She pushes it, sloughing through sodden sand towards the crashing sea.

'Should you even be doing that in your condition?' As soon as I've said it, I'm aware that it's unlikely to go down well.

Melissa looks as though she's going to thump me.

'I've been cleared for "strenuous exercise" before treatment starts by my *actual* doctor, thanks very much. I don't need medical advice from a *dentist.*'

Touché.

I try another approach and point to the black wilderness of water. 'But just look, it's not safe!' It isn't that I'm scared, you understand (though, also: *that*) – I just have no intention of losing my sister now that I'm on the very cusp of finding her. *It's a total shitblizzard out there...* 'Why don't we postpone until daylight? Or the weather's better? Tomorrow, maybe?'

But Melissa isn't listening. A purple haze has descended – otherwise known as The Ray Family Stubborn Streak. She's already wading in the shallows, then making a move to mount the boat, as only a squat five foot two woman in adverse conditions can try, and fail, to do. Three times.

'I can do this,' she mutters to herself, trying various manoeuvres. Our clothes are sopping wet and I'm becoming convinced that this would officially be classed as A Terrible Idea by any impartial observers. But really, what choice is there? *I have to go with her,* I tell myself – a statement of fact – *I can't desert her now.*

I'm just hoping that *two* floundering Ray sisters might be better than one.

Here goes nothing, I think, as the wind lashes my face. I fling a leg over the side, with as much dignity as a woman in wet yoga pants can possibly muster, and take up an oar, determined to play my part. 'OK, I tell her, I'm in. Here, give me your hand, I'll help you up. Then we can go—'

'Wait!' a voice sounds out from the darkness. 'Stop!'

It isn't Melissa.

It also isn't, as I'd been secretly hoping, Inge, come to demand that we abandon this clearly foolhardy mission.

'*Tricia?*'

'Hi!' she pants, resting her hands on her knees for a few moments and hacking up any residual tar that may conceivably be lurking after a lifetime's dedication to Marlborough Lights.

'Hang on!' She holds up a hand, head still between her legs, heaving before one almighty hock brings up the last of the sputum. 'Bear with me ... There, that's better. Right ...'

'Are you OK?' Melissa looks concerned.

'Fine, fine.' Tricia waves a hand, struggling to get her breath back as she coughs one more gravelly and alarmingly 'productive' cough before carrying on 'S'OK, I've got another lung if I need it! Inge said you'd probably be here, thought we should clear the air ...' Tricia doesn't elaborate on whether it's her or Inge who've been doing the thinking. 'So, here I am!'

I'm glad she's thinking about speaking to me again. And I want to make it right. *But now? Really?*

'You know, Tricia, I'm very, very sorry about last night, but I just need to talk to my sister right now. Do you think you could give us a moment?'

The damp has now seeped to my underwear.

I knew I was going to get a wet bottom again. I just knew it ...

'There's nothing you can say to me that you can't say in front of Tricia,' Melissa says briskly.

Is she kidding?

'I know you're angry with me, Melissa,' I start, then add, 'and you, Tricia,' before turning back to my sister. 'But if we could talk, just the two of us ... ?' She leaves me hanging so I try Tricia again. 'And if you could go back to the house, Tricia—'

'Why don't *you* go back—' Melissa starts.

'Sorry?'

'You go back! If it's an issue, *Alice.*'

Oh, it is an issue ...

'Just leave, if that's what you want to do, *Alice,*' Melissa goes on. 'You're good at that: leaving ...'

My mouth hangs open as I struggle to respond. *It's like a workshop in passive aggression. She's turning into ME ... I've created a monster!*

'All right, I get the picture,' I tell her. '*Pass-agg* correspondent, Alice, here – reporting for duty. I understand that you're pissed off with me, but I'm not going anywhere.'

'Well, neither am I,' says Melissa.

'Or me,' Tricia adds, before looking around doubtfully. 'Mostly because I'm not sure my body can take another rain-lashed run today ...' she says, before stumbling towards the boat 'for a sit down'.

'Right.' This is not how I pictured my grand reunion scene going. 'And Inge doesn't mind?' I try a different approach. 'Everyone taking off like this? Before *supper*?' I'm still hoping to dissuade both of them by appealing to their better natures – or their stomachs. I also can't help thinking about how cross I get when I've prepared food back home and everyone buggers off to do something else instead.

'Nope.' Tricia lifts up a leg, exposing her gusset, and I get a bottom in my face as she flings a limb overboard with surprising mobility for a woman in her ... *fifties? Sixties?* 'Magnus cooked and it was all a bit ... *brown*. We ate a little, then Inge said we were free to go off and do whatever we liked. Whispered that she'd leave some bread and cheese out for us later.'

I won't lie: the thought of this cheers me immeasurably, despite our current predicament. *My world is threatening to fall apart and I'm excited by cheese? I've definitely changed.*

'Then Inge went off to bath the kids. And Magnus. Which was peculiar ...' Tricia adds, looking troubled by the recollection, as though now utterly cured of her crush from earlier in the week.

'Well then, that's settled,' says Melissa smartly.

'Will you even tell us where we're going?' I ask, but she shakes her head.

'Need-to-know basis only. Trunk out, Dumbo,' is all she says.

'So you just want us to row with you to the middle of Scandi-nowhere?'

'No,' she corrects me. 'What I want is for you, Alice, to get out of the boat and go home. But since that's not happening, I'm going anyway. OK?'

'OK,' I mumble.

'Right then. All aboard!' she calls out, as she dips an oar in the water and instructs me to do the same.

'Isn't that what they say on trains?' I ask. She gives me a look that tells me it's 'too soon'. So I shut up and row.

Tricia is also silent, though this has less to do with picking up on the tension and more to do with still being out of breath from her exertions. But she takes on the rudder with surprising ease and an aptitude that suggests she's done this before. *As though she may even know where we're going.*

The water is choppy and the boat rocks, far more than it had earlier.

A storm. There's definitely a storm brewing.

It's harder to pull the oars through the water, too, and the volume of the rain – in both senses – makes it difficult to use our senses as Inge instructed. *Water*, I observe, *is noisy* – both the stuff underneath us, lapping occasionally over the side of the boat, and the icy droplets currently being tipped on our heads. My overriding sense is 'cold' but I still row for all I'm worth and we move in jerks, further and further from the shore.

'OK, let's get the sail … err … going,' Melissa says, having forgotten some of the lingo. There follows a discussion with Tricia about the best ways of doing this alongside some gargling sounds and yelps. I had resolved to stay well out of it, keeping my head down and concentrating on the task allocated to me: ironically as the 'muscle' of the operation, rowing with both oars while the others are preoccupied with the giant white sheet. But I allow myself the scarcest of glances up when the cries begin to sound more pronounced, more water-logged and more desperate. Looking around, I'm alarmed to discover that these sounds aren't coming from *inside* the boat at all.

'Can you hear something?' I ask, worrying now.

'What?' Melissa looks at me, crossly.

'*Nng*— help!' a stifled voice can be heard, just, above the tumult.

'Someone's out there!' I peer into the nothingness, scanning the water for ... I'm not sure what.

Tricia leans over the side to get a better look. 'I think she's right ...'

Melissa squints into the black water, then bellows. 'ARE YOU OK?'

'N-no,' is all that can be heard by way of response.

'Bloody hell ...' I murmur.

'WHO'S THERE?' Melissa shouts out.

Nothing. No human sounds can be heard now, and I wonder whether perhaps we have been experiencing a collective auditory hallucination.

That or whoever it was is no longer above water ...

'Hello?' I try, again, tentatively.

'Help!' the voice, gulps. 'It's me! I can't ...' The speech gets drowned out once more but not before we spot a body in the water, struggling.

Thirteen

'It's me!'

'Who's "me"?' There's no answer, but the body continues to thrash about.

'Do you know,' Tricia starts, 'it sounds a little like—'

'*Margot*?' Melissa frowns into the darkness.

'Yes!' Tricia exclaims. 'Is that you, Margot?'

'Ye—' the lashing creature yells before getting a mouthful of water and going under. It resurfaces, bobbing, then attempts a, 'Yes!'

'Oh my God!' Tricia squeals.

'It IS Margot!' Melissa processes this new development.

'Don't just stand around looking,' I shout. 'DO something! Melissa, can you get the sail going to move us any faster? And Tricia, doesn't that thing turn us around?' I gesture to the 'boaty steering wheel' that I latterly remember is called a rudder and start rowing with all my might to accelerate a change of course. It isn't easy, and the sea is rougher than usual, the wind having got up considerably so that it now appears to be blowing from all directions. The current is strong and the tide is going out, so we're drifting away from shore, even without my poor efforts with the oars.

But we're not that far out, I calculate. *No casual swimmer should be struggling to this extent ...*

We get close enough to the spluttering, bedraggled figure for me to extend an oar and tow her in. But the effort of staying partially afloat has exhausted our youngest trainee Viking and she's a husk of her former self.

'Are you OK?' I ask, hauling Margot's torso over the side, then assisting with the clambering on of those never-ending legs.

'*Mmm-nnnn* ...' She can only manage a shiver in response, teeth chattering, so I go into medic mode. We take it in turns to rub her hands and feet, in danger of turning into pruned slabs of ice far more quickly than the rest of ours are. There's nothing dry to wrap around her and we're all pretty wet from the rain, so the only thing I can think of to stave off hypothermia is human contact.

'Do you mean like a *group hug*?' Tricia looks surprised when I suggest this and even Melissa eyes me with incredulity.

'Yes.' I sigh. 'I suppose I do.' So they oblige. There is a unanimous dereliction of duties as we all surround Margot like penguins huddled in the Antarctic. We stay like this for a good fifteen minutes until our youngest member is marginally less frozen. The experience seems to embarrass Margot almost as much as it does me, and when we finally release her from our collective embrace, she can only manage a nervous smile.

'So, what happened?' I ask, in as gentle a voice as I can manage.

Margot, tucking wet tendrils of hair behind her ears as if her life depends on it, looks mortified.

'Were you, like, *drowning*?' Melissa gets straight to the bones of the matter and I notice Margot stiffen, though this could be the cold.

'You seemed to be really struggling,' Tricia narrates, obligingly, 'almost as if you couldn't ...' She leaves the sentence hanging, until Margot drops her shoulders and opens up her hands so that her palms are facing upwards in a rare moment of vulnerability.

'Yes,' she says. 'I was ... I mean. And no, I can't ...' She speaks without full stops. 'But then, four-time America's Cup winner Dennis Conner can't either and it's just never been a problem before ... I just ... didn't think it would get deep so quickly ...'

'What? You can't *swim*?' Melissa is keen to clarify. Tactfully or otherwise.

'No,' says Margot, looking down. 'I can't.'

None of us are quite sure what to say, but my inner monologue runs something like this:

Margot can't swim? Margot can't swim!

Margot has a flaw? Margot has a flaw!

As I said, I'm not proud.

'So, why were you in the water ... ?' Tricia looks at her as though she is deranged. Which, to be fair, we might all be by this stage.

'I ... I didn't want to be left behind,' says Margot, once she's got her breath back, 'with Magnus and all the brown food, I mean. I wanted to join in. See what you were all up to. Not be left out ...' The rest of us exchange a look. 'Well?' Margot asks, with a final cough up of seaweed mixed with mucus. And brown food. Probably. 'What have you all been up to?'

'Oh, nothing much,' I say, instinctively, sensing my window for a heart to heart with my sister about her illness slamming shut.

'That's not *quite* true,' Melissa corrects me.

'It's not?'

Really? She wants to do this here? She wouldn't even tell her own sister that she has cancer – but now Melissa wants to discuss it in front of a couple of women we'd never even met this time last week?

I must have really let her down.

'No!' she goes on. 'You were going to *apologise*, to Tricia. Again. For snooping. And generally being an arse—'

'I don't think I said that last part—' I start, but Melissa fixes me with such a glower that I hear myself agreeing. 'Yes, that's right.' I'm still being punished – justifiably – so I offer an: 'I'm *extremely* sorry, Tricia.'

'That's OK,' The older woman gives a small shrug, adding, 'I wanted to explain how things ended up like that, anyway. You know, Doug, gin-in-a-mug-at-noon ... That's why I came.'

'Right.' I nod. 'Yes'.

'And where are you going?' Margot asks Melissa, quite reasonably. I look to my sister, who feigns blissful oblivion in the face of the question that's just been posed and merely squints into the driving rain.

I try to follow her eye line, squeegeeing water off my forehead with my free hand in the hope that I might be able to actually see something between drips.

Nope, nothing.

So I echo Margot's line of enquiry. 'Yes, Melissa, where *are* we going?'

'Where are any of us going?' she replies, echoing Magnus's infuriating response from day one.

I'm not buying what she's selling ...

'Yes, yes, but *specifically*? As in, *now*?' I ask, as a sizeable swell sways and spins us. 'We all seem to be headed there, so isn't it only fair you let us in on where "there" is ... ?'

Melissa sucks her teeth and makes a face like a mechanic informing you that they *could* fix your car, but that *it'll cost you*. 'I'll be honest; I'm not sure any more.'

'What?' I say sharply.

'Well,' my sister goes on, 'in all the kerfuffle of Margot's rescue—'

'Sorry.' Margot sniffs.

"S'OK.' Melissa nods. 'But in all the kerfuffle and the penguin hugging ... I *may* have lost track of which direction we should be aiming for. Or which direction we're currently *in* ... Or even—' and here she winces slightly '—what direction we should take if we wanted to go back ...'

As my stomach nosedives – a sensation increased ten-fold by the pitching of the boat – I can almost feel the collective anxiety ramping up. Each of us in turn looks around, to verify Melissa's concerns and see ... *nothing*. No lights, no land, *nothing*.

We're in foreign waters. We're lost. We're wet. And we're cold. Unimaginably, face-achingly, cold.

The moon is faint, a slim crescent partially obscured by clouds that also cloak any helpful stars we might be otherwise able to navigate by.

If any of us actually knew how to navigate by stars, that is. Although Margot's probably done a Duke of Edinburgh taster course in this somewhere along the line ...

What she hasn't done, apparently, is 'basic swimming' and none of us have our 'how to find your way home safely in the middle of a storm at night' Brownie badge.

'So we're lost?' Tricia asks, sounding scared. She's answered by a distant brattle of thunder.

'We might just be,' Melissa admits. 'What? It was a very long group hug!' she adds defensively, wiping rain off her face with a sleeve as the boat keels and rocks in the squall.

'Right ...' I have no idea what to do next.

What would a Viking do? I wrack my brains but draw a blank. My sister misinterprets my silence as hostility.

'Oh yes, I know what you're thinking,' she tells me. 'You're thinking, "Melissa's fucked up again", that it's all my fault—'

'That's not what I was thinking—'

'That I'm the irresponsible one, next to "perfect Alice" who never does anything wrong—'

'No! Honestly, I wasn't—'

'Are we going die?' Tricia interjects, lips now a blue-ish tinge and hands fluttering at her throat.

'No,' I tell her, with as much authority as I can muster. 'We are not going to die.'

'Well, we're all going to die eventually,' Melissa deadpans, then catching my expression, adds: 'What? Spoiler alert, but none of us are getting out of this alive.'

'Fine, but no one is going to die *now*,' I insist, addressing my sister directly. 'And listen, I never claimed to be perfect! I don't know where you got this from—'

'From you! You've always had this rule book the rest of us haven't seen copies of and have no hope of living up to!' Melissa goes on. 'You were always the one who got fussed over when we were little! Petted by Mum, driven to violin lessons—'

'Oh, I learned the violin, too!' Margot pipes up. 'And the cello ...'

Shut up, Margot! But she goes on wittering something about musical grades as Tricia starts up again, too, until it's as though we're all immersed in our own private conversations. Our own private hell.

'I find it helps to keep talking when I'm worried,' Tricia goes on, looking around her into the darkness, fear leaching into her voice now. 'You know what they say: once a broadcaster, always a broadcaster!' She laughs nervously as my sister continues her diatribe:

'Do you know what it was like growing up not being as clever or thin or as "gifted" as Mum wanted me to be? As you were? I grew up terrified of taking up too much space. Scared, even, of bumping into people in the street – ducking and weaving out of people's way. All the time. It was knackering. Once, I decided not to move out of anyone's way for a week and bumped into 200 people. Rammed right into them – because no one held open doors for me or stepped aside to let me pass or drove me to *VIOLIN LESSONS!*'

I had no idea that the violin had been such a big deal. I can only recall making an extraordinary, strangled sound until Mum and Dad eventually agreed that I was so prodigiously untalented that I should stop. That it 'might be best' to 'focus my efforts elsewhere'. For everyone's sake. What I somehow failed to notice was a younger sister watching longingly and waiting for the day it would be her turn to take up the stringed instrument and get that one-on-one parental attention. A day that never came, once tragedy struck and Dad descended into his decade of mourning.

'Why didn't you tell me any of this?' I demand now.

'I shouldn't have had to!' Melissa retorts. 'You should've seen something was up.'

'But you looked ... *fine*,' I tell her.

'But I wasn't!'

I try to absorb this and say simply, 'I'm sorry. I didn't *get it* ...'

'Tricia, apparently, doesn't get it either. 'I feel I should explain a few things, too,' she addresses me, 'about the video ...'

Now, Tricia? Really? Timing is not this woman's forte ...

'Well, what it *was*, was, that work had dried up a bit, and an old timer told me I should try going walking on the beach one day wearing something skimpy. "no-make-up" make-up – you know: heavy lip, big eyes etc. etc. I did some "frolicking", ate a Mivvy suggestively, the usual. Then we got this friend to call the paps and made out as though a seagull attacked me. Thought it might up my profile ahead of *Strictly*—'

'Paps?' Margot asks.

'Photographers. Anyway, total hatchet job. Said I'd had ... *"cosmetic assistance"* ... I mean, really!' Tricia sounds offended. 'So I had one heavy night – two, max – a few bad shows. Station said I was slurring – whatever *that* means! Then there was the to-do over cashews ... I split up with Doug after a heated exchange in the Burgess Hill branch of B&Q. And then my former sidekick went on a confidence-building course and got a bit pleased with herself. Got new hair. And my show. And Doug, though frankly she's welcome to him. But the show part stung. I mean – she hasn't even got her own Wikipedia page! I realise now that it wasn't her fault – any of it. She's just a girl trying to get on in the world. I blame the system. Down with the patriarchy. Anyway, I don't know where I was in my pill/wine/coffee cycle, but, wherever it was, I'd had enough. Thus the reel-to-reel ultimate Frisbee—' She's cut off by a slap in the face from a Baltic blast of ocean spray.

This is too much, I think, as Melissa takes up the baton once more:

'Then after Mum died, you just left!' she gasps through the cold, turning on me to continue her indictments. 'You didn't wait for me. Or even *talk* to me. And I was sad – all on my own. And you went off and had all the fun—'

'It wasn't fun,' I tell her, thinking back to the first year away from home: alone, lonely, skint,[27] and a year younger than all my classmates so that I had to do a lot of pretending to make it seem as though I knew what was going on. As though I had

---

[27.] Student grants: retrospectively generous, still meagre-seeming at the time

a clue – about anything. 'Not all of it, anyway,' I add, in case she doesn't believe me.

She doesn't.

'It hurt. A lot. And you should know that,' she tells me. 'I'm over it, now,' she adds. 'I'm over *you*. I've tried and tried, all these years, only to have it thrown back in my face. I planned this trip as one more go at saving something – anything – between us. But you *still* treat me as though I'm a joke. Your plan B. Well, I'm no one's Plan bloody B.' she shouts.

'I'm sorry.' I hadn't realised that she felt like this. I hadn't realised that she could *read me* so astutely – that she'd been doing so for years. All the assumptions and prejudices I thought I'd concealed so slickly with my camouflage of 'busy' have apparently been as conspicuous as a peacock in full plumage. *I am an appalling human being.* 'You've … you've been so good to me,' I say, struggling to get the words out. 'I know I don't always make it easy.' I want to give her a hug. And not let go. So I do. She doesn't seem thrilled by the idea at first but eventually relents and wraps her damp, sex-fleeced arms around me too.

I can see why she's so obsessed with this polyethylene terephthalate zip-up jumper, I think, admiring the way the synthetic fibres have protected her from the worst of the weather while remaining surprisingly soft. And although not exactly 'warm', I definitely feel less ice-cream-headache cold than before. *My sister gives good hug …*

'You know, what you said in your letter, about keeping a lid on things? Well, really, don't,' I mumble into her hair, which now smells a lot like wet dog. 'Your way is better. You were right to be honest about how you're feeling. To get sad when you need to. I'm sorry I ever made you doubt that. I'm the one who's been wrong. I've nearly given myself a hernia trying to push everything back down for years – but it doesn't work. It always comes out, somewhere.'

'Do you mean like in a Premier Inn en suite loo?' Melissa asks.

I nod. 'Among other places, yes.'

I close my eyes to stem the tide of tears currently threatening to add to our waterlogged situation, but can still hear Tricia, talking agitatedly above the crashing of the water.

'Everyone says it – they say, "Tricia, you've been doing this for years! You must be rich!" They say. "Why are you spending Christmas in Hull on a wire playing the wicked queen in panto?" And I tell them, "Because I love it!" But of course I don't bloody love it! I'm spending Christmas in Hull. On a wire! The only booking I had over Easter was judging a cat show ... all hissing and arching their spines – and that was just the owners ... But that's show business! If you're not Gyles Bloody Brandreth or Sue Perkins, it's all your agent can find you, that time of year,' she says, her teeth chattering.

'Mmm.' Margot responds out of courtesy, as Tricia's only 'audience member', and eventually my sister and I disengage. Melissa stares at me.

'Are you crying?' She looks pleased.

'No!' I half-laugh, half-sob. 'It's just raining ... on my face.'

'Yeah, same here,' she says, dabbing at very wet eyes and then blowing her nose with her hand and wiping what comes out on her combat trousers.

That's my girl, I think with love.

The boat tips and rears like a bucking bronco under a new barrage of 'weather' until we're forced to sit, and I'm startled to find my bottom sluiced anew with waves of bracingly cold sea, slapping over the side. We seem to be far lower down in the water than we were during the test run earlier today.

Uh-oh, this isn't good. This isn't good at all ...

'What was it Inge said about this being a *two-man* boat?' I ask, fearful of the answer.

'She meant massive Vikings, didn't she ... ?' Melissa starts. 'Three of us should be fine ...'

'Yes, but there are four of us now ...' I look around the boat and see my sister's mouth moving as she does the calculation. I lean over the side. 'And I'm pretty sure she said something about the water being no higher than two fingers below the top plank ...' I feel my way down but am immersed in icy water before I can trace a single ridge in the wooden panelling.

'Christ, are we ... ?' Tricia murmurs.

'Sinking?' Margot looks worried. 'As well as lost?'

'We might just be.' I shiver to get the circulation going, then start scooping out water with my hands as fast as I can. I spy the plug at the bottom of the boat, now refracted and magnified by the sheer volume of water on top of it, as though taunting us along the lines of: *Ha! You thought I worked like a plug in a bath! Fools!*

'Stupid pissing plug,' I mutter to myself.

'What?' Melissa frowns, also scooping out water with her hands now.

'Nothing.' I shake my head and hunt for the actual, official 'bailer' that I'm sure I saw earlier today.

'Bloody hell, has it come to this?' says Tricia, evidently choosing panic over bailing. 'I've never been in actual danger on one of these retreats before! No matter how much I complained when they made me do burpee circuits in Ibiza!' She wails now. 'I don't want to end my days here! I'd rather be in John Lewis! Shoplifting!'

This is new ...

'You're not going to end your days at sea in a Viking boat,' I tell her, firmly. 'Not on my watch, anyway. But right now, we need to focus and STAY CALM! What we have to do is get more of the water *outside* the boat than in and work at reducing our weight ...' Melissa looks up, outraged. 'I mean of water and any ... er ... surplus cargo,' I quickly clarify, casting around for anything that might qualify.

'Like *this*!' Tricia holds up a bucket and makes to throw it overboard.

'No! Wait!' I howl. But it's too late: a faint splash can be heard over the din of the storm and our bailer bucket bobs away into the cold black nothingness. 'Great. Anyone got any suggestions for what we bail with now?'

I keep going with my hands and Melissa does the same but when she's close enough to be sure we're not going to be overheard, she looks at me, pleading, and whispers, '*Is this it?*'

'I don't know,' I confess. We could swim for it, I reason. But someone would have to carry/tow Margot as our resident non-swimmer. And the only one of us strong enough and fit enough to tow Margot is ... *Margot*. What's more, we have no idea which direction to aim for. Plus the water is cold. So cold that we'd probably be debilitated within fifteen minutes. By the half-hour mark, I calculate, hypothermia would set in. I've seen *Titanic*.

A deep, heavy feeling takes over my core at this sobering train of thought. I carry on scooping out water as fast as my now-numb cupped hands are able, but on reflection I have – if not given up – then certainly made peace with whatever is to come. *At least we're together*, I think, as we all scoop in silence for some moments.

Cold is something you can handle when you know you'll get warm again soon. Or dry. I've been a fan of cold showers in my time, in an attempt to boost circulation or tauten the skin or make my hair shinier (at least, that's what the magazines tell me). I can even bear those bitter winter days where you have to muffle up before leaving the house to make it to the car or the tube without frostbite. Primarily because you know that soon you'll be rewarded with a hot fug of fan heating, or the communal perspiration and expelled carbon dioxide of a dozen or so other commuters. But this? With no end in sight? I don't know how much longer I can stand it. I'm frightened that it really might be game over.

'Wait!' Tricia sits bolt upright, then starts wriggling her arms inside her sodden sweatshirt.

'What are you doing?'

'This!' She releases and then dangles a sizeable padded bra an inch from my face.

'What?'

'Nothing gets through this,' Tricia point, then bends over to demonstrate and begins to scoop. 'See?' She tips a good two litres of water over the side from her DD-cups and then repeats the motion. It's an improvement on hand-scooping, and I find my sports bra also does an adequate job, if I'm quick. Melissa's M&S cotton number isn't much use, however – and Margot, as she insists on reminding us, 'doesn't wear a bra'. So we're two underwear bailers down, but it at least feels as though we're doing something. *Anything* ...

Lightning slaps and cracks on the horizon and then the thunder rolls in, closer now. *Perhaps death by lightning would be preferable ... Quicker, at least. And it would certainly warm us up*, I muse, as another fire bolt pierces the blackness and Tricia shrieks in terror. But then I notice something.

Could it ... ? Would it ... ?

It's our only hope. So I say nothing, but cross everything.

By the time the third strike comes, I'm ready, braced to look all around me for the fraction of the second that the sky is lit up by electrostatic discharge. Straight ahead of me I see a straight line, clear now, where sea turns to sky, but to my left the horizon is stippled and prickles with ... *trees.*

'Land!' I yelp, a mouthful of seawater making its way in simultaneous with my outburst. 'There's land! Over there!' I point. 'And trees!' The other women scan the nothingness, struggling to share my enthusiasm, until another bolt of lightning flicks the temporary switch and illuminates the world once more.

'Land!' Melissa echoes me. 'I fucking love land!'

'Me too!' Margot can't even be brought down by profanities this time.

'We're going to make it, we can do this!' I tell myself as much as anyone else.

What did Inge say? I scroll back through the events of the past couple of days and start downloading, rapidly. 'OK, we need two oarswomen and a steerswoman and bailer, so Margot, you're the strongest, if you and Melissa row first then Tricia and I can steer and bail to try to keep us afloat, then we'll keep switching until we're close enough to wade in.'

We jostle into position to battle the elements for a final, bone-crushingly exhausting and by now sub-zero push.

We take it in turns to row and bail, alternately, until the trees get bigger and lights can be seen twinkling between a dense tapestry of fir. We heave on the oars until we can heave no more and the base of the boat hits a welcome barrier of sand.

'Oh, thank God.' Tricia collapses and then proceeds to vomit with relief, exuberantly and over the very section of the boat that Melissa has just swung herself out of.

'Thanks very much,' pants Melissa, ducking away from the worst of it but not wavering in her mission to heave what's left of the boat up on to the beach.

Together, we drag the wooden carcass ashore. And while I'm slowly analysing the various 'next-step' options open to almost-shipwreck survivors – a scant knowledge gleaned exclusively from children's' books featuring tropical beaches, coconuts and monkeys – Melissa appears ... confident.

'Come on,' she says, wiping a few lingering chunks of Tricia's stomach lining off her sex fleece. 'It's this way.'

Tricia too appears relaxed, post-puke. She wrings out her bailer bra, flings it over her shoulder, then follows Melissa up the waterlogged sand dunes and towards a light in the distance.

Margot and I look at each other, still in the dark – in all senses. But with few options open to us, chilled to the marrow, and – secretly – consumed by curiosity, we slowly make to follow in their soggy footsteps.

Fourteen

Trees glisten with wet, refracting a light now shimmering in the distance. Margot strikes ahead, holding back a bushy branch of fir *not quite* long enough to let me pass, so that it pings back in my face, showering me with chilly droplets afresh.

FFS … I look upwards: *Seriously? I need to get even wetter?*

Still shivering and distinctly briny – lips, fingers, everything in fact shrivelled by seawater – I can't manage much more than a stagger to follow my leaders.

Melissa and Tricia are a long way ahead now, tiny doll-like figures disappearing into the woods as Margot and I struggle to keep up. But beyond the final barrier of pine-scented foliage, we're rewarded with a celestial vision: a bleached wood cabin with a terrace extending out onto a ridge of boulders. Candlelight flickers in the windows and there's evidence of a fire within, with smoke trickling valiantly through the rain from a small chimneystack.

Warmth! I scream silently. *If we can just get inside, we could get warm!* This is all I can think about as I keep putting one foot in front of the other, urging on every sinew in my exhausted body.

Amidst the timpani of raindrops, I can hear music now – upbeat and poppy but with a base that thuds through the earth, competing with the gamelan of weather so that my feet seem to be vibrating. *Either that or I've still got sea legs*, I think, feeling unsteady.

'You OK?' Margot asks, extending a hand to help me up the final steep incline.

'Yes, fine,' I insist, but take her hand anyway, reasoning that dented pride is a small price to pay for getting dry, sooner. *Besides*, I think, *we've all had a few bubbles burst in the past twenty-four hours, haven't we? I don't suppose that any of us are feeling particularly proud.* None of this seems to matter any more, either, because the golden light is drawing us in, ever closer, to the majestic fortress up ahead. A wooden sign, creaking and swaying in the wind, reads:

'*Welcome to Valhalla.*'

We push open heavy golden doors to reveal a crowded room, dominated by a vast stone fireplace (*Vikings + fire obsession, exhibit #9*) with logs popping on the hearth. Whitewashed walls give way to rough hewn beams, festooned with low-slung lamps. A dozen or so obscenely photogenic Vikings – all looking as though they've stepped out of a catalogue – lounge against walls or perch on sheepskin-lined benches. Lean, tanned necks disappear into crisp cotton collars, beautifully knitted confections, or simple white T-shirts and the clientele turn, as one, to take in the two bedraggled forms who've just let in a draft of icy cold air.

'Err, hi!' I try, in my best 'pan-Nordic' accent (i.e. talking slowly, loudly, and with a lilt of *Borgen*). 'Has anyone seen my sister?'

I skim their faces for Melissa – or rather, the gaps between their faces, since I'm guessing my sister is a good foot shorter than all of them. My extremities burn with relief at being out of the cold and I smooth back my hair, attempting to make myself presentable and failing miserably. *I am not cool enough for this place,* I acknowledge.

But my sister, apparently, is.

'Is *that* ... Melissa?' Margot points and my eyes follow her outstretched arm. Peering, I make out two diminutive figures in the centre of what is now officially a Scandi-throng, being welcomed like old friends. Blankets are flung around their shoulders, drinks are placed in their hands, and Melissa ... I screw up my eyes to check that they aren't playing tricks on me ... Melissa is being ... *kissed.* Full on the mouth.

'Isn't that ... Inge's cousin?' Margot, a regular oracle, as it turns out, observes. I try to get a better look at the man my sister is currently having mouth-sex with, but what I can mostly make out is *beard* and a mass of brown curly hair. I think back to the man to whom Margot is referring, striving to conjure up a clear image.

Didn't we meet him the day Magnus got poisoned sick? The day of the Terry's Chocolate Orange Proustian-tart? The day I drank all the beer and let slip about Mr Teeth? The day Melissa officially stopped talking to me? A lot's happened since then, I conclude. *I can be forgiven for poor facial recognition. Can't I?*

I look again. It's a shock to see my sister *in flagrante.* I'm also experiencing mild disbelief at the unlikely pairing.

'Him? Really? The guy channelling Peter Jackson who smelled of buns?' I somehow murmur out loud, still staring at my sister who is now on tiptoes and touching foreheads with the bear-man, staring into his eyes.

'That's the one,' Margot confirms, 'Otto? Wasn't his name?'

'Yes, I think so ...' I respond, before experiencing a hearty slap on the shoulder.

'There you are!' It's Tricia, who has broken away from the couple and clearly absorbed a few of Melissa's mannerisms.

'Here.' She presents Margot and me with a blanket each. 'Let's get you both warmed up. I'm drying my bra in front of the fire if you want me to take yours? No? OK then; well, how about a drink?'

It's taking me a while to process all this. 'Where *are* we?' I look around, puzzled. 'And what's happening *here*, please?'

'Here?' Tricia echoes my words, gesturing all around her. 'Or *here*?' She points at the scene ahead, the one entitled, *Massive Viking currently snogging Melissa*'.

'Both?' I reply. 'But mainly, *that*.' I nod at my sister.

'Right. Yes. *This* is our local, in case you were wondering. Great place, isn't it? And *that*—' she inclines her head towards Melissa '—well, join the dots ...'

Nope, I'm still drawing blanks. Perhaps the cold has numbed my mind and dulled my faculties.

'Have you heard of *knullruffs*?' Tricia continues.

What is she ON about? I think. *Is she suffering from brain-freeze, too?*

'Don't worry,' Tricia assures me. 'I hadn't either before this week, but apparently it's a Swedish word meaning "messy hair after sex". Don't Scandinavians have the best words? Did you know the Finns have a term for drinking at home in just your underwear?'

'I did not know that,' I freely confess.

'Yes! *Kalsarikännit*.'

'Right, good.' I try to return us to the matter in hand. 'But what's this got to do with my sister?'

'Oh yes. Well, what I *meant* was ...' Tricia gets back on track. 'Haven't you noticed? Melissa's been rocking up with some great *knullruffs* most mornings ...'

'Oh?' I say, and then the kroner drops. '*Ohhhh* ...' I draw the word out.

How could I have been so slow? My sister? And the Viking? 'Doing it', as they say in Charlotte's class at school? My little sister has sex ... ?

My SISTER has SEX.

I repeat the phrase a few times in my head to try and make it stick. It seems unlikely, somehow, that the younger sibling I have known and yet not known forever – my sister who likes horses and dogs and old black-and-white films and Enid Blyton – also likes to hop on the good foot and do the bad thing. Regularly, if Tricia is to be believed. I think about whether I have been blind to the signs – the clues that my sister has been a fully fledged 'sexual being' for some time now. And conclude that the answer is 'yes'.

The summer she locked herself away in her room for long stretches of time with a poster of Jeff Goldblum and insisted on doing her own laundry is suddenly framed in a whole new light. The time during her GCSEs when she told us she was staying the night with her friend, Jodie ... before Jodie turned up on our doorstep, was, in retrospect, a poorly planned dirty stop out. I have, it seems, been wilfully blind.

This has been quite the day of revelations ...

'Drink?' Tricia goes on, as though appreciating that I might need one.

'Yes,' I say, emphatically. 'Please.'

My de facto wing woman Margot also nods at the offer, and so, thickly wrapped in woollen blankets, Tricia leads us to a wall of wooden shelves in the far corner of the bar.

It looks like something out of a Dickensian apothecary, laden with ancient glass bottles bearing brown luggage labels and what appears to be a selection of red wine already 'breathing' in decanters. Behind a low wall of sandblasted wood stands a man so dashing that I don't know where to look. But Tricia greets him in a most familiar manner, then turns to us and whispers, 'Isn't this place *To. Die. For*? It's like a tree house for grown-ups, but with hot people and booze!' She whips back around and gives the barman her most winning of winning smiles.

'So what'll it be?' she asks us while still beaming at him.

'What have they got?' I respond, a little (a lot) overwhelmed. I feel as though I'm in a language tape from the 1980s and should just be asking for 'three drinks of alcohol please'. Fortunately, Tricia is an experienced and willing guide.

'Well, I've been rather enjoying aquavit,' she tells me. 'A Scandinavian spirit distilled from potatoes ...'

I have flashbacks to a particularly punitive detox diet I tried once that involved drinking potato juice (a real low), and so ask if perhaps there might be an alternative. '*Or?*'

'Or beer, or wine, or ... no! I've got it! There's something you just *have* to try ...' Tricia tells us and orders on our behalf. I recognise that this is dangerous when we're handed two tumblers of brown liquid.

'What's *this*?' Margot wrinkles her nose at her glass.

'It's G&T, but they make their own tonic from quinine bark!' Tricia gushes.

Of course they do! It's like a hipster masterclass ... I bet they can all secretly tell that the first album I ever bought was Simply Red's Stars.

'Quinine bark?'

'Yes! The owner told me it means you can use cheaper gin,' Tricia adds as I almost choke on the concoction.

Sweet Jesus ...

'Strong?' Tricia asks, innocently

'It's like *lighter fluid*,' I gasp in a voice that is not my own. After a second sip, I feel as though I've been tasered. '*Oh god, it's burning ...*' I press my free hand to my mouth then add a lisping, '*I think my teeth are melting. That can't be good ...*'

'Don't think too much, just drink! It'll warm you up. I've ordered food, too,' Tricia assures me. 'For *soakage*. So come on, bottoms up!'

Margot does as she's told before a platter of pickled fish, rye bread and knobbly-looking vegetables arrive on a wooden slab.

'This'll sort us out,' Tricia announces, digging in, and she's right. It does. There's also a strange sort of respite that comes halfway down the second tumbler of brown-tinted lighter fluid when I don't feel so cold any more and I'm also not afraid. This is unusual. More Euro pop starts up and the cool kids start pogo-ing in insouciant formation.

'I love the music here, don't you?' Tricia asks, bobbing chaotically. 'They play exclusively Scandinavian pop.'

'That's a good thing?' My eyebrows arc.

Maybe my Simply Red admission wouldn't go down like such a shit sandwich after all. I could even confess to my Billy Joel collection ...

'Of course!' Tricia retorts as though this much was obvious. 'It's only in the UK that we don't fully appreciate its charms.'

'Is that right?'

'Yes,' she tells me very definitely. 'It is. When ABBA won Eurovision in nineteen seventy-four with Waterloo, they got nil points from the UK. And look how they turned out. So who do you think knows more about music?'

I see I'm not going to win this one, so I eat, drink, and find that, soon, I don't care any more.

'Have you been coming here a lot?' I ask Tricia.

She guffaws. 'Are you asking if I come here often?'

I snort 70 per cent proof alcohol and brown tree juice out of my nose until it hurts. 'I suppose I am,' I reply when the burning sensation has subsided.

'We may have stopped by last night in the boat ...' Tricia says with a practised nonchalance, taking a swig from her tumbler.

'And when did it start? With Otto, I mean. And how did you find this place? Did *everyone* know about all this apart from me?'

'I didn't know,' Margot pipes up and I realise that by 'everyone' I meant Tricia and Inge. Melissa not confiding in a model-esque semi-stranger ten years her junior is one thing. *But Melissa not confiding in her sister? Again? That's something else.*

Of course, it pales into insignificance in comparison to the letter I read earlier today, but still ...

I want her to be able to share things with me, don't I?

It's at this moment that the lighter fluid/brown unction hits my ... my – *neurotransmitters, is it?* – in earnest. So I down the remainder of the scalding liquor until I tingle from my oesophagus to my groin – and decide to find out for myself what's been happening.

I move towards my sister but am blocked by Tricia, now dancing wildly to Roxette. After a tussle, I manage to break free from her attempts to embroil me in a duet and leave Margot to fend for herself. Edging through the beautiful people until I'm close enough to see Melissa, I notice she's considerably more preoccupied than anticipated. My sister's arms appear to have been cut off at the wrists, the rest of them disappearing down Otto's trousers.

Oh my, I think, and then, surprising myself: *good for her!*

Melissa finally disengages and with a final squeeze of his bottom (at least, I hope it's his bottom ...). She dodges through the mob in the direction of what I guess to be the ladies' loo, thanks to a wooden arrow with a carving of a She-Viking on it.

I hope she hasn't got cystitis, is my instant, unfiltered response. *All that cold water, wet pants and 'action'.* I wonder whether I've got a spare sodium citrate sachet in my wash bag to help make her urine less acidic. Then I realise that this is horribly unromantic and probably says more about my own disappointing sexual encounters to date than the likely state of my sister's urethra.

I attempt to follow Melissa, without giving much thought to what'll come next. I shuffle through the crowd as swiftly as an awkward Brit still suffering from the after effects of shock/hypothermia/home-made tonic and cheap gin can. After dispensing the odd, 'excuse me?' and 'please may I just get past ... ?', I slur an uncharacteristically yobbish. '*OI!*' and push my way through to the loos just in time to catch Melissa pre-wee.

'Hello you!' I start, in what I hope is a casual tone.

'Oh hi!' Melissa gestures to the free cubicle. 'Want to go first? I can wait.' She nods at the other, occupied stall. 'Until they're done.'

'Oh no!' I tell her. 'I only came in to see you!'

'Because that's not weird at all ...' she replies.

'Is it?' I'm genuinely not sure any more. *I should start making a list ... Maybe I could start a running document in the Notes app on my iPhone. 'Weird stuff I do that apparently isn't socially acceptable'?*

'Yes,' Melissa assures me. 'It is. Following people into the loos when you don't want a wee is definitely weird ...'

'Right,' I acknowledge my gaffe, then add, 'Noted. Sorry. I just wanted to say ... congratulations.' *Is that the right word? The appropriate response to the revelation that your sister has been getting a good seeing to with Thor's hammer?* 'I mean, I had no idea about your *friend* ...'

What am I? A middle-aged maiden aunt from the nineteenth century?

'Congratulations? On what?'

'Otto?'

'Oh, yeah,' is all she says.

'So, are you two ... *an item?*' I say this, inexplicably, in an American accent. As though trying to disassociate myself from the cheesiness of the enquiry. *I am truly terrible at this 'talking' business ...*

'It's only been a few days – no hats just yet! Sure you don't want to go?' She nods her head towards the loo.

'No, thanks,' I tell her. Then, in the hope of fostering a confessional mood, I add, 'I went in the water before we got to shore – helped warm myself up.'

At this, she gives a *pfftt* of laughter. 'OK, well, mind if I?' She's already peeling down trousers as she says this and proceeds to urinate, with the cubicle door open.

She's not even hovering or putting loo roll down on the seat first! I shake my head at my sister's brio. *I haven't touched a bowl since 1998, let alone the rim of a public convenience! Doesn't she know how many germs could be lurking?*

'So,' I ask, averting my eyes and casting around the rest of the white panelled washroom, 'are you OK?'

'Me? Yeah, I'm OK, I just needed to wee ...'

This wasn't what I'd meant. Although ... *uh-oh.* A klaxon goes off in my head. *Recent intercourse? Urgency to pass water? Urinary tract infection alert! Must search for that sachet ...*

'I mean, about what will happen when we get back. Are you booked in for surgery?'

She nods.

'Are you feeling all right about it?'

'Yeah, brilliant.' She makes a sarcastic face. 'I'm going to have a chunk cut out of my left breast. Which has never been my favourite, but still.'

I don't know what to say to this.

'Have they given you any lifestyle advice?' is the best I can come up with. She looks at me defensively.

'This isn't because I'm fat, in case that's what you're thinking—' she starts.

'Oh no, I wasn't!' I protest.

'Apparently using deodorant has nothing to do with it, either. Or space. Or Wi-Fi ... In fact, the main risk factors for breast cancer seem to be the things none of us can do anything about,' she goes on. 'Like getting older, genes, and just having breasts – yeah, that seems to be the main one. Which is a kicker.'

I know this already after the research I did at our local library once Mum was diagnosed. That and all the questions I asked doctors because Mum was too depressed and Dad was too upset to think of them. Jotting everything down in a yellow notebook that always looked far too cheery – inappropriately upbeat, I realised – whenever I got it out at hospital.

'Basically, it's all going to be a bit crap for a while,' Melissa concludes.

'Yes, sorry,' I stutter. I wish we were both marginally more sober for this conversation. Then again, maybe this was just what we needed – to let go. 'Have they given you a treatment programme? Will you have chemotherapy?'

She nods. 'And hormone therapy, and the rest ...'

'Good,' I say and watch Melissa's eyebrows shoot up. 'I don't mean "good". What I mean is, I'm glad they've got a plan in place. For what'll happen next. And I'm here for you, whatever you need.' She nods. 'It's OK to be scared, you know—'

'Good, because I am!' she wobbles. 'I'm scared of going bald. I'm scared of looking weird after. I'm scared of not feeling like me any more.'

'I'm so sorry,' I tell her, again, my heart in my throat.

'No! Don't look at me like that.' She points at my face. 'This is why I couldn't imagine telling you, watching your expression change. I didn't want to give you the opportunity to feel trapped again. To have to make a sacrifice—'

'It's no sacrifice!' I tell her. 'You're my sister!' She looks up at me. 'What? I mean it,' I insist again. 'I miss you. I miss not knowing things about your life. I never know about your relationships or what's going on—'

Melissa shakes her head, and then her *bottom* to eliminate drips pre-wipe. *Efficient,* I think, impressed. Tugging up her trousers, she says, 'I don't tell you about my life because for years you didn't seem interested!' She flushes – literally, I mean, not in terms of cheek reddening – then says, 'I don't tell you because you never ask. Never wanted to know!' She raises her voice to be heard above the sluice.

'I'm sorry. Really I am,' I tell her, then add, 'I've been a crap sister.'

There is a long pause after this.

'If you're waiting for me to disagree with you, that's not going to happen ...'

'No, OK, fair enough.' I nod. But I still feel the need to explain. 'I didn't mean to block you out. It's just ... you were ... always so down on Mum. And when she died, I was just so sad—'

'You didn't show it—'

'No. I was an idiot.'

'You were staying in control,' Melissa corrects me, parroting the phrase I've used in my defence for the past twenty years.

'I was an idiot.'

'I missed her too, you know,' Melissa says, wiping just-washed hands on her still-wet trousers. 'I lost *my* mum as well, even though she could be … well—' She stops herself. 'And I hated seeing Dad hurting like that. But then it felt as though you abandoned us. Like there was nothing to keep you there – like I wasn't good enough.' Then she adds, quietly, 'Which is just how Mum always made me feel.'

'She did?' I'm taken aback.

'Always!' Melissa says. 'She was different with you. Whether she meant to be or not. I loved her but she wasn't always … *nice* to me.'

I prickle at this. Because my idealised Saint Mum was always fair and just. I got used to defending her – from Melissa, from Dad, even, once, from Greg.

He never made that mistake again …

But could I have been wrong about her, too? Or at least, not wholly right? Scandinavia has already taught me that there are shades of grey.

Perhaps Mum beetled around the 'battle ship' end of the spectrum … Supposing she wasn't 'all good'? Supposing she was only human? Like the rest of us?

I remember being very young, sitting on our mother's lap, wrapped in a towel after a bath. She would sing songs that she made up, just for me, and I felt like I was wrapped in love. But when I picture this scene, it doesn't include Melissa. *Wasn't she there?* I wonder. So I ask.

'Hell, no – I don't remember her doing anything like that with me.' Melissa snorts. 'Maybe she was already a bit knackered. Used up. Or she didn't like me as much.'

'What, like I got the "best bits" of Mum?' I ask her.

'Maybe it's a firstborn thing.' She shrugs.

I think about this. *Have I been nicer to Charlotte than I have been to Thomas?* I scroll through the highlight reel of my own parenting. Of endless nappy changes. Of weaning (*the mess!*).

Of getting Charlotte and Thomas out of the bath when they were small, fighting to get them dried and dressed while they wriggled and shouted and drove me mad. 'Like wrestling croco-diles,' is how Greg described my post-bath technique. I'm not sure I've been beatifically nurturing with either of them.

I remember Mum as this shiny beacon of motherhood, but I doubt my children will ever think of me that way, I realise. *They'll probably remember that I was always cross, busy, and a bit useless ...*

I've never made a rocket out of loo rolls, or done anything Pinterest-y with yoghurt pots. Or made up lullabies. Or tried to encourage either of them to take up the sodding violin. *I've failed. On an epic scale ...* I worry, now.

I try to relay this to Melissa. 'I think I've been equally rubbish with both of my children.'

She does not dispute the statement, but says instead, 'Well, you've got time to change all that.'

'I have, haven't I? With your help?'

'You mean if I do my best not to die?' She looks at me, very sincerely, as though she is peering into my very soul. Then she sputters a *pffft*. 'Just messing with you!' and punches me on the arm. It hurts, a lot, but I know, in Melissa-world, that this means we're at peace.

'Anything I can do, or that you want to talk about, with the diagnosis or treatment or anything, I'll be there,' I tell her. 'I mean it.' I tense up in anticipation of another wallop. But it doesn't come. Instead, she says, 'Thanks.'

'I don't want people to be all careful around me though, or do that thing where they tilt their head to one side like I'm a toddler that's crapped itself and needs wiping,' Melissa adds.

'No. Right. Of course you don't.' I hold my head unnaturally upright. 'But I can come to your appointments, help out around the house – whatever you need.'

'All right then,' she agrees, then with a glint in her eye, adds, 'but you might have to look after the house rabbits. And walk the dogs.'

I gulp.

'That's OK. Charlotte and Thomas would love to help with the rabbits.' I hope this is true. 'And I can Google "best way to walk dogs".'

'It's not about doing it "the best way".' She stares at me in amusement. 'It's about giving them some exercise and letting them take a dump!'

'Got it.' I nod.

'And wearing a high visibility vest and a bum bag with dog biscuits in it,' Melissa says, sounding blasé.

'OK,' I concede, resigned to my fate.

'Just kidding about that last part – you only need to carry around treats or wear a tabard if you want to!'

'Oh! Right!' I exhale with relief – as Melissa near undulates with mirth.

'Ha! You should see your face! I got you that time! Wow, you really are sorry.'

I look at her with damp eyes, trying to smile.

'And you're crying!' Melissa points now.

'I'm not crying, *you're* crying,' I tell her, laughing. 'And I'm not going anywhere ever again – you're stuck with me.' Then I add as an afterthought, 'So don't go leaving me with sodding Margot while you and Tricia talk to boys and hang out in bars!'

'All right, all right,' Melissa agrees. 'But you know, the only reason you don't like Margot is that you two are similar in a lot of ways.' She says this as though it is fact – undisputed and apparent to everyone but me.

'What?' I scoff. 'No, we're not!'

'Yes, you are,' Melissa says.

'We're not!'

'You are!' she tells me. 'Margot's not a bad person: she's just a hotter, smarter, *younger* version of you – of course you hate her!'

'I don't *hate* her!' I retort, then modify this with a 'much' and 'any more'. 'Anyway I'm nothing like Margot!' *Am I?*

Could it be that she represents everything I hoped I could be, once?

I have a horrible feeling my little sister has been Very Wise Indeed. Again. 'Well, maybe I *might* have tried to win at things a bit too much in the past,' I concede, glossing over the fact that I'm counting 'the past' as being 'up to and including the last hour'. 'But I'm not the one with an inherited sense of entitlement, no idea about the real world, and tits so perky they don't need upholstery!' I try to make my tone light-hearted, to get back to the place where we were just a few moments ago and make my sister laugh. 'I'm not the one who's a pain in the arse, knob-head, Little Miss Perfect at *everything* – but who can't bloody swim and nearly made us all drown!' It's at this point that I decide to embark upon an ill-advised impersonation of our youngest trainee Viking. '*Ooh, I'm Margot! Look at me! Help, help! I can't swim!*'

Just at this moment, there's a lull in the Scandi-pop background music and a sob so loud it can be heard from the cubicle behind us. It's then I remember that the stall has been occupied since our arrival, and that someone has been in there for a *really* long time.

Melissa breaks away from me, hesitates for a moment, then knocks at the door. 'Everything OK?' A muffled snuffle can be heard in response, and so Melissa, with no regard for privacy or personal space – as usual – stands on the loo seat of the adjacent cubicle to peer over the top of the plywood wall. Finding she's too short to see, she summons me to try.

'No way!' I hiss.

'*Yes* way!' Melissa insists.

The crying game continues as the bawls ramp up a gear.

'Come on!' my sister beckons. 'Whoever it is might need help!'

I'm not convinced this is wise, but unwilling to jeopardise our newfound sisterly equilibrium, I do as I'm bid.

You are putting your bare feet on a loo seat, my inner monologue castigates me. But Melissa appears unconcerned, edging around the oval throne to give me a better foothold until I can extend my fingers to gain purchase on the top of the stall and then, finally, poke my head over to see what's the other side.

Shit ...

I experience another of the sinking feelings with which I've become exceedingly familiar of late.

'Oh god,' says Melissa. 'It's her, isn't it?'

An open, unlined face registers shock, then dismay, mottling slightly on seeing me, before crumpling into a further onslaught of tears.

'Sorry, Margot,' is all I can think of to say.

Fifteen

'Every … time …' Margot gulps to get the words out between sobs ' … I spend time … with people … I like—' she dissolves into hiccups and does some loud sniffing before she can resume her sentence ' —they never … like … *me*.'

There is an awkward silence, at least on my part. Then Melissa pipes up. 'Of course we *like* you!' She pokes at my thigh, urging me to follow her lead.

'Yes!' I blurt. 'I didn't mean it, that stuff I said – it was the gin talking!'

But Margot won't be consoled. Her bottom lip is trembling and she's battling snot now, so I scrunch up some loo roll for her to have a wipe with. Once I've leant over the top of the toilet door and delivered my gift of several sheets of two-ply, I poke at Melissa.

'Go on!' I tell her.

'What?' Melissa hushes me.

'Say something else! Something nice! Please?' I beg. 'You're good at all that.'

'*What?*'

'You know, talking and stuff – words coming out of your face …' I'm floundering now.

'No!' she hisses. 'This is your crap-storm, you clean it up!'

Must everything relate to excrement with my sister? Seemingly so …

'Margot?' I try, looking back over the plywood wall. 'Margot! Listen – what you just heard ... Ignore me. Forget about it. I shouldn't have said—'

'But you *meant* it!' she wails.

'No! Not really.' I glance back at my sister, still hoping for backup. She makes a V-sign with her fingers and points them at me, then at the cubicle next door. *What?* 'What does that even mean?' I hiss. 'I have no idea what you're on about!'

Melissa shakes her head in despair. 'Just keep talking! To *her*!' she whispers back.

So I do.

'I didn't *mean* mean it,' I go on. 'It's just that you can sometimes come across a bit ... *perfect* ... what with your hair and your face and your tiny bottom and nice arms and your no-bra policy—'

'What?' Margot cups her hands to her chest defensively and Melissa mimes slitting her throat to indicate that I might just be making things worse.

'Sorry, that's not important right now,' I say, trying to dismiss my previous point. 'You're also clever and good at things and *young*. So young ...' I lose my train of thought momentarily.

'That's not my fault ...' Margot retaliates, quite rightly.

'No, it isn't,' I say. 'I think I was just—' I take a deep breath before I can bring myself to say the words '—a bit *jealous*.'

'Jealous?' She looks wide-eyed. 'Of me?'

'Mmm,' I murmur, embarrassed now. 'As though we were somehow in competition—' I break off, aware that I'm flattering myself by even entertaining this notion.

'Basically, I think my sister would quite like to *be* you.' Melissa cups her hands and speaks into the wall. *Oh, so NOW she's joining in? Thanks a lot ...* 'Isn't that right, Alice?' Melissa raises her eyebrows at me encouragingly.

Really? Is my vilification to be quite so complete? Thank god for the gin, I think. *This would be far too much, sober ...*

'Yes,' I manage, jaw clenched. 'Yes, that's right.'

'See?' Melissa beams. 'That wasn't so hard, was it?' She hops off the loo seat looking pleased with herself.

I step down, tentatively, and between us we coax Margot out of the stall. Her feline eyes are pink from prolonged crying and her brow is crinkled with confusion.

And yet ... still pretty! How does that work?!

'Come here, come to mama bear,' Melissa says, inexplicably maternal all of a sudden. She holds out her arms and envelops Margot into one of her best hugs as the younger woman attempts to compose herself.

'I'm sorry,' I say again – for what must be the twentieth time today.

"S'OK,' Margot mumbles, wiping away tears. 'But you would tell me, wouldn't you?' she asks. 'If there are things I do that put people off? Because this happens a lot ...' She's crying again. 'At school ...' She sniffs. 'University ...' Her sentence is further punctuated by a nose blow. ' ... even the Duke of Edinburgh Awards! Though of course Phil would never say anything to Daddy ...'

'Of course he wouldn't.' Melissa strokes Margot's hair and *shushes* her as I fight the urge to roll my eyes. 'But perhaps,' my sister offers, 'you could do with ... relaxing a bit more?'

'Mmm.' I make a tentative 'agreeing' noise then try to get in on the hugging and head-stroking action.

Is this what girls do in these sorts of situations?

But Melissa breaks away and both women stare at me.

'I mean you as well,' Melissa tells me. 'No one likes a smart-arse and there's no need to make everything a competition.'

Oh …

'No …' Margot and I say in unison, struggling to take on these new life lessons.

'But it's never too late to change.' She turns back to Margot. 'Look at my sister? She's been uptight for thirty-seven years—'

'I have not!' I retort on reflex.

'You have,' Melissa corrects me.

'*Not* … ?' I'm less sure now.

'OK, what was the last party you went to where you let your too-long hair down?' she asks.

'The last *party*? That's your metric? Are we fifteen?' I flash her my best 'teenage'look and wonder aloud whether a dentistry conference counts. Melissa shakes her head and a pitying expression comes over her.'In that case,I don't know,' I concede. *In truth, it may have been the millennium.* 'I used to be fun once, didn't I?' There is silence. 'Then suddenly, one day, I woke up with two kids and a Renault Espace …'

'You both just need to … loosen up more,' Melissa goes on, giving a – possibly drunken – shimmy to illustrate 'optimal loosening'.

'Like how?' I ask, cautiously.

'Like …'Melissa thinks of a suitable example, before settling on, 'Like Tricia! Come on, I'll show you.' With this, she boots open the toilet door, links an arm in each of ours, and leads us back out into the now buzzing bar where a bouffant blonde bob is just visible amidst a crowd of cheering Vikings. She stands, legs apart, breasts hoiked together like buns by a fire-warmed brassiere, a clutch of silverware in one hand and tumbler of 'brown liquid' in the other.

'*Tricia?*'

'There you are!' she greets us enthusiastically. 'Are you having a marvellous time? I'm having a *marvellous* time! It turns out that when I get drunk, I can speak *Danish*!' She slurs something incomprehensible at a passing Viking who looks perplexed.

'What are you doing with those?' I point to the knives in her hand.

'Ah! Well.' She looks pleased to have the opportunity to explain her cunning ploy. 'I've been chatting to the indigenous, and with the help of my push-up bra, I have negotiated a deal whereby we'll all get a free beverage of our choosing, every time I can hit that corkboard, over—' she squints at the far side of the room '—*there*! At least, I think that's where it is ... I was telling everyone all about our axe-throwing lesson and then I thought, "Why not show them?" Here, hold my drink ...' A glass is deposited in my sister's hands as Tricia turns to take aim, before any of us can form the words to dissuade her. I reach out, in what feels like slow motion, to catch her right arm as it swings back to launch weaponry in the direction of the immaculate clientele, when a voice from the entrance halts Tricia in her tracks.

'Stop!'

Silhouetted by a crack of lightning from the outside world stands a statuesque figure: her mane of glossy hair apparently undiminished by a pounding from the elements.

Sleek and surefooted, Inge gusts into the bar as a ripple of awareness follows her. Even the catalogue-esque clientele pale in comparison with her Amazonian form and self-assured presence, and one by one they greet her, vying for her attention. But Inge's eyes are only on Tricia. The crowd parts as she marches over and confiscates the cutlery.

'I'll take those, thanks,' says Inge, returning them to their rightful place behind the bar.

'Sorry,' mumbles Tricia.

'Never apologise,' Inge holds up a hand. 'Just keep your axe-throwing for outside.'

'Right, yes. Got it.' Tricia nods. 'But for all of us running off, too ... and for taking the boat ...'

'Yeah, that was a little dumb,' Inge concedes. 'In a storm. When there was no hope of seeing a swan ... But I must congratulate you all on your wanderlust and seafaring spirit.'

'You must?' I'm stupefied.

'Of course,' she says.

'Even though we almost drowned?' Margot asks.

'None of you died, did you?' Inge clarifies, doing a quick headcount.

'But we *nearly* did. Twice, in my case ...' Margot starts up again, before Melissa gives her a look that says, '*You know that thing we talked about when you can be a massive goody-goody who takes things too literally and puts people off? Yeah, this is one of those times. Stop talking. Now.*'

'You were *Vikings*,' Inge tells us. We all stand a little taller on hearing this. 'You survived. Otto gave me the heads up that I'd find you here – and that you'd made it together. Which means you're ready – for tomorrow. For the final stage of your training. You're ready for—' even before she can say the word, I tense up '—berserking!'

Bile rises in my throat. Because in spite of all we've been through and everything I've learned, I still don't feel as though 'me' and 'berserking' are entities that should ever go together. *How am I going to be able to slough off thirty-seven years' worth of 'uptightness' – as Melissa puts it – to be able to do the whole running, shouting, naked thing in a few short hours?* I'm fretting now, so I'm relieved when Inge tells us that there's a supplementary step we'll be taking together first.

'Although I'm proud of you for making your own way here and getting through the week, we still have some work to do around honesty. Wouldn't you say?' She looks at each of us in turn. 'There have been secrets. Lies. Concealments – even from yourselves. To be a Viking, you need to be true to yourself. To finally go berserk, you need to know who you are and what you stand for.'

This is all sounding a little more earnest than I'm normally comfortable with. But somehow, I can't think of any cynical quips. Maybe it's the gin. Maybe it's the quinine. Maybe it's the ABBA playing on loop ... Or maybe, just maybe, it's the fact that already today I have reckoned with the prospect of losing my sister, fought my way back to her, battled storms – literal and metaphorical – and been humbled in ways I could never have imagined when I woke up this morning. It's as though I've been broken down, only to be built back up, better than before. So if there were ever a time to embrace my 'inner truth' and bare my soul in as un-British a way as possible, it's probably around now, I reason.

'I want you all to focus on what's holding you back and what you're going to do about it,' Inge tells us, taking a seat at the head of a table and gesturing for us to join her on the wooden benches. 'Because we all have to share a world. So anything you're preoccupied with on the inside, now's the time to get it out. Own up to it here, tonight, so we can move on.'

'Like a sort of honesty arms amnesty?' Melissa asks.

'A little like that, yes,' Inge indulges her.

'Ooh, can we have a mantra?' Tricia requests. 'I love a mantra on a retreat. Or a *manifesto!*'

'The Viking Convention!' Margot pipes up. 'Like the Geneva Convention,' she adds for the benefit of the rest of us in case we don't quite 'get it'.

I get it, Margot, I think. But I let it lie. *Because I am the NEW, improved Alice!*

'Sure.' Inge shrugs, as though aware she only has to humour us for another twenty-four hours. 'So *The Viking Convention "Protocol I".'*

'I plan to stop being a – what was it, Alice?' Margot looks at me, then remembers. 'Oh, "a pain in the arse knob-head". And to try relaxing more.'

She says this totally innocently, apparently unaware she is landing me in it, even deeper than I'm already mired.

Inge is appalled and even Tricia looks as though she's trying very hard to raise her eyebrows where the effects of the latest batch of botulism are starting to wear off.

'I SAID, I was REALLY sorry about that,' I clarify for the rest of the party.

'No, it's OK,' Margot assures me, eyes still wide. 'Feedback's a gift, as they said on my gold DofE—'

The rest of us look blank.

'Oh, sorry, the Gold Duke of Edinburgh Award – to complete the process, you have to meet your assessors and talk about what you've done and what you can do better in future. A bit like this! Only with fewer near-death experiences. Usually.'

Margot, I understand now, isn't a bad person. She's just inexperienced of the ways of the world beyond her £36,000-a-year boarding school and (en)titled social circle. And yes, I know exactly how much her schooling cost because *old* Alice Googled it. Back when she had a contraband phone and hadn't learned about things like 'honesty', 'humility' and shades of grey.

'So anyway, I'm going to cut loose more!' Margot announces with a flourish, beckoning over a heart-stopping beautiful barman bearing a tray of aquavit and downing two shots in quick succession. 'Mmm, *umami* ...'

'Good for you!' Melissa gives Margot a slap on the back that almost makes her aquavit go down the wrong way, before adding, 'And maybe tell people you can't swim next time you're near open water, OK?'

'Oh yes, that.' Margot blushes.

Inge looks momentarily surprised. Then she nods sagely, murmuring something in Danish.

'What's that?' Melissa demands.

'I said, "textbook stuff",' Inge clarifies. 'It's your classic overachiever: self-conscious about the seemingly simple skills or activities they haven't yet mastered. A lot of highly successful people can't drive, for instance—'

I experience a momentary a tinge of disappointment that I can both swim *and* drive.

'Or cook,' Inge goes on. I ruffle my feathers with tentative pride, wondering whether I can put my sub-par culinary skills down to overcompensating in other areas of life. 'Though of course, this can just be laziness,' Inge continues.

Oh ...

'Well, I'm going to sign up for swimming lessons as soon as we get home,' Margot announces. 'And stop treating life like one long competition for who can accrue the most House Points ...' She tails off in what I suspect is a rose-tinted recollection of her glory days at school. *Playing lacrosse and snaffling buns in the prefects' common room, probably,* I think. Although it's also possible that I'm projecting my own *Mallory Towers* fantasies here. Melissa wasn't the only one who liked Enid Blyton, I am now prepared to admit.

'Great,' Inge moves us on. 'And you, Tricia?'

'Oh, god, *me* ...' Tricia puffs out her cheeks and adjusts her bra. *Those padded T-shirt bras take an age to dry. She'll catch a chill if she's not careful ...* I worry. Then I stop: *Shut up, Alice! You're boring yourself ...*

The beautiful barman passes back with a depleted tray of shots so I take one to silence my inner monologue. The potato liquor is as much of an assault on my senses as expected. *It's almost ... chewy.* I try not to gag.

'I'm going to think about what's really important rather than running away all the time,' Tricia starts, 'to Ibiza, or Arizona, or ... well ... here. In fact, I might stop running all together – doesn't do anything for the knees at my age: makes me want to throw up most of the time and I'm pretty sure it's contributed to making my face look like a collapsed mineshaft – without "help",' she adds, tapping the area underneath her eye and feeling her brow to check it's still eerily smooth. 'I've spent the past thirty years grafting, seeking out the celebrity *waft* – Phil Collins, Anneka Rice, *et al* – dry ice machine turned up to *eleven*. But all it got me was fired from a job I hated and dumped by a man with a hairy back (and I mean *really* hairy – like he was wearing a jumper. Clogged up the shower no end – as if a woodland creature had taken up residence in the plughole). Anyway, the point is, it wasn't great. Overall, I mean. So maybe it's time for change. To think about what comes next.' We nod, supportively. 'I'm no good at doing nothing – *The Shipping Forecast* followed by *Gardeners' Question Time* banging on about a pensioner's bush? No thanks. I need to work. I'll get another job, somewhere. And it'll be marginally more interesting than the previous one. But I'll stop running. Spend more time with the dogs. And my son.'

'Right, yes,' I say, in as supportive a tone as I can, trying not to dwell on the fact that her son came after the dogs in Tricia's list of priorities. Again.

'He's all grown-up now, of course. Married, even. Pretty girl, nice eyes. Works as an accountant,' She pulls a face. 'But in general, a good egg. And he's turned into a very pleasant human being, in spite of his parents. So it would be nice to see more of him ...' She looks wistful and Inge lays a hand on her arm.

'Reconciling with your son would be a very good plan,' she says. 'However much they annoy us, kids are for life and family is important.' Here, Inge shoots me a look. 'So we need to work at these relationships,' she adds.

Melissa gives me an arm punch. 'D'you think she means us, too?'

'Ow! Yes, yes I do.' I sigh. 'But you have to stop doing that – it *really hurts!*'

'Oh, come on! Build a bridge. Get over it!' Melissa scoffs as I resolve to work on my own unique Melissa-greeting. *A sisterly Chinese burn perhaps?* I wonder. *A sibling wedgie?*

'Melissa? Are you volunteering to go next?' Inge interrupts.

'Me?' Melissa asks.

'Yes, go on: what's your plan for moving forward?'

'Erm ...' she hesitates for a moment before coming up with. 'Carry on being a legend'?'

'Try again,' Inge tells her, firmly though not unkindly.

'Umm, OK ... well.' Melissa frowns. 'Well, I suppose, I'm going to try not to live in the past so much. What with all that's coming up—' she looks at me here '—I need to get better at taking each day as it comes. Living in the now.'

Inge looks as though someone has just presented her with Alexander Skarsgård, starkers – a bottle of schnapps in each hand. 'That's *it!*' she tells Melissa, slapping the table in triumph. 'Well done.'

'Have we left anyone out?' Tricia asks, looking around as I try to shrink further down into the bench to evade scrutiny. 'We've done Margot, me, Melissa ...' Her eyes rest on me. 'Alice!'

'Ah yes, Alice!' Inge turns to me. 'Anything you'd like to share?'

I've learned so much over the past few days. *Where to start?*

'I'm going to stop being an idiot. I'm going to put my own oxygen mask on first—' I nod to Inge, then catch sight of Melissa '—and I'm going to spend time with the people I care about.'

'And forget about perfection,' Inge adds, swishing her unicorn's mane.

Margot spills some of her spud juice at this. 'Easy for you to say ...' she slurs, as four pairs of eyes swivel towards her, surprised by this outburst.

Inge smiles. 'Ah, you and Alice and your perfection!' She shakes her head. 'I said it to her and I'll say it to you: perfection doesn't exist.'

'Show her your arse!' I heckle, remembering what first won me around to Inge's way of thinking. Then I realise the inappropriateness of what I've just demanded and backtrack. 'Sorry, sorry, I—'

'*No apologies!*' the other women bark at me in unison.

'Right. No. As you were – bum out! Or not, whatever you like ...' Befuddled, I drink more, instead – as Inge obliges. Standing up to give us the full benefit of her impressive stature, she drops her trousers and bends over to flash Margot her behind.

'Battle scars!' she tells her, adding, 'we all have them, whether you can see them or not. And we need to *own* them.' At this moment, the insanely hot barman passes again, replenishing our glasses, followed by Otto, delivering snacks (for all of us) and snogs (exclusively for Melissa). Inge pulls her trousers up, in no sort of hurry and as though it were the most normal thing in the world to get your arse out in public, then sits, slowly, as Tricia, Margot and I down our drinks for fortification.

Stubble-rashed and light-headed on lust, my sister promises she'll see Otto before she goes before turning back to the group.

We finish a final round of drinks in comfortable, companionable silence, each contemplating all that has happened and cementing the pledges we have made for the future: to be more honest. To be more Viking.

'You've done well.' Inge stands finally and announces that it's time to leave. 'You have a big day tomorrow, you'll want to rest up.' She tells us that Magnus – here we all pull a face – is back on his feet so he'll be leading the running part and pushing us hard. 'So come on, I'll drive us home.'

'Did you say drive?' Tricia is baffled. 'Aren't we on an island?'

Inge looks at her. 'No?'

'What?' Melissa's head snaps up. 'But we came by boat ...'

'I thought you just wanted the adventure,' says Inge, frowning. 'We're not on an island, it's a tombolo.'

'A tom ... what?' Tricia asks again as Margot slaps her forehead.

'A tombolo! Of course!' Margot exclaims, delighted at the opportunity to finally make use of her first class (Hons) Geography degree. 'A land mass attached to the mainland, by a spit or, in this case, a road—'

'Wait, so hang on, there was no need come by boat?' Melissa checks, doubtfully. Inge shakes her head. '*Shit a brick* ...' is Melissa's instant, unguarded response. Her eyes widen as she turns, slowly, to face the rest of us. 'Sorry ...' she starts to say, before Margot interrupts by walloping my sister on the arm.

'Never apologise!' she says, before adding, 'I wouldn't have missed tonight for the world!'

Sixteen

Burr-burrr-burrrr! Burr-burrr-burrrr!

A piercing, penetrating, din makes me wrap the pillow around my head.

BURR-BURRR-BURRRR!

Swimming up through layers of sleep, pain splices my temples and the terrible brass cacophony seems to sear my very soul.

Make it stop, I beg, silently: *MAKE THE HURTY STOP!*

Peering out from the underside of my goose-down armour, I blink, tentatively, then screw my eyes shut in an attempt to un-see the spectre of Magnus, bearing down on the bunk beds, traditional Viking horn in hand.

Oh dear god, no …

His man-bun is standing proud; his beard, spreading out like a frizzy cloud after forays into braiding over recent days, fish-hook and holestone necklaces dangling, chest, exposed.

Urgh …

'Rise and shine!' he gloats.

I want to tell him to piss off and that I'd prefer to *caffeinate and hope for the best* rather than any rising and shining right now, but find my tongue still hasn't woken up. I feel desiccated, dehydrated, drained of tears and – possibly – still drunk. It's a mere three hours after our bumpy ride home from Valhalla and our sadistic leader, now fully recovered, apparently, is tooting his trumpet with glee.

BURR-BURRR-BURRRR!

Tricia sits bolt upright in the opposite bunk, looking dishevelled, disturbed and with a hint of the *Hellraiser* about her.

'You OK?' Margot swings down from the top bunk. She, at least, still looks relatively fresh.

'Yeah, I'm OK ... I just had an *awful* dream.' Tricia cradles her head in her hands, trying to protect it from the noise.

'You poor thing!' Margot looks concerned. 'What happened?'

'We were going to have to go running barefoot through the woods on no breakfast.' Tricia shudders at the recollection.

'Well, bad luck.' Magnus grins. 'Because today is your Halloween! Now, up! No talking! Just moving! All of you!'

I roll my way out of bed and attempt to stand, unsteady on my legs as a young, hungover, foal.

'Where's Melissa?' Tricia whispers, looking around. 'Shagging again?'

'No!' There's a growl from the top bunk and the blanket ripples into life to reveal my sister.

'It's the final stage of your Viking challenge, ladies. Get ready to go berserk!' Magnus broadcasts, back on infuriatingly irrepressible form.

Where are the rogue berries when you need them? I wonder, blackly. But there's no time to ponder. We're shooed out of the house just as Inge and the children are beginning to stir, then loaded like cattle into the family's bumpy trailer.

Empty stomachs gurgle as we rumble along the road to the forest. Margot pukes over the side of the truck and then wipes her mouth with a sleeve.

'That's better,' she says, as the rest of us look on in alarm.

Tricia begins rummaging for something in her pocket, retrieving a small, gold cylinder that she twists up to reveal a waxy, crimson stump.

'Are you putting *lipstick* on?' Melissa asks, mystified.

'It's not lipstick, it's war paint,' Tricia tells Melissa, pursing her lips and applying a thick layer. 'You need more of it as you get older—'

'Vikings!' She's cut off by a holler from the driver's seat. 'Be at one with your thoughts!'

'You what?' Melissa yells back.

'*Shh*!' Magnus motions.

'Oh! OK. Sorry!'

We comply, exchanging only the odd smile or nod of camaraderie. There's an overwhelming sense of anticipation buzzing between us – as though this really is the moment we've been building up to – not just over the course of this week, but in our lives to date. As though going berserk really might turn out to be the purest expression of *who* we are and *what* we're here for.

We are each to be 'released' at various points in the vast woodland with the simple instruction to find ourselves and so our way home, by embracing the 'intense psychical and mental training' we've received so far.

Today, we prove our mettle, I think. *Today, we test our basic animal instinct to run for our lives. Or, at the very least, for our next meal ...*

Today, we go *berserk*.

'Right,' Magnus announces, as he screeches the truck to a stop. 'Proud Chest? You're first!'

At this, Tricia stands unsteadily makes to wriggle out of her leggings. Magnus looks horrified.

'What are you doing?'

'Getting undressed?' Tricia whispers, as though aware she's still not supposed to be talking. 'Don't we do this bit naked?'

'No!' He blinks rapidly.

'No?'

No!'

'Oh.'

'Why do people always assume Scandinavians want to get naked all the time?' Magnus looks bewildered.

'It's not that—' Tricia remonstrates, at which point I think, *Yes: that. Exactly that.* 'It's just,' she appeals to the group, 'didn't Inge say something about getting nude?' We nod in support.

'Well,' Magnus moderates his tone, 'there may be an *element* of nudity. Inge always goes on about the nakedness—' he shakes his head as though this is just another of their marital spats writ large '—but that's just an added extra. It comes later,' is all he'll reveal. *'Ancillary' nudity? Everyone's favourite kind* ... 'For now, clothes on. ALL OF YOU,' he instructs, sternly, lest the rest of us are overcome by the urge to show him our bits.[28] 'And no talking!' he adds, though on this one I fear several of the Icelandic horses have already bolted. Still, since it's currently so cold I can see my own breath, I'm relieved that we aren't expected to disrobe just yet. 'Get ready to run and we'll see you when – or should I say *if* – you make it back!'

There is an audible gulp.

'Good luck ...' Melissa whispers, as Tricia clambers over the side, presenting her arse to my face for the second time in twenty-four hours. 'Or rather, make your own luck, Viking style!' she adds, disregarding Magnus's no-talking policy. Tricia

---

28. We're not.

gives a half smile and lowers herself down to ground level, telling us all earnestly that she'll see us on the other side.

'Run! Run like you stole something!' Melissa yells after her as Tricia jogs towards the forest.

'Shhh!' Magnus hisses.

'Sorry!' Melissa shouts, then turning back to us, adds, '*Not* sorry!'

Once Tricia has vanished from view, we drive on, further into unknown territory. 'Night Wolf' is next. Margot vaults over the side of the vehicle effortlessly and sprints into the distance with a double thumbs-up before disappearing into the dark forest.

'Just you and me then,' Melissa whispers, slinging an arm around my shoulders as we judder off, driving cross-country for another few minutes.

Eventually, the truck slows to a stop and Magnus twists his head to look back from the driver's seat. 'Strong Legs? Are you ready?'

'I was *born* ready!' is Melissa's bravado-fuelled reply. 'Let's do this!' She executes an elaborate commando roll to the forest floor before bouncing up and doing a few air punches to psyche herself up.

She's a loon, but I love her. I watch my sister go bumbling off and hope against hope that we all come out of this in one piece.

And then there was one.

Light begins spiking through the trees and I take in great lungfuls of cool morning air in an attempt to stave off carsickness/alcohol-induced nausea before I'm delivered to my drop-off point.

'Time to shine, Aslög!' Magnus says, finally, as I am unceremoniously turfed out.

*

Twigs snap beneath my feet as I bat away branches and run. Really run. Heart pounding so hard it's threatening to break free from my chest and outstrip me at any moment. My sense of direction has improved slightly since the start of my Viking training but, if anything, my spatial awareness appears to have regressed with the addition of a hangover. I ricochet off trees, adrenaline surging around my body until it stings – almost like sunburn. And then ... and then ...

Something amazing happens.

Momentum takes over and despite an angry pain in my shoulders, feet that have been lacerated and shins currently seizing up, I carry on, impervious to any obstacles now. My legs blur beneath me and – suddenly – I'm flying. Suddenly, I am an uplifting montage at the end of a film: a hero chasing through a crowded airport to stop the plane in time to get his girl; the boy in a rites of passage classic breaking free from his parents; Butch Cassidy and/or the Sundance Kid, charging out, guns blazing. I am Forrest Gump. I am Rocky, I, II, III and IV. I am the entire cast of *Chariots of Fire*. I am ... *Hang on, why they always men?* I think, outraged. *Don't women ever run in films? Unless they're being chased by a serial killer? Where are the badass women?* Incensed to find that I can't think of a single example of sisters running for themselves, I experience a surge of extra vigour at the injustice until I am a ball of kinetic energy.

The forest holds no fear for me now, and that terrified girl who got lost in the woods all those years ago becomes just that: a girl unsure of her way in unfamiliar woodland who got scared. As anyone would, in the circumstances and with all she had to contend with at the time. She's still a part of me, but I feel almost maternal towards her now. I surrender to the fear I felt then and the exhilaration I'm currently experiencing and – somehow – reconcile them both.

Because I am Viking!

I run and I run and I don't stop, even when stones, slugs and God knows what else lodge themselves between my toes. Branches whip my face and brambles attack me from all angles, but I keep going.

Come and get me thorns!

I can hear the blood pulsing in my ears and feel a juddering heartbeat. Time loses all meaning and I am only aware that I have been doing this for what feels like An Eternity when I see two figures ahead of me in the clearing. Fire-lit torches are burning, and with my breath escaping in puffs now, I manage a *'Hello?'*

Then I 'shout my rage', as instructed.

'Arghhh!'

'Arghhhhh!' Melissa shouts back. Flushed, with a strand of dark hair stuck to her forehead with sweat, my sister is buzzing.

'That was *insane*! Wasn't that insane?' she pulls at her T-shirt to create a flow of cool air down her top. 'I mean, wow! I felt like Kate Bush pushing through a forest! Or Bilbo Baggins showing Mirkwood who's BOSS! I LOVE berserking! I want to do it again! Right now! I want to go and ... and ... break rocks or something!' she tells me excitedly, rain dripping from her nose.

Margot is similarly euphoric and somehow manages to look like a film star, despite being covered in mud (*How does she do it?* I marvel*). Then a third woman limps into view.

'I think I screamed so hard I strained my groin ...' Tricia proclaims to all, rubbing at her pelvis before dissolving into a coughing fit.

The Hills are Alive with the Sound of Wheezing, I think, affectionately. *Again*.

We hear a slow hand clap, and then a barrel-chested man wearing nothing but harem pants deftly descends from a tree.

He swings down branches with simian grace, then strides across the clearing as the rest of us roll our eyes, as one.

'The children have built a fire in your honour,' he tells us, as we move out of the woods. He quickens his pace to keep up with us, keen to claw back his audience. 'It's big!' His voice goes up a notch in desperation: 'And fiery!'

Ahhh ... Viking pyromania ... how I'll miss you!

We charge towards a plume of smoke in the mid-distance until we can see a vast bonfire on the beach, now crackling and licking upwards, expelling heat and light for yards around. The children are daring each other to throw kindling on top of the flaming stack. Their woody missiles are aimed ever more haphazardly until, inevitably – like a giant game of high-stakes Jenga – one falls, whereby they all beat a hasty retreat, cackling like the miniature lunatics that they are.

Inge is preoccupied with pulling down birch twigs and binding them together with twine, but when she sees us, she sets down her bundle and spreads her arms wide, inviting us all into her warrior-ess embrace.

Two group hugs in as many days and I'm not even flinching. I take comfort from the warmth of my sister on one side and Inge on the other.

'My Vikings! You've done it,' she says. This is enough. This is all we need to hear from our *real* leader – the one who's taught us more about life than any of us can yet appreciate. But there's more. 'Now, we celebrate.' She collects buckets of water then gestures to a small wooden cubicle up shore that I'd merely taken for another outhouse up until now. 'Who's for a sauna?'

'Vikings do spa treatments?' Melissa asks in disbelief.

'Of course.' is Inge's response. 'Heat is good for the muscles after a run, plus Vikings invented saunas – we built them wherever we went! Hot stones? Water? Communal sweating?

It's practically our religion! More important decisions get made in saunas than in meetings!' I've never seen Inge this animated. 'In Finland, they even have a Burger King sauna! To share a sauna is to share the essence of someone! To be a true Viking,' Inge summarises, 'you must *sweat*.'

'I sweat on a winter's day in Kidderminster!' Melissa exclaims. 'I always knew I had a Viking heart!'

'Are you sure you're allowed saunas—' I start, looking at my sister protectively.

'Listen, *dentist*: I'm fine,' she tells me with a grin. 'I asked about spa treatments after you kept harping on about fluffy towels, so yes: I'm sure. Let's do this!'

Magnus shepherds the children back to the house and, as soon as he's out of earshot, Inge instructs. 'Clothes off!'

This time, it's for real and Tricia isn't a woman who needs to be asked twice. She strips off layers of muddied Lycra and, as advertised, the mahogany tan extends to every nook and cranny that the ultraviolet rays of her personal Solar 5000™ Stand Up Sunbed can penetrate. Her enhanced chest is so taut, it looks like it's on loan from a younger woman, and she's also completely hair free … *down there* …

She catches me looking and explains. 'My last gentleman caller liked a clean work surface.'

'Right. Yes …'

Margot, as expected, looks like a live action cover of *Women's Health* magazine and Inge is just as toned and magnificent as I might have imagined – battle scars and all. And then there's me.

I'm typically hyper-aware of my body – of the way my thighs must look, the way my arms go rigid, refusing to swing, and of my hands, just … *hanging* there. But for the first time post puberty, when faced with the prospect of getting naked,

I don't demur. *This is OK,* I think, *these women are my friends. We've dodged death together. We've thrown axes. We've shared more than I've ever shared with another human being. Ever. So this? This feels ... fine.* Something I was so scared of at the start of the week now seems inconsequential. Not prurient or salacious: simply *sans* clothes. So I disrobe.

I'm just peeling off a sodden sleeve when I notice a bump on my right arm that moves and grows as I flex at the elbow. At first I presume it's another bruise from the hours spent colliding with forestry and falling over, or an injury sustained when I ever-so-slightly fainted post-run.[29] But then I notice the same thing on my left arm.

Could it be ... ? Have I got ... BICEPS now?![30]

Amazed and elated, I tense then relax these strange new additions.

I've got guns! Muscles! All of my very own! Michelle Obama, here I come ...

I strip off swiftly after this, keen to check if there are any more muscles lurking (there aren't. But still, it's ridiculously exciting ...).

Here I am, world! Nude! Enjoying the air around my arse! The wind on my nipples! The breeze on my BICEPS! I am Viking! Hear me roar!

I tune back in to my surroundings to hear Tricia telling everyone about the time she presented a series of naturist videos. 'Great gig on the Costa del Sol,' she reminisces. 'You can still find a few of them on YouTube. Though once you've seen that many naked bodies, you realise no one's very interested in yours. More's the pity ...'

[29.] I'm still harder than Simon from *Lord of the Flies*. Fact.

[30.] Yeah, that's right: in a WEEK #GoVikings

I hadn't thought about it like this, but as we near the shed-sauna, I find I am completely relaxed. *Inge's right*, I think. *It is freeing, somehow.* Surrounded by four other exposed bodies, each moving and undulating in its own way, it's easier to get a sense of perspective. *Look how far we've all come!* I cast my eyes around our group, affectionately.

The sauna is dimly lit, with no fluffy towels in sight and definitely no whale music. But I find I don't mind – in fact, I'm enjoying myself.

'Hot ...' mumbles Melissa as we blink our way in and take a seat on wooden benches.

'Relax into it,' Inge instructs. 'The heat forces you to slow down.' She throws a scoop of water on the stove, releasing a wave of steam until I feel as though I am being broiled alive. 'Just make sure you drink a lot,' she adds.

I eye up the cool box in the corner of the hut. 'Is there water in there?'

Inge lifts the lid to reveal a row of neatly packed bottles, glistening with condensation. 'Better than water,' she tells us. 'Beer!'

I'm so thirsty by now that I'll pretty much drink anything, so I accept, gratefully. Within minutes, my muscles – and my mind – begin to pleasantly loosen.

And ... breathe ...

I do this, on repeat, until a lovely lax sensation takes over. I feel tenderised to the world anew. Memories and emotions that have been firmly locked up for decades seem to swirl around me, returning 'home' once more.

I remember the time I cried so much that I threw up.

And ... breathe ...

I remember the night I drunk myself sober.

And ... breathe ...

I remember the summer I had my heart broken by a French exchange student.

Breathe ...

I remember the morning Charlotte was born. And Thomas. Even the day Mum and Dad bought Melissa home from hospital.

Home isn't anything to be scared of, I see now – and it isn't a building, either. It's on the inside of us. *And it's been there all along.* I feel as though, finally, I'm coming home to my body. To me.

I find I'm crying: big, fat, happy tears mixing with the sweat that's rolling down my face now. Without saying anything, Melissa shuffles closer and a hand slips into mine. I look up at her as she mouths the words. 'It's OK.'

Inge ladles more water on the sizzling stove and then – once I'm pretty sure my eyelids are in danger of burning off – we're led out into the chilly evening air, down to the pier, and told to jump.

A week ago, this would have terrified me. But after last night's epic adventure and our graduation through the seven stages of Viking training, a quick dip in the icy North Sea seems easy.

Inge is the first to take the plunge, followed by Tricia, then Margot – who quite sensibly elects to lower herself in and hold on to the side of the pier to avoid the risk of drowning for the third time in twenty-four hours. Melissa and I opt for a running jump in tandem, and as toes touch water, I let out an involuntary yelp. There is a burst of hysterical laughter as we flounder, delirious, before wading out and rubbing at skin now burgundy with cold.

The process is repeated after another stint in the sauna and by the third watery-dunk, the sea no longer feels chilly, even.

Between us, we support Margot and in a strange and totally inelegant synchronised swimming move, we coax her away from her wooden safety ledge and out into the open water. And then ... We all simply float, like leaves in the wind or animals that have finally found their true home.

We emerge together, glistening in the moonlight, butterflies from a chrysalis: reborn.

Then the birch twigs come out.

'Oh my!' I can't help exclaiming and even Melissa expresses some surprise.

'Whipping makes the skin soft,' Inge explains, brandishing her homemade switch.

'I use exfoliating shower gloves,' Margot sounds apprehensive. 'Won't they do?'

'No.' Inge is insistent.

Tricia gamely volunteers to go first, before suggesting that we all 'have a go on the cat-o'nine-tails' – both administering and being administered to. So we do. The smack of birch on flesh takes some getting used to, but after several *Fifty Shades of Grey* references and some exclamations that would have done Frankie Howard proud, I warm to the discipline (pun intended).

Reader: I whipped a girl and I liked it.

Afterwards, Tricia and Melissa compare skin smoothness while Inge retrieves several large foil parcels from the cool box and throws them on the hot coals. A few minutes later, dinner is served. For women who haven't eaten all day, there is no finer sentence in the English language. A few minutes later, we unwrap charred aluminium bundles to reveal thick, sizzling and delicious-smelling ... sausages.

'I'm still a vegetaria—' I start and then think, *Sod it.* I forget about any previous dietary peccadillos and fall upon the juicy provender (#justetff).

'So, is this, like, *a thing*?' Melissa asks through a mouthful of semi-chewed pork.

'Sorry?' Inge asks.

'Sauna sausages?'

'Oh, yes,' she says. 'Cooked the traditional way on the coals and eaten in situ.'

'*Naked*?' I ask surprised.

'Course.' Inge nods, taking another bite.

Once we are sufficiently sausaged-up, we are released back into the night air and a bear-like figure in a grey beanie materialises from the gloam: Otto.

'Oh, Otto fancy seeing you here ...' Melissa grins before taking his hand and towing him off to the woods to have her wicked way with him one last time. Otto is a willing supplicant, and the two break into a near-sprint to get to where they're going faster.

Inge and Margot are just plundering the depths of the cool box when Tricia reappears with a ghetto blaster, of the kind that was probably last sold some time in the 1980s.

'Found it in the woodshed!' she shouts with delight. 'Shall we?'

Pressing play on the clunky cassette player, we are rewarded with forty-five minutes of the best retro Scandinavian pop one could ever have the fortune to stumble across.

Stark naked, Tricia demonstrates some of her finest moves, including 'air push ups', and – what has long been a personal favourite – 'the two-fingered pointy dance'. It's all done with such joy and a lack of inhibition that I can't help but smile – and neither can the others. So when Inge and Margot join in with some equally inexpert shuffling, shoulder shimmies, and elbow dancing, I do too. And I've never felt so free.

Melissa returns with some serious *knullruffs* and sex stamped all over her face. She's wearing her fleece again, but not much else. She plucks at imaginary lapels to indicate that the 'hit rate' of her polyester pulling-jumper remains undiminished. I give her an approving nod and a grin. After expressing delight that the party appears to be 'going off like a frog in a sock', she joins in the frenzied dancing, spinning and zooming around like a drunk bee. There is singing, too, an activity that Inge declares is prime Viking. Feeling safe, soothed, yet also invigorated and stronger than I think I've ever been, I open my mouth and get my *song* on – for the first time since my Whitney Houston shower sessions as a child. My voice is ... loud, I realise. And pretty bad, I can now concede. *The pop world hasn't been unduly deprived of my services after all* ... There may well be a good dose of what Melissa termed warbling on the top notes. But it *feels* great, and this, I'm learning, is the point. We sing and dance and spin until we collapse in the sand, semi-hysterical, cheeks aching from laughter.

'Have you been having a *nice time*?' I ask Melissa. 'You look as though you have!'

'I've had a very nice time, thank you.' She nods and I smile. I'm pleased for her. I'm also aware that I haven't had that glow for a very long time now. *Something to work on*, I think to myself.

'Are you going to miss Otto?' I ask.

My sister shrugs. 'Yeah. But I'll be OK.'

And I believe her. I give her a hug that swiftly morphs into a wrestle (her idea, not mine) before at least one of us has a mouthful of sand (me).

While Inge arbitrates over a cartwheeling competition that Margot appears to have initiated (old competitive habits die hard), I slip an arm through Melissa's. I take the opportunity to draw her away for a long overdue sister-to-sister (the new 'deep and meaningful').

The fire has mellowed from 'raging inferno-Jenga' status to 'warming glow' and so we settle down to toast ourselves, feeling dizzy and decidedly dehydrated (read 'drunk'), but cleansed of body and mind.

By the darty light of the licking flames, Melissa looks different somehow. As though perhaps I've never really seen her, properly, before. Her pupils are threatening to overtake her irises and her hair is now essentially a thatch, but I also see now that she isn't the same little sister I took for granted all these years. I study the blocks of shadow under her cheekbones, just above deeply etched dimples, and the sculpted contours of her face. And I see, now, that she's a grown woman. And she's beautiful.

Melissa catches me looking and tells me with sisterly love to 'stop being an insane weirdo'. I tell her I'm beginning to realise that sanity is overrated.

'Fair point.' She shrugs, and we contemplate this. 'If I die,' Melissa says, staring into the fire now, 'I want you to give me a proper Viking funeral. I mean flames, boats, hot men with beards – the works.'

I feel a stab in the heart just hearing her talk like this, so I take her hands and address her head on. 'Listen to me when I say that everything's going to be OK. And if it's not, I will make it OK,' I promise. Wisely or otherwise.

Melissa starts to well up at this and sniffs, loudly. She attempts to wipe her nose on her arm, but because I'm still holding her hands, she takes me with her, depositing a residue of salty snot up my wrist.

'Oh, sorry!' she says.

'It doesn't matter,' I say, eyes pricking with tears and my own nose running now.

'You look like a snotty mermaid,' Melissa half laughs, half sobs, 'with your too-long hair ...'

'Thanks,' I laugh-snuffle back.

'I mean, maybe one that's had quite a hard life and lost its sea-shell comb, but a mermaid nonetheless.'

I shrug. 'I'll take that.'

'My Vikings!' Inge comes over, with Tricia and Margot in wobbly drunken pursuit. She moves to where we're sitting with the careful, deliberate tread of a mildly intoxicated woman and I'm overjoyed to discover that even Amazonian goddesses lose it sometimes, too. She sits down with us and passes around a bag of nuts that have materialised from the depths of her snack pack. 'This is hygge, by the way,' she tells us. 'I told you you'd find it on your own: relaxing, together.'

'And the nakedness?' Margot slurs.

'Optional,' Inge responds.

'And the booze?' Tricia checks.

Inge gives this one more thought. 'Recommended. That or coffee. And snacks. Obviously.'

'Excellent.' Tricia claps her hands together and nearly misses.

'So are you happy?' Inge asks us all. 'Just at this moment, I mean?'

'Yes.' Melissa nods and I find I have to admit that, in spite of everything – my sister's illness, Greg, what'll become of us when I get back – I am, too. Here. Now.

'That's all there is, isn't there?' I say. 'This. Right now. We're all just carbon, aren't we? We get one go at life, then we make dust and become something else ...'

At this, Inge smiles.

'What?' I demand.

'There's nothing left for me to teach you! My work is done.'

I feel suddenly peaceful, and ... heavy. *Happily ... heavy*, I think, pressing my hands down on the sand around me to ground myself. Then Melissa gives my arm a punch, so I give her a Chinese burn, before lying back to take in the panoply of stars above, experiencing a strange, bone-deep, contentment. There is a slackening off of tension, somewhere deep within – a tension I've never appreciated the extent of before, until it isn't there any more. One by one, the others recline until we are five women, sprawled out in the sand under the stars, naked but for a sex fleece, a rough-hewn blanket and a Sweaty Betty hoodie between us. Lying together in the warmth of the fire, talking and laughing until our ribs hurt, I vow never to forget this moment. Whatever happens next.

In the morning, heads are sore, hair is dreadlocked, faces are filthy and Margot somehow has a charred scrap of sausage foil adhering to her left cheek, but we are strangely serene.

I look in the mirror and smile at the woman looking back at me. She has a split lip from some particularly exuberant berserking, unruly hair, and eyebrows in dire need of a tweezer. But her eyes are bright and alive. And she looks, I recognise now, *happy*. The kind of woman I wanted to be when I was a girl. *There you are!* I tell myself, and then, *Here, I am! Battle scars and all …*

We pack up what's left of our belongings, wash and dress. It's strange to see my fellow Vikings in their 'real world' clothes for going home. Tricia's strappy wedge sandals and white Capri pants look out of place in a Scandi farmhouse and my skinny-jeans and navy blazer combo make me look 'a lot like a Boden catalogue reject or someone who runs a dry cleaning franchise', as Melissa kindly points out.[31]

---

31. She's a tonic, my sister …

Wearing shoes again is an odd experience. My feet feel as though they've grown a size – swollen by trench foot and scarring, probably – so that footwear is constraining and I can't stop wriggling my toes in a bid for freedom. *I might just take them off again*, I think. We're also reunited with our phones, to far less fanfare than any of us would have anticipated if you'd asked us a week ago.

Inge presents all of us with our very own grey hessian bags to remember the week by, each containing a candle and a hunk of rye bread 'for the journey'.

'Travel light – but never go hungry,' is how she explains this.

'And keep burning stuff, Viking style?' Melissa asks, holding the candle aloft.

'Always!' Inge grins.

At this, Melissa initiates a group hug, hauling me in and near-crushing my lungs. The usual.

After breakfast and several cups of strong coffee (what else?), Inge sends the children out with Magnus so we can have 'proper goodbyes'. She speaks to each of us in turn, imparting her final, private words of wisdom and encouragement.

When she holds me by the shoulders, I feel like I'm going to cry. I can't wait to see Charlotte and Thomas but a part of me doesn't want to leave this place.

'You're strong,' Inge tells me. 'You're ready.'

'Are you sure?' I can't help asking, at which point her expression shifts and I see a flash of the steeliness I've come to admire so much.

'I'm speaking, aren't I?' she says.

I nod. 'Yes.'

'Then I'm sure.' She smiles.

And I believe her. Because, now, I'm a Viking.

Epilogue

Six months later ...

I push open a heavy door, unsure of what I'll find the other side, this time. The corridor smells strongly of hand sanitiser and sweat. But then I realise that the latter might just be me. I'm out of breath after a sprint from the car in the rain and anxious about being late. I'm still not a late person.

And yet here I am.

Late.

Bloody Greg, I think. *It's Greg's fault.* He had told me he'd pick the kids up at 9am – leaving plenty of time for me to get here. *But was he there at 9am? Or even 9.30am? Was he* Newsnight ...

I still have a few of what Inge would term 'anger issues', but these days they're out in the open. I don't bury things, any more; I vent. And I've stopped making that constant series of self-adjustments, monitoring what I say or do to please other people. I'm slowly learning to let down my guard, thanks to my Viking education. Because whatever backstory we construct for ourselves, I've realised, it's what we actually do, moving forward, that matters.

When I got home from the retreat, Greg and I embarked upon a last-ditch attempt to save our marriage, by talking openly and honestly. I was mindful of becoming one of those women you read about in magazines who jacks in their marriage after a weekend in Magaluf, or during a mid-life crisis post magic mushroom trip – then spends the next decade regretting it. Though when I mentioned these fears to Melissa, she laughed for a good hour.

'Have you met yourself?' She pointed out that, Mr Teeth aside, I had never done anything rash in my life. This was a slight reassurance. Greg and I decided to postpone the extension and – shortly after that – our marriage, with a trial separation. We even saw a marriage counsellor but she told us, unprompted, that we'd be better off calling it a day. And strangely, since then, there's been an overwhelming sense of relief all around. I like living alone, or at least, just me and the kids. I can now do a shop to fill the fridge and feel confident that it won't all be eaten by nightfall. Plus there's no one judging me on how many cushions I have. As a result, I feel about ten years' younger and half a stone lighter (despite all bathroom scale evidence to the contrary).

Only this morning, I called my soon-to-be-ex-husband a 'pube-face' – a delightfully puerile insult I'm currently enjoying that Charlotte told me she'd learned in the playground at school. A term that I pretended to be cross about but secretly relished. Greg looked sincerely apologetic, said he was 'really, really sorry' for being so late and that he had a job interview next week. This was something of a breakthrough and I was genuinely delighted for him. Had I a klaxon to hand, I'd have sounded it. Hard. But I didn't. So instead we all ended up laughing. Greg and I get on better as co-parents living apart than we ever did as *News 24*-addict husband and uptight wife. So when he offered to take the kids this morning, I said 'yes please'. I kissed Thomas and Charlotte goodbye, gave them a hug 'big enough to last until I'm back' and tore out of the door.

Then I drove. Fast. Up the M40 without a single convenience break. I couldn't park so I had to dump the car miles
away and run in the rain. I didn't even have time to walk
the dogs beforehand. *I only hope they haven't crapped everywhere,* I think. They have form in this area.[32] But I can handle
all of these things now. Because I am Viking. I can handle
anything.

Melissa told me not to worry about coming today ('I know
how it all works by now – I know where the loos are and the
best mags ...') but I referred her to *The Viking Convention,
Protocol II*. Namely, the agreement made that we will both be
there for each other no matter what – whether we're prepared
to ask for help or not.[33]

I also know that if it were me in her size-six shoes, I would,
were I being honest, want someone with me. And this is
something I can do for her, physically, as well as being there –
as they say in the self-help community – *'emotionally'*. This
last word still makes me want to vomit slightly, but only
slightly. So, you know: progress. Dad was with her yesterday
and we were all together last weekend. Turns out the kids
love having their granddad and Fun Aunt Melissa around.
And so do I. Dad and I worked out a rota for helping with
Melissa's animals and around the house and now like to
overlap our shifts, so that we get to spend time together, too.
We've even talked – really talked – about Mum. About how

[32.] I don't know how Melissa gets the dogs to defecate exclusively in woodland,
but it's a trick they appear reluctant to repeat. It's as though they can tell
the substitute teacher's in charge and are deliberately playing up ...

[33.] *Protocol I* being our pledges to be more honest with ourselves and take a
break from our various modes of self-sabotage. No more covert 'car picnics'
at 3am ...

he felt, and about how I didn't allow myself to feel. It's been great. I only wish I'd made an effort sooner and I'm sorry I deprived all parties of each other's company for so long. But there's no point beating myself up over this now. *Never apologise*, I remember Inge's words. Instead, I just plan to do better. From now on.

A woman with red cheeks who's always sniffing passes me in the hospital corridor and we exchange a brief smile – in the way British people who've encountered each other a few times but have yet to be formally introduced have down to a fine art. Then I begin scouring the ward for my sister.

I worry that she'll be unrecognisable. I worry that my expression on seeing her will give me away, before I can reassure her that she still looks like herself.

The previous round of treatment took its toll and she described to me the disorientating fog of her 'chemo brain'. The last time, Melissa told me she couldn't stand the smell of bins any more and had just projectile vomited while trying to empty the dishwasher I bought her ('Onto clean plates?' I couldn't help asking. ''Fraid so ...' was her response). My hardy sister now needs a hand emptying her refuse before it reaches 'puke-level-full' and washes up manually again.

I've been pet-sitting, as often as possible, along with a whole host of well-wishing neighbours who have helped out in more ways than I could ever have anticipated. *She's popular, my sister*, I think, proudly: *a good person, who other people want to be around*.

I'm trying to be more like that.

And I think I'm getting there, too. I asked one of the mums at school over for coffee this weekend and had lunch with the new dentist at the practice twice this week. We had tapas together – so it definitely counts. Plus he has really good teeth. And hands. And he keeps a bag for life in his car at all times ... (just the one, mind, but still: impressive). I even reconnected with an old schoolmate recently. I may just be 'slamming it', as Melissa would say. At the very least, it's a start. I'm trying to be less prickly, too. Although I still think people who wear harem pants are, largely, bell ends. As Melissa also says: some things should never change.

Now, I smooth down my rain-tangled hair and keep looking for signs of my sister.

Of course, she may be oblivious to the fact that I'm not there yet ... I remind myself. 'I like a nap while I'm plugged in,' she told me last time before dozing off like a cat for the duration. I spent the time sifting through work emails, then put my phone away and read a book. For the first time in years. Turns out there's a lot of sitting around to be done. What they never quite get across in TV soaps is how cancer treatment can be very much like waiting for a plane in an airport. But not today.

'Oi! Over here!' a familiar voice rings out.

I squint to see where it came from and realise the time has come to admit that I need glasses for seeing anything further away than a patient's mouth. Peering, I spot a small semi-circle to the left of seated figures. Most have magazines open on their laps. Some are chatting and a couple are sleeping, snoring gently. My sister, along with the woman next to her, appears to be sporting a space helmet with a nozzle coming out of it, attached to an elaborate-looking machine.

'Well, don't you look like a wet rescue dog!' A pale but upbeat Melissa greets me from underneath her contraption.

'Well, don't you look like you're visiting a hair salon from the seventies.' I point to the device. 'What *is* that?'

'It's got ice in it to keep my head cold; apparently it might save some hair. Otherwise—' she gestures for me to pass the tote bag currently resting by her ankles '—it's this!'

She pulls out what I initially mistake for a guinea pig, but then she shakes it, more vigorously than an animal lover ever should. A mass of hair unravels to reveal a curly, auburn wig that even Cher might shirk at.

'Ta da!'

'Blimey!' is all I can think of to say.

'Yes. I told them I wanted to try something a bit different. But, well ... there's different, and there's ...'

'Yes. Quite.'

'Anyway, it'll be good to dress the dogs up in. I put them in the Viking helmets last week!'

'Did the dogs like to be dressed up?'

'Doesn't everyone?'

'*No?*' My sister and I are still very different. In many ways. But I'm learning that This Is A Good Thing. And I'm delighted the dogs are getting some wear out of the horned helmets. I apologise for being late and hand over the cool bag of grapes I've frozen for her.

'In case I wasn't cold enough already?' She flicks her eyes up to the top of her head.

'I read that they're good for nausea,' I explain. The last round left Melissa with mouth ulcers and she's been complaining of a tongue like cotton wool. 'And I've brought more magazines.' I unload my haul from one of the bags-for-life I've filled for the occasion. 'Some moisturiser, snacks, new, un-stinky socks ...' I glance at the 'lucky socks' that Melissa still insists on wearing and crinkle my nose. 'And of course, the acerbic wit that only a sister like me can provide ...'

'Of course! Like human sandpaper.' She smiles, flashing her dimples, then gives my arm a punch.

'Ow!' *How come my little sister, who's currently having chemotherapy and her head frozen to minus four degrees, can still beat me up?* Melissa's strength = one of life's mysteries. 'So how are you feeling now?'

'Honestly?' she asks.

'Honestly.'

'Shattered. Sick of having a big shiny moon-face and aching bones and permanent reflux. But it's OK. It's out. The cancer, I mean. So this is my life for a while,' she says. 'It could be worse. I spoke to a woman named Barbara who said she had the kind of chemo that turns your pee red. And see that woman in the purple?' She points to a sleeping figure wearing a turban. 'Lost all her hair – eyelashes, eyebrows – the lot. Even down there,' Melissa adds in a too-loud whisper, pointing at her genitals. 'She showed us, last time – bald as a coot.'

'That's some sharing,' is all I can think of to say before realising that this is probably a poor response.

'And my nails haven't fallen off,' she adds. 'So that's a result. Plus I've got ink, now – more battle scars, Viking style!'

'Sorry?' I frown.

Melissa sets down her magazine bounty to tug at her loose-fitting jumper, lowering it at the front. 'They tattoo dots on you to line up the lasers for radiotherapy, make sure they don't zap the wrong bit. One in the middle and one under each armpit. Pretty cool, right?' She beams.

My sister is incredible.

I fear that in her position, I would still spend the majority of my time feeling sorry for myself. But not Melissa. Apart from some initial howls at the injustice of it all once she'd started chemo ('I felt *fine*! Then they *told* me I was ill, and then they gave me '*treatment*' that made me *feel* ill! I KNEW I hated medics!') she swiftly reconciled herself to the idea that the experts were only trying to help. Since then, she has even embraced 'science 'n' medicine 'n' stuff' in something approaching a *Damoclean* conversion.

Next step – space, I think. *The final frontier* ...

Her treatment is progressing and time is passing, faster than she had expected it to. 'As long as I keep on keeping on, I'll be OK,' she said on my last visit. 'Won't I?'

'You will,' I told her, as confidently as I could. Because the alternative still isn't worth thinking about. So I don't. Instead we settle into our routine of chatting – about other patients, the dogs, the state of everyone's bowels (hers: because the treat-ment can do peculiar things to a girl's poo, apparently. And mine: because, peculiarly yet happily, I'm far more regular and relaxed post Viking retreat – much to Melissa's delight and endless fascination). Then I get my book out and have a read while she sleeps, safe in the knowledge that I'm here beside her.

Afterwards, it's a race to get home, get the anti-nausea drugs inside her, and get both of us into pyjamas to take up residence on the sofa where I will stay with her overnight. Ostensibly this is to pet-sit and walk the dogs. But really, we both know, it's to be a familiar body in the house.

The rain has stopped by the time we walk out of the hospital together, slowly and under a weak sun. Once we've located the car among the rows of tin boxes, Melissa teases that it looks like I've just driven here from a showroom.

'I'm surprised there isn't plastic wrapping on the seats for extra cleanliness!' she says and I laugh. What I don't tell her is that I spent much of last night valeting the car – with a dedication to disinfection seldom seen outside of the dental room. I've read that Melissa's at greater risk of infection than normal after treatment and despite my obsession with anti-bacterial gel and latex gloves, my children appear to be magnets for mud, ringworm and – most recently – head lice (that's karma …). Parenting is not for sissies.

Melissa, on the other hand, is still spectacularly unconcerned about dirt, despite leaflets from 'actual professionals' advising her otherwise – leaflets that I have 'liberated' duplicate copies of from the hospital and left lying around her house in a nonchalant fashion. But to no avail. So I'm cleansing by stealth, on her behalf.

'How are the kids?' she asks, after a cursory rummage around in my glove compartment for sweets and a *harrumph* that there are none lurking.

'The kids are well! Ish …' I tell her. 'I mean, they still hate me for confiscating the iPad and think their dad's more fun because he lets them watch TV all the time when they stay with him. But they're helping to lay the table now and can even get their own cereal in the morning! Laundry's still a struggle, but since I set up a trampoline in the garden, they're so exhausted most days, they haven't got the energy to fight me on it. And they've got those kind of round, rosy cheeks, like kids in story books!' I say, with pride.

'Wow!'

'I know!'

'No, I mean, are they OK?'

'Oh yes – I think it's just from the fresh air and exercise. Not slapped cheek syndrome,' I say with some certainty, having Googled this ferociously ahead of my previous visit for fear of contaminating Melissa.

'Huh. And you set up that trampoline all by yourself?' She looks doubtfully at my admittedly still sub-Viking physique.

'Yes!' I tell her. 'I've been working out, honestly!' She nods, impressed. 'I also think that trampoline assembly might be my one of my secret special skills,' I tell her.

'Like sword-forging?' she jokes. 'Or axe-throwing?'

'Ha ha! Very droll – no. But, listen to this: I now have the ability to tell if a trampoline is the optimum tensile strength just by looking at it!' I enthuse. 'I've tested it out at friends' houses, too,' I add with a note of pride, because I have *friends* now!

'Optimum tensile strength, eh?' Melissa is mocking me but I don't care.

'Yes! It's pretty exciting stuff. At the very least, it's something you want to get right – otherwise the kids end up in next door's garden ...'

'Did you learn this the hard way?'

I keep my eyes fixed on the road.

'Al?'

'Yes. Yes, I did ... Anyway ...' I gloss over this last part, ' ... are you proud of me?'

'I am,' Melissa agrees, generously. 'You're practically a Viking. What next? Building them their own bunk beds out of whittled wood, like Inge?'

'Who knows?' I enthuse, 'Maybe!'

We pull up outside her cottage and the dogs start up a cacophony of greetings before I can even slot my key in the lock.

'Mama's home!' Melissa ruffles their fur and allows herself to be mauled by them before wincing slightly at one of the bigger dog's enthusiastic reception.

'Is Silas trying to hump you?' I frown.

'Only a little ...' she waves a hand in dismissal.

'All right, all right, get down,' I tell him firmly as we make it in through the front door. Melissa's house is cheerfully shambolic, playing host to a miscellany of country life with bits of old shell, stones and what she terms her '*knickknacks*', generously scattered around. The floor is, again, littered with clothes after my last big tidy up. I'm still not sure how much of the mess is because my sister's been in and out of hospital and how much is down to baseline detritus and her own personal housekeeping standards (still low). Fortunately, the rabbits are safely ensconced in the neighbour's kitchen, spreading straw and shredded newspaper to their heart's delight there. It turns out that Charlotte has inherited my allergies and Thomas took an instant dislike to 'the bunny that looks at me funny'. Still, we tried. And dirty protests aside, the dogs and I have been getting on surprisingly well during my visits and stick-throwing sessions.

If anything, Silas is a tad too keen ..

Now, taking her hand in mine, I help Melissa inside and upstairs to get her fully-pyjama-d and ready for some serious sofa time. A cursory rifle around her Tracey-Emin-d bed reveals some semi-clean pyjamas and we make it back downstairs. A couple of the smaller dogs curl into tight coils on her lap as she settles into the freshly plumped and laundered (by me) cushions.

I light candles – because, well, that's something else both of us like to do now, to make a space feel like home – then I boil the kettle on the hob until it screams.

'Tea?' I ask and she nods. 'Fancy eating anything? I brought miso soup and kale?' I've read that these are healing foods but Melissa's not biting.

'Urggh, no thanks.' She pulls a face. 'I'm not hungry.'

'Right ...' I suspected that this might be the response. Fortunately, I have a back-up plan. 'Not even ... for a Marks and Spencer tuna pasta cheesy bake?' I ask, retrieving a satisfyingly weighty cardboard box from a second bag-for-life.

'Oh ... well—' I can see she's tempted '—OK, then! Thanks.'

'I'll just heat it up,' I tell her, feeling pleased I remembered to stock up on a few of her favourites during yesterday's supermarket sweep. *It's a good thing I did*, I think, noticing that the rest of the fridge is bare but for bottles of beer and a few forgotten-looking bowls of ... something or other. I lift tin foil off one to have a sniff, then recoil and hold it as far from my nose as possible to convey it to the bin, silently. After putting the rest of the provender away (*maybe she'll feel like the kale later*, I kid myself), I sling the ready meal in the microwave – a modern contraption that Melissa has finally been won around to on account of 'having cancer anyway'. While I wait for the food to heat up, I take in the new batch of postcards from well-wishers and friends, stuck on to the front of the fridge with a variety of canine and equine themed magnets.

Because I am now a Viking, I ask Melissa before I read these – apparently it doesn't count as snooping this way and my curiosity can be sated with a clean conscience.

'Sure,' she mumbles drowsily, 'if I can have a go on your phone?' My sister has recently discovered the delights of online Solitaire, a mere two decades after everyone else. She takes my mobile, still suspicious of its square icons and sounds, then unlocks the game and begins to play, furiously.

Weirdo ...

One of the postcards is of turquoise seas, white sands and expensive-looking people wearing exclusively beige. It's from Margot, who's doing a swimming course in St Barts.

All right for some, I think, and then correct myself. *You know what? Good for her.*

We've agreed to meet up next month, ahead of our Viking reunion later this year. She's growing on me, Margot, and I'll never forget her parting words to me on the retreat. 'You *are*

an older version of me!' Then she added with similar guilelessness. 'So I'm going to be your friend whether you like it or
not.' I couldn't stop smiling at this. And I felt strangely
honoured. *So now I have Tricia, Margot, New Dentist (Ben),
School Mum (Sara), Former Classmate (Emily)* ... I tally them
up: *FIVE friends!*

The second postcard is from Tricia, bearing a Brighton
beachfront and announcing that she's been seeing Ed – her
son – more and 'doing some parenting'. She's also got a job
interview next Tuesday and has been further getting her craft
on with a local crocheting group, delightfully named 'The
Happy Hookers'.

A third is from Otto, written in neat, block lettering with
a Danish postmark. I feel oddly embarrassed to be reading
this one but he simply says he misses her, that he's forging a
sword in her honour, and he hopes she'll come back and visit
him one day. And that's it.

I wonder whether Melissa minds this – whether she had
hoped for more. So when the microwave pings and I return
to her with a bowl of pasta, I enquire, gently.

'Otto? Oh no! I'm good,' she assures me. 'He's great and
all but I've got a lot on. Long distance suits me just fine. Plus
he sent me two packets of artisanal bacon last week.'

'Is that a good thing?' I ask carefully.

Now my sister looks at me as if I'm the weirdo. 'Did you
not hear what I said, about the bacon? Of course it's a good
thing! If anything, he's a little eager, don't you think?'

'What, a postcard and some cured pig?'

'I know, right?!' Melissa rolls her eyes. 'But maybe I'll
invite him over sometime soon,' she softens. 'Maybe ...' Then
she puts her arms out to receive her tuna bake. 'Anyway,
quick! Gimme gimme!' She forks in two mouthfuls in quick

succession before murmuring, 'Mmm, penne: like slimy panpipes ...' in semi-rapture.

I'm glad she's OK with the whole Otto situation. I love how relaxed she's always managed to be – and I'm learning from her, every day. In fact, speaking of relaxing ...

'Mind if I help myself to a beer?' I say this casually, as if unaware that it will raise much of a response.

Yes, I now drink beer. And eat pasta. And my life is a good 30 per cent better. Basically, I give fewer fucks.

'Be my guest!' Melissa approves. 'Are you taking a break from being an arch perfectionist?'

'Something like that,' I tell her. She knows all about my 'issues' with eating now. And although Melissa may not be the apotheosis of anorexia recovery support, talking to her has definitely helped. 'Mainly though, it's that I don't want the entire brewing economy to suffer just because you're off the sauce for a while ...'

'That's very noble of you, thank you.'

'You're welcome.'

Warm comforting bowls of pasta in hand, we huddle up on the sofa to eat – in a way I never let Charlotte and Thomas get away with these days back home. Hot wax trickles down white candles and pools on the bronze geometric candlestick that Melissa admired at the airport on our way back from our retreat. I distracted her at the time by telling her there was a Lego model of a dog in the shop next door (true) then snuck back and bought it before presenting it to her as a 'thank you' for the trip. It was the first thing I'd ever given her that she actually wanted – and it felt good. I resolved to try doing more of it.

Cocooned under a blanket now and wearing the new, matching woolly socks I treated us both to (thoughtful present

#2), the remains of the day are spent watching films and chatting like teenagers. Something we never did growing up.

We're not regressing, I tell myself. *We're making up for lost time.*

They say that if you suffer a loss, life goes on hold until you make peace with your personal brand of angst – and we all have one of those. Even Vikings.

For us, the hurt came to a crescendo that endless summer back when I was sixteen and Melissa was fourteen. Everyone else was hanging out in parks, learning to smoke and have casual sex, but we were inside, *not* coping with our mother's death in our different ways. Not speaking – not feeling, in my case. For weeks, months, decades, even, after. Our relationship stopped that summer – until this year. Until our Viking Spring awakening.

I watch Melissa now, curled up like a cat, barely needing a fork and simply inhaling tubes of pasta one by one. She's laughing intermittently at the TV, talking with her mouthful whenever possible, and nuzzling one of the dogs with her foot. Another of the canine companions has made a dreadful smell, while a third laps contentedly at his own penis. And yet ... I feel a wave of love, like the kind I experience when I see, hear, or even think about Thomas and Charlotte. *This is it*, I realise. *This is what it's all about. Having my sister, here, with me now – hopefully at the end of her treatment – as well as my children happy and healthy and a career I care about, is enough.* The addition of a masterfully taut-strung trampoline in the garden is merely the icing on the cake (which I also now eat, just FYI).

Melissa draws me back out of myself by starting up what turns into an impassioned debate about whether *Back to the Future I* is superior to *Back to the Future II* (Answer: Yes.

Clearly ...) before widening out the discussion to include such seminal topics as the best way to serve eggs (me: 'poached'. Melissa: 'Are you insane? *Fried!* Obviously!') and 'if you could only have one type of carbohydrate for the rest of your life, what would it be' (jury's still out on this one, but 'potato' definitely has a shot). We talk about old friends, making new ones, family, work and the milestones that each of us missed out on in each other's lives. I feel sad that it's taken us so long to come around to this, but also grateful that I'm getting the chance to make up for it, now. Here. With my wonderful, caring, courageous and chaotic sister, who somehow planes the edges off me.

The light outside fades and the air blackens to reveal a million tiny specks of light, luminous dust that fills the sky, visible from every window of Melissa's cottage. She now eschews curtains or blinds in favour of 'The Viking Way', insisting that she prefers to see what's going on in the world around her, rather than the pattern of something floral from John Lewis. The results are a little drafty, but I can live with that. *And she was right about one thing*, I think. *It is beautiful out here.* Turns out nature isn't so bad, after all. So after a couple of hours, we turn off the TV and watch the night, instead. And chat some more. And then some more. Because, you see, we have more than twenty years' of conversation to catch up on.

Acknowledgements

I wrote this while being kicked to kingdom come, from the inside, by four legs. Four. That's a ridiculous number. Human beings cannot, I feel sure, have been designed for BOGOF reproduction. Fortunately, I love them very much, even though one just puked on me and the other is currently fixing me with a look that says, 'Get ready to put another load of laundry on ...' But if there's one thing that doing something a bit hard and hurty does, it's make you stronger – so thank you to the two mini-Vikings now out, proud, loud and marauding on the outside. Hear them roar, every two hours (with extra decibels at night). My husband, the Lego Man, did some first-rate latte-papa parenting to allow me to write this and our toddler, Little Red, proved invaluable at fetching 'warm paper' from the printer when needed (though he's still mightily cheesed off that this book isn't about diggers).

The biggest of thank yous must go to the team at Ebury for bringing *Gone Viking* to the world – to my fabulous commissioning editor Emily Yau; to Gillian Green, the phenomenal publishing director for fiction; plus Steph Naulls and Tessa Henderson for publicity and marketing wizardry.

I am ever grateful to my splendid agent, Anna Power, for her support, assistance and general superwoman credentials.

My traditional Viking education came courtesy of the Kongernes Jelling Museum in Jutland, as well as Diana, Karen, Gudrun, Bjarne and the team at Ribe Viking centre, who were unbelievably patient while teaching a heavily pregnant Brit how to axe-throw and make authentic Viking tar. Roskilde Viking Ship Museum sailing instructor and navigation teacher Karen Andersen opened my eyes to a brave new world of 'being in touch with nature 'n' that' and is the source of my new favourite swan fact. Go visit all these places: they are fascinating and you'll see A LOT of excellent beard-work.

I'm hugely grateful for the help of the information nurse team at Cancer Research UK for checking factual accuracy (visit www.cancerresearchuk.org for more information and those affected by cancer can call CRUK's nurses on 0808 800 4040). My chats with Alexandra King from Cancer Research UK were instrumental – and she's an inspiration (#Viking).

And thanks as always to my tribe for showing me how modern-day Vikings roll. For introducing me to Icelandic horses and lambs in cupboards (Katie); for insight into dentistry (Jill); for opening my eyes to contemporary retreat options (Matthew); and for crucial help with character names (Rob, who's miffed that he hasn't been mentioned in previous books. So there. R.O.B.). To Emily, Chrissy, Caroline, Sarah and Joe for unflagging support from the motherland as well as my actual mother, for bringing me up to believe that girls can do anything. To Tara and Fen for early brainstorming over gin; to Frauke and Jackie for sanity breaks when I was nearing the end of my housebound tether; and to every badass Viking I've been inspired by during five years of living Danishly: you rock.